Praise for

"I flew through this creative ar[...]y
absorbed by the world Kate C[...]
felt so real and their joys and sorrows and struggles and triumphs
felt so relatable that I forgot I was reading fiction. I can't wait
for the whole world to fall in love with *Love Lettering!*"
—Jasmine Guillory, *New York Times* bestselling author of *The Proposal*

"*Love Lettering* is delicious and beautiful and perfect."
—*New York Times* bestselling author Sarah MacLean

"Kate Clayborn's writing is uniquely, intensely beautiful.
This book will wake you up in the middle of the night
aching for these perfectly imperfect characters. It's
layered, nuanced, and unrelenting in how deep it digs."
—Sonali Dev, author of *Pride, Prejudice, and Other Flavors*

"*Love Lettering* made me laugh and made me cry. Kate
Clayborn is my new go-to romance author."
—*New York Times* bestselling author Stacy Finz

Praise for Kate Clayborn

"Emotional and real." —*O, The Oprah Magazine* on *Beginner's Luck*

"Warm and lively romance." —*The New York Times* on *Luck of the Draw*

"Breathtaking . . . easily one of the best I have ever read."
—*BookPage* on *Best of Luck*

"This book is hilarious and moving and sexy, with a focus on strong
female friendship, guilt that's hard to let go of, and one of the most
realistic, and ultimately romantic, fake fiancé setups I've ever read."
—*Buzzfeed* on *Luck of the Draw*

"In the hands of a lesser author, this setup could be preachy and
heavy, but Clayborn's characters are bright and nuanced, her
dialogue quick and clever, and the world she builds warm and
welcoming. Zoe and Aiden slide into love, healing themselves along
the way." —*The Washington Post* on *Luck of the Draw*

Also by Kate Clayborn

The Chance of a Lifetime Series
Beginner's Luck
Luck of the Draw
Best of Luck

Love Lettering

kate clayborn

KENSINGTON BOOKS
www.kensingtonbooks.com

KENSINGTON BOOKS are published by

Kensington Publishing Corp.
119 West 40th Street
New York, NY 10018

All Kensington titles, imprints, and distributed lines are available at special quantity discounts for bulk purchases for sales promotion, premiums, fund-raising, educational, or institutional use.

Special book excerpts or customized printings can also be created to fit specific needs. For details, write or phone the office of the Kensington Sales Manager: Attn.: Sales Department. Kensington Publishing Corp., 119 West 40th Street, New York, NY 10018. Phone: 1-800-221-2647.

Kensington and the K logo Reg. U.S. Pat. & TM Off.

First Printing: January 2020

ISBN-13: 978-1-4967-2517-2
ISBN-10: 1-4967-2517-4

ISBN-13: 978-1-4967-2518-9 (ebook)
ISBN-10: 1-4967-2518-2 (ebook)

10 9 8 7 6 5 4 3 2 1

Printed in the United States of America

For Mom, who taught me everything I know about being an artist

Chapter 1

On Sunday I work in sans serif.

Boldface for all the headers, because that's what the client wants, apexes and vertexes flattened way out into big floors and tables for every letter, each one stretching and counting and demanding to be seen.

All caps, not because she's into shouting—at least I don't think, though one time I saw her husband give their toddler a drink of his coffee and the look she gave him probably made all his beard hairs fall out within twelve to twenty-four hours. No, I think it's because she doesn't like anything falling below the descender line. She wants it all on the level, no distraction, nothing that'll disrupt her focus or pull her eye away.

Black and gray ink, that's all she'll stand for, and she means it. One time I widened the tracking and added a metallic, a fine-pointed thread of gold to the stems, an almost art deco look I thought for sure she'd tolerate, but when she opened the journal—black, A4, dot grid, nothing fancy—she'd closed it after barely ten seconds and slid it back across the table with two fingers, the sleeve of her black cashmere sweater obviously part of the admonishment.

"Meg," she'd said, "I don't pay you to be *decorative*," as if being decorative was the same as being a toenail clipping hoarder or a murderer-for-hire.

She's a sans serif kind of woman.

Me? Well, it's not really the Mackworth brand, all these big, bold, no-nonsense letters. It's not my usual—what was it *The New York Times* had written last year? *Whimsical? Buoyant? Frolicsome?* Right, not my usual whimsical, buoyant, frolicsome style.

But I can do anything with letters, that's also what *The New York Times* said, and that's what people pay me for, so on Sunday I do this.

I sigh and stare down at the page in front of me, where I've used my oldest Staedtler pencil to grid and sketch out the letters

M-A-Y

for the upcoming month, big enough that the *A* crosses the center line. It's such a . . . such a *short* word, not a lot of possibility in it, not like my clients who've wanted a nice spring motif before their monthly spread, big swashes and swooping terminal curves for cheerful sayings ushering in the new month. Already I've done four *Bloom Where You're Planted*s, three *May Flowers!* and one special request for a *Lusty Month of May*, from the sex therapist who has an office on Prospect Park West and who once told me I should think about whether my vast collection of pens is a "symbol" for something.

"Other than for my work?" I'd asked, and she'd only raised a very judgmental, very expertly threaded eyebrow. The Sex Therapist Eyebrow of Knowing How Rarely You Date. Her planner, it's a soft pink leather with a gold button closure, and I hope she sees the irony.

Now I pick up my favorite pen, a fine-tipped Micron—not symbolic, I hope, of any future dating prospects—and tap it idly against the weathered wood countertop that's functioning as my work surface today. It's quiet in the shop, only thirty minutes to close on a Sunday. The neighborhood regulars don't come around much on the weekends, knowing the place will be overrun by visitors from across the Bridge, or tourists who've read about the cozy Brooklyn paperie that Cecelia's managed to turn into something of a must-see attraction, at least for those who are looking to shop. But they're long gone by now, too, bags stuffed full of pretty notecards, slim boxes of custom paper, specialty pens, leather notebooks, maybe even a few of the pricey designer gifts Cecelia stocks at the front of the store.

Back when I worked here more regularly, I relished the quiet moments—the shop empty but for me and my not-symbolic pen and whatever paper I had in front of me, my only job to create. To play with those letters, to experiment with their shapes, to reveal their possibilities.

But today I'm not so welcoming of the quiet. Instead I'm wishing for some of those Sunday shoppers to come back, because I liked it—all the noise, all the people, being face-to-face with brand-new faces. At first I thought it was simply the novelty of having my phone put away for so long—a forced hiatus from those red notification circles that stack up in my social media apps, likes and comments on the videos I post, the ones I used to do for fun but now are mostly for sponsors. Me showing off brush-lettering pens I don't even use all that regularly, me swooping my hand through a perfect flourish, me thumbing through the thick, foil-edged pages of some luxury journal I'll probably end up giving away.

Eventually, though, I realized it was more than being away from the phone. It was the break from that master task list I've got tacked above the desk in my small bedroom, the one that's whimsically lettered but weighted with expectation—my biggest, most important deadline ratcheting ever nearer and no closer to being met. It was the relief of being away from the chilly atmosphere in my once-homey, laugh-filled apartment, where these days Sibby's distant politeness cuts me like a knife, makes me restless with sadness and frustration.

So now the quiet in the shop seems heavy, isolating. A reminder that a rare moment of quiet is full of dread for me lately, my mind utterly blank of inspiration. Right now, it's just me and this word, **M-A-Y**, and it *should* be easy. It should be plain and simple and custom-made and low stakes, nothing like the job I've been avoiding for weeks and weeks. Nothing that requires my ideas, my creativity, my specialty.

Sans serif, bold, all caps, no frolicking.

But I *feel* something, staring down at this little word. Feel something familiar, something I've been trying to avoid these days.

MAY*be you're blocked*, the letters say to me, and I try to blink them away. For a few seconds I blur my vision, try to imagine being *decorative*, try to imagine what I'd do if I didn't have to keep my promises to the client. Something in those wide vertexes? Play with the negative space, or . . .

MAY*be you're lonely*, the letters interrupt, and my vision sharpens again.

MAY*be*, they seem to say, *you can't do this after all.*

I set down the Micron and take a step back.

And that's when he comes in.

♥ ♥ ♥

The thing is, the letters don't always tell me truths about myself.

Sometimes they tell me truths about other people, and Reid Sutherland is—*was*—one of those people.

I remember him straightaway, even though it's been over a year since the first and only time I ever saw him, even though I must've only spent a grand total of forty-five minutes in his quiet, forbidding presence. That day, he'd come in late—his fiancée already here in the shop, their final appointment to approve the treatment I'd done for their wedding. Save the dates, invitations, place cards, the program—anything that needed letters, I was doing it, and the truth is, by then I'd been almost desperate to finish the job, to get a break. I'd been freelancing for a few years before I came to Brooklyn, but once I started contracting for Cecelia exclusively, handling all the engagement and wedding jobs that came through the shop, word about my work had spread with a speed that was equal parts thrilling and overwhelming. Jobs coming so quickly I'd had to turn more than a few down, which only seemed to increase interest. During the day my head would teem with my clients' demands and deadlines; at night my hands would ache with tension and fatigue. I'd sit on the couch, my right hand weighted with a heated bag of uncooked rice to ease its cramping, and I'd breathe out the stress from meetings that would sometimes see couples and future in-laws turn brittle with wedding-related tension, my job to smile and smooth ruffled feathers, sketching out soft, romantic things that would please everyone. I'd wonder whether it was time to get out of the wedding business altogether.

The fiancée—Avery, her name was, blond and willowy and almost always dressed in something blush or cream or ice blue or whatever color I'd be just as likely to ruin with ink or coffee or ketchup—had been nice to work with, focused and polite, a good sense of herself and what she wanted, but not resistant to Cecelia's suggestions about paper or my suggestions about the lettering. A few times, in our initial meetings, I'd asked about her fiancé, whether she'd want me to send scans to his e-mail, too, or whether she'd want to try to find a weekend meeting time if it'd make it easier for him to come. She'd always wave her slim-fingered left hand, the one with the tiny ice rink on it that looked almost identical to the rings of at least three other brides I'd been working with that spring, and she'd say, pleasantly, "Reid will like whatever I like."

But I'd insisted on it, him being there for the final meeting.

And I'd regretted it later. Meeting him. Meeting them together.

I regret it even more now.

We'd settled on a Sunday afternoon for that final meeting, and now it seems doubly strange to find him here again on another Sunday, my life so different now than it was then, even though I'm in the same store, standing behind the same counter, wearing some version of what's always, pretty much, been my style aesthetic—a knit dress, a little slouchy in fit, patterned, this particular one with tiny, friendly fox faces. Slightly wrinkled cardigan that, until an hour ago, was shoved into my bag. Navy tights and low-heeled, wine-red booties that Sibby would probably say make my feet look big but that also make me smile at least once a day, even without Sibby willing to tease me anymore.

Last year, *he'd* been wearing what other people call "business casual" and what I'd privately call "weekend-stick-up-your ass": tan chinos pressed so sharply they'd looked starched, white collared shirt under a slim cut, expensive-looking navyblue V-neck sweater. A double-take face, that was for sure—so handsome half of you is wondering if you've seen him on your television and the other half of you is wondering why anyone would put a head like that on top of what looked like a debate team uniform.

But now he looks different. Same head, okay—a square, clean-shaven jaw; high cheekbones that seem to carve swooping, shadowed lines down to his chin; a full-lipped mouth with corners turning slightly down; a nose bold enough to match the rest of his strong features; bright, clear blue eyes beneath a set of brows a shade lighter than his dark reddish-blond hair. Neck down, though, not so business casual anymore: olive green T-shirt underneath a hip-length, navy-blue jacket, faded around the zipper. Dark jeans, the edges of the front pockets where he has his hands tucked slightly frayed, and I don't think it's the kind of fraying you pay for. Gray sneakers, a bit batteredlooking.

MAY*be*, I think, *his life is pretty different now, too.*

But then he says, "Good evening," which I guess means he's still got the stick up his ass. Who says *Good evening*? Your grandad, that's who. When you call him on his land line.

I feel like if I say a casual "Hi" or "Hey," I'll open up some crack in the space-time continuum, or at least make him want to straighten the tie he's not wearing. I shouldn't be deceived by the clothes. Maybe he got mugged on the way over by a rogue debate team captain in need of a new outfit and that's why he looks the way he does.

I settle for a "Hello," but I keep it light and cheerful—*buoyant*, if you will—and I'm pretty sure he *nods*. As if he's saying, "This greeting is acceptable to me." I have a fleeting image of how it must have been at his wedding. Probably he did that nod when the officiant said "man and wife." Probably he shook Avery's hand instead of kissing her. I really don't think she would've minded. Her lipstick always looked so nice.

"Welcome to—" I begin, at the same time he speaks again.

"You still work here," he says. It's flat, the same as everything I've ever heard him say, but there's a hint of question, of surprise in it.

So maybe he knows something of what I've done since I lettered every single scrap of paper for his wedding.

But surely he can't know—he absolutely *can't* know—why I'd decided his wedding would be my last.

I swallow. "I'm filling in," I say, and it's—less buoyant. Cautious. "The owner's on vacation."

He's still standing right inside the door, underneath the bright paper cranes Cecelia has hung from the ceiling near the entrance. Behind him, the window displays feature various sheaths of the new custom wrapping paper she'd told me about two weeks ago, the last time I'd stopped in for supplies. It's all so colorful, a springtime celebration of pinks and greens and pale yellows, a cheery haven from the mostly gray tones of the city street outside, and now it looks like a human skyscraper has walked in.

It reminds me of one of those truths about Reid Sutherland.

It reminds me of how he'd seemed a little lost that day. A little sad.

I swallow again and take a step forward, pick up my Micron from the crease of my client's notebook, prepare to close it and set it aside. **M-A-Y**, it calls, and this time something else occurs to me. It'd be close now to Reid and Avery's first anniversary. June 2nd, that was the wedding date, and sure he's planning way ahead, but probably he's that kind of guy in general. Probably he's got a reminder on his phone. And he'd be the type to follow the rules, too, all the conventions. Paper, that's the traditional first anniversary gift, and that's probably what brought him here. Very sweet, to come all the way to Brooklyn, to the place where they'd chosen their first paper together. Or I guess where she chose it, and he sort of . . . blinked at it in what she'd taken for approval.

I feel a blooming sense of relief. There's an *explanation* for this, for him being here. It's *not* because he knows.

No one but me could know.

I push the notebook out of the way and fold my hands on top of the counter, look up to offer help. Of course in the face of a human-shaped piece of granite I find myself struggling to muster the cheerful informality that's always made me such a hit in here, that had lifted my low spirits throughout today's shift. Ridiculously, I can only think of phrases that seem straight out of Jane Austen. *Are you in need of assistance, sir? What do you require this evening? Which of our parchment-like wares appeals most to you?*

"I suppose it's to be expected," he says, before I can settle on a question. "You wouldn't need this job, what with all the success you've had."

He's not looking at me when he says it. He's turned his head slightly, looking to the wall on his left, where there's a display of greeting cards that Lachelle, one of Cecelia's regular calligraphers, has designed. They're bright, bold colors, too—Lachelle uses mostly jewel tones for her projects, adding tiny beads with a small pair of tweezers that she wields as though she's doing surgery. I love them, have three of them tacked on the wall above my nightstand, but Reid doesn't even seem to register them before his eyes shift back to me.

"I saw the *Times* article," he says, I guess by way of explanation. "And the piece on . . ." He swallows, gearing up for something. "*Buzzfeed.*"

LOL, I think, or maybe I see it: sans serif, bold, all caps, a bright yellow background. Reid Sutherland scrolling through *Buzzfeed*, the twenty gifs they'd embedded of me drawing various letters with pithy captions about how it was almost pornograph-ically satisfying, watching me draw a perfect, brush-lettered cursive *E* so smoothly.

He probably got an eye twitch from it. Then he probably cleared his browser history.

"Thank you," I say, even though I don't think he was compli-menting me.

"Avery is very proud. She feels as though she got on the ground floor, hiring you when she did. Before you became . . ."

He trails off, but both of us seem to fill in the blank. *The Plan-ner of Park Slope*, that's what I'm called now. That's what got me out of the wedding business, that's what the *Times* wrote about late last year, that's what's had me on three conference calls in the last month alone, that's what's brought me the deadline I'm avoiding. Custom-designed datebooks and journals and desk calendars, the occasional chalk-drawn wall calendar inside the fully renovated brownstones of my most handcraft-obsessed cli-ents, the ones who have toddlers with names like Agatha and Sebastian, the ones with white subway-tile kitchens and fresh flowers on farmhouse-style tables that never once saw the inside of a farmhouse, let alone the outside of a farm. I don't so much organize their lives as I do make that organization—work re-treats and weekend holidays and playdates and music lessons—look special, beautiful, uncomplicated.

"Are you looking to have me design something for her?"

I haven't been taking on new clients lately, trying to put this new opportunity first, but it's clever, I guess, for the one-year paper anniversary. A custom journal, maybe, and it's not as if I don't secretly owe him an apology-favor. Of course, if this is what he wants, he's cutting it close, especially if he wants me to design the full year up front, which some clients prefer. Those here in Brooklyn I've mostly got on a monthly schedule, but Reid and Avery, I'm guessing they stay in Manhattan most of the time. Avery had a tony address on East 62nd when she was engaged; she's got the kind of money I don't even understand on a theoretical level, much less a practical one.

For the first time something in his face changes, a twitch of those turned-down corners. A . . . smile? It's possible I forgot what smiles are since he came in here, jeez. But even that brief flash of expression, of emotion—it changes him. Double-take face turns to triple-take face. Take-a-photo-and-show-it-to-your-friends-later face.

He's very tall. Exceptionally tall. I hate myself for thinking about the symbolism of my pens.

In the context of a *married* person, no less.

"No," he says, and the sort-of smile is gone.

"Well," I say, *extra* cheerful, "we have other gifts and—"

"I'm not looking for a shopgirl," he says, cutting me off.

A . . . *shopgirl?*

Now it's him that's made a crack in the space-time continuum, or maybe some kind of crack in my normally frolicsome façade. I wish I could unzip my forehead and release the Valkyries on his person. It'd be worse than the debate team captain mugging, I can tell you that.

I blink across the counter at him, trying to wait out my annoyance. But then, before I can plaster over the crack, I press up on my tiptoes, exaggeratedly looking over his shoulder (one of two excellent shoulders, not that I should care) to the street beyond, the dark green awning of a fancy shave shop flapping gently in the spring breeze.

"Did you come here in a time machine?" I ask sweetly. I lower back down to my heels, meet his eyes so I can catch the expression I'll see there.

Blank, flat. No anger or amusement. The *most* sans serif person.

"A time machine," he repeats.

"Yes, a time machine. Because no one has said 'shopgirl' since—" *Parchment wares*, is all I can think, annoyingly. So I finish with an exceedingly disappointing, "A long time ago."

I think my shoulders sag. I am truly terrible at confrontation, though this man, with his blank handsome face, seems unusually capable of making me at least want to try getting better.

He clears his throat. He has fair skin, an aesthetic match for the ruddy tone in the dark blond of his hair, and part of me hopes he flushes in shame or embarrassment, some physical reaction that would remind me of what I'd seen in him all those months ago. Something that would remind me he's not a man-sized thundercloud, come to monsoon on the rainy disposition I already felt taking hold before he walked in here.

But his complexion stays even.

I could've been wrong that day, thinking he was lost or sad. It could be that he's just a smug, stick-up-his-ass drone. Thinking of him this way—I wish it made me feel better about what I did, but it doesn't, not really. It was so . . .

It was so *presumptuous*. So unprofessional.

But I'm all out of patience now, no matter the error I made, especially since he doesn't even know about it. I may not be good with confrontation, but I am exceedingly, expertly good at avoiding it. I can paste on a smile and finish this shift for Cecelia and get him out of here, back to whatever doorman-guarded high-rise he lives in with his fancy wife who never has ketchup stains on her clothing. A *shopgirl*, for God's sake.

"Anyway," I say, clenching my teeth in what I hope is an approximation of a smile. "May I help you with something?"

M-A-Y, I think, in the pause he leaves there. Flat, flat, flat.

"Maybe," he says, and for the first time he removes his hands from his pockets.

And I don't think I could say, really, what it is that makes me realize that *monsoon* was an understatement, that this is about to be a tidal wave. I don't think I could say what I notice first: the fact that there's no wedding ring on his left hand? The corner of that thick paper he begins to pull from the inside of his jacket? The matte finish, the antique cream color I remember Avery stroking her thumb over, her smile close-lipped and pleased? The flash of color—*colors*—I used on the final version, the vines and leaves, the iridescence of the wings I'd sketched . . . ?

But I know. I know what he's come to ask.

MAY*be*, I think, the word an echo and a premonition.

He doesn't speak again until he's set the single sheet in front of me.

His wedding program.

I watch as his eyes trace briefly over the letters, and I know what he's seeing. I know what I left there; I know the way those letters worked on me.

But I didn't think anyone else ever would.

Then he looks up and meets my eyes again. Clear blue. A tidal wave when he speaks.

"Maybe you could tell me how you knew my marriage would fail."

Chapter 2

Talk about whimsical.

Not this moment, obviously. This moment is more like: *How noticeable would it be if I stress-vomited in the wastebasket underneath this counter?*

But the program that Reid's set down between us? The one that's sucking all the available air out of the room while reminding me of my recklessness?

That is definitely whimsical.

It'd been Avery's suggestion, the *A Midsummer Night's Dream* theme, inspired by her first date with Reid. "Shakespeare in the Park?" she'd said, as though maybe I hadn't heard of it, though I definitely had. Sibby and I had gone once, not long after I'd moved here and she was still acting as both my best friend and my expert tour guide/distractor-in-chief. I wouldn't necessarily have pegged it as a good first date activity, but that's because when we went it had been ten thousand degrees outside and the play had been *Troilus and Cressida*, which so far as I could tell was basically about sex trafficking.

But *A Midsummer Night's Dream*—that was romantic, I guess,

at least in some parts. Forests and fairies and couples coupling, and Avery seemed important enough to control weather patterns, so the date with Reid had probably been perfect.

It'd been easy, really, to develop the treatment. Lots of ornate lettering, illustrative details overlaying or weaved in. I frolicked my face off for this job, and everyone I'd shown it to had loved it.

Except Reid.

Right now his face looks very similar to how it had the first time he'd seen all the preliminaries that day we met. Like he's taken a professional brow-furrowing class and like his mouth has had a turn-down service. He is laser focused. He would definitely notice if I stress-vomited.

"I don't know what you're talking about," I try, but I am as bad at moderating my voice as Reid is good at moderating pretty much every single thing about his physical presence. It sounds almost cartoonish; I half expect to blurt, *I would've gotten away with it, too, if it weren't for you crazy kids!* next. My hands are clasped so tightly together, the braided-together fist of them backing off from where the program lies between us, as though it'll burn my skin if it touches me.

But clearly Reid has no such reluctance. He reaches out a hand—a big hand, broad palm, long fingers, *forget about the symbolism*—and touches two fingers to the corner of the paper. I don't look at him, but I'm hoping the pause is him rethinking this. I'm hoping it's him deciding that what he saw isn't really there after all. I don't know what happened with him and Avery, but hey, breakups can be messy. You can start looking for all kinds of reasons things went wrong, right? Two years ago, Sibby developed an elaborate theory that the banjo player she'd been dating couldn't commit to her because the banjo as an instrument has a "wanderer's sound."

It's not a reasonable hope, though, not judging by the way Reid is staring down at the program. He is not the type—unlike me, I guess—to lie to himself.

"There's a code in this program," he says, still looking down. "A pattern."

Oh, God. A half hour ago I was lamenting the end-of-day quiet in the shop, but now I'm so glad for it. If Cecelia heard this, if any shoppers heard this—*God*, if this got out on social media—I can't imagine it'd do anything good for my career. Those conference calls where I've been making all sorts of professional promises I'm not even sure I can keep.

I can imagine, in fact, that it'd wreck everything.

"I—"

Before I can even attempt another very unconvincing denial, his hand moves, his index finger tracking to the first line of the program, second word: *Marriage.* The tip of his finger rests right above the *M*, the letter over which I drew the first fairy—she's facing left, the very tip of one of her slim, delicate feet touching down on the second shoulder of the letter, her veiny wings—I'd used the finest tip for those—still fully extended as she descends. I'd made her blond, same as Avery, though she's tiny enough that nothing about her simple facial features suggests a resemblance.

His finger moves again. Second line, where their names were side by side, joined by a viney ampersand I'd been particularly proud of. *Reid,* that's where his finger pauses, and he taps over the *i*, which I'd dotted with a delicate, golden drop of the love potion from Act Two, a mischievous-looking Puck drawn above, his hand still extended, as if he's only just finished the job.

Third line, where I made something of the first *S* in *Four Seasons*, the lower curve turned into a leafy hammock, a sleeping Titania's long, wavy hair draped over the terminal curve.

M-I-S . . .

He keeps tapping. The *t* in *Wedding Party*, another blushing, smiling fairy hanging by one hand on the cross-stroke. The capital *A* in *Andrew*, the name of the violinist, a raised-eyebrow fairy tucked into the triangular counter, a tiny, slim finger raised to her smirking mouth, good-humoredly reminding everyone to be quiet. The *k* in *Thank you*, a confident Oberon leaning against the high ascender. The *e* in *special day*, Bottom's ass's head peeking from the eye, one of his long ears slightly bent. It's all spread out, over the course of a lot of letters, but still . . . still, it's there.

M-I-S-T-A-K-E

"There's other drawings," I say. I'm still too afraid to touch the thing, but I nod my head toward the flowered arch over the first line. There's additional sketches, too, worked in throughout, some of them even on or inside the letters themselves. The flowers and vines, the—

"Not like these," he says, and he traces his finger up, working backward over the hidden word now, until he taps again at the *M*. "Not fair—" He stumbles over the *f* there, the furrow in his brow almost a trench at this point. I don't imagine he's had much occasion in his life to talk about fairies, I guess other than his first date with his ex-wife. He clears his throat. "Not— characters. This is a pattern."

"It's random. A coincidence."

Even as I say it, I feel a pang of unpleasantness in my stomach, different from the stress-vomiting feeling. Bad enough that I'd done this in the first place, now I'm going to gaslight him about it? Gross. This reminds me of a plotline from *Troilus and Cressida*, or maybe it reminds me of something closer to home.

"No." It's the most emphatic syllable he's uttered since he walked through the door, and he raises his eyes from the program so he's looking right at me, and *there*. That's it, that's what had made me think Reid Sutherland seemed lost, sad. *That* look in his eyes.

"I see it," he says. "I *know* patterns."

I feel my own brow crinkle at the way he's said this, as though I'd been dumb enough to hide the word *MISTAKE* in the wedding program of the guy who invented Morse code or something.

"Aren't you a banker?" I ask. I've got a vague memory of Avery saying something about Reid working on Wall Street, which I functionally understand as a beeswarm of bankers, a bunch of black- and navy-suited people with dollar signs in their eyes instead of pupils.

"I'm a quant," he says, as if that explains everything.

"A what?"

He shakes his head minutely, answers quickly. "Math models for investments. Risk management. Numbers, code. You know what I mean."

Uh, I do not know what he means. He said "math models" and all I could think of was the time my tenth-grade geometry teacher built a cube out of cafeteria straws and silly putty. I'm guessing that's not the kind of work Reid does.

"Sure," I say, which is, interestingly, also what I told Mr. Mesteller when he asked if I understood his lesson with the straws and silly putty. I got a D in geometry.

There's a stretch of silence. It feels long, but it must be only a matter of seconds, that program lying between us like a headstone. Inscription, *not* frolicsome: *Here lies everything you've worked for. Dead by your own unruly, interfering hand.*

I take a silent breath through my nose before I speak again.

"I'm sorry to hear about your divorce."

"There's no divorce. I didn't—we didn't have the wedding."

So, forget getting sick in the trash can. I'll just move in there like the piece of garbage I truly am.

"I am so—"

"It's not because of this," he says, touching the corner of the program again before tucking his hands back in his pockets and taking a small step back. "Or rather, it's not only because of this."

I wonder if I could fit a blanket with me in the trash can. I definitely do not deserve a pillow.

"But I would still like to know. I would like to know how you knew."

He's looking at me with that stern face, those sad eyes, and I think I could say a lot of things. I could say, *I was talking about myself; it was always a mistake for me to do weddings. This is an old habit. Sometimes I don't always know when I'm doing it. I didn't mean for it to come out in your program the way it did. You and Avery were a nice couple.*

I can almost see it, how it would go. I'd tell his triple-take face and he'd know I was lying about half of it, but he's too reserved or too uptight to press, and maybe I don't seem all that reserved or uptight to him, but still. Still, I know how that goes. I know how easy it is to avoid saying anything important at all. I can already see, by the way he holds his jaw—his ears seem to sit higher with the tension—that he came to ask me this question once and once only, and he'll give me one of those nods (this one not so approving) before he leaves. I'll close up and go home. I'll walk in the front door and I'll tell Sibby, *You will not* believe *what happened today—*

No, that's not right. I won't tell Sibby, because Sibby barely acknowledges that I exist for anything other than half of rent and utilities anymore. Instead I'll tell Reid one of those lies and he'll leave and I'll stare down at **M-A-Y** until my eyes blur, worrying about my unruly hands and my encroaching deadline and my missing inspiration. I'll wait here until I'm reasonably sure Sibby's gone to her room for the night and *then* I'll go home, and I'll still feel all the things I felt before Reid walked through that door, **MAY***be*-ing myself into a personal and professional crisis while I wait to find out whether this man is going to spread the word about what I've done.

So instead I unclasp my hands and pick up the program. I don't think I could meet his eyes for this, so I keep focused on the letters, the ones only he was able to see. The pattern, the code. The mistake.

"How about I buy you a coffee and we can talk about it?"

♥ ♥ ♥

We go to a slick espresso bar on the corner of Fifth and Berkeley. There's one closer, only a block and a half from the shop, but it closes earlier and it's also one of the places in the neighborhood where I regularly meet clients, so I'd decided that even though it would mean a longer awkward walk, there'd at least be less of a chance someone would overhear whatever conversation Reid and I are about to have.

Of course it'd been more awkward than I'd anticipated, completely silent except for one blindingly difficult moment of conversation after I'd stepped away from locking the shop's front door and gripped the edges of my cardigan to wrap it more tightly around myself against a lingering winter chill in the air.

Reid had cleared his throat and said, "Would you like my jacket?" and it hadn't even been grudging. It had been automatic, sort of the same as his very well-mannered "Good evening." I'd been so taken aback that I'd said, "Don't be *nice* to me." Then he'd done another nod and we'd both pretended to be invisible to each other until we got to our destination. Where he opened the door for me.

In our seats he seems as stiff as he had in the shop, his back and (still very nice) shoulders straight and his elbows tucked into his sides, God forbid he puts them on the table like a normal person. He's still got that slight air of distaste about him—he seems suspicious of every surface in this place, had peered at the heavy-lidded glass jars of biscotti and extra-large cookies and chocolate balls rolled in shredded coconut as though they were exceptionally disgusting dead insects pinned inside a display case for the express purpose of grossing him out. When I'd asked him what kind of coffee he'd wanted, he'd said it was "quite late for coffee" (*quite late!*) and had ordered an herbal tea instead.

I feel like I'm doing *Masterpiece Theatre* cosplay.

"It'll take me some time to get back to the city," Reid says when I'm in the middle of the first sip of my cortado (bad choice; I'll be up all night, but what else could I do in the face of that *quite late?*), and as a conversation-starter it seems entirely like a non sequitur until I realize he's urging me to get on with my explanation.

"Um," I begin, and suppress a wince at this tic, something I never realized I did so prominently until I started seriously with videos on social media. The first one I'd ever recorded had it pretty much every third word—*some letterers prefer,* um, *a classic Blackwing Pearl,* um, *with a nice,* um, *balanced graphite*—and it took me four takes to eradicate the "ums" to a tolerable level.

My last video—proof of how far I've come—had none, even in a single take.

I try again.

"I don't know if I'll have an answer that's satisfying to you."

"You may not." He lifts his hands, a palm-up gesture to indicate our surroundings. It's a we-had-that-awkward-walk-so-you-might-as-well-try gesture.

I readjust in my seat, a slight shift from side to side that's really nothing more than a poor attempt at loosening the fabric of my dress, which right now feels sweat-sealed to my ass and thighs. I think about what to say, how to casually communicate the *feeling* I'd had that day, seeing him and Avery together. How I'd felt later, when I was designing their program.

"It isn't that I've never seen an uninterested party before," I begin. "I used to sit in meetings with couples where a groom has never once looked up from his phone to have an opinion."

"I don't believe I brought my phone to our meeting."

"They probably don't have phones where you come from."

In the Masterpiece Theatre *movie you live in*, I'm thinking, but he says, "I'm from Maryland."

I cannot tell if he is joking. But if he was, he's certainly blanked the humor from his face before I can recognize it, and now all that's clear to me is that he wants to get back to business, and I guess I owe him that. None of my usual chipper, customer-servicey distractions.

"I guess I thought you were . . . um. You were . . . you had a way of being absent, I guess, even though you'd finally come. You seemed very unhappy, and honestly . . . she did, too. She hadn't seemed that way before, when it was only the two of us meeting."

He sits back. It's maybe the first time his spine has made contact with the chair.

"You didn't like anything she'd picked; I could tell just by looking at you. But then you blinked once and wiped all opinions from your face." It had looked so familiar to me, that blanking. I'd seen it between my own parents for years and years, a practiced disconnection after one of their fights. "She wanted you to have an opinion, too. She was disappointed."

"Yes," he says, completely matter-of-fact. "I did disappoint her. Often."

On instinct, I want to backtrack, to soften all the hard edges of this conversation, to keep the peace.

"Listen, I don't know you. And I don't know her. Maybe you'd had an off day. Or, I don't know, maybe you had some kind of arrangement together, how your relationship worked, and I misunderstood. It was completely wrong of me to—"

"You didn't misunderstand," he says quickly. Then he moves his hand, curls his thumb and fingers around his cup, turns it in a move that's precise, like a quarter-turn to mark the time. I don't imagine he'll say anything else, and I stare down at my own cup. I'm surprised when he speaks again, his voice lower now, almost as though he's not talking to me at all.

"I . . . went along. She led, and I followed, because it took less effort. It's how it was with us."

I blink across the table at him, a smooth, small, Spencerian script unfurling in the space between us, probably the first spark of creativity I've had in weeks. *I know how that feels*, it spells, but I don't say anything. In the silence, we both sip our drinks, and since mine is basically a defibrillator in a cup, I'm the first to get back in the game.

"I didn't intend it," I say plainly, my voice an eraser over that script connection between us. "Sometimes it just happens, and I realize it later." I feel a strange, unfamiliar temptation to tell him the whole thing. *The letters, they work on me sometimes. When I'm stressed, when I'm tired, when I'm lonely. When I'm blocked . . . I can't draw at all, or when I try—I end up saying too much.*

But telling him all that, what good would it do? It's nothing to him, and it's detrimental to me. I don't need him leaving here and spreading the word, not after everything I've worked for and am still working for. I thought maybe I'd fixed the problem when I stopped with the wedding work; I thought all the effort I'd put into my own business would give me a sense of ownership, a sense of control. Sure, it'd be other people's plans, but the idea for the planners, the execution—it had been my idea, my vision.

But I've started to slip again, at such a critical time, and Reid doesn't need to know it.

"I loved doing the job," I say, back in that cheery register. "I really did. The play, the tribute to your first date—"

Trench-brow, back again. "What first date?"

"Your first date with Avery. *A Midsummer Night's Dream.* Shakespeare in the Park?"

"That wasn't our first date. Our first date was coffee in the lobby of my office building."

"Oh," I say. Meanwhile, this coffee shop now feels like an inferno to me. I wish I had asked him to do whatever the opposite of going to a coffee shop is. An outdoor vending machine that dispenses sleeping pills? Literally anything but an echo of his first date with his ex-fiancée, whose life I have possibly ruined.

"Her father arranged it."

"That's . . . nice."

It is not nice, not judging by the way trench-brow disappears, replaced with a single quirk of the left one. *Do you really believe that?* Left Quirk says.

"He is also my boss."

"Oh, *God*," I groan. "Did you get *fired*?"

"No, I am"—he blinks down toward his tea again—"valuable to him. And it was amicable."

"Must be awkward." Probably not more awkward than this meeting, but still.

He shrugs, a slight lift of those broad shoulders, and it's a sloppy-looking, uncharacteristic gesture on him. Unexpected. "It's business."

He must be speaking of the work he does, but somehow, it seems "It's business" is also what he means by Avery, by their engagement. Their breakup, however amicable it was.

"I apologize for calling you a shopgirl," he says, a change of subject abrupt enough that it takes me a second to realize what he's said. "I obviously think you're very talented."

It's so surprising that I make a quiet snort of disbelief. If nothing else has been confirmed by this extremely wrenching conversation, at least it's fair to say that I've got a pretty good instinct when it comes to Reid Sutherland, and no part of our interactions today or a year ago have indicated that he thinks I have any talent at all.

"Obviously?"

"Yes," he says. "Everything was . . . well, Avery was very pleased with all of it."

"But *you* weren't." As soon as it's out of my mouth, I regret it. What am I doing? Baiting a very messy hook, fishing for compliments from a guy I mostly need to forget me five minutes after he leaves here? I need him to never think about my talent again, given what he knows about how I've used it.

"I was . . ." He moves his cup again, another quarter-turn. "I was affected by it. I looked down at your letters and—they felt like numbers to me. Something I could read. They felt like a sign."

I know how that feels. The first time I saw—well, *really* saw, really paid attention to—a hand-drawn letter, it was on an old sign in this city. And that's how it'd felt to me—something I could read, sure. But also something that was full of possibility. *Look at all the ways this letter* says *something.* It gives me a strange, secret pleasure to hear Reid say this about some of my own letters.

But I can't and shouldn't take what he's said—that my work affected him—as a compliment. What I do—it's petty, secretive, immature. I'm not meant to be writing *signs* for people. I'm meant to be writing *plans* for them, plans they've already made for themselves.

I have to stop this. I have to find a way to break the habit for good. Get back on track, get unblocked. Make my deadline, the one that could take my still-in-startup-mode small business to the next level.

"I won't do it again," I say, more to myself than to him, but immediately I wish I'd made this declaration privately. Stand-in-front-of-the-mirror-in-my-bathroom privately. I sound as if I'm begging for his silence with this promise, and the way his mouth flattens even further tells me he doesn't appreciate the shakedown.

"I assure you, I have no interest in talking to anyone about this ever again."

That's his promise back, I guess—his version of *I'll never tell,* and it should make me happy, or at least relieved. Instead I feel like I've done whatever the *Masterpiece Theatre* version of a drug deal is. I guess it would still be a drug deal, but an old-timey one.

When Reid moves, as though to stand, I get a strange sense of panic at leaving it this way, with this clandestine promise between us, and so I speak—the first question I can think of.

"Why now?"

Left Quirk is the only response he gives me before straightening in his chair again. He turns the cup one-quarter and looks at me.

"I mean, why come to me now, if you saw this then? Before the . . . before the wedding, I mean."

"It wasn't the most urgent thing on my to-do list," he says dryly, but somehow he has managed to telegraph directly into my brain every single way I probably screwed up his life—his relationship, surely his living situation, his job, possibly his friendships. "And I suppose I'm running out of time."

"You're running out of *time*?" This last part is high-pitched enough to sound almost hysterical. Is there something *wrong* with him? Am I on this man's bucket list? My eyeballs feel like they're in a 3D movie, jumping right across the table into his face.

Please, don't let something be wrong with him, I think, with a startling amount of feeling.

"Ah, no," he says quickly, obviously disconcerted by my 3D eyeballs. "I'm leaving New York. Probably by the end of the summer."

"Oh. I'm sorry."

I'm sorry? What do I have to be sorry for? This is good for me, that he's leaving. This is the best possible outcome for this meeting, short of Reid developing spontaneous, highly specific amnesia about me and his wedding program.

The noise he makes—it is a scoff. Nothing so sloppy as a snort. "I'm not."

"You don't like New York?"

"I hate New York."

It almost makes me recoil, the way he's said this. Bold, sans serif. No caps, but italics for the **hate**. It's not a harmless, pedestrian "I hate this song" or "I hate those chocolate balls rolled in shredded coconut." It's not one of those small, meaningless hatreds that shear the word of its meaning.

When Reid Sutherland says he hates New York, he really, really means it.

"Why?" In my head I see a very whimsical arrangement of letters asking me "why" I would even want to know this. It's unusual for me to press this way—to *want* to press this way. I keep it light; I keep it cheerful.

I keep the peace.

But everything between me and Reid feels a little unusual.

He still has his hand on his cup, but he hasn't turned it, not yet, and I sense that when he does, it'll be the end of this, whatever *this* is. He pulls his lips to the side, and I may have no earthly idea what his job entails, but I've got a feeling this is the expression he wears when he's doing one of those math models. That he wore when he looked at my letters for the first time.

"Let's just say it has not been an easy place for me to understand," he says, finally. He makes the last turn of his cup and lifts his eyes to mine. "There haven't been many signs for me here."

I have a sudden, shocking urge to protest. *But there are signs everywhere here! Street signs, business signs, billboards, subway ads, window decals, graffiti . . .*

Of course I know it's not what he means. But it's part of what the city means to me.

But I can't get my thoughts together before he stands, taking his cup and saucer with him in one hand.

"I am grateful for yours, I suppose," he says, and then he holds out his free hand. On autopilot I shake it, feel the warm, dry strength of his palm enveloping mine, a gesture that feels shockingly unbusinesslike to I'm sure me alone. Good thing I'll never see him again, because these are highly inappropriate feelings to have for this particular man.

When he releases my hand he gives me one of those devastating nods.

"Goodbye, Meg," he says, and with one stop by the counter, tidily returning his cup and saucer to the bussing tray, tall, triple-take-face, time-machine-transported Reid Sutherland walks right out the door.

Chapter 3

I wake up to three unusual things: a hangover-sized headache, the rectangular press of my phone underneath my left shoulder, and the sound of Sibby still in the apartment.

I can thank the evening espresso for the headache, that plus staying awake until 3:30 a.m., finishing up the May spread I'd stumbled over, determined to keep my renewed promise to myself—no tricks, no codes, no signs allowed.

I'd tried to sleep after, but that had been futile, my head full of Reid Sutherland's words and manners and shoulders and face, my hands fairly itching with the need to make headway on my new project. When that had been another creative bust (**MAY**be you've lost your touch), I'd still worked late, as though I was doing penance, crossing off item after item on my regular task list, first at the small desk I have shoved underneath the lone window in my room, then eventually—uncharacteristically— from my bed. I'd lain in the dark with my phone, tapping out generic but friendly replies to the commenters on my latest videos (*xoxo, thanks! —M; keep practicing! XO —M; try using a bigger drop shadow! <3 M*), scheduling posts for today, organizing some deliveries for planners I'd finished over the weekend. Usually I keep a hard and fast rule about working this way, doing my level best to follow all the advice out there about screen time at night, about setting work-life boundaries in your space, particularly when you often work from home, but last night I'd been doing anything, everything, to get that meeting with Reid out of my head.

They felt like a sign, he'd said.

I roll to the side and unstick my phone from my skin (Reid is clearly not out of my head, since I picture the face of mild to moderate disgust he'd make at this), squinting at the screen to confirm my suspicion that it's way too late for Sibby not to be at work on a Monday, and yeah—9:30, when she's usually out the door by 7:00. On instinct I sit up quickly, grabbing for my sweatshirt off the back of my desk chair. I'm still pulling it over my head when I open the door, still pushing a cloud of wavy frizz off my face when I step out.

She's coming from the kitchen, her laptop closed and tucked under one arm, a mug of coffee in her other hand as she crosses to the couch. Her curly black hair is piled high and messy on top of her head, her face clean of the winged eyeliner and red lipstick she wears almost every day, no matter that the five- and seven-year-old she spends most of her waking hours with could give a shit about how she looks. But Sibby loves a dramatic face, always has, and it's jarring for me to see her this way at this time of day.

"Are you okay?" I ask her, arrested in my spot outside my bedroom door, the small square of floor that Sibby and I always joked led to the "sleeping wing" of our place, which had seemed huge to us when we first moved in, a luxurious comparison to our previous apartments in the city.

"Yeah, I'm good." She sets down her coffee, settles herself on one end of the couch, laptop in the cradle of the legs she crosses underneath her. No further explanation forthcoming, I guess, but even so—it's too rare these days, having time alone here with Sibby where she doesn't seem so determined to be in a different room than me. She doesn't even make a move to put earbuds in.

I feel the familiar stir of hope I've felt so many times over the past few months, since this plane of distance between us opened. *This is it*, I'm thinking. *This is when we'll work it out, whatever's gone wrong between us. This is when it'll go back to normal.* I walk the length of the living space, make a stop at the refrigerator that's to the right of our front door—it's bigger here, sure, but it's still got one-quarter of a kitchen in the living room—and reach in for a cup of yogurt. We keep our stuff separate these days, as if there's a chalk line down the middle of all the shelves. It is thoroughly inane, especially because we still shop at the same bodega, buy almost all the same foods.

"Aren't you late?" I lob casually.

"I asked for the morning off. Tilda's getting the kids ready for school."

"That'll be a disaster," I say, and it's a slow pitch I'm sending her way, an easy hit for once-familiar unloading about Sibby's boss, who doesn't work but who manages to stay out for twelve to fifteen hours a day and who seems startlingly unfamiliar with both of her children's routines. The last time Sibby was sick, Tilda forgot about the youngest's lactose intolerance and the results of an impulsive, tantrum-preventing ice-cream cone were felt for days and days.

But Sibby only says, "She's good with them," and there's a thread of censure to it, as though she needs to defend a woman who once made her stay overnight and sleep in the bathtub closest to Spencer's room in case he had another nightmare about *Frozen*. Another way I've been shut out: not even worthy of a good, old-fashioned "my job sucks" diatribe.

"Yeah, of course," I say, because I basically agree with anything now when she deigns to talk to me.

I went along, I think, Reid's voice so clear in my mind that I speed my pace gathering my breakfast, trying to flush it out with the tinkle of silverware in the drawer, the clink of a glass on the countertop, an unnecessary shake of a box of granola.

My face feels flushed, and at this moment I'm grateful that she avoids me so thoroughly. Whatever it is she's doing now, hanging out in the same space as me, she'll probably soon enough go back to her room or take a shower.

But she doesn't leave. She says, "Meg," and it almost, *almost* sounds the way it used to. It almost sounds everyday, the sound of your name in your best friend's voice, surely one of the best sounds there is. I'm so glad I wasn't pouring the granola when she said it.

"Yeah?"

"I wanted to talk to you about something."

Finally, I'm thinking, that stir of hope something closer to a swirl now, and I wish I was more prepared. For the first couple of months after Sibby had started pulling away—not home as frequently, answering my texts with friendly but bland, noncommittal replies, passing on offers to watch a favorite show or visit a neighborhood bar or restaurant—I'd tried so hard to connect. Lightly, at first, with jokes about how busy she always was, or once a clever, hand-drawn ransom note on her bedroom door: *The Bachelorette season finale tonight or your cashmere sweater gets the dryer.* Later, more serious efforts to talk it through, efforts that made me feel sweaty and sick with nerves, Sibby always brushing me off with a laughing reply, "I'm just busy, Meg! You worry too much." A quick hug or promise to find some time soon would always have me feeling both vaguely better and vaguely unsatisfied, a disquieting familiarity in her brush-offs. I knew Sibby too well to think we'd gotten to the root of whatever the problem is, but after so many months I've become passive about it, locked in an old, painful fear of what pressing her might lead to.

"What's up?" I lean back against the counter so I face where she's sitting on the couch, the whole width of our apartment between us, but I'm sure this is the right move—not too eager, not too pressured.

"You know Elijah, right?"

This is an absurd question. He sleeps here three nights a week and has for the last three months; of course I know him.

I know what kind of razor he uses. Frankly, in a thin-walled apartment, I am way too familiar with some of his most not-for-public-consumption noises.

"Sure." It's casual, but inside I'm steeling myself. The three-nights-a-week stuff has already been a concession, particularly since when he's here I always worry I'm interrupting by breathing, and because I know—from one of my few longer-than-five-minute conversations with him—he prefers our place to the studio he's got in Bed-Stuy, I'm expecting a big ask. Probably his lease is up, probably he wants to crash here for a while—

"He and I are moving in together."

I almost drop the yogurt.

"We got a place in the Village. Not far from that oyster bar you used to like . . ."

What. The. Fuck.

Sibby keeps talking, something about tiny square footage but an updated kitchen, but I'm stuck on the essentials: she's moving in with a guy she's been dating for a few months, she's moving out of *here*, she's moving out of *Brooklyn*, she's had the gall to reference an oyster bar I did not in fact like but *did* go to for a date awkward enough to deserve an entire *Cosmo* article.

"But don't worry, I'm here until the end of summer, so you've got plenty of notice."

I can't seem to do anything but stare.

"I don't figure you'll bring in another roommate," she continues, "but I wanted to give you lead time in case. You can take my room when I go, make yours an office. Run your business out of here, you know?"

Run my business? Sibby barely knows the half of it with my business, knows nothing about how many regulars I've picked up since the *Times* article, and she certainly knows nothing about the massive potential of the contract I'm trying out for, which now I absolutely have to get if I have any real hope of affording this place alone, even temporarily. Sure, I'm doing well with clients, have a couple of regular sponsors for my social media—but I'm a twenty-six-year-old artist living in one of the most expensive cities in the world.

What is she *thinking?*

I can hardly process what we're talking about here, can hardly process that this conversation is so transactional, that we're not going to talk about the fact that we've lived together in this city since we were nineteen, that every big move we made here—apartments, jobs, changing our regular laundromat—we've made them as a unit. That there'll be a whole body of water separating us now.

My hold on the yogurt container now feels less a drop risk and more a smash risk. I breathe through my nose, try to settle down.

"What about your job?"

Sibby waves a hand. "I'm going to start with a new family in the city after Labor Day. It's all set."

"You love the Whalens, though," I protest weakly. Not Tilda, but those kids—Sibby's poured her whole heart into those kids for the last four years she's worked for the Whalens.

Sibby looks down, rubs her thumb against the outer edge of her laptop. "They'll be okay. Spence'll be in school full time soon. And anyway, I've probably only got a year or two left in me for nannying. Besides, that was never the dream."

"Will you start auditioning again?"

She purses her lips, shifts her eyes toward the front window. It's sunny out, a slant of light passing through the thick pane of glass, and I see the crinkles at the corners of Sibby's eyes. Tiny, cheerful lines from a big, honking laugh I haven't heard in months.

"No, Eli got a producing gig at NBC, a pretty good one. I may not even have to work forever."

"Sib," I say. That nickname, it's always felt special. *Sib*, short for Sibby, short for Sibyl. But to me, it always felt—short for *sibling*. Short for the sister I never had. But this isn't the sister I know. "I don't understand this."

This is such a profound understatement that it's almost funny. It isn't that I thought Sibby and I would live together forever; it isn't even that we haven't considered separate places before. After all, when she took the job here, it was me who thought of staying behind in Manhattan, where I was getting steady work even without the benefit of a home shop like Cecelia's, in demand enough to be able to dodge noncompetes for the shops I did work with. But how did we get to this place, a place where we haven't even *talked* about this massive change? How is it simply an announcement, and not the culmination of hours of conversation, including at least a few hours devoted to my ambitious, determined friend saying she *may not even have to work* anymore? How did this *happen?*

She led, and I followed. Reid's deep voice again, and all I can think is: *I wish I had a code for this. I wish I had a sign.*

"It's a big change, I know," Sibby says lightly, opening her laptop and tapping a few keys. "Here, I'll pull up the listing for you so you can—"

"No. No, that's all right." I've only taken two bites of my yogurt, but I hastily put it back in the fridge, spoon and all. Let's face it, I'm definitely not going to eat that later. It's going to get that weird yogurt skin that makes you wonder why yogurt exists, period. But right now, I don't care about anything but getting out of here before Sibby can see I've got frustrated tears pricking behind my eyes. "I'm actually filling in at the shop again today, so I'd better get going."

"Meg, listen, it'll be fine! I'll come visit, and you'll come visit."

I pause, briefly, feeling another inconvenient spike of anger toward her. *That's it,* I think. That small, casual "It'll be fine." That's the way she's managed it, this distance between us. She's kept it so friendly. She's never let on she notices that anything at all has changed.

She knows, more than anyone, why this would work on me so well. Why I wouldn't want to press too hard about what has, without a doubt, changed.

"Yeah, of course." My voice sounds the same as it always does, but I feel as if I'm speaking through clenched teeth. "I'm happy for you, Sib." I'm an *I-went-along* broken record.

For a split second we look at each other, and to me it feels like a mountain of letters between us, all jumbled up and unmatched, a thousand things I need to say to her but can't figure out how to say. Not without starting some kind of terrible avalanche. Not without getting buried beneath them.

So I blink first, right before Sibby's quiet "Thanks," and after that I decide it's my turn to do the avoiding for a while.

♥ ♥ ♥

Here's the thing: *I* used to hate New York, too.

When I was thirteen years old, my eighth-grade class got split into two groups: in the spring, only three weeks before the last day of middle school, half of us would take a four-day trip to Washington, D.C., and half of us would take a four-day trip to New York City. In the days leading up to the October announcement about the trip rosters, I would lie in my twin-size bed and make promises to a god I wasn't even quite sure I believed in, swearing to do all my chores early for a whole year, to lay off my parents about finally letting me get a cell phone. Anything, *anything* so I wouldn't get picked for the New York trip.

I got picked for the New York trip.

I was scared; that's the long and short of it. I'd never traveled outside the state of Ohio, and even inside of Ohio I'd only really ever left home to visit Cincinnati, which is where my dad's parents lived. Both trips seemed overwhelming, but in pictures D.C. seemed mostly comprised of clean, white, official-looking buildings surrounded by evenly cut, extremely green grass, and since I grew up in the suburbs, evenly cut, extremely green grass was basically my understanding of nature in general.

But in pictures—not to mention in TV shows and movies—New York seemed huge, unpredictable, gray and crowded and noisy and mismatching. There was Central Park, sure, but in the aerial photographs our social studies teacher showed us, even that seemed overwhelming—thick-topped trees hiding what, I didn't know, but probably not a bunch of suburban-looking grass, and all of it surrounded by that gray maze of buildings.

When I'd come home and told my parents, neither of them seemed to register the wobble in my voice, instead almost immediately—as was their tradition—taking up diametrically opposed positions on the whole thing. My mother was appalled that a place as "unsafe" as New York was even an option, and my father rolled his eyes and complained about how sheltered I was. By the time they were done, a few slammed cabinet doors later, the wobble had been out of my voice. I'd told my mom all about how many chaperones would be with us; I'd told my dad how excited I was.

A few months later, I'd taken my seat on that spring day with a sketchpad clutched to my chest and two full bottles of Pepto-Bismol in my backpack, remembering my dad's advice to "stay tough" and my mom's to keep all my money in the flat fanny pack she'd bought me to wear beneath my pants.

And then Sibyl Michelucci sat down next to me.

She was new, had moved to our school from Chicago, and basically she was one hundred times cooler than anyone in our class. By extension, she was also obviously one million times cooler than the person with two bottles of Pepto-Bismol in her backpack. She'd been to New York "uh, a *lot*" of times, because her dad was an architect and also because the entire dream of her life was to be on Broadway, and her parents were "like, *so* supportive" and took her to see a show at least twice a year. On the bus ride she started sing-a-longs that no one hated (*magic!*) and a game of truth or dare where no one got embarrassed (*sorcery!*).

I'd had friends before Sibby, of course—kids I'd been in school with for years, kids who knew me to be polite, upbeat, always drawing or coloring something. But as soon as I was old enough to recognize them, I'd been cautious about cliques, about the rivalries and conflicts that always seemed to brew beneath the surface of them, and I suppose I'd kept my distance. But there was nothing cautious about Sibby, no one—including me—she kept her distance from. She was easygoing and fun-loving and curious, and she had a way of bringing me into the fold without making me feel overexposed.

And on the New York trip, she became my best friend.

But even having Sibby by my side didn't change my mind about the city, not really. I was still overwhelmed; I still wore that flat fanny pack as if it was a medical device keeping me alive; I still drank two tablespoons of Pepto every morning before we left the hotel for the heavily scheduled and chaperoned days of sightseeing we had; I still thought I was in imminent danger of being mugged every time I was in the open air. I managed to enjoy parts of it (the park did, after all, have a lot of nice grass), but I didn't *own* it.

I *went along.*

When Sibby decided to move here right after graduation, we'd hugged and cried and made promises never ever to lose touch, but there was really no question I'd ever go with her. I had a partial scholarship to the Columbus College of Art and Design, and planned to grin and bear it at home with my parents until I could save up enough for a small apartment. I was going to graduate and get a job doing graphic design, first for my dad's business and then, I hoped, for others. New York would be a place I visited, for Sibby, but not—not *ever*—a place I lived.

But when everything fell apart, it was Sibby who I needed, Sibby who gave me a fresh start. That I hated the city was irrelevant. I didn't hate it as much as what had happened at home—that final, terrible fight between me and my parents. The one where for once, they'd been on the same side. The one where I'd finally, finally pushed them into telling me the truth—about them, about me, about all of the things they'd kept from me for years.

Talk about an avalanche. Some days I think I'm still shaking off the snow and rocks.

So at first—numb and sad and scared—I followed her lead. She offered me a spot on her small, uncomfortable couch; I took it. The catering company where she worked at night needed more servers; I signed up. She needed to go to auditions; I rode the subway with her, helping her carry extra clothes and waiting in hallways and lobbies while she anxiously read sides. She made plans with the friends she'd met since her arrival; I tagged along.

When I was ready, though—when I finally went out on my own—it was signs and letters that taught me how to love the city for myself.

To make it my new home.

So maybe that's why, after my awful, stomach-churning conversation with Sibby, I take the extra-long way to the shop, so extra-long that it's not really the way at all. It's just a big, zigzaggy detour that kills time before I really have to be there for the shift that doesn't start for another hour and that lets me see more of what I want to see: letters making sense.

There's not much at first, or at least not much most people would notice. The signs on my street are about how to function in a space, reminders of how to be a resident: **NO PARKING, CONSTRUCTION AHEAD, YIELD TO PEDESTRIANS.** They're mostly all caps, mostly sans serif, sizes varying depending on the seriousness of the problem you'll have if you don't pay attention to them. Then west toward Fifth, a left to take me past where I sat with Reid Sutherland last night, more of his words ringing in my ears.

There haven't been many signs for me here.

I go down Union, where it's all about to change, where it's not so much about functioning in a space as it is about figuring out what to visit or eat or buy once you're in it. There's a red awning marking out a restaurant known for using almost all local ingredients; their sign looks carelessly, charmingly handwritten, a heavy, uneven tittle over an *i*, an all-lowercase web address that looks scribbled out as an afterthought, a messy accommodation to modernity. Union and Sixth, a good corner for signage—a veterinary clinic with a slim sans serif, clean and safe-looking. A market with a lime-green star to replace the *A*, a standout against the black background—it's hip, it's expensive, it's probably got a bunch of food you've never heard of but you'd definitely be hip, too, if you tried it.

Past the neighborhood food co-op there's a block that gets exceptionally good for signs, for letters. A creamy script on the maroon awning of an Italian restaurant. Across the way, cream again, but this one for a laundromat, bold and plain against a dark green backdrop trimmed in yellow, the letters stacked vertically, efficiently, exactly how you'd want your laundry to be folded. A favorite: the jumbled cacophony of the multiple signs for a local, longstanding bike shop—some Gothic printing on the sign for the building, a decorative serif for the bright red sign hanging over the street. That one, it looks hand-painted, as does the window lettering—white, trimmed in blue—over the front door. *We've been here a long time*, these signs say. *It doesn't matter if we match.*

I keep walking, head up, and I feel as if I'm counting, noticing signs I've never looked at before, and that's saying something. It soothes me in the same way it did back then, when I learned the city by walking it, by paying attention. I learned neighborhoods letter by letter, sign by sign. It's how I got inspired; it's how I fell in love with the city but also how I learned to make it here. It's how I taught myself that I could be someone other than the sheltered, suburban girl from the perfect-on-the-surface family. It's what I sketched late at night on the subway, stinking of food and dead tired, distracting myself from thoughts of my parents and also my chances of getting mugged—signs and letters I'd seen, new ideas that rattled loudly in my head like the tracks beneath my feet. It's what convinced me to take the first commission I ever got offered, twenty-five birthday party invitations for my catering manager's son's eighth birthday party.

It's what convinced me to go out on my own, to start the business that turned Meg Mackworth into The Planner of Park Slope.

There are *signs*, I'm thinking, to the invisible Reid who won't get out of my head. *You just don't know how to read them.*

I'm a few blocks from the shop when the idea hits me. I can't seem to do anything about Sibby, about the path she's going down that'll take her even further away from me, but I can do something about myself, about the way I've been feeling lonely and blocked, restless with the need to say too much in the jobs I'm doing, reluctant to even attempt a start on the job that could change everything for me.

Maybe I can remember that every single letter I draw is a sign. No reckless, inappropriate codes necessary.

I need to get out here again, walk the streets, see the signs, remember what really brought me to lettering in the first place.

Inspiration for this new job, some bonus content for my social media. A series of walks, inspired by the city's best hand-lettered signs. A bit of research and planning, the warmer months coming—it's *something*, something to help me get unblocked.

Some of the weight from this morning has lifted as I approach the shop's front door, as I unlock the two heavy bolts for the old storefront gate, a relic from back when this place was a jewelry repair shop. Inside I leave the lights off for now, the shop's interior lit enough by the nearly midday sun. Before it's time to open, I figure I can straighten all the stock, double-check the register, make sure the back room is tidy for meetings the freelance calligraphers and letterers will have here today. Lachelle at noon, Yoshiko at two, David at three thirty. Tomorrow Cecelia will be back, and the distraction of these temporary shifts will be at an end.

But I've got a plan now. I wish fleetingly that I had someone else here I felt close enough to call up, to say, *Hey, want to go with me on these inspiration walks?* But one of the worst outcomes of the distance between Sibby and me is how quickly it revealed the shallowness of so many of my connections here—colleagues and clients, people I like and respect and enjoy, but people who know me only as cheerful, frolicsome Meg, drawing and working with ease, quick with a smile, good for a laugh and some light conversation.

Calling any of them now—when I'm so blocked, when my reckless, ridiculous habit seems determined to make a reappearance—seems, somehow, impossible.

Still, going it alone will maybe be a good reminder. This city is mine, too, whether Sibby's my roommate or not, whether Sibby's my *friend* or not. This city is home.

A flash of white on the worn oak floor catches the edge of my vision as I approach the counter, a scrap of paper someone must've dropped, and I reach down to pick it up. I should've swept last night, one of the items on the evening closeout list, but I'd been distracted by Reid waiting for our Incredibly Uncomfortable Espresso-Herbal Tea Summit, standing by the door like a statue in my periphery.

Once it's between my fingers, though, I get that same ripple of feeling I had when he'd stood right across from me, the counter and my secret between us. It's not a piece of scrap paper at all. It's a perfect, pristine rectangle. It's cardstock, extra thick, rounded corners you pay extra for. Black ink, raised, so you can run the pad of your thumb over it and feel each letter. A lovely, Glyphic serif—what a surprise.

It's simple. A name, a title, a place, an e-mail address.

A sign.

For the first time in months, my mind sparks with an idea. An outrageous idea, maybe, but still—an idea.

To write to Reid Sutherland, and to ask him if he wants to be part of my plan.

Chapter 4

For the next six days, I am haunted not by a word, not by a letter; not even, really, by a name.

Instead I am haunted by a single sound: that brief, airy swoosh that came from my phone when I pressed send on my impulsive e-mail to Reid.

I hear it all through my last fill-in shift at Cecelia's, when the sound is fresh, when I'm still in the headspace where it seems completely rational to navigate to my Sent folder so I can read my short, hastily drafted message every—oh, say twelve to fifteen minutes. I hear it all that night and the next day, when I try desperately to focus on work, when I resort to tasks like designing new color-coding systems for my pens (my old system was fine, really), when I do a six-part Instagram story on how to draw a black letter *R*. I tell myself it stands for *Regret* rather than a certain person who has not yet returned my e-mail. I do get a direct message that tells me my black letter *R* is "lol, boring," which is only comforting in that I can't imagine Reid had any such reaction to my e-mail.

I hear it Wednesday evening when I'm sitting on my couch,

my browser open with approximately ten thousand Google Maps tabs open, research for the city walks I may very well be doing alone. That one is so real-seeming, even in spite of the headphones I have in my ears, that I look up, only to find Sibby opening the door to our apartment, her eyes down on her own phone, her eventual smile of greeting bland and noncommittal. I hear it again Thursday morning when she leaves for work, while I stay still and quiet in my bed, still groggy from a restless sleep.

On Friday I think I may get a respite from this twenty-first century Tell-Tale Heart sideshow, because Reid finally, *finally* e-mails me back, his message time-stamped at 5:01 p.m., because *of course* it is. It's brief, efficient (more shock and awe, obviously), barely more than a recitation of my own offer to meet again. *I'll find you at the Promenade,* he'd written. *Sunday, four o'clock.* I stare at that e-mail for a long time. *Maybe he's hidden a code,* I think, though there aren't enough *f*'s for "fuck off," which, you know. Would be fair enough, I guess.

But I hear it again now, a tiny echo of it.

Because it's Sunday, one week since he showed me that program. Because it's three p.m., and if I'm going to make it to the Promenade by four, I need to leave the shop soon and catch the R train ("lol, boring") to Court Street. Because in one hour (you know he'll be right on time!), I need to make a pitch to a man who has very real reasons to dislike me. Because if he takes me up on this, I might be seeing him semiregularly for the foreseeable future.

"You seem antsy," says Lachelle, which I appreciate, because at least it stops the phantom swooshing in my brain. Across from me, she pulls her nib away from her sharpening stone and picks up the small magnifying glass she's wearing around her neck to check the sloping edge. She makes a noise of frustration and drops the glass again, adding a few more drops of water to the stone.

"Oh, not at all," I say casually, my voice customer service cheerful in spite of the fact that we're in the rear of the shop. Lachelle's in to try out a new brand of walnut ink Cecelia's ordered, some museum benefit job they're collaborating on. I'm in to pretend I need to test out Cecelia's metallic pen inventory, but really I'm here because Sibby and Elijah are at our place watching a show about people making terrible baking errors, and my nerves are too jangled to act normal around them *or* around the baking errors. And since I couldn't really decide what would be worse—Sibby noticing my nerves and asking me about it, Sibby noticing and not asking me about it, or Sibby not noticing at all—I figured visiting the shop made sense.

A return to the scene of the swoosh, if you will.

"What I mean is," Lachelle clarifies, "your leg shaking is making this table move."

I feel my face flush as I still my unruly right leg. "Oh! I'm so sorry."

Lachelle looks up at me and smiles. "Do you have a date or something?"

Swoooooooooosh, my brain says, loudly. I use the silver Tombow I've been testing to represent this noise on the page. It looks disappointingly similar to the famous logo, which is strike one million against my creativity lately.

"Uh. No."

I don't think she buys it, her lips pursing skeptically, and for the barest, most deranged of seconds, I think of telling her. *There's this guy,* I'd say. *He's a former client who picked up on a bad habit I've got.* We don't know each other all that well, Lachelle and me, but we've got a friendly rapport whenever we're at the shop together. She's fun and kind and as talented as anyone I know, and maybe—

"Good, you're still here," Cecelia says to me, breezing into the room and breaking the spell, her arms full of a stack of look-books, various paper and writing samples she's constantly assembling and reassembling for clients who come in needing ideas. "I got a call about you yesterday."

There's a thud of nerves in my stomach. What if he changed his mind? What if he decided Cecelia—she is, after all, the owner of the shop those programs came out of—needed to know what I'd done? What if his agreement to meet me was his way of putting me off the scent of this, his eventual truth-telling to my former boss?

"Oh?" I manage to make that single syllable into three.

Cecelia gives me a curious look but keeps moving, setting the books onto one of the white shelves lining the walls back here, all of them tidily organized and gorgeously color-schemed, two of Cecelia's many strengths. "Yes, a new client. She's *desperate* to hire you."

My body sags in relief. *It wasn't him. Thank God, it wasn't him.*

Cecelia turns to me, the long curtain of her straight black hair—not even a whisper of gray in there, no matter that she's nearing fifty—slipping over one shoulder, her hands going to her hips. "*Desperate*," she repeats, her smile proud.

"I'm sorry. I don't know why people don't use the web form I have set up on my site." Even as I say it, I know this isn't *really* what I'm apologizing for, since Cecelia's never acted annoyed by the calls she sometimes still gets about me and my work. I'm apologizing for that thud of nerves. For the cause of that thud, and the trouble it could have caused her.

Cecelia lifts a hand from her waist, waves it dismissively. "It's no problem. She said she's cautious about e-mail." She pauses, peeks out toward the front of the shop to make sure it's still only the three of us here. "I think it's someone *famous*."

"Don't do it," says Lachelle immediately, raising the glass to her eye again and squinting. "Three months ago, I did party invitations for one of the Real Housewives and it was a nightmare. Three redos from the time I started the job and I didn't even see anyone get a drink thrown in their face. What a waste."

"It's not a Real Housewife," says Cecelia, moving to peek over Lachelle's shoulder. She hums approval at the practice Lachelle has already done. "I could tell."

"She didn't give you a name?" I don't know why I'm even asking. New clients are not part of the plan, not until I make my deadline.

She looks over at me, shakes her head. "She left the name and number of her assistant. Said to call anytime."

"Oooh, an assistant," says Lachelle. "Yeah, definitely call her."

"She seemed nice," Cecelia says. "I don't think she'd throw a drink in anyone's face. She'd probably pay a *lot*. If she's some huge star, it could be a big deal for you."

"Yeah, I'm—" I pause, make a show of gathering my things while I gather myself. I haven't told Cecelia yet about what I've been working on, especially since—given my gummed-up creativity—it may not come to anything. "I'm probably too swamped right now," I finish, and it's about as convincing as my denial about not having a date. Lachelle gives me that same mouth-purse.

"You're sure?"

I cross my bag over my body, smooth down the front of my dress. No patterns, in case they make the situation with Reid worse, who'll probably be back to the debate team thing today. A short-sleeved T-shirt dress, an emerald green that Sibby always says looks nice with my light brown hair, a denim jacket over top. Probably I should've considered whether the various enamel pins and buttons I have decorating the front pockets will be a distraction. One of them says *Keep NYC Weird*, which I'm guessing Reid won't find hugely endearing given that New York's weirdness has to be numbers one through one hundred on the "Reasons Why He Hates It" list.

When I look up again, Cecelia and Lachelle are both watching me, their expressions twinned in confusion, probably at my uncharacteristic quiet. They're good friends, the two of them— about five or so years ago Lachelle took one of Cecelia's calligraphy classes, and Lachelle was such a quick study that now they collaborate often. But they also hang out—they're both married, both have kids, though Lachelle's are younger than Cecelia's teenagers. Together they have what I think of as the general magic of calligraphers—a smooth confidence, a steadiness, the same quality that allows them to set an ink-dipped nib to a page and create something beautiful. No stopping the stroke, no pauses to erase and try again.

I feel another gripping pain of loneliness, of longing. I came here this afternoon for company, for respite from the *swoosh*. But even small talk seems risky—I can't really talk about Reid without explaining how I know him, which would be disastrous. I'm not confident enough at the moment to talk about my deadline, and I'm embarrassed to tell them about my block.

"I'm *totally* sure," I say lightly.

Cecelia shrugs, pulls out the chair that's next to Lachelle. "I'll hang on to it anyway. Just in case."

"She'll change her mind," Lachelle says, looking up at me and smiling, giving me a teasing wink. "She's distracted by this date she's got."

Cecelia pauses, mid-sit, her eyes lighting up. "Oh, a date? That's nice!"

"That's nice" is what married people always say when they find out you have a date. As though a good eighty-six percent of dates in this city don't end with you considering a blood pact with yourself to give up men in general.

"It is *not* a date." This is the most conviction I have put into any sentence since I've arrived here. Cecelia, sitting now, nudges Lachelle with her elbow, and they both smile at me. I roll my eyes genially, check my phone. I'll still make it on time, but I don't feel any less nervous than when I showed up here. "I'll take the Tombow," I tell Cecelia, dropping it in my bag. "Put it on my account?"

"Sure," says Cecelia, but she's distracted now, reaching for a fresh sheet of the paper Lachelle's been using.

"I'll see you guys," I say, moving around the table.

"Meg." Lachelle's voice stops me as I'm about to cross into the front part of the shop. "Someone knows where you're going, right?"

I still in place, wishing I could toss back a light reply immediately. But that small expression of care—that code of friendship that insists on these kinds of safety hatches—I feel a brief press of tears behind my eyes. It takes me a second to swallow them back before I look over my shoulder, smiling brightly.

"Oh, sure," I lie. But I'm so grateful that I add, "The Promenade. Public place, and all that."

"Have fun!" she calls back, but she and Cecelia already have their heads bent together, looking over the ink, a picture of the kind of comfortable friendship I don't know if I'll ever have again.

When I'm pushing out the door, Cecelia's bright laugh rings out behind me, and I feel as alone as I have in months.

Swoosh, I hear as the door closes behind me.

♥   ♥   ♥

In the end I make it a whole six minutes early.

It's a busy walk down Montague—the sun's out, the weather's warm, and everyone's got that slightly dazed "oh my God, it finally stopped raining" look about them. Instead of focusing on signs—almost as though I don't want to jinx it before I talk to Reid—I focus on people. I pass the Häagen-Dazs and see a man staring down at his chocolate shake like he's a groom at the end of the aisle and he's just seen his bride walk through the doors. I see a kid joyfully swinging her mother's hand while she licks at a cone, what's probably thirty percent of the original serving spread across both her cheeks and down the front of her shirt. I see an older couple standing outside a café, both of them squinting at the menu that's tacked up in the window, and the shorter man says, "They've got a club sandwich; you love a club sandwich!" as though a club sandwich is a really great surprise to come across and not a menu item you could find within five blocks of any place you're standing.

Once I get to Pierrepont Place I can see the blue of the East River ahead. With the sun shining, the water is a brighter shade than I've seen in months and months, and the breeze across my face is enough to cool me down, but not enough to make me worried about getting hair stuck in my lip gloss, which, as everyone knows, is the ideal type of breeze. There's a woman hanging around the bike racks, juggling four balls of yarn and singing a song about cat astronauts (*Keep NYC Weird,* obviously), and while I'd normally think of this as an ideal opportunity to avert my eyes and pretend there's something interesting on my phone, this stretch of people-watching I've been indulging in means I'm somehow charmed and not vaguely on alert for one of those yarn balls to hit me in the head. For a few seconds I feel a bit like chocolate milkshake guy or club sandwich man, remembering for the first time since the *swoosh* why I'd thought this was a good idea. Even if Reid says no, getting out here, around all these people, will be good for me.

I just need to get through this one meeting, which I am, again, six minutes early for, an absolute advantage since I can set myself—

Except of course! He's already here.

He's twenty or so yards down the Promenade, his forearms resting along the railing, hands clasped in front of him as he looks across the river toward the city. He's definitely not doing business casual, wearing instead something similar to what I saw him in a week ago—sneakers, jeans, jacket. Maybe this is his Sunday outfit. It's probably labeled that way in his extremely anal-retentive closet. His profile, even at a distance, is ridiculously handsome.

I subtract a few letters from that word that's been haunting me. His face looks like the word *swoon*.

He straightens as I draw closer to him, as though he's sensed me coming, and when he turns toward me there's an awkward few steps where there's nothing happening except him standing there waiting for me. I feel as if I'm walking the plank toward those blue eyes, flat and fixed on me. I wonder if he'll say, "Good afternoon."

"Hey," he says instead. I try not to let my eyebrows raise in surprise.

"Thanks for coming." For the first time, I notice there's a woman sitting on the bench closest to us. She's got a travel mug in one hand and her phone in the other, and she's staring at Reid with her mouth slightly open, which is probably what I would be doing if I were in her position and was seeing him for the first time. He doesn't seem to notice, but still I say, "Want to walk?" and I'm relieved when he nods, lifting an arm in a gesture that tells me to go ahead. Maybe the woman behind us sighs.

"So," I say, trying to squeeze right into that casual "Hey" he offered me. "How's your weekend been?"

He looks over at me, blinks once. He is definitely not going to dignify small talk with a response. I might as well have asked him which sexually transmitted diseases he's been tested for.

"Mine's been okay," I continue, as though he's answered me. "Of course, it rained all day yesterday, so I didn't get out much. Pretty nice out here today, though."

If Sibby were here, she would remind me that talking about the weather in this way is functionally the same as having "I'm a Midwesterner" tattooed onto my face. For my next trick, why not bring up a garage sale I heard about? Or perhaps point out that I got the bag I'm carrying at a fifty percent off sale, with an extra five percent deducted for a temperamental zipper? Would Reid be interested in knowing my opinions on mayonnaise versus Miracle Whip?

"You mentioned you had an idea," Reid says, and he is obviously not referring to the mayonnaise-Miracle Whip thing.

I clear my throat, committed to dispensing with the small talk for both our sakes. "Right. Right, well. I was thinking about what you said last week. About there not being signs for you here?"

I slide my eyes his way. His hands are in his jacket pockets. His head is tipped down. He's listening, but he's keeping his distance about it.

"Well, signs are sort of . . . my thing. Given my job and all, I'm always interested in signs—what they say, how they say it."

He stops, and I'm a half step ahead before I pause, too, turning to look back at him. His face is so serious, the kind of face that should be stamped on a coin.

"I was not speaking literally." I think the slight softness to his voice is sympathy. *Dear Diary,* I imagine him writing later. *Today I met a woman wearing too many buttons who does not understand what a metaphor is.*

"No, I mean . . . of course, I realize that. But when I first moved here, the actual signs, they sort of, um"—I look out toward the Manhattan skyline, all its huge gray-and-glass chaos—"they organized my experience."

There's a long stretch of silence while Reid simply looks at me. I'm guessing my sense of organization is different from his, what with the days-of-the-week outfits and daily diary entries I have assigned to him, but for some reason—maybe for the same reason I felt that odd connection to him last week and last year, too—I have the sense he gets it. That he wants me to keep going.

We start walking again.

"I have this project. My deadline is in July, which is a long way away, but also not, because I'm . . ." I pause, a heavy swallow in my throat. Too blocked to even say the word out loud, which is I guess whatever the opposite of irony is. "Because I've been having some trouble focusing on my work lately," I say instead.

"That seems hard to believe."

"Why's that?"

He looks out at one of the piers beneath us, where there's some kind of kickball game going on, the occasional distant shout of celebration or objection filtering up to us. "Because you—the lettering projects, I mean. They're very . . . creative."

My lips press together in annoyance. Something about the way he's said *creative*—as if he's using air quotes around the word—makes it sound like I'm hobbying around, not serious. I tell myself to let it go, but then my mouth uncharacteristically trots ahead of my brain.

"You think creative people don't have to focus?"

"I didn't say that."

"What I do, it's a business, and—"

"I meant that it seems like it would be interesting, what you do. Lots of variation."

"Oh." I think about explaining all the *Bloom Where You're Planted*s, everyone lately wanting the same kind of brush lettering—swooping, upright scripts with fat, washed-out downstrokes. But it's probably petty to get into it. At least I've been switching up the color schemes.

"Is it not that way?" he asks, and the thing is, even though I don't really know Reid at all, I once again get that sense about him, something essential. He never asks a question he doesn't want to know the answer to. In a world of the standard, unthinking "How are you?" where the only real acceptable answer seems to be a neutral "Fine," Reid's attention feels special. Acute.

I shrug. "It's the same as anything else, I suppose. It can get rote, or frustrating. When that happens, it's easy to make a mistake."

He coughs. Because I said *mistake*. I wonder if the dive into the river from here would kill me, or just maim me. I think my steps actually falter for a second, as though my body's really considering it. It can't be as dirty in there as everyone's always saying.

"It's okay," he says, keeping his eyes ahead. "It's a common word."

"I'm sure your work is interesting!" I blurt. "Variation, or whatever." I try to think of some keywords from the absolutely impenetrable Wikipedia page on "quantitative analysts" I read last week in preparation for this meeting. I think I quit reading at the word *stochastic*, which actually sort of reminded me of Reid, if what it means is a combination of *stoic* and *sarcastic*. But I'm pretty sure it has to do with calculus.

"What kind of project?" Reid asks, and it is absolutely a deliberate cutoff. He is not interested in talking about his work with me, which I suppose I should be grateful for. It is both too math adjacent and too ex-fiancée adjacent.

I stop, gesture to one of the few empty benches on this busier part of the Promenade. Once I'm seated, I pull my bag onto my lap, reach in for the slim, soft-covered notebook I've been using for my ideas. When Reid sits beside me, I wince at the crinkle of stuff inside—a half-eaten bag of pretzels, probably ten balled-up receipts from Target. I start talking immediately to cover it, and maybe it's a gift—having to rush this out. It ensures that I don't think too hard about Reid being the first person I've told.

"There's this company, Make It Happyn? 'Happen' but with a *y*, so it's—uh, 'happy' also."

"I don't get it."

Frankly, I don't get it, either. It is cheesy in a way that makes me slightly embarrassed, but I don't want to admit that to Reid, so I move on. "They're a big brand for most of the major craft retailers. They make build-your-own planner materials. Folios and accessories and calendar pages."

"Like what you make."

"Not really," I say, thinking of the big, neon-signed store on Atlantic Avenue that I visited after my first phone call with the artistic director, a bold-voiced, fast-talking woman named Ivonne. The Make It Happyn aisle had been crowded with shoppers, some displays nearly sold out. I'd felt uncertain initially, seeing some of the more generic stuff. A January spread done all in ice blue. February, pinks and reds. March, all green. April, raindrops. May? An actual Maypole, which made *Bloom Where You're Planted* feel damned subtle by comparison.

But I'd been excited, too, by the possibilities, by the treatments I could create. It could be career-changing, this job, giving me the kind of opportunities most people in my position would love to have. Life-changing, especially now, if it means I can stay in my place on my own, at least for a while.

"I mean, yes," I correct, raising my chin. "They're mass-produced, obviously. Not . . ." I trail off. *Not containing subtle commentary on the status of anyone's relationship*, is what I'm thinking. That's another benefit to the job, frankly. Surely I won't be tempted to weave ridiculous, reckless codes into work I'm submitting for a general audience.

"Unique," Reid says, and it's a kindness, I think. The most generous completion of that sentence possible.

I stroke the front of my bag, my face flushing, but stop when I hear the crinkling again.

"So," I say brightly, to cover the crinkling, "They've asked me and a few other artists to produce three treatments, full-year planner pages. If they choose me, they'd produce a line with my work, using my name."

"Aha," he says quietly, barely a murmur. "A business opportunity."

"You say that as if it's a bad thing."

He turns his head, looks vacantly across the river. "It isn't."

He lifts a hand, gestures toward the Manhattan skyline. "Obviously."

But that *Obviously*—he's sure made it sound as if it's a bad thing. He's made it sound like business opportunities are the worst thing. Like that skyline is Sauron.

When he looks at me, his blue eyes washed pale with the bright sun, his expression looks harder, closer to the way it had been when he'd come to the shop last week.

"Despite what you may think about my work," he says, "I'm not some kind of business consultant. That isn't the work I do."

"I have no idea what you do."

"I told you. I'm a qu—"

It's my turn to wave a hand. "I looked it up. I still don't understand it. Math, that's the extent of it. You're probably very smart."

His mouth lifts, higher on the right side, and it makes a gorgeous decorative line on his cheek, a curve up from his chin, a gentle swoop outward toward his cheek. That curve—it only lasts a second, maybe two, but it's enough to feel seared into my brain. I'll probably try to draw it later. *Swoonsh*.

"I don't want you to help me with my business," I say, looking away. "That's not what this is for."

"What's it for, then?"

I take a deep, courage-gathering inhale. "It's for me to get some ideas."

I tell him briefly about the signs, about how they inspired me, how the letters on them, especially in this city, are *full* of variation. I show him the page in my notebook, where I've made a bulleted list of some of the most famous hand-lettered signs around the city. I reach for my phone, to show him the map I've saved, tiny red pins marking all the places I plan to go, but before I can unlock it, he speaks.

"I don't see why you'd want me involved. I don't know anything about letters."

"Because you're a numbers guy." A statement, not a question, and he doesn't respond other than with another polite tip of his head. It's as much an agreement as it is an invitation for me to continue, to well and truly explain myself.

But I'm not sure if I can do that. I'm not sure if I can be as honest, as direct as he was. *I found your card, and it felt like a sign.*

So I shrug casually, as if I do this kind of thing all the time. "Last time we talked, you said you hated this city. And it seemed to me I could h—"

He stiffens. That's saying something, because he is a stiff guy in general. "You feel sorry for me." His tone is sharp.

"What? No!" I think fleetingly of opening my bag to show him the pretzels and Target receipts. *Do I look like a person who would feel sorry for you?* I would say.

"Because I am not . . . I am not brokenhearted. About Avery." That tiny point of clarification. God.

"I wanted some company," I blurt, and that, I realize, is what I should've said from the beginning. It isn't the whole truth, but it's certainly part of it. I *do* want some company, and Reid— the only man in this city, in this *world*, who knows my secret— might, oddly enough, be the right man for the job.

He doesn't say anything for a few seconds. Then he stands, tucking his hands in his jacket pockets and turning back to me. From anyone else, I'd read this as a dick move, a way for someone to literally talk down to me. But Reid's face is contemplative, his posture looser. I think he simply needed to move, even that small amount.

"Someone did tell me recently I ought to try keeping my mind occupied."

I know he wouldn't appreciate it, but I definitely feel sorry for him now. This feeling intensifies when Reid takes one hand from his pocket and tugs at the sleeves of his jacket—a small, unconscious gesture that spells out a whole page of feeling to me. His discomfort. His disorientation at this whole entire prospect.

"Well, you see?" My voice is so . . . *buoyant.* "It could be a great idea. Even if it's awful, your mind will be occupied with how awful it is." I smile up at him, and he *swooshes* at me fleetingly. Then it's quiet again, Reid looking down at the gray pavers while I wait, notebook clutched in my hands.

"It's a *y* instead of an *e*?" he says, finally.

I blink up at him, and it takes me a second to catch up. *Make It Happyn*, of course.

"Yes."

"Because having the planner makes you happy." He says this so flatly. Stochastically. What if he had been in the marketing meeting where this idea was proposed? Probably everyone would have vaporized from the sheer force of his displeasure.

"I think that's the idea."

"It's ridiculous."

I nod, look down at my notebook. It'll be fine, to do this alone. Good for me, even.

He clears his throat, waits for me to look up at him. He fixes me with eyes that are, for the moment, not so sad. And then he says, "It's ridiculous, but I'll do it."

Chapter 5

I text Reid to meet me by The Garment Worker, a big, bronze statue of an older man in a yarmulke, bent in work over a hand-operated sewing machine, a loving tribute to the workers who made the textile industry in New York what it once was. It soothes me to wait by this particular piece of art, since in general Midtown has never been my speed—even when it's blocks away Times Square is still a shouty, ocular migraine-inducing shadow, too many honking horns and flashing lights and tourists doing incomprehensible things like actually enjoying themselves in the madness. But even though this is still a pretty loud spot, especially on a Wednesday afternoon, I'm comforted by the quiet stillness of the sculpture. And since I've arrived a half hour early—as if I'm trying to out-anal-retentive my companion—I've had a lot of time to be comforted.

I've spent most of that time considering two things: one is the list of addresses I copied out, comparing it to the map on my phone and reviewing the path I've set out for our walk. If I've got it right—and this is questionable, since one never really knows whether a hand-painted sign will have faded into oblivion, or whether some new build has since blocked its visibility—Reid and I should be able to see at least a dozen signs today. Whether I like the neighborhood or not, the Garment District has a lot to offer in the way of signage, and there's even a few—one from a 1960s dress shop in particular—that have drawings included. My list makes me feel productive, prepared. Ready to meet the challenge and to meet Reid on firmer ground, a shared goal between us.

The other consideration is the fact that, as a human woman, I would of course wake up with two new pimples on my forehead on the same day I have something important to do, and with someone I want to look presentable for. This latter consideration, obviously, is not a productive line of thinking, unless you consider my reaching up to touch them every forty-five seconds productive.

That's what I am doing, in fact, when Reid arrives. Today he's fallen way off the casual clothes wagon, as in he has set the wagon on fire and spit on the ashes, because he's wearing a suit. Dark blue, almost black. Slim cut. White shirt, gray tie. A gray messenger bag crossing his chest.

Wall Street Reid.

It shouldn't really be a surprise. Reid picked the day and time, coordinating with a meeting he mentioned having in the area, and it makes sense that the meeting would have to do with his fancy job. But somehow it still startles me to see him this way, and it's almost as though he knows it, because for a few seconds after nodding a greeting he simply stands, looking up at the still, serious, sewing man.

I clutch my list so tightly it's nearly folded in half in my hand. "Neat, right?" I finally say, moving to stand beside him. "Is this your first time seeing it?"

"No." He looks over at me, then turns his head to stare across Seventh. "There's a bridal shop over there I've been to."

He hasn't said it with any malice, but it's possible we've released some kind of awkward nerve gas into the air. Everyone within a half-mile radius probably pauses where they stand and winces.

"Right," I say, hoping my whole head hasn't turned into the cringe emoji. "Lots of bridal shops and fabric shops around here." The strangeness of our agreement, of our being together in any context at all, washes over me again, and part of me wants to bolt, to forget the whole thing.

I'm jolted by the shoulder of a passing pedestrian, part of a small group of tourists who are laughing and staring down at one of their phones, and when I bump into Reid's side from the impact, he steadies me with a hand on my elbow and snaps, "Watch it, asshole," at the pedestrian. I'm pretty sure the guy doesn't hear him, but the line is enough of a surprise to shake me out of my inhibitions.

"*Whoa*," I say, my eyes wide as I look up at Reid. "You called that guy an asshole!"

That flush I waited for the other night in the shop—it shows up now, faintly, right at the outer swoop of Reid's cheekbones.

"I mean, I don't imagine you saying a word like *asshole*." He furrows his brow, so I clarify. "I thought your insults would be—I don't know. 'Rogue.' 'Scoundrel.'" *Old-timey.*

"Why would they be like that?" His voice is still flat, but his eyes are interested, and his hand is definitely still on my elbow, which is a brand-new erogenous zone I've never known about.

I shrug, dislodging his hand. Probably I shouldn't share the *Masterpiece Theatre* thing. "You sounded like a New Yorker."

The muscles in his jaw tick. "You mentioned there was a lot to see around here."

"Yes, right!" Too cheerful, again. I try to less cheerfully pass him my list, and he looks down at it for a few seconds, his brows still lowered.

"We should switch the first three with the last two," he says. "It's more efficient."

I peek over his shoulder at the list, then swipe my thumb across my phone, stare down at my map. *Shoot.* He is correct.

"That was rude," he says suddenly, and I look up at him. He looks tired around his eyes, the bright, piercing blue somehow wearier. "To use that word."

I smile. I know which word he means—I'd pictured it written out, *very* sans serif, as soon as it had come out of his mouth. *Asshole.* But I feign ignorance.

"Efficient?" I say, widening my eyes dramatically.

He seems to appreciate that, the *swoonsh* back briefly, and it doesn't quite break the tension between us, but it makes it more manageable. I have a flashback to every time a teacher made the class count off into partners: those initial minutes where you're sitting next to someone who *feels* new to you, no matter that they've only been sitting a few rows away for the whole school year.

It starts out well, it really does. The first three signs— efficient, indeed!—are still visible, and while the first one is a little bland, not much more than different sizes of the same basic block lettering, the second and third are winners, basically giant, hand-painted banners on the brick sides of buildings, multiple advertisements stacked on top of one another with lots of lettering styles. For both of those, we stop, tucking ourselves out of the way as best we can so I can take photos without getting in the way of people walking, and it becomes a sort of rhythm between us as we move through the next few on the list. A couple of times, Reid takes my phone from me and gets a better angle, his height and long arms a real advantage. Sometimes he crosses the street or straightens himself beside a parked car to get closer. When we talk, it feels safe, focused— he asks me what I call a certain type of lettering, or asks me to explain some term I use for a specific part of a letter. At one point, I tease him about watching some of the short tutorials I've done so he can practice the basics, handing him one of my own business cards and directing him to my website. For some reason, it makes my stomach flutter to see him holding it, to see him looking down at its careful design. It's as though I'm peeking in on the same private moment I'd had when I'd held his card in the shop.

He carefully tucks it inside the inner pocket of his suit jacket, giving it a single, serious pat, as though he's really planning to watch one of those videos, and I feel my face flush in pleasure.

But sometime around the sixth sign, things start to take a

turn for the worse. Two in a row, we can't find—either because I've got something wrong from my searching or because they're covered up. The next is too faded to see. After that, my dressmaker sign, the one with so much potential—I don't know if I've written the address wrong, but nothing from the image I saw online looks familiar around the address I've written down. I check the map again, zoom in on various satellite views; I ask Reid to try a different app while I'm looking. I feel pressured, embarrassed, and it's Reid who has to suggest we move on.

And on top of that, the sidewalks seem to grow steadily more crowded. Our strategy of staying out of the way now seems more difficult to master. Reid's already always-stiff demeanor stiffens; he looks tense and impatient—*I* hate *New York*—and I'm flustered, too. I see signs that aren't on my list, wonder if I should stop, then struggle to refocus. The sky has turned grayer than it was when I arrived, as gray as the buildings that seem to loom on all sides, and this seems to make the signs harder to discern.

Around Sixth and 36th, there's a sign I caught sight of on a blog, but when we get close, my heart sinks—the parts I can see are faded, and there's construction scaffolding everywhere, obscuring the view. The noise is unreal—grinding, metallic, miserable. Reid and I have to shout at each other to suggest angles at which we might see better; at one point, misunderstanding each other completely, we turn in the exact opposite direction from each other, and I have to reach out to tug on his sleeve so that he follows me under a scaffold sidewalk to get closer to the sign. Through the brief length of it, the noise from the construction seems even louder, inside-your-bones loud, and the space is warm with the body heat of everyone passing through it. I look up at Reid when we emerge, see his jaw work, as though he'd been clenching his teeth the whole way through.

"We'll just try and see this one." I'm already opening the camera app on my phone.

"You still can't see it. Maybe two of the letters."

He's right, but I don't want to give in to it. I look around, as though some new route will open up, some new staircase to the sky that'll let me get closer. This one, it feels important—the background a deep red; the one *W* I can see has a drop-shadow, which none of the other signs had, and beneath that, I'm almost sure there's a script. "What if I—"

And then it starts raining.

It's not a drip-drop kind of situation, either. It's the kind that starts right in the middle of things, big, soaking sheets all at once. People-scattering rain, and everyone around Reid and me is running to duck for cover, most of them cramming back under the scaffolding Reid was so relieved to be free of. One advantage to the massive, slouchy bag I carry is that I can put it over my head, though this feels pretty silly when Reid shifts his own bag long enough to pull out an umbrella. Even though he knows words like *asshole*, he definitely isn't one, because he puts it over my head instead of his own, and points across the street to a blue awning, where a short, harried-looking woman is tugging a rack of fabric bolts back into her store. As we jog, our feet slapping against wet concrete, our clothes misted by the cars we dodge, Reid stays a half step behind me. I can't say for sure, but I think I feel the way he keeps his hand hovering at my back.

Not touching. But hovering.

When we're finally undercover, there's a few seconds where we're both surveying the damage. My tights soaked up to the knees, my dress stuck wetly to my thighs. His suit blackened with moisture, his hair copper-brown. I look up at him, feel a solidarity smile spread over my mouth. It's *funny*, isn't it? It's funny how this went?

"You don't have an umbrella?" he says, and it's . . . not funny. It's *scolding*.

I stare at him, a long second of censure at his tone, at that haughty way he's looking at me.

"Yes, I *have* one. But not on my person, obviously." I think about my crinkly bag full of stuff. On the train I reached in for my box of Altoids and found a single sock, one of those half-foot ones that you can't see beneath sneakers. It's truly appalling that I don't have an umbrella in there, but it's also truly appalling that he's pointing this out.

"It wasn't supposed to rain," I say.

Reid mumbles something from beside me.

"What?"

"I said forty percent."

I keep staring. There is a single droplet of rain quivering on the end of the hair that curls at his temple.

"Forty percent chance of rain," he clarifies. "On my weather app."

"Forty percent isn't one hundred, is it?"

The drop of rain falls onto the collar of his suit jacket. He looks entirely confused by what I have said, and his jaw clenches again. As if we've been cued, both of us turn to stare out at the street in front of us, the rain coming down impossibly faster. There's a slice of space between us that's charged with the strange energy crackling between us.

"This new project," he says eventually, his voice louder to compensate for the thudding rain on the awning above us. "Will you give up your clients, if you get it?"

A gust of wind blows a mist at us, and I take a step back, watching the pavement get wetter around the toes of my shoes. I feel defensive, prickly—the walk getting off track, the umbrella censure, the way I can still feel where he touched me.

I shrug, playing at a flippancy I don't feel. "Probably not. I like working with my hands. But there's only one of me. This job would give me a cushion, and new opportunities. I definitely could take on fewer clients."

"Everything you do now, it's freelance?"

I look over and up at him, but he's giving me his profile, his eyes still on the street. "Yes," I answer, slowly. Suspiciously. I don't know how much longer I can play at flippancy in the face of this.

"What if you have a lean month?"

I purse my lips. On the one hand, I don't want to sound like a pompous jerk. On the other, Reid is being one with this question. "I pick up work easily. I'm in demand."

He nods. "But if there were lean times," he says. "You have an LLC, or something? Do you pay yourself a salary out of that?"

Oh my *God*. Whatever is worse than man-splaining, this is it.

This is man-terrogating. Before, at the Promenade, his ques-tions—they were blunt, too abrupt. But they didn't feel this way, at least. These are vaguely accusatory and not-so-vaguely supe-rior.

"Remember how you said you weren't a business consultant?"

"Yes," he says, grimly; then he goes quiet. But when there's a long stretch of silence, the rain slowing to a steady but still seri-ous shower, Reid clears his throat and speaks again. "What do you do for health insurance?"

"Hey, look," I say, nodding my head across the street. My voice is still cheerful, but nothing inside of me is. "There's the None of Your Business Store. And right beside it, the boutique called Things You Have No Right to Ask."

I don't look at him, but I know—I *know* what he's doing. He's looking across the street, too. He knows those aren't real signs, but he's looking anyway.

"I only meant that health care costs are at a premium, and many people in creative industries—"

"Reid." I turn to face him, crossing my arms over my chest and feeling a fresh mist of rain blow against my whole right side—my clothes, my face, my hair. I never really knew what people meant before when they said someone was "pushing their buttons." Right now, I am *made* of buttons.

I take a deep breath, wait for him to look at me. I feel *electric*.

"Let's get something straight between us. I don't feel sorry for you, and you have no reason to feel sorry for me, either. I'm not some manic pixie dream girl who needs your stabilizing influence. I'm good at my job. I built a business in one of the toughest cities in the world that now people are coming to *me* to expand. I only thought it'd be nice to have a—"

I break off, startled, my face heating. I was going to say *friend*. Jesus, what am I *doing*? Why am I saying all these things to him?

"A what?" he asks.

"Company," I finish, limply. "Like I said before."

"You do have a company."

"No—" Oh, my God. This is so . . . it's so *frustrating*, how it is between us. How he presses me on every single thing, how he baits me into saying what I shouldn't say. How he doesn't *let* me keep it light.

"That's not what I meant," I say.

The whole world seems to quiet around us, the rain suddenly slowing, barely a drizzle now. Fat globes of it drop from the edge of the awning we stand under, and within seconds there's twice the number of people on the street, emerging from whatever shelter they took during the downpour. Reid watches them, looking tense and handsome and sad, and even in spite of the frustration, I still feel that thing—that sympathy, that connection.

But I'm wrong, clearly.

I step out from underneath the awning. A big drop of rain falls from the edge of it and hits me on the forehead, right where the pimples are. No umbrella, no dignity. What a freaking *day*.

"Meg," he says softly, and for a second, I think his eyes might be—pleading? But his mouth closes again. He's got nothing at all to add. This whole thing has been painful for him, from start to finish.

He tries to hand me his umbrella, but I wave it off.

"This was a mistake," I say, and this time he doesn't cough when he hears me say the word. *That* word.

He only looks at me, holding that stupid forty-percent-chance umbrella, and I guess it's as good as an agreement.

I turn and walk away, and I feel as if I'm trailing the letters of that fateful word behind me.

♥ ♥ ♥

By the time I get home, I'm a wet, straggly-haired, angry mess. I am basically a feral cat, if feral cats got harassed two times on the subway, once by a man who kept insisting I take his seat and then called me a "rude bitch" when I finally told him I really preferred to stand, and once by his friend, who said he always liked a "gal" with a temper and then stared meaningfully—disgustingly—at my crotch. On my way off I discreetly stuck my gum to the strap of his backpack, but unless it has the power to expand and seal him and his douchebag friend into a suffocating, chewed-up cocoon of my feminist rage, it's a pretty hollow victory.

"Hey, you're home!"

It's a sign of how angry, how not myself I am that I don't even feel a spark of gratitude or relief or hope to find Sibby here, greeting me as though it's a welcome part of her day to have me home. She's sitting at the small, two-seat table we have off the kitchen, a takeout box of noodles in front of her, and all I feel is annoyed. Her hair is not only dry but also not at all straggly. Her winged eyeliner is back in top form, whereas I'm well aware that half my mascara is half down my face. Don't get me started on the fact that her skin is clear. Plus those noodles are from my favorite place.

"I need a shower," I say, and she looks slightly startled. For the last couple of months, I've been a lot of things with Sibby— questioning, polite, probably even desperate. But never angry or curt.

"Oh, sure," she says, waving her plastic chopsticks. Actually, they are *my* plastic chopsticks, which is obviously not as bad as getting harassed on the subway, but even so I wish I had a piece of gum in my mouth.

"Do you think you'll be out in twenty? I'm headed to Elijah's, but wanted to go over something with you first."

I want to heave the world's biggest sigh. Whatever she's about to say isn't going to make this day any better, but even though that shower is calling my name, I'd rather get this over with. Then I can cry about my shitty fight with Reid *and* this conversation, all at the same time. Take that, Reid! Who's efficient now?

I lift my bag from across my chest and let it thunk to the floor unceremoniously, which earns me another look of surprise. I'm not the tidiest person in the world, but early on in our shared living situation, I learned to keep my messes contained, to keep them mostly out of Sibby's sight. She's always preferred tidiness, so I've always—*ugh*—gone along.

"Just tell me now. I'm sure it won't take long." *Nothing takes long with you lately.* I am being so passive-aggressive that I almost wish I was recording this. I could send it to my mom later. I think she'd be proud.

"Okay," Sibby says slowly. "Well, I know I said the end of the summer." She ends it there.

I—quietly, imperceptibly—let out the sigh.

"But a different unit in the same building opened, and, Meg, it's *so* much better. There's this window in the kitchen, and—"

"Those chopsticks are mine," I blurt, and she blinks quickly. "Never mind. Take the chopsticks. I don't care."

"Meg, come on." Her voice is so gentle. But what right does she have to be gentle with me, when it's been death by a thousand cuts for me in this apartment for months? I press a thumb to my temple, rub my fingers over my still-damp forehead, feel the soreness of the pimples assert themselves. There's a dull throb of exhaustion in my shoulders, my back, my feet. The truth is, we both know I'm not going to argue with her. Especially not about this. If she wants to go now, she *should* go. Given the way I grew up—my parents white-knuckling their entire marriage from the time I was born, a "staying together for the kid" cautionary tale—I know that more than anyone.

"Listen, it's been a lousy day." I reach down, pick up my discarded bag, try to seem casual and not like I'm thinking of my efficient wash-and-cry coming right up. "So if not the end of summer . . . ?"

She looks down at her noodles. So *this* is the hard part, then. I tighten my already tight shoulders in preparation.

"We can get in at the end of June."

"That is . . . soon." Tough-to-find-a-non-creepy-subletter soon, and anyway, the hope was that by the time Sibby moved out, I wouldn't need a subletter right away. I'd have landed the Make It Happyn job.

A fresh wave of anger rises within me, and I feel desperate to get away from her, to shove it down.

"I was thinking I could call my dad," Sibby says. "Then I could pay you for the rest of the summer, even though I'm leaving earlier than I said."

It's my turn to blink in surprise. Sibby broke financial ties with her dad about four years ago, when he'd come to the city for a conference. She'd met him for dinner and a show, some musical Sibby had already seen three times, and afterward at the hotel bar, Mr. Michelucci told Sibby he couldn't see her up there, not ever. "You're not like those girls up there, Sibyl," he'd said to her. "You don't have the voice or the face or the body. It's time to get serious."

When she'd come home that night, she'd cried and cried, choking on the words he'd said to her, and my heart had broken. All the connections and commonalities Sibby and I had, the ones we relished and celebrated as each other's very best friend—I would have never wished this one on her, a fractured relationship with one of her parents, especially her dad. She'd always been closer to him, had always felt he was in her corner.

So I know exactly what it would cost her to ask him for this.

"Don't call him," I say. I'm mad at Sibby, and I'm confused by her. But I love her, still. I want her to be happy. And if she'd propose something this desperate, then obviously what she needs to be happy is this move. "I can cover it."

"Yeah?" she says, her voice lilting, musical. Her dad, he can get in my gum cocoon, too. He was so wrong about her. She *does* have the voice and the face and the body, whatever that means. It's only that a whole lot of other people in this city do, too.

"Oh, yeah," I sort of . . . chirp. "It'll be fine."

Already I'm thinking about what's in my bank account right now (my *business* bank account, thank you very much), how much savings I have, how many regular jobs I have lined up in the next few weeks, when my next quarterly tax payment is. It is supremely, face-punchingly annoying that I'm thinking about how useful a quantitative analyst who does math in his head quickly might be right now. A handsome pocket calculator on demand.

"Can we work out the details later? I *really* need a shower."

"Sure, of course." She picks up her phone from where it sits beside her box of noodles, checks the time before she speaks. "Why was your day so lousy?"

I stare at her for a long moment. What can I even say in the remaining minutes she's got to give me? What would even make sense, what with all these long gaps of time between our interactions? I think, painfully, about Reid and his blunt, no-nonsense questions. The ones I said he had no right to ask. He doesn't, but still.

It wasn't the worst thing, to be asked.

I don't really answer her. I shrug and gesture to my wet, bedraggled face and body and tell her to have a good time at Elijah's. I go to my bedroom and close the door behind me.

But before I strip off my clothes, I pull my phone from my bag, hold it in my hand for a few minutes while I look around my room. For weeks all I've been able to see in it is the cramped chaos of my desk, the work I've been trying to do and redo as I struggle with the Make It Happyn job. The rest of it, though—sure, it's small and it's messy, but it's also lovingly, carefully curated. The perfect, pale-blue down comforter with fluffy, pin-tucked-style squares. The big white pillows with a gray monogram that I designed, an indulgence after the *Times* article came out. The sheer pink scarf I have draped over my bedside lamp. The small, rose gold statuette Cecelia bought me for Christmas a couple years ago, a bird at rest, its rounded body perfect for cooling the palm of your hand. The silhouette I did of the Manhattan skyline—instead of lines defining the buildings, I'd done a tiny, pristine roman print, snippets of conversations I'd overheard on the subway, a simple dot separating them.

I don't want to have to move from here right now. I don't want another upheaval.

But I need more money—and soon—to make it work. And since I won't have any more walks with Reid on the agenda, I guess I'll have the time. *I pick up work easily,* I hear myself telling him. *I'm in demand.*

I swipe my thumb across the screen and navigate to my contacts.

"Cecelia," I say, when she picks up the phone. "Do you still have that number you mentioned?"

Chapter 6

I don't mean to be dramatic, but: It's a motherfucking movie star!

I mean, it's not like it's Meryl Streep. But it is a person who has been in at least one movie, and it is also a movie I have seen. Said movie was called *The Princess Tent*, and not only did Sibby and I see it together in the theater when we were fourteen years old, we also each had our own copy, and we watched it at probably sixty percent of our sleepovers.

The Princess Tent was pretty objectively Not A Good Movie, with lines such as, "You're a princess where it counts. On the *inside*," and "My tent may have been small, but this castle is a prison!" For years afterward, Sibby and I would say these lines to each other at moments both appropriate and not, and always dissolve into laughter afterward.

But even if we teased about it, we also loved it—a long-lost princess, believing herself orphaned, fed up with the system that shuffled her in and out of foster homes. Living on her own at the edge of a forest, strong and resourceful. Hiding her circumstances from everyone at her high school, including the handsome boy in her English class who wrote noncreepy poetry—a feat, let's face it—and always packed an extra sandwich for her just because. Sibby and I were so invested that we probably would have burned the movie theater down if Princess Freddie (real name: Frederica, of freaking course) didn't get her happy ending (crown, castle, tent on the grounds, poet-sandwich boyfriend), so it's a good thing it all worked out for her.

And I guess it also worked out for the young starlet who made Princess Freddie a household name, because on Friday afternoon I'm standing in the doorway of her and her actor-turned-director husband's brand-new row house in Red Hook—part of a line of buildings that are similar to brownstones in that they're shoved all together, but dissimilar to brownstones in that they are brutally modern, some faced with wood siding dry-burned black, some with what reminds me of the dull side of aluminum foil, some—including this one—with orange-rusted steel. They all have huge, high windows on the second and third floors, the kind a fancy decorator would tell you absolutely *cannot* have curtains. It's not my taste, but I've lived in this city long enough to know that this sucker costs at least two million, more depending on what's beyond this doorway.

I'm sure I'll get a peek at it soon, but right now I'm still too busy concentrating on keeping my mouth from hanging open as Lark Tannen-Fisher's assistant, Jade, shows me a piece of paper that she "totally promises" is not legally binding but that also contains scary words like *practitioner* (which I think means me) and *termination* (which I don't think means murder, but who knows). I've only been here for three minutes, tops, and even though I know I'm not going to take this job until I have an attorney (yeah, I know when to call an attorney! Suck it, Reid!) look over this thing, I'm still having trouble moving past that first minute, when Jade explained who I was about to meet.

Again: a motherfucking movie star!

Jade smiles an extra-white smile at me when I look up from the non-legally-binding paper. "Lark is *so* excited to meet you. She *loves* your Insta."

"Great!" I say, but my mind is a sieve for anything other than *IS THERE A TENT SOMEWHERE IN HERE?* I'm thinking it all the way down the long front hallway, which smells of fresh paint and money, and I'd probably continue to think it if we didn't step into a massive kitchen-dining-living room, open and airy and bright. There's not much furniture yet, but everything that's built in is gorgeous—sleek, dark-stained wood cabinets lining one whole wall, steel hardware that matches the appliances, a massive white marble island, glass-blown pendant lights hung above. Beyond it, a work-of-art chandelier, tangled branches of wood beautifully intertwined with delicate glass prisms. And where the living room furniture will surely go, a low, rectangular fireplace, built into a white brick half-wall, windows above and flanking it on either side, overlooking the kind of landscaped patio that half the population of Brooklyn would terminate someone for.

In spite of the fact that Jade has spoken to me in sentences that include at least twelve more words in italics, I don't know if I'm processing it; I am absolutely not playing it cool when she pulls out a fancy acrylic chair away from the island and invites me to sit and "set up." She asks if I want anything to drink and when I decline, she gives me another blinding smile and says she'll see me later.

I'm going to meet Princess Freddie, I think as I sit there, my client notebook and my Micron in my hand. Neither are pink or have sparkles, and under the circumstances I consider this a profound failure.

"Meg?"

Lark looks remarkably the same as she had on-screen all those years ago—shorter than I thought, the planes of her face sharper with adulthood, but she's still got all that long dark brown hair, brown eyes to match, a smattering of freckles across the bridge of her nose and cheeks. Her smile is Princess Freddie's, closemouthed and cautious, and after the movie came out I remember reading an interview where she'd said she'd always gotten teased for how big her mouth was. Since I'd had a face full of braces at the time, I'd felt a kinship.

Lark shakes my hand when I stand from my chair, and I make a real effort not to curtsey, holding the Micron in my other hand so tightly my knuckles ache. "Thanks for having me," I say, as though I've shown up to her wedding shower or a cocktail party.

"I'm thrilled you came. I've been following you for ages!"

Given that I spent a good portion of my freshman year drawing sketches of her magical forest tent, this is a moment of cognitive dissonance for me, so I'm pretty sure I smile goofily, feeling as if my braces have grown back.

But when we sit at the gigantic island and Lark tells me about the work she wants me to do, something about her makes my smile start to feel frozen and awkward in a different way. She's light, cheerful, a mode I know all too well and usually feel comfortable with, but everything she says seems littered with the name of her husband. Cameron wanted to leave LA because it was a wasteland. Cameron picked Red Hook because it's "gritty." Cameron wanted this house because its simplicity won't interfere with his "process." Cameron supports her acting but also doesn't approve of the rom-coms she gets offered, and *definitely* doesn't want her doing TV. Cameron wants kids, two boys. Cameron wishes she was a better cook.

So I low-key hate Cameron, which is awkward since Lark doesn't want me to do *only* a custom planner for her. She also wants me to do two large walls in her house, because Cameron is into inspirational quotations (here's hoping he's not a fan of *Bloom Where You're Planted*!). One of them is a larger-scale version of something I've done before, a narrow panel in the kitchen that they want done in chalk, but the other—which Lark leads me to—is a massive, high-ceilinged wall in the master bedroom that they want done in paint.

"I don't usually work with paint," I tell her as we stand in front of all the blank whiteness. This isn't entirely true—about a year and a half ago I took a four-weekend sign-painting workshop in Williamsburg to get some practice with retro-style lettering and composition. I'd translated most of what I'd learned there into my regular ink-and-paper practice, but I'd also done a couple of painted signs for Cecelia and the shop, and one for little Spencer Whalen, mostly because I didn't want Sibby to get in trouble if I'd said no to the request.

So I could probably do this, could brush up on my brush skills, and as long as they don't want anything too complicated, it'd probably be fine, if more time-consuming than I'd hoped. But something makes me uneasy about it. At first I think it's a whisper of my most recent outing with Reid, staring up at walls, even though those weren't blank. After a few seconds, though, I realize it's another type of familiarity. It's the sense that if I do this job, I'll want to say things I have absolutely no place saying. The sense that I'll break my promise to myself—to Reid, not that I should care—if I take it.

"I could give you some names of people who do that kind of work full time," I add, once I realize the silence has stretched too long. There's hardly anything in this room yet—a big California king with all-white linens and a large black-and-white framed photo from Lark and Cameron's wedding leaning against the wall beside it. In it, Lark's face is almost totally obscured, and Cameron is wearing a slouchy knit cap and wide black leather cuffs on both his wrists. On the beach! I feel newly committed to my decision to pass. How would I ever get through this job without hiding a message about how much I disapprove of Cameron's wedding attire?

I would not, probably.

But then Lark says, "Oh," and she sounds so genuinely disappointed. "Maybe I'll skip it. I was kind of trying to avoid—" She breaks off, tucks her hands inside the front pocket of the hoodie she's practically swimming in. "I'd rather have fewer people coming in and out of the house, I guess?"

I look over at her and she gives me a sheepish shrug.

"I get nervous about privacy stuff."

"Oh, of course," I say, as if I somehow know how it is to be a child star. I look back up at the wall, now feeling decidedly less committed about why I should pass. All through the mini-tour of this massive house, I couldn't help but think, *This castle is a prison!* Except this time, it hadn't seemed funny at all. When I first saw Lark in that movie years ago, the three-year age gap between Freddie and me seemed huge. She was a *real* teenager, not the kind of teenager I was—emerging and awkward, parties and proms and joyrides on a very distant horizon. But right now, with Lark standing beside me in this huge, sterile room, *I* feel like the older one, the real adult in the room.

Maybe I could do this part of the job, to help her out. I can ignore whatever she says about Cameron, keep my promise to myself, and give her what she's asked for. And this will be good for me, too. Even aside from the money I stand to make, this will be a good challenge to set alongside the Make It Happyn job. A place to put all the excess inspiration I am *absolutely* still going to get out of my city walks.

I take a big breath, speak with all the cheery, casual confidence I'm still mustering about this.

"You know what? Why not, right? I like trying new things."

She smiles at me, big and genuine. Then she says, "Cameron," and I resist the urge to groan. "He's always encouraging me to try new things."

"Such as cooking," I blurt, and right after it comes out of my mouth I grimace. First of all, I sound like Reid, whom I should not be (a) thinking about, or (b) imitating in any way. Second of all, I barely know this woman, and I've also just committed to keeping my mouth—well, my hands—shut about whatever she has going on in her life. And who knows, Lark/Princess Freddie might have a tyrannical streak and I could be five seconds from getting thrown out. Jade had a really firm handshake; she could probably do it.

But Lark surprises me with a snort of laughter that she brings a hand to her mouth to cover. When she composes herself she huffs a small sigh. "It can be exhausting, trying new things. You know?"

Boy, do I. I wonder if she'd want to know about trying a new thing where you call a man who doesn't like you, ask him to indulge in your probably useless efforts at artistic inspiration, de-

velop an inappropriate fondness for his face, and then get into
a fight with him in the rain on a crowded street in Midtown.

Exhausting indeed!

"I absolutely do," I say.

For a second, we both look up at the wall, and I try to convince myself that all this blankness won't turn into another
block.

♥ ♥ ♥

I call Cecelia when I'm on my way home.

I don't do it because I want to disrespect Lark—or, God forbid, that piece of paper—but because Cecelia helped me out
by hanging on to her number, and she'll want to know how it
worked out.

"Oh, Meg!" she says, her voice high. "Was it a Real Housewife?"

I laugh, but then I feel sad again at the mention of it, thinking of Lark in that big house, Cameron wanting boys-only kids
and cooking and his knit-cap/leather cuffs portrait, and Lark
looking a bit shell-shocked by it all. I push the thought away.

"No, definitely not. She's got a pretty big following, so it'd be
great if she showcases any of my stuff on her social media."

"See, that's exactly what I hoped for. Another planner?"

I tell her briefly about the planner, the two walls, and she's
interested but also distracted, probably counting stock or looking over new samples.

"So I wanted to say thanks, and—"

"I'm glad you called, actually," she interrupts. "Can you stop
by the shop? There's a package for you here, delivered by messenger a few minutes ago."

"Ugh. Is it from ink•scribe again?" Another overly stylized
name for a company that's always sending me free stuff care of
the shop, except this free stuff is garbage. Pens that last a literal
day and a half, and I think they've sent me fifty since the *Times*
article. "I guess hang on to it, if so." I'll pick it up tomorrow and
donate it to the day care two blocks from me.

There's rustling on the other end of the phone. Cecelia
mumbles something about needing her glasses, which I know

without seeing her are tucked into the neck of her shirt. "Oh, here they are," she says, a half second later. "No, this one— Sutherland, it says. Who's that?"

My face heats. "Oh, uh—"

"Your date maybe, hmmm?"

I immediately change direction, heading toward the Smith Street station so I can get over to the shop.

"No, jeez. I wouldn't have a date send something there. He's a—" I break off. Can't risk it. Out of context, his name isn't that memorable. But if I say *former client* maybe it'll ring a bell for her. "He's a small business consultant."

How *annoying*, that this is what I've said. All his man-terrogating got in my head. That package probably has a bunch of information about health insurance that I already know. What a *jerk*.

"Oh, what a good idea," Cecelia says.

I tell her I'll be there soon and for the rest of the trip over, I'm doing that thing I indulge myself in sometimes, where I compose a lengthy, highly organized but incredibly witty lecture of censure to someone who has done me wrong. Except in this version, I'm seeing it all written out. I'd make it chaotic, haphazard, all different fonts blended together. Something that would really annoy Reid. Bubble letters, definitely; that'd probably make his face melt off. *I set up the LLC months ago*, I'd write. *And I have a health savings account. I even looked into one of those asset insurance policies for my hands.* I'd leave out the part where those policies are expensive enough to have made me laugh out loud.

By the time I'm close, my mind has wandered, and all I can do is wonder what that *Sutherland* looks like on the package. Did he address it himself? Seeing his handwriting—the possibility feels at turns exciting and unnerving. Intimate. It's rare to see people's handwriting these days. Surprising as it may sound, no one ever really sees mine, since what I draw isn't really similar to my natural writing. Even my own planner, it's stylized—my headers for task lists in a wide, all-lowercase script, no slant, the tasks themselves blocked with a slim, all-caps roman. It looks good in photos.

But once I have what Reid's sent in my hands—Cecelia pausing briefly in her consultation with a customer to wave me to where it sits on the back worktable—I see that both the labels on the front have been typed, probably by someone who works for Reid. I ignore the disappointment I feel and tear open the package—it's slim but stiff, nothing more than a standard, legal-size envelope, the kind of thing a contract comes in. So probably it is annoying I-didn't-ask-for-this business advice. Well, at least if Cecelia comes back, my lie will be convincing.

Except it's not business advice.

It's a letter. A4, white, nothing special, though thicker than average printer paper.

And it's handwritten.

Dear Meg, it begins, and for a second I can't get beyond those two words. Despite my *Masterpiece Theatre* imaginings, Reid doesn't write in some kind of eighteenth-century cursive; instead, like most people these days, he has a sort of half-print, half-script style—the *M* of my name separate from the *e*, but the *e* joined to the *g* with a smooth garland. The letters are close together, but the words themselves are given room to breathe— wide, even kernings that make me think of the way Reid's jaw unclenched outside that crowded scaffold sidewalk.

Dark black ink. Even pressure. A rightward slant, a low vertical. I resist the urge to trace it with my finger. *Dear Meg.* I force myself to read on.

> *I apologize for the questions I asked you on Wednesday. I'm sure you've noticed that I'm not the most natural conversationalist, and I was nervous. I relied on discussing matters I know more about. Matters I know more about than art, at least. This is no excuse for what bad company I was.*
>
> *Yesterday morning I went back to the building we got stuck on. Before 7 a.m., it's different, as I'm sure you know.*

Traffic noise, construction noise, people noise: It's all still there, but quieter, which is why I should not have suggested meeting when we did. The light wasn't great, and the scaffolding is still there, so I still couldn't see the letters, but I made a trip somewhere else after work and found what I've enclosed here. I hope it helps.

For whatever it's worth, I enjoyed watching you work. I wish you every success.

Reid Sutherland

I stare at what he's written for a long time, ignoring for now whatever it is he's enclosed. I'm not looking for a code, because I know now Reid wouldn't leave one. If he asks, he wants to know. If he says something, he means it. If he writes to you, he's written exactly what he wants *you* to know.

Instead I pick out the phrases I like most, the ones that make me want to agree with him, answer him, ask him. *I was nervous,* I read again, and I want to say: *I was, too. No excuse,* and I think: *No, but I forgive you. Before 7 a.m.,* and I wonder: *What time do you get up in the morning? What time do you have to be at your weird calculator job?*

I enjoyed watching you work. I love that word, *enjoyed.* It sounds small and polite, but it contains something big, passionate. In my head I see it as it should be, I think. The *en-* and the *-ed* should be small, but sturdy. Like bookends, or like hands, supporting something that's lean and tall, but fragile and new. A fawn's legs. *J-O-Y.*

It's a photograph he's enclosed, or a photocopy of one, but I can tell that the original is black and white. On the bottom right corner I can see a snippet of a label, something that must've gotten caught in the copier, a *YPL* that I know must have an *N* before it. Photo archives in the New York Public Library. That's the trip Reid took after work. To the *library.*

It's a ribbon cutting of some sort, though it must be a pre–big scissors and smiles moment, men in dark suits standing around behind a long, thin line of fabric. Behind them is a newer version of the building that had, only a few days ago now, been covered in scaffolding. But if you let your eyes drift up, up and over, you can see it. Top left corner. Three-quarters of the sign we squinted at. Not *freshly* painted, I don't think, but newish. Clear and bright, and though I can't see it all, I can see enough of what we'd missed on the street. The script I'd strained so hard to see is for a brand of men's clothing, nothing I've heard of before, but I can picture the clothes, somehow, from that script—cap lines and ascender lines almost the same, swooping cross-strokes that nevertheless stay within the boundaries. Organized and elegant and aspirational.

Beneath it, the line of lettering that had faded almost completely, that I almost hadn't known was there. An unassuming, narrow all caps. What's written there makes me smile, and I wonder if it made Reid do the opposite. I wonder what this line of text means to him.

IN THE NEW YORK STYLE, it reads.

A literal sign, but maybe the other kind, too.

♥ ♥ ♥

I stall on the way home, not wanting to seem too eager. I stop for a few groceries and get caught up talking to Trina, who works the register most Fridays and who was hilariously insistent about showing me the infection she's got from her belly button ring. On my walk home I bump into one of my clients who's coming out of her Zumba class, and when I compliment her on her extremely fashionable exercise outfit, she is thrilled to give me a coupon code for a friends and family event at her favorite athleisure store. When I'm finally on my street, I see my neighbor Artem crouched outside the front door with his young daughter, valiantly attempting to draw a unicorn for her with sidewalk chalk. The head resembles a thigh with a dagger sticking out of it, so I am professionally obligated to take over, fixing it up and drawing his daughter's name so it curves over the unicorn's back, all the way down its windswept tail. She claps and hugs my knees, and Artem gives me a grateful smile, and for the first time in a while I feel as if I've had a good hour of my own brand of THE NEW YORK STYLE.

Upstairs I carefully unpack my groceries, not giving in to the petty temptation I have to put a few of my things on Sibby's side. I make my notes for the job with Lark, catch up with a few social media comments, sort a giveaway for a new set of notebooks.

Then I take out the envelope and set the photograph Reid sent me on the center of my bed. I sit on my desk chair, put my feet up on the mattress, and take a deep breath.

He answers on the first ring. His *hello* is exactly as I'd expect it. It's a declarative rather than an inquisitive hello.

Hello, period.

"Hi. I got the photograph."

"Good," he says. "I'll thank my guy." The messenger, I guess he means. I wonder what people who work for Reid think of him. Probably they think a lot of wrong things, like that he's never, ever nervous.

"Thank you. For the photograph, and for the letter."

There's a couple of seconds of silence, and I wonder if he'll repeat the apology, say it out loud, too. The thought is so jarring that I reach a hand beside me, absently feeling for the cord of my headphones. If he says it when I have the phone pressed right up against my ear—I don't know. It feels too close.

He only says, "You're welcome."

But I still put in the headphones, set my phone on the desk so I don't stare at the shape of his name on my screen.

"So. You went to the library."

"I did." After a beat, he adds, "I like research. I did a lot of it, in graduate school."

"You went to graduate school?"

"Yes. Masters and doctorate. Both in mathematics." It's not a boast, just a completion, an anticipation of the follow-up I would've certainly asked if he'd only said yes. I know I'm not great at numbers, and it's not that I think he's lying, but it's hard to believe that Reid—who doesn't look much over thirty—has both of those degrees. Maybe I am also not great at estimating age.

"Will it be helpful?" he asks, before I can follow up. "The picture, I mean."

"Oh, yes. It's amazing. I can't imagine doing something this big."

"You could, though. You could do it."

I feel a warm flush of pleasure at his quick, unfiltered confidence in me, but deflate when I think of that big, blank wall in Lark and Cameron's bedroom. "I like the scale I work in, usually. But these, they have something to teach me."

"How do you mean?"

"They have to make such an impact, so quickly. Striking enough to make a pedestrian look up, but not so striking that they have to stop and decode it. Memorable but simple. There's a real balance to that."

Reid makes a slight humming noise, a thoughtful assent. "The librarian I spoke to—she had a lot of materials to recommend about sign painters. Books about the profession, and also some old volumes about the craft itself. I could send you her information. I should have done that."

I'm quiet for a few seconds, and so is he. If I say, *Yes, send it to me,* I think this would end with an e-mail, or a text message, my last communication from Reid the name and number of a librarian. He wouldn't push it. He thinks he's done enough to end this. *I wish you every success.*

I hate thinking of him out there, miserable in his misunderstanding of this city.

"Reid," I say, not ready yet to hang up, but also not ready yet to ask him what I want to ask him. I look down at the photograph, at the letters there. "Tell me one thing you like about it here. One thing."

I hear him take a breath. A big inhale, a quick, almost frustrated-sounding exhale. Damn these earphones. They're just as intimate.

"I like the food," he finally says. His voice—I'd thought of it as flat before. But it's not, not really. It's deep and quiet and purposeful, nothing wasted. "Not the fancy, expensive restaurants. I like that you can walk into some tiny place that's three-quarters kitchen and get a huge plate of food for cheap, and it's good, too. It has to be good, for it to survive in this city. The food here, in those kinds of places—it's a meritocracy."

I can picture the exact kind of place Reid is talking about. I've been in and out of those places the whole time I've lived here, and I like them, too. Places so worn-out and dumpy looking you can't imagine at first why your mailman or your bodega guy or your brow waxer or your boss basically shouted in your face about how you *have* to try it; you're an absolute philistine because you haven't yet.

But then you do. You wait in the long line, you stumble through your order while all the regulars are rolling their eyes at what a rookie you are. You stand at a narrow counter inside with a plastic fork and taste food that's better than anything you've ever eaten, or at least anything you've ever eaten before the last place you went into like this. You get ready to shout in the face of the next person you see.

Reid probably doesn't do that last part, but still. Handwritten letter of apology, photocopied photograph from the library, phone pressed to my ear: None of it makes me feel more connected to Reid than this small piece of information about his preferences in this place he says he hates so much.

"Okay," I say softly, and I wonder if he can hear the smile in my voice. "You want to try again?"

Chapter 7

"I admit," he says dryly, hunching his wide shoulders yet again to let another customer by, "that I generally get the food to go."

Reid and I are standing—standing *close*—inside a narrow corner storefront in Nolita, an Israeli place that ticks every box he and I discussed on the phone last night: tiny place. Big portions. Cheap. It's a place he comes to somewhat regularly, he'd told me, and I'd checked my list and said I was certain I could find some good signs in the area.

It'd all seemed a good start for my suggestion to try again, a way for us to loosen up around each other with a meal we're both likely to enjoy before we get out on another letter quest.

But now I suspect, given how stiffly both of us are taking the forced proximity, that neither of us really thought about the practical consequences of this reboot, because in the last five minutes alone, we have learned things about each other that are probably, at the very least, second-date territory for me personally. Reid, for example—thanks to the line that at first extended out the propped-open front door and a strong, warm spring breeze—knows how it feels to have a strand of my long hair against the skin of his neck, a development he greeted with what can only be described as aloof tolerance. He may have even winced as he leaned back on the heels of those same gray sneakers.

As for me? I now have been adjacent to Reid's body for long enough to realize that there's a faint smell of chlorine on him, a summer-day-at-the-pool smell, and between that and the light, spicy scent of his soap, I feel sort of the same way I did the first time I slow-danced with a boy in seventh grade. *Boys smell like* this? I'd thought, new to the wonders of a modestly applied cologne, new to the feeling of wanting to press my face into another person's skin.

"Do you live near here?" I say, determined not to think about pressing my face anywhere untoward, but when Reid looks down at me, his brow furrowed, I can only think about pressing my face into an ice bucket or an invisibility cloak. My cheeks heat in embarrassment.

"I mean, not because we'd take the food back there! I wasn't . . . inviting myself over. Or trying to get into your business."

His lips twitch, an almost smile. "Business," he says, deadpan. "Dicey territory." The almost smile grows. Crooked and a little sheepish. God, he is handsome.

"Reid," I say, fighting my own smile and further face-pressing thoughts. "Did you make a joke?"

"Probably not," he says, ducking his head and tugging on the sleeve of his jacket, pulling it over his watch. "I'm not known for my sense of humor."

What are you known for? I'm thinking, but before I can ask anything, a loud voice shouts "MAG!" in our general direction.

I roll my eyes. "Mag," I mumble to myself, moving through the crowd toward the counter, where a young man has set two gigantic cardboard squares of food. I'm pretty sure he knows my name isn't "Mag," but I've learned that mispronunciation of this nature is some kind of New York food-service ritual. I feel Reid at my back, hear him say "Pardon me," as we move through a particularly dense clump of teenagers near the register. They'll probably have to Google what that means.

We luck out, finding two stools side by side along the shop's front window, the bar in front of us exactly deep enough for our plates. Despite our general awkwardness together, I'm comforted by the way we competently perform a familiar, casual-dining-out routine: I set my bag on Reid's stool when he goes to the counter along the wall and grabs us napkins and plastic forks; I straighten our plates and reach an arm down the bar and grab one of the bottles of extra hot sauce that rests there, while Reid makes his way back and distributes his take between us.

Two friends, out for an early dinner. *Company.*

I finally find an outlet for my face-pressing once we're settled, forks in hand, bending my head to take in the smells of my food—the best-looking falafel I've ever seen, garlicky sautéed carrots, a tomato-and-cucumber salad that I plan to mix with the hummus that's sitting right beside it. *Yum.*

"Is your name Megan?" Reid says, interrupting my small ritual. I straighten in my seat and look over at him. He's got his fork poised right above his plate, as though knowing my full name is really necessary for going forward. I super-hope he isn't asking so he can do some kind of formal prayer involving me, or else this meal is going to feel extremely weird. Extremely weird-er, I guess.

"Uh. No," I say, starting the hummus-cucumber-tomato stir-up. I can feel Reid watching me do it, and I'd bet the farm he thinks it's disgusting. I shrug. "It's Margaret."

"Margaret," he repeats.

"Old-fashioned, I know." A family name, sort of, though who wants to get into it. I take a bite of my food. Holy smokes. Maybe we should do a prayer. These carrots taste like an orgasm feels.

"I like old-fashioned," says Reid, and I think about offering up a jokey, flippant "*Huge* surprise!" in response. But when I look over at him, I see he's stirring his hummus into his salad, his brow-furrow in full force, and I turn back to my food, letting my hair fall over my shoulder so I can hide my smile.

He's *trying.* Trying again.

For a few minutes, we eat in silence, and maybe that wouldn't be so bad except that it's not silence at all. The line's still out the door and there're people on either side of us, the pair beside me punctuating their conversation with boisterous laughter. Outside the window, a dump truck rumbles by, releasing puffs of dark smoke into the air behind it, all the pedestrians in its wake ducking their faces as they walk. I feel oddly, uncomfortably responsible—I want to say, *Do better, New York,* so that Reid doesn't get that look on his face from last time. That tense, I'm-barely-tolerating-this look. I think about his letter to me, all the times he wrote the word *noise* in his tidy half-script.

This city's noise is all caps, all the time. Written with a big, chisel-tip, permanent black marker. Impossible to ignore.

"Hey," he says, surprising me. "Look over there." He's gesturing out the window, not to where the dump-truck smoke lingers, but across the way, to a somewhat run-down-looking bar catty-corner to where we sit. "That's hand-lettered, isn't it?"

It *is*. The awning is black vinyl, and that's obviously been screen-printed, but below the molding that separates the building's brick upper floors from the bar beneath, there's a length of faded black paint, not far off in color from the chalk paint I'll use in Lark's kitchen. Painted across it is the bar's name in an inexpert serif, uneven beaks on the *S*, the foot of the *T* slanting upward. The letters are filled in a dark marigold, traced out with a brick red that picks up the color from the building above. I feel the nudge of an idea—this rich, unexpected color scheme and that elegant script from the photo Reid sent me.

"Good eye," I say, reaching for my phone to snap a photo. I could wait until we're outside again, but this has the echo of one of those rare moments, the ones that sometimes come when I'm in the thick of a project—when my mind is so busy that I've got to sleep with my sketchpad by my bed in case I wake up in the night inspired. I haven't had that kind of moment in a long time.

When I set down the phone, I think I might wriggle on the stool. "Thank you," I say, picking up my fork again.

Reid clears his throat. "Have you ever heard of John Horton Conway?"

I've got a mouth full of falafel so I can't really answer. I shake my head and hope that John Horton Conway is not a Founding Father or any other historical person I should definitely know about but can't remember because this food is so good.

"He's a mathematician."

"Like you," I say, or sort of mumble around the falafel.

Reid shakes his head. "No, he's a professor." He pushes his hummus-tomato-cucumber mixture around—I don't think that was a successful endeavor for him—looking wistful for a second. But then he speaks again. "He's brilliant. He can do the kind of math that seems unbelievable."

"Huh," I say, not acknowledging that I'm pretty unsure about what qualifies as "unbelievable" math. Long division, probably.

"He also plays a lot of games. They say he's always got dice, or a Slinky, or playing cards. For years, when he was first starting out, it's how he would spend all his time. Backgammon. Chess. New games he'd make up."

"He sounds fun." I pause for a half second before I add something, a tentative effort. This meet-up, this meal—it's a game all its own, the one with the long, rectangular blocks you pull from the bottom and stack on top, making a taller and taller tower. Taking a risk, watching to see if it'll topple. "Probably has a *great* sense of humor."

Reid looks over at me, gives me that crooked almost smile. The tower holds, and I could clap for myself.

"People used to think—even he used to think—he was wasting time, playing games. But he was really . . . he was working out math all along. Loosening up his mind for ideas that were on their way."

"Do you do that?"

"No, not lately. But I was thinking about your . . ." He trails off.

I can almost see it, him pulling his own block from the bottom. "Reid. Are you about to give me a business idea?"

He shifts on his stool. "No."

I wait. He was absolutely about to give me a business idea.

"It's more of an . . . *ideas* idea." He's got that block hovering right at the top of the tower.

I give a dramatic sigh, but on the inside, I'm smiling. I want the *ideas* idea the same way I wanted to see his handwriting. "Okay. Let's hear it."

He picks up his napkin—which he'd actually draped over one of his thighs, as if we're somewhere fancy—and swipes it across his mouth before setting it neatly beside his cardboard plate. "I was thinking about your list."

I must get a look on my face.

"Which is a great list," he adds, hastily. "Very efficient."

"*Bu-ut,*" I say, prompting him before I take my last bite of food.

"It seemed stressful. Following the list and looking for . . . expected things." He clears his throat again. "It struck me that—it could be useful to remember that signs are, ah." He pauses, looks across the street again. "Often unexpected."

Like you, I want to say again.

"I know you have a goal, to get your inspiration. But what if you . . . made it more fun? Like a game."

I blink, swallowing my food heavily. Anyone looking at me and Reid right now—anyone who notices his excellent table manners and good posture and tasteful weekend clothing, and my Clever Girl dinosaur T-shirt and the way I slouch over my plate and how I never thought to put my napkin in my lap— anyone would think it'd be me who'd suggest something fun, something light. A game.

"It isn't my business," he says in the silence I leave there. He makes a move to gather his plate.

"Wait," I say, and his hands still. Anyone *would* think that, even me. But having Reid for a fr—for *company*—it's probably going to mean that I stop thinking that way. We've built up quite a tower of blocks here, the two of us, in this small, inexpensive, delicious restaurant.

"It's sort of your business," I say. "If you're still doing this with me."

For a second, we look at each other, the tower tall and quivering between us. The corners of his mouth are tight, as though he's making an effort to control his expression. It's still so noisy in here, but not so much that I can't hear his next two words, a quiet, simple promise.

Of company. Maybe even of friendship.

"I am," he says.

♥   ♥   ♥

"Margaret," Reid says an hour and a half later, staring down at his phone. "We got it."

"All of them?" There's a note of disappointment in my voice. *Over so soon?* I'm thinking, even though the light's fading and my feet are getting tired.

I move next to him easily, more familiarly now, and peer over his shoulder, but still make sure I don't let any of my unruly hair blow onto his person. And there it is, spread out over the eight photos on the grid of Reid's photo library—all the letters of my name, my *full* name, the one no one ever really uses, but the one that's been half of our quest since we left the restaurant.

We'd picked something easy for our first try at Reid's game idea. Each of us, we'd decided, would have to try to find versions of all the letters in the other's name, Reid including his middle name—Hale, from his mother's side of the family, he tells me—to even things out. The rules were simple: no using the same sign for more than one letter, and nothing that's not hand-lettered.

We haven't really been competing; it's not the kind of game where we've been trying to one-up each other. It's like sharing the Sunday crossword, I guess—instead of passing the folded newspaper back and forth, trading clues and guesses, Reid and I had pointed out to each other the signs we noticed as we'd walked. And the same way the Sunday crossword-share never finishes without at least one concession to a Google search, Reid and I had adjusted some of the rules as we went along. A particularly impressive *H* on a vinyl sign inspired the "wild card" exception: one letter from a sign that's not hand-drawn. A best out of three rock-paper-scissors practice implemented for when one of us would spot a good example that matched with one of the letters—*A, E, R*—that we both have in our names.

"The *E*," Reid says, nodding up toward the mural he's standing in front of on Bleecker, an amazing red, white, black, and gold image of Debbie Harry of Blondie wearing a leopard-print blouse and a look of challenge in her black-rimmed eyes. There's a lot of lettering on this mural—a crooked version of the CBGB logo minus the decorative serifs, a narrow black script against a deep-red background, a blocky, clean all caps in the lower right corner.

Reid's zoomed in and snapped the *E* in BLONDIE as it appears on a rendering of a concert ticket—*1979; gates open at 6 p.m.; no bottles, cans, coolers, or pets.* It's red, the *E*, and the top arm is shorter than the bottom, a sturdy-looking thing, and even though all the images on his phone are out of order—no rule for having to find consecutive letters—it's easy to reconstruct my name from these eight snapshots, to rearrange them. Here, *Margaret* doesn't look so old-fashioned. It looks bright, colorful, cheerful. It somehow looks more *Meg* than *Margaret*.

I swipe my thumb over my own screen, tip it toward Reid so he can see the various building blocks of my own take. *Reid Hale.* His name, it sounds kind of . . . new-fashioned. And also stuck-up. But as with the letters from my own name, *R-e-i-d* looks different in the pictures. Noisy and alive and *fun*, like the game itself and the Bowery around us, coming to life on a Saturday evening.

My hands feel restless to sketch. I don't even notice that my hair's blown against him again until he clears his throat and straightens.

"I can send these to you," he says, moving to tug down the sleeve of his jacket again. It's stayed warm tonight, warm enough that I've never even taken my own be-buttoned jacket from where it's stuffed inside my bag, but Reid has left his on the whole time.

"Yeah, that would be great!" I've basically cheered it, because now that the game is over, Reid and I seem to have slipped back into our familiar roles. I resist the urge to sigh. During our walk, Reid wasn't exactly loose, but he was engaged, and interested, and determined. His version of excitement is basically— pointing, I guess, with the occasional attractive eyebrow raise, but still, there's something about it. Something friendly, and comforting, and nice to be around.

"That was a really good . . . *ideas* idea," I say.

"It helped?"

"It did."

Reid nods once, that firm tip of his head, a piece of punctuation. An end to the sentence we've kept going between us for a while now.

We've moved back to the corner, where a crowd is waiting to cross Bowery. We could say our goodbyes here and I could turn, keep walking, see a few more signs on my own, walk through a neighborhood where the letters change, become characters for a language I don't know. I could call for a Lyft when I get to the Manhattan Bridge. An indulgence, surge pricing for sure, but I feel I've earned it.

Except . . . I also want to stop for a few minutes. Take in the results of the game, look over the pictures and see what strikes me as interesting, as inspiration. There's a coffee shop beside us—*quite late for coffee*—and I look toward it, see tables open. Even as I'm picturing it, as I'm thinking of me and my notebook and my Staedtler and these pictures, a familiar pressure builds. That twitching in my hands—what if I sit there, and it all comes to nothing? What if it's another block, and I can't—

"You should choose one of the letters," Reid says, interrupting my thoughts. I blink away from the coffee shop and look up at him. "Choose one, and do one of our names, or—a month name, for your project. All from that one letter's style. Another game."

"Wow," I say, chuckling at the way he seems to have read my mind. "Maybe you *should* be a business consultant."

"Maybe," he says, with a small, self-deprecating smile.

I stare down at my phone again, my grid of pictures. The nice thing about the game was the way we created it together, *played* it together, the way neither one of us was following or playing along. I wonder whether it feels as good to him as it does to me.

So before I can think about it too hard, I push my phone into his hands.

"Pick one," I say. "Pick one, and follow me."

Then I move past him into the coffee shop, not ready for the game to be over yet.

♥ ♥ ♥

"You are not serious," I say, looking down at Reid's selection.

He shrugs, lifts his cup, and takes a sip of the herbal tea he ordered. Across the small, round table, his posture is nearly as impeccable as it had been the first time we sat together in a place like this.

But it's not like that time. For one thing, I have *also* ordered an herbal tea, and even though I think it tastes like licking the bottom of a flowerpot, at least I know I won't wake up tomorrow with a caffeine hangover.

For another, Reid and I are *playing*.

"This is extremely unexpected," I say, tapping my pencil against my open notebook.

His mouth curves fleetingly as he sets down his cup. "If you'll recall, unexpected was the point."

The lowercase *a* that's pictured on my phone is strange, misshapen. It's a double-storey, the kind of *a* with a hook-and-eye look to it that's common in roman fonts but uncommon in handwriting. But where most double-storey *a*'s have a circular counter, this one's counter is triangular, made that way by the odd proportions elsewhere in the letter. Flat along the bottom, thick and blocky outlines, not at all consistent or familiar.

I'm surprised he picked it—orderly, well-shaped Reid—but I'm not displeased. In fact, as I still my pencil and flip it easily to rest in my usual drawing grip, a smile tugs at my mouth, because I already know what I'll do with it. A month name, the first I've attempted outside of client jobs for *weeks*.

Within two minutes I've copied the *a*—I'm quicker, usually, but it takes me a couple of tries to get the proportions right, and by the time I've got a version I'm satisfied with, I'm working on the lower quarter of the page. I can feel Reid's eyes on my hands, and while it sometimes makes me self-conscious to have people watch me work, I find I don't mind. He's so quiet that it's not all that different from when I set my phone up on its tiny stand and take a video of myself sketching.

The hard part—the game, really—is not the copying, but the mimicking, the way I'm supposed to take this one letter and use it as inspiration for something new. That takes me longer— more experimentation, more mistakes as I struggle to get those over-broad shoulders on the top edges of the letters right, as I play with options to give them more dimension, more texture. I feel my mind going blank, my hand working more smoothly, confidently.

Ten minutes and two pages later, I've got a rough sketch of it. This isn't where I'd stop—if I were home, if I had more time, if I had all my stuff with me. I'm already thinking of colors I'd use to fill it in, and of how those big shoulders could become tiny canvases all their own, the tiny, clever sketches I could put inside. . . .

"March?" Reid says, reading what I've written. It's the first time he's spoken since I started sketching.

I blink up at him. He's leaned forward, elbows resting on the table, his empty cup of tea in the space between. If this is how he sat while I worked, then I guess our heads were bent together, and it makes me feel strangely powerful, to know that my sketching was drawing him closer. Now that I'm finished, I'm free to notice things about close-up Reid: In the low light of this place, his eyes are darker blue. The lashes that frame them are long, but they aren't showy about it—dark blond, lighter at the tips so that the true length of them is hidden from the casual observer. He has a single, small light brown freckle on his left cheekbone.

I realize, snapping myself out of it, that his lean-back method is very effective for stopping spontaneous face-pressing feelings—not that he has those to worry about.

"March," I repeat. "Only sensible choice, for this kind of letter."

His brow furrows, his mouth pulling to the side. "How do you figure?"

I shift in my seat, unsure about how to explain this part to someone else, how I try to read letters for more than the words they spell out.

"Did you notice the store this came from?"

He opens his mouth, then closes it again before making that furrow in his brow even deeper. Then he says, even more formally than usual, "I did not."

I resist the urge to smile. "I mean, don't worry about it. It's not as if that was one of the rules."

"Right."

"Anyway, the store was for western-style clothing. Boots, and clothes, and those—you know those ties that aren't ties? With the . . . leather, and the thingy." I gesture at my neck.

"Those don't sound like something I'd wear." He seems disgusted by the very idea, and I have to bite my lip to keep from laughing.

"The point is," I say, once I've got it under control, "the store is sort of . . . odd. What it sells, in this city, in that neighborhood—you wouldn't think of it, would you? So the sign, the letters—they should feel that way, too. Unexpected."

"Okay." Somehow he makes it sound like *Go on.*

"And March, that's definitely the most unexpected month. So it *had* to be March."

He looks down at the word, then back up at me. "I don't get it. It comes every year. Right after February."

"Yes, but it's, you know—every year, you're all, 'March! This is going to be *great*! Start of spring!' But it's definitely not, right? Because there will be a weird, freak snowstorm, and it's like winter's started all over. Unexpected things happen in March."

He stares at me, and I think he might argue. He might say, for example, that if one feels this way *every* March, then it can't be truly unexpected. Which would be a good point, but I'm telling you. My *M-A-R-C-H* is making the case.

Instead he says, "You match the lettering to the"—he turns his teacup—"the feeling."

"Yes," I say, relieved. I take a sip of my soil-flavored tea. The warmth I feel—it's not from the drink. It's from this evening, these games, this moment. This understanding, or at least the attempt at it.

But then Reid says something that makes everything turn cold again.

"Avery," he says, his voice steady. "I can see why you picked those letters for her. The ones on our . . . on the wedding things."

"Oh," I say, stunned. Reid is so—*direct*, really. Being with him sometimes—it's as if I'm learning a whole new language.

"The fairies, those suited her. She was—" He pauses, looks down at the notebook between us. I don't remember doing it, but at some point in the last few seconds I've closed it. My right hand is resting on top, palm flat, bracing myself against everything about this that is uncomfortable.

"Unreal, in a way," he finishes. "Beautiful, and powerful."

The only thing I can seem to do is nod. She *was* those things. Even I thought so, and I barely knew her.

He looks up at me, that trace of sadness in his eyes until he seems to see something in mine. His gaze sharpens, and he straightens in his chair. "I apologize."

"No!" I say, too hastily. "I'm the one who . . ."

I trail off, pressing that hand flatter against my notebook. I doubt I'll open it again tonight. The *a* that Reid chose—right now it doesn't feel all that unexpected. It doesn't feel like he chose it because he was curious about what I'd do with it. It feels like he chose it because it's a way into this—this constant, looming confrontation between us. What I did. What I put into those letters.

It's so *hard* to have that confrontation looming there.

The tower we started building—it's near collapse.

"It's getting late," he says, seeming to know.

Quite late, is all I can think. I nod, but don't move to pack up.

"Shall I walk you to the train?" Those starchy, lovely manners. I wonder if he knows how unexpected he is. How unreal, in this city.

I smile up at him. My truest talent, this feigned lightness, no matter what this book of sketches resting underneath my hand contains. "I'm going to stick around. I'll call for a Lyft in a while."

He tips his head in a nod, but he seems disappointed. "I hope you"—he gestures at my notebook—"I hope your work goes well."

"Thanks." I still feel shaken, as if I'm the tower now, wobbly and uncertain. *Game over*, I see in my mind, blinking and computerized, not a hand-drawn letter in sight.

Then I think Reid takes a risk of his own.

"I had fun," he says, as serious as ever, and I look up at him. The severity in the lines of his face now looks to me like sincerity. *Hope*.

"Me too," I say honestly, the memory of all those photos on my phone a blinking, deleting cursor, backspacing over that *Game over.*

"Maybe we can play again sometime."

Maybe, I'm repeating in my head, still wobbly. I tuck one of my fingers inside the notebook, feeling the indentations my sketches have left there, the slight grit of the graphite on my skin.

But he turns to go before I can answer.

Chapter 8

"Yes. No, wait. No, I think. Or—I don't know?"

Beside me, Lark is staring down at nine different sheets of paper, all of them covered in some of my most common lettering styles, the ones I seem to rotate through my various clients' planners and wall calendars. It *may* be true that I have left out the most popular brush lettering, but it also may be true that if I have to do one more client project with that as the sole focus, I will find some way to break my own fingers, and where's that going to leave me?

Nowhere, that's where.

Nowhere, however, is also where this appointment is going, because Lark is having an incredibly difficult time making literally any decision. The question that has prompted this latest round of existential dread is whether she wants black accents. It's Tuesday afternoon at three thirty and we've been here since shortly after noon, or, perhaps, since the actual birth of Christ. I raise my gritty eyes toward the front of the shop, where Lachelle is standing behind the front desk. Every once in a while she looks back here and gives me a sort of cringe of sympathy.

At Lark's house last week, I'd realized she seemed tentative, preoccupied with her husband's opinions, small and lost-looking in that big townhouse. In fact, that's partly why I'd suggested we meet elsewhere today, our first effort at going through possibilities for the two walls—I thought it might be less overwhelming for both of us not to stand before the full, blank canvas, more blank somehow by virtue of the unfinished space of the house.

Of course I'd also suggested it partly because what if Cameron had been there in the awful beanie and black wrist cuffs? What if he'd brought up not liking rom-coms in front of me? I've got to keep clear of temptation, is the thing.

Initially I'd proposed one of my standard haunts for client meetings, but Lark had been hesitant; then I'd remembered what she'd said about privacy, so I'd papered over my misstep quickly, promising that the shop's back workspace would let us review ideas "uninterrupted." Since Lachelle has never seen *The Princess Tent* ("What do you mean a poet-sandwich boyfriend?" she'd said, when I'd tried to explain after showing up early to prep her), so far that's seemed to work out fine.

Except for, you know. The fact that my leg bones are calcifying under this table. The fact that I'd thought I'd be out of here an hour ago. The fact that I'd wanted to already be back at my apartment and in front of my desk, working on the new sketches I've started for Make It Happyn.

Since Saturday night, I've done more sketches for Make It Happyn than I've done in all the weeks since I first got the call. The game I'd played with Reid—however awkwardly it had ended—seemed to ignite something in me. For each of the sixteen letters we'd gathered together, I'd tried a word—sometimes a month name, sometimes a day name, sometimes the sort of banal general terms that show up in planners and on calendar pages: "TASKS," "REMINDERS," "TO DOS," "BIRTHDAYS," filling them out with decorative details and sketches. None of them yet seem exactly right for the job, but they're all—on the *way* to something, I guess. On Sunday, I'd been so absorbed that I hadn't even heard Sibby rustling around the apartment.

When I'd finally come out of my room late in the afternoon, determined to forage for snacks, I'd blinked in shock to find a set of boxes already lining our narrow hallway.

"Oh," I'd said, nearly bumping into her as she was emerging from her room. "I didn't realize . . ."

There'd really been nothing to do but trail off. It'd been painful, of course it had been. But it hadn't been stomachache painful; it hadn't been I'd-better-get-back-behind-a-closed-door-to-cry painful. I'd even helped her—once I'd shoved a granola bar in my mouth—take apart an old, particle-board bookshelf that we'd put together a couple of years ago over slices of pizza and too-sweet cans of wine, her phone blaring music as we'd worked. This time, though, we'd worked quietly, politely. I'd suggested she wrap some of the shelves in a couple of the old beach towels she has under her bed, and she'd thanked me. She'd asked if I'd maybe want to keep one of the nightstands she won't be needing in her new place, and I'd said no.

Then I'd gone back to my room, eager to keep working.

Now I shift in my seat, my eyes tracking down to the pages in front of Lark. I really shouldn't be frustrated—I've agreed to this job, and I need this job, *especially* because of all those boxes lining my hallway. Most of my clients these days have a pretty firm sense of what they want already, or they're happy for me to keep doing what I've been doing for them. But Lark's new to this, and new to town, and also I guess new to being asked to make decisions on behalf of herself and her new husband.

So I need to be patient.

"I know it's ridiculous," she says, raising a hand to her forehead, rubbing two fingers along her hairline, right by her temple. I've learned in these last three hours that she does this when she's particularly stumped. Which is often.

Really often.

"It's only that—it's going to be on the *walls*."

I smile gently. In this kind of situation, all my cheery lightness is useful, and I deploy it fully.

"But if you don't like it," I say airily, "you can always paint over it. And the chalk? *Pffft.*" I wave my hand casually. "Bit of special cleaner and a big sponge, and you've got a blank canvas again. No problem!"

Lark blinks at me. "I couldn't do that," she says, sounding shocked. She is really not at all like Princess Freddie, who was defiant, unflappable, subversive. "To all your work?"

It's nice, that she feels this way, that she takes what I do so seriously. But if this is the problem, she's definitely overthinking it. A fundamental quality of my work is its impermanence. Sure, my planners are inked, and sure, clients could always page back through and admire a particular spread. But really, the *point* of the planners, of the calendars, is that you make your way through them, that you check off the days and turn the page. That you move on.

I open my mouth to reassure her, but then I have a thought. A memory.

What if you made it more fun?

It's not the first time I've thought of Reid since Saturday night—his low, serious voice and his stern, handsome face, his secret eyelashes and his soft *swoonsh* of pleasure. Each letter I'd sketched had been a reminder of the fun we'd had, the game we'd played. But inevitably, I'd remember those last, painful few minutes in the coffee shop, the way we'd left it up in the air, and I'd try to put him out of my head for a while.

But now, I cling to the memory of him in the restaurant, to the walk we'd taken, working out our rules. Without saying anything to Lark, I reach my hands out and messily gather the nine sheets of paper toward me, wrinkling a few. She makes a small noise of distress, but I ignore it, hastily stacking the sheets.

"Okay," I say. "We're going to try something." I look toward the front of the shop, see that Lachelle's leaning over the counter, casually flipping through a supplies catalog, and I call out to her. She rushes back as though she needs to rescue me from the purgatory I've been in, and I give her a grateful smile before explaining my plan.

The rules I make are messy, a bit nonsensical. We each get three sheets, and we've got ten minutes—*only* ten minutes, because I don't want Lark getting trapped in another decision vacuum—to make some kind of flying projectile out of each one. After the time is up, we're all going to stand in a line behind this table and, one by one, launch them out into the shop.

The two that go the farthest?

Those are the ones I'll use for the initial lettering treatments.

I don't put conditions on it, don't tell Lark that treatments aren't final, don't tell her that I can mix and match pretty much any of the various styles I have spread across these nine sheets. At this point, none of that matters, same as it didn't matter at first with what I'd ended up doing with the letters Reid and I had gathered up on Saturday night. It only matters that Lark gets out of her own head for a few minutes.

"Am I allowed to use my phone?" Lachelle blurts. You'd think I've announced a ten-thousand-dollar prize. I should've known; Lachelle has a real competitive streak. Last year some of the local businesses along this street had a window-decorating contest for Halloween, and Lachelle had basically conscripted Cecelia—who'd really had no interest in this kind of contest— and I to work late into the night before the judging. When the shop got runner-up instead of first place, she accused the judges of vote tampering. Every once in a while she still brings it up. "Crooks," she'll say, shaking her head.

"Sure, why not?" I say, and before I have it all the way out Lachelle is tapping away, surely searching for how-to videos on paper airplane designs.

I start folding, using the kind of rudimentary tactics you learn in elementary school, and for a few seconds Lark simply looks back and forth between me and Lachelle, as if our different approaches are now the newest, freshest dilemma of her life. But eventually, she takes out her phone, and after a quick search she starts folding, too. Every once in a while Lachelle makes a noise of satisfaction; one time she says, "You'd better get yourself ready, Meg," and Lark laughs softly.

By the time we line up behind the table, we've formed some kind of strange paper-airplane adversarial bond. Lachelle says I have "noodle arms" when my first attempt fails miserably. Lark puts a hand over her mouth when Lachelle squares up the first time like we're on an actual Olympic field, and when Lachelle sees her doing it she says, "You won't be laughing when I win, princess!" but that makes us all laugh harder. It's clear that I am the worst at this game, which provides pretty good fodder for both of my competitors. I don't really mind their teasing, but before I can stop myself I think about Reid again, guessing that all his math knowledge would probably make him an extremely skilled projectile designer. His broad shoulders, those would be good for the throwing.

But I shouldn't be thinking about those.

"It's you and me, princess," says Lachelle, giving an exaggerated side-eye to Lark before throwing her last sheet. As far as I can tell, it lands right past her first effort, which means two of her three might be the winners. I look over at Lark, and notice her last sheet isn't folded yet. She looks at me sheepishly.

"I ran out of time." She's holding the sheet close to her, the writing facing her body, and even though I don't know her well, I can tell something.

She didn't run out of time.

Before I can say anything, before I can tell her to hang on to it, that I can definitely work with that one, no matter the rules of the game—she sets her face and crumples the sheet into a tight ball.

And then she throws it—as if she's standing on a pitcher's mound—out into the shop. Almost all the way to the front door.

"Damn," Lachelle says. "I didn't know we could do just—*balls!*"

I shrug. "Wasn't a rule against it."

Lark's smile is huge, and she doesn't bother covering it.

"Chalk or paint for the winner?" I say, before she can think too hard.

"Paint." She looks surprised with herself.

I want to raise my fists in the air in victory. Lachelle actually does it, even though she's probably going to ride me about the balls rule every time I see her for the next few months.

But finally, finally—we've gotten somewhere.

♥　♥　♥

By the time Lark has left the shop and I've packed up all my things and said goodbye to Lachelle (she does bring up the balls thing again), it's past four thirty, and while I'm still feeling pretty satisfied, I'm also exhausted. Most of my burning desire to get back to my desk has now left me, since the idea of sitting in a chair again sounds like the worst possible idea. It's possible my ass has turned into a pancake, or a tortilla. Or a pizza.

Also, I am hungry.

In spite of the fact that I did pretty well over the weekend with Sibby's packing, I'm not up to heading back to the apartment now. If I'm not planning to shut myself up in my room to work it's likely I'll feel her impending absence more acutely, and anyway, it's a nice afternoon, warm and breezy, and I sort of want to . . .

Walk.

Play.

My slouchy bag bumps rhythmically against my upper thigh as I head down the street, and each time I think of my phone in there, about taking it out and sending a message to Reid. I'd been frustrated with Lark and her decision paralysis this afternoon, but had I done any different, working so hard to avoid thinking about Reid, about that almost confrontation? Had he left that coffee shop wondering whether I'd call him again? Has my laser focus on the Make It Happyn job these last few days been, in part, some version of staring down at a table of options, unwilling to make a decision about our . . . arrangement?

I've made my way down to Joe's on Fifth without really thinking, unless "smelling pizza" is a form of thinking. Inside the narrow store—not quite busy with the dinner rush yet—I order a slice, then decide to take it back outside on its already limp paper plate. Reid would like this place, and this pizza. He would not like the paper plate, or the fact that I got only two napkins for what I'm sure is a four-napkin slice, but you can't win them all, I guess.

I sit on the red wooden bench that's been constructed around the tree outside of Joe's and stare up at the crooked awning, the white vinyl sign above. Truthfully, there's not much interesting to see here—*maybe* the little serifs on the sign stuck to the cooler in front, advertising some prepackaged Italian ices. But as I finish my last bite and wipe my fingers (two napkins were not enough), I make a decision.

It'd been uncomfortable, those last few minutes with Reid, the reminder of how we came together. It'd been uncomfortable to confront again, even in such a small way, what I'd done.

But so much of it, before that, had been the opposite of uncomfortable. It'd been easy to play those games with him. And it'd made it easier to draw for Make It Happyn. It'd made it easier with Lark today.

So maybe that discomfort—that risk of confrontation—is worth it.

I pitch my trash and snag another napkin, cleaning up more before I take my phone from my bag. Then I snap a few pictures, all from Joe's storefront. The *P* from *pizza,* the *L* and the *A* from the Italian ice sign, the *Y* from the *open 7 days.* I wait until my phone's clock turns from 4:59 to 5:00, and then I attach all four of the pictures in a message to Reid.

I type a single question mark, press send, and wait.

Within a few minutes my phone rings, and I can't help but smile, knowing it's him even without looking at the screen. I press the tab on my headphones, hoping my cheery "Hiya" chases away any of the lingering heaviness from our last conversation.

"So," he says, and from that one syllable I realize that I've missed his voice. "You couldn't find a question mark on a sign?"

My smile widens. *It's worth it.* "Damn. You got me."

There's a small silence during which I hope Reid is smiling, too, though not at anyone in his immediate proximity, since I also realize that I'd feel more than a little jealous if someone else got to see the full force of a smile *I* caused. It can't be good, some of these stray, soft things I feel about Reid, but it's so good to feel something other than stressed or lonely or blocked.

"You're out walking?" On the other end of the line, there's

suddenly more noise, as though Reid's only now stepped out onto the street. It's nice, thinking he might've called me while he was still inside his office building, wherever it is. Nice to think he might've been excited.

"Yeah. In Brooklyn, though."

"Ah." Does he sound—maybe disappointed? It's hard to tell over the phone.

"I thought maybe if you're walking home from work, maybe we could . . ." I trail off, stopped at a crosswalk. I don't want these two people waiting beside me—even though they are definitely not even paying any attention to me—to be witnesses to my potential rejection.

"Walk together?"

I look beside me, at the two people who are still simply staring down at their phones. One of them is tapping a thumb frantically on tiny, fuzzy monsters that float and scramble across his screen, which seems to me to be a terrible game.

See? I want to say to both of them, feeling smug. *It* was *a good idea that I reached out to him.*

"Yes," I say, starting to cross the street. "I mean, we need a game, obviously."

"Obviously," he repeats, and actually I think I *can* tell something over the phone. I think he might be enjoying this already.

I feel sheepish now, not having thought of an idea before I called him. Doing our names had been easy, obvious, safe. I could suggest something similarly bland—spell out your birthday month, or the name of your first pet. But that feels ludicrously like the beginnings of an identity theft scheme, and anyway, I find myself wanting to have a different kind of conversation with Reid.

"Okay," I say, taking a deep breath. "One word to describe your day."

I think the sound Reid makes is a groan, and it makes me break stride, hearing that noise from him. It's so—*unbuttoned.*

I swallow, collect myself. Collect a lot of unruly thoughts about Reid being unbuttoned.

"We can pick something else."

"No, one word is"—there's a pause—"fair. Hand-lettered only?"

"You trying to take the easy way out?"

"Alas," he says, and I worry I'm going to start developing some kind of *Masterpiece Theatre* library of sexual fantasies. *Alas, alas, alas.* I'm thinking about the word *cravats* when he finishes his sentence. "I am not in an area known for its hands-craftsmanship."

I'm guessing that means he's downtown. Phallic-skyscraper city, dollar-sign-eyed people all around him. Neckties, not cravats, which is a shame.

"Not hand-lettered only," I say, but I'm already snapping a picture of a chalk-drawn sandwich board, focusing on the *S*. I already know what my word is going to be. "I can be flexible."

Reid and I decide we've got fifteen minutes to find the letters for our respective words; then we'll send them to each other all at once when the time is up. At first, I feel a pang of nervousness—will we hang up, find our letters separately? Or will we stay on the phone, a distant sort of togetherness, trying to find something to talk about?

But Reid settles that for us, because as soon as we start the time he asks where I am, what it's like in the neighborhood I'm walking through, as though he wants to minimize the distance between us. I snap photos as I walk, do my best to describe the particular flavor of Park Slope on a Tuesday early evening. Strollers and schoolkids on the sidewalks, Subaru wagons on already-clogged streets. I tell him about how I was surprised, when I first moved here, that some of the shops close so early, and I tell him—as I make my way all the way down Twelfth— about my favorite bakery, which stays open until seven. When I get there, I tell him my cupcake options and ask him what I should pick, and he says, "I don't eat many sweets," which makes me laugh.

I order a Brooklyn Blackout—four different kinds of chocolate—but decide not to eat it while we talk.

Reid tells me, too, about where he is. But he says he's not as good at describing things as I am. He says that when he looks around, he has a hard time seeing anything that stands out.

"It looks uniform to me. Everything is tall. Gray. Busy. Dirty."

"That's what I used to think, too." I snap another photo, the lovely, lowercase blue *r* from the bakery's front window. "Before I moved here."

"Yes, but you're in Brooklyn. It's different."

"I didn't always live in Brooklyn. I used to live in Manhattan, when I first came."

"You did?"

"Sure, Hotshot," I say, teasing. "You and your fancy job. You think I'm not cut out for Gotham, or something?" I snap another picture, not quite believing the way Reid and I are talking. It's even better than the game. For all I'm walking along by myself here, I don't feel lonely at all.

"That's not what I mean." There's another long pause, and I wonder if he's taking a picture. "But . . . I don't associate you with here."

The way he says "here" somehow makes this feel like a point in my favor, and maybe I should take it that way. Maybe a place that Reid sees as gray and dirty is not a place I should want to be associated with in his mind. But maybe it's only that he met me here, in the shop I'm still only blocks from, drawing out wedding programs for a wedding that never happened.

I hear a series of tinny beeps and Reid says, "Time's up," which is something of a relief. I'm not sure where I would've taken the conversation after that. "Ladies first."

I duck under an awning, tuck myself close to a building so I can send him my photos. A mix between hand-lettered and not, but I don't really mind. In fact, I appreciate the look; it suits the word I've chosen.

S-U-R-P-R-I-S-I-N-G.

It takes a minute for all the photos to go through, and once they do there's a few seconds of silence while I'm guessing Reid looks them over.

"I like the *G* best," he says, and I smile. That's my favorite, too. It's the third letter I snapped and right away I thought of it for *August*. Also my birth month, not that we're doing the identity theft thing. Then he says, "Why surprising?"

"I met with a new client," I tell him, leaving out the part where I'm still repeatedly surprised about knowing Princess Freddie in real life. I'm guessing that he, like Lachelle, would not understand what a poet-sandwich boyfriend is. "I used a game to help her make a decision." I pause, clear my throat. "You inspired me."

He doesn't say anything for what feels like forever. But then he says the nicest thing.

"That's quite a compliment. To be an artist's inspiration."

Quite a compliment. An artist.

I almost say, from some old, knee-jerk place too many women have within them, *I'm not an artist!* But I stop myself. Of course I'm an artist, and a good one. Instead I'm grateful he can't see my pink face and I say, "Your turn."

"Mine seem somewhat inadequate. Only five letters."

"Quit stalling. Cough up your winnings."

He maybe sighs.

When the letters come through, I can add another reason why my day's been surprising.

"What the heck!" I say loudly, and a woman pushing an extremely fancy stroller gives me a startled glance. I give her back a brief, apologetic smile before looking back at my phone screen. "These are *all* hand-done!"

"I walked to South Street Seaport," he says, and I think I detect a note of self-satisfaction there. "Many painted signs here."

"I feel like you've cheated me, somehow! You're a card sharp, but with this incredibly nerdy game that only we know about." I wish Lachelle were here; she would definitely have something to say about this.

But I also don't wish that. Because then I wouldn't be alone, in on this secret game with Reid. Then I wouldn't be alone the first time I hear him laugh. Even through the phone, it's lovely. Soft, low, hardly a laugh at all. A *chuckle*. I see that word, drawn out. I'd make it so there were no ascenders, so all the letters were on the level. I'd make it so there was hardly any space between them, so that the word would look as snug and as warm as the sound feels.

Then I really look at what he's sent. What he's spelled. *T-E-N-S-E*.

"Oh. Not a good day, huh?"

"It was—as I said. Or, as I spelled, I suppose."

"You want to ta—"

"No," he says quickly. "That word about covers it."

Reid says so little about his work that it almost makes me wish I understood that Wikipedia page better. But maybe I should be grateful, given how tied Reid's work is to the things that made our last meeting so awkward: Avery, and Avery's father.

"I'm sorry," I say.

"It isn't your fault."

I wonder if he's standing still where he is, too. People and cars and buses rushing by, but a tiny, cozy pocket of quiet in the lines between our phones. Maybe *I'm sorry* and *It isn't your fault* are things Reid and I should've already said to each other, in other contexts, but it doesn't matter.

It matters that we're saying them now.

"So," I say, after the quiet stretches a beat too long. "South Street Seaport, huh?"

"Yes, it's not that far from my office."

"That's not gray. Or dirty, really." I like it down there, in fact. Sibby and I went to a fall stall market down there a couple of years ago and bought a bunch of misshapen but colorful root vegetables that, as happens to most casual farmers' market visitors with no talent for cooking, we only ended up using half of. In the shadow of the Financial District, South Street feels . . . *low*. Pleasantly so. Low to the ground, and at the edge of the water. The buildings are older—washed-out brick, charming stretches of storefronts. A respite from the sometimes dizzying heights of what stands at its back. I open my mouth to tell Reid about the Big Gay Ice Cream parlor that's opened down there, but then I remember he doesn't eat sweets.

"No, I guess it's not." I think I hear him start to take a deep inhale, as if he can finally breathe, but the honk of a horn intrudes at almost the same time.

I feel . . . disappointed. I wanted to hear the full range of that deep breath.

"Unfortunately," Reid says, "I have to head to another meeting. A work thing."

Alas, I think.

But I also feel a bold stroke of pleasure swoop across my middle, thinking of Reid leaving work for a few minutes, only to play. Maybe he'll go back in there, some of what was tense about his day slightly less so. Maybe I gave some of the surprise of my day to him.

"Sure. Thanks for the company." Then I add something, something honest, something Reid once said to me. It feels right to add it, like I'm helping us build some kind of routine.

Like we're more than just company. Like we're *friends*.

"I had fun."

There's a pause on the other end of the phone, and I hope I haven't somehow made it weird. Something I've learned over the last couple of weeks is that I am extremely talented at making it weird with Reid.

"Are you free on Saturday?" he asks. Bluntly. Directly. Reid-ly.

I smile.

This time I don't hesitate to answer.

Chapter 9

When I hung up the phone with Reid on Tuesday evening, I felt a lot of things.

Eager, for one: about going back to my apartment, and getting back to Make It Happyn, armed with newly formed ideas and newly loosened leg muscles.

Confident, for two: I hadn't *needed* Reid to tell me I'm an artist, but it'd been nice to have the reminder anyway, especially building off the work I'd been doing as a result of our first game.

Hopeful, for three: about the progress I'd made with Lark, about some of the pain and anger I seemed to be sloughing off about Sibby, about how I'd taken a risk, playing another game with Reid.

Excited, for four: We'd made *plans*. We were going to play again, and in some ways, we've *been* playing since. We send photos back and forth to each other, mine mostly of local business signs and Reid's mostly of faded advertisements from the sides of buildings, the kind of relics we'd looked for on our first walk together. We don't even say much in the messages—sometimes

we add an address, or a note about which letter is our favorite—
yet they feel full of the promise of our next meeting.

But by the time Saturday comes, I feel exactly one thing.

My period.

I should've known, and not only because The Planner of Park
Slope *obviously* has a very specific method by which she tracks
her cycle—an extremely genius tiny red dot next to the expected
date in my monthly log. I should've known because I woke up on
Friday morning in the kind of mood that swings wildly between
"ten seconds from murdering someone" and "three seconds
from crying because you noticed a layer of dust on your window-
sill, you absolute filthy *pig.*" Lucky for the world at large I did not
have to leave the apartment all day, but unlucky for me there
was a marathon of *House Hunters* on, during which I listlessly
made my way through a few regular client jobs while fantasiz-
ing about murdering every single house hunter who complained
about paint colors. Then I cried about the per-square-foot cost
of housing in Missouri (it's really very affordable!).

At one point I'd rallied, trying again to finish the sketches
I'd been working on since Tuesday night, when my phone had
honked with the obnoxious horn sound I've assigned to my
dad's text messages, which come in pretty rarely. I'd swiped it
open and there'd been a photo of him, tanned and smiling,
shaking the hand of some man in a suit with a flag pin on the
lapel, a framed certificate between them. Behind my dad was
Jennifer, the woman he married two weeks after he and my
mom officially divorced, which was also, as it turned out, barely
three months after I'd left home.

*Local businessman of the year from the Chamber of
Commerce,* was my dad's caption, bland and informative, and
I'd felt a spike of old, awful anger. I'd opened my notebook and
swept my hand through a single word, adding a few dramatic
swashes for decoration, and snapped a photo to send back to him.

Congratulations! it read, beautiful and celebratory, but four of
the letters there—*L-I-A-R*—fell minutely beneath the baseline,
so minutely that only I would notice.

And then I'd thought: *Reid would notice.*

I'd felt so bad to have done it, so petty and small, that I'd almost, *almost* texted him to cancel, my fingers hovering over the keypad on my phone.

But then I'd thought of him spelling out that word to me—*T-E-N-S-E*—and I'd known—in some certain, specific place inside of me—that I didn't want him spending his Saturday alone. I'd gone to bed early with that dull, anticipatory ache in my lower belly, hoping for better luck with the premenstrual mood pendulum in the morning.

And when I wake up, I *do* feel less like murdering or crying. Of course, that's because the main event has arrived, which means the dull ache has turned into something heavier and sharper. My lower back aches, everything I put on feels a half size too small, and I would very much like to attach a vacuum hose to my mouth that connects directly to a bag of chocolate, clutch a heating pad to my middle, and watch a series of romcoms where no one ever seems to get a period, ever.

But I said yes to Reid, and I don't want to go back on my answer—not only for him, but for me, too. I *want* to walk and play and get inspired again.

So I shove a few extra tampons in a small purse—I can't imagine hauling my bag today—knock back a couple Advil, and take a long subway ride to the Village.

He's waiting for me when I walk up the steps from the station, as he'd promised he would be, his casual-Reid uniform in place: sneakers, jeans, T-shirt, jacket. His face, obviously, looks fan-fucking-tastic, which I'd appreciate more if he didn't look immediately at my own and wrinkle his brow.

"What's wrong?" he asks, in lieu of a greeting.

The only solace I take in this question is the private speculation I indulge in about what would happen if I loudly announced to Reid on a public street that I got my period. Imagine the throat clearing! It would be legend.

"Oh, you know," I say, waving a hand back toward the station. "Long ride over."

He straightens his already straight posture. "I would've come to Brooklyn."

He'd offered, actually, when we'd first made these plans, but it'd been my suggestion to meet in the Village, where I know there're tons of examples of old, painted signs. I force a smile, try to smooth over the wrong-footed start—whatever my face was doing when Reid first saw it, that note of embarrassed defensiveness in his voice.

"I know," I say lightly. "Your turn to come up with a game."

I start walking, not really caring if he had another direction in mind. I've just had a fresh bout of cramping, the kind that snakes all the way down the front of my legs. If this is going to work out today, I need to clench my teeth and keep moving.

So it's a good thing Reid does, in fact, have a game in mind. This time, we'll each pick a color, and then we'll try to get as many letters of the alphabet as we can in that one color over the course of an hour. No limits on type of letter or sign, but we know the game—or each other—well enough now to know we're both going to try finding the more interesting stuff. The hand-lettered, the hand-painted, the stuff that'll give me something to draw about.

Reid offers me first pick and I choose blue, which gives me my first genuine smile of the afternoon because I absolutely know he was going to pick blue; I can tell by the look on his face when I say it. He chooses green, and I tell him that's basically cheating because green is a *version* of blue, and he definitely does not like being called a cheater because he says, "Fine. I choose red, then."

For the first couple of blocks, I tease him about that, too, because red is *obviously* the easiest color for sign-watching. He does the *swoonsh* and keeps snapping his photos, while I grumble about being the more nuanced competitor. We both get a win on the old, cracked-paint C.O. Bigelow sign, tall and huge on the side of a brick building, though Reid gloats about how the red paint is holding up better than the pale blue. "Gloating" for Reid basically involves him stating a fact, but still.

But we're only a half hour in when I start to flag. That Advil I took must've been stale candy, because I'm pretty sure my uterus weighs thirty-five pounds and everything from my waistband down is uncomfortable. I am *miserable* and too far from home to do anything about it immediately. I definitely should've canceled, or at the very least picked red before Reid could and—

"Meg?" I hear him say.

I look up at him, realize I've missed something, and since Reid doesn't talk much in general, it's a real loss.

"I'm sorry. I zoned out."

"We could stop." Then he does that thing again, tugging down the sleeve of his unnecessary-for-the-weather jacket. Maybe the sleeve tugging is the same as Lark's two fingers along her hairline, or maybe it's the same as me wanting to lie down in the middle of this sidewalk to contemplate the various horrors and indignities of my childbearing years. "If this isn't helping, I mean."

My shoulders slump in defeat. I've done such a bad job of pretending today, of being my normal, cheerful self, and even the ideas I'm getting from the signs can't compensate for the way I feel.

"It's only that—" I break off, sigh heavily. He looks over at me, his brow wrinkled in that same way as it'd been when I'd gotten off the train. "I don't feel very well today," I admit.

I barely have time to feel embarrassed, because Reid stops, sets a hand under my elbow—*whoops*, still an erogenous zone—and gently guides me to the edge of the sidewalk, out of the way of the pedestrians behind us.

The move is so—immediate. So instinctive and concerned and direct, and so very *Reid*, and that gives me the three-seconds-from-crying feeling again. I lower my eyes, stare down at my shoes, which now feel more than a half size too small. He smells the same as he did last weekend—soap and that whisper of swimming pool—and if this turns into actual crying I don't trust myself to resist the face-pressing instinct.

"I knew it," he says. "You're sick?"

"Not really." Without thinking, I smooth a hand over my stomach, low where it aches.

"You have—" He breaks off, puts his hands in the front pockets of his jeans. "Aha," he says, softly.

I can't help but laugh. This is all very *Masterpiece Theatre*, like old-timey times when people couldn't say the word *leg* or *ankle* because it was too morally disturbing. It feels as though he's invited me—with all his serious, starchy caution—to say it out loud.

"If that 'aha,' means 'your period,' then yes. You are correct."

He doesn't clear his throat or set his jaw or get a wash of pink across his cheeks. He gives a skeptical glance to the small purse—a real miscalculation, I admit, since I can't fit a military-grade heating pad inside of it—and says, "Do you have everything you need?" as though he's planning to go into the nearest Duane Reade and buy me a bag of supplies.

The funny thing is, I think he actually would. *In which aisle would I find tampons?* he would say, in that very serious voice.

I tug on the hem of my favorite shirt, an old striped button-up that's been washed so many times it's as soft as the sheets on my bed. "I'm okay. I don't want to quit yet. I'm just feeling . . . yuck."

I fully expect him to furrow at that description, but he only nods and looks up ahead, where there's a small, tree-canopied enclosure, black wrought-iron gating separating it from the busy sidewalk and street.

"Let's go sit for a while. You can put your feet up."

I stare at him, and this time he actually does flush a little.

"My sister always does that. When she feels . . ." He trails off.

"Yuck?" I finish for him, smiling softly, less at the word than at what Reid has told me—something about his private life, something that's not tied up with his broken engagement. "You have a sister?"

Another nod while he keeps those blue eyes so focused on me, his fan-fucking-tastic face fixed in concern.

"She's younger. She still lives at home with my parents."

"Oh," I say, but suddenly I have ten thousand questions, so many questions about Reid and his life that the weight of them distracts me from the extremely unpleasant weight in my abdomen. It *would* be nice to sit for a while, to put my feet up. I'll rest and drink some water, and if it doesn't help, I'll make my way back to the train and go home to sleep it off, ask Reid if he can meet again in a couple of days.

But for now, while I'm waiting it out—why not play a game of twenty questions?

♥ ♥ ♥

"There are *seven* of you?" I say, my voice high-pitched.

Reid flattens his lips, but this is the kind of lip flattening that I now know means he's hiding a smile.

"There are."

I adjust my ass on the hard slats of the bench beneath me. It may not be all that comfortable in terms of furniture, but it's lovely, this enclosure—small and shady and quiet, even though it's only a few steps off the busy traffic on Sixth. Around the various landscaped beds are low, arched black fences, and while the landscaping is still sparse this early, most of the bushes are full and green, and the trees above us rustle with a light breeze.

Best of all? There're two signs that seemed to greet us when we came in, both on the same wall of the building that forms one edge of the park. They're old, faded, and partially obscured by the trees, both advertising the same local pharmacy that's no longer in business. One has white letters on a black background; the other, black letters on white. Sans serif fonts, sturdy and practical, more lovely for the wear and tear, and every time I ask Reid a question, he looks up at them.

"Do you all look the *same*?" I ask now, my eyes wide. Seven Sutherland siblings, he'd told me. Six boys and one girl. After this I'm going to ask if they ever performed a concert in Austria, or had a series of romance novels written about them.

It is ridiculous how much better I feel.

Reid looks at the sign, his brow furrowed. "Some of us do, I suppose. Connor and Garrett and I, we all have this hair color, same as my dad."

Do they all have your jawline?! I want to ask.

"But Owen and Ryan and Seth and Cady all have my mom's dark hair."

"How do you remember all their names?" I'm only half-joking. A family that big—I can't really imagine.

He smiles over at me. "You don't forget your siblings' names. No matter how many of them there are."

"Yeah, of course." I add an awkward laugh, but then I lower my eyes and press my hands into my thighs, rubbing at the aching that's mostly dissipated now. When we got here, Reid insisted that I stretch my legs out in front of me along the bench's slats, and then—a stroke of magic—he'd produced a small blister pack of (not stale) ibuprofen from his jacket pocket. My first of the twenty questions had thus almost been *Will you marry me?* but instead I'd settled for asking whether he always has pocket-sized pain relief.

"The occasional tension headache," he'd said as he settled his tall, lean form right up against the bench's other side, leaving me most of the space. Something had closed off in his face when he'd answered, an echo of that *T-E-N-S-E*, so I'd stayed on the sibling stuff he'd introduced with the mention of his sister.

"Do you have any brothers or sisters?" Reid asks, and I guess it's only fair, but I really preferred when this game of twenty questions was focused on him.

"Uh, no." It comes out more sharply than I intend. But not having siblings—it's a sore spot in my family history, nearly as sore as my dad having a decade-long affair with Jennifer, and my mom knowing about it the whole time.

"I always wondered what it'd be like, though," I add, trying to soften the edge.

"Crowded," he says flatly. Then he looks over at me, his mouth curving upward, and I think it's his own way of softening that edge.

"Do you miss them? Living here, I mean?"

"Yes," he says immediately. He looks back at the signs. "But it's a relief, sometimes. To live alone."

"I've never lived alone," I admit, and in my surprise at having said it, I clutch tighter at the muscles of my thighs, kneading up and down. When I look up, I catch Reid watching the movement, and something in my middle warms pleasantly.

But he seems to catch himself, and he raises his eyes, his blue gaze tangling with mine briefly. That warmth spreads out, seems to exist in the space between us.

He clears his throat. "Never?"

I shake my head. "I left my parents' house to come here. And I've lived with Sibby"—I knead more aggressively—"ever since."

"Sibby is your . . . ?"

I take a deep breath, struck by how quickly the conversation has turned. It's strange, how sitting here in the quiet with Reid feels similar to walking out there in the loud beside him. A different kind of game, leading to a different kind of unblocking.

But an unblocking all the same.

"She's my best friend. We grew up together."

"That must be nice. To have someone here from home. Someone you know so well." There's a melancholy note to his voice, and I wonder how much of Reid's disdain for New York is about this—not having someone from that big, crowded family he misses here with him.

"It has been. But . . . um, she's moving out soon, into a place with her boyfriend." I look out toward the park entrance. "To this neighborhood, actually. So I guess I'll have that living alone experience, at least for a while."

For a second, all I can think of is the first apartment Sibby had, the one I came to after I left home. It was in Hell's Kitchen (also an appropriate name for the feeling in my stomach at the time)—one room, longer than it was wide, with Sibby's compact sofa pushed against the same wall as her twin-size bed. The first few nights, when she could hear me crying, she would only have to reach out from there to grab my hand. In the mornings I'd fold my blankets and we'd sit side by side, eating instant oats Sibby would make in the tiny microwave that sat on top of the mini-fridge. Usually my phone would ring, my mom or dad calling, and Sibby would say, "Want me to answer today?" but she never pressed me, no matter how many times I'd say no.

"You're not happy about it." It's less a question than a statement.

I stop kneading, smooth my palms to a stop on my thighs, pretend to check the chipped, pale-green polish on my nails. "We've had some trouble recently. Not a fight or anything, but we've grown apart. Or . . . she's grown apart from me, I guess. I'm not sure she wants to be my friend anymore."

It's the first time I've said it out loud, to anyone. And surprisingly, it's such a *relief*. It's a bit like when I fessed up that I had my period and wanted to stop walking for a while, or like when we walked into this park to sit and my whole body had sagged in anticipation of the comfort.

"I'm sorry," Reid says, after a few seconds of quiet. "It must be difficult."

And that—that *acknowledgment*—has the same effect as that blister pack of pills, helping to chase the ache away.

"Thanks." I feel an inconvenient pendulum swing back to the crying feeling. I may be relieved to have said it, but I don't want to go full catharsis out here in the open air, particularly since Reid probably doesn't carry a vacuum hose and a bag of chocolate in that jacket.

"You've never asked her?" Reid says. "Whether she wants to be your friend anymore?"

When I look up at him, he's watching me, as though he's asked the easiest question. As though that would be the easiest question for *me* to ask of Sibby. As though when you ask people things—the really, really hard things—you don't have anything to fear from their answer. You don't have anything to fear from how you'll react to it.

"Not in so many words," I say, and it's terrible, the way my voice cracks. I blink back down at my legs, mortified.

And then, after a long pause, Reid speaks again. "I don't suppose I know how it is, with a friend like that. That you've had for so long, I mean. I had my siblings, but not really—not friends I grew up with, I guess."

I don't know how to explain what happens in those few seconds after he finishes speaking, except to say that it's as if a piece of my heart breaks off and leaves my body. It's as if that tiny, vulnerable piece beats its way right across the bench and attaches itself to Reid.

All because of this gentle confession, this effort at making me feel better.

I clear my throat, watch as he looks back toward the signs.

"No one from school?" I ask.

He shakes his head. "It's my own fault. I was . . . difficult in school."

Difficult? I try to picture it: Reid launching spitballs, mouthing off to teachers, not doing his homework. I can't see it, and something must show on my face, because when he looks over, he smiles briefly and speaks again.

"I was bored. Always done with my work early. It frustrated my teachers, and obviously . . . ah, did not endear me to other students."

I can picture that better. Serious, studious Reid. Probably cracking whatever code they gave him, and getting no reward for it. Getting the kind of mystified, slightly put-off responses that'd make a kid feel small, embarrassed. That particular mouth-pulling on Reid's little-boy face.

Pendulum swing, firmly to the murder feeling. Basically for all of Reid's former teachers and any kid that did not . . . feel endeared to him. I should probably be extremely worried about how fully endeared *I* am, except that I'm too invested in asking more questions. It's not a game anymore; it's not for inspiration. But it still feels so, so important.

"But it must've been better," I say. "When you went to college? Or—your graduate school?"

Reid looks up at the signs again, waits a long moment. "I was fifteen when I went to college."

"Fifteen?!" I still slept with a stuffed animal at fifteen, which I have the good sense not to say out loud.

"Community college for the first semester. An extension program through my high school."

"Oh, sure," I say, still processing my shock. "*That* makes it better!"

He gives me the sad eyes. Those are the worst. They make my stomach feel like Hell's Kitchen.

"Not better. I only mean . . . it doesn't make it any less surprising. Or less impressive. It's—wow. You are *smart*, huh?"

He *swooshes*, and I'll bet if I scooted closer, I could watch that blush spread across his cheekbones.

"At math," he says.

"Well, you must be in hog heaven now, at your job. Surrounded by math people!"

The *swoosh* fades, his face closing off again. T-E-N-S-E.

"Money people. It's different."

For a second he looks so drawn and hollow that all I can think about is making him feel better. Some blister pack of something to take that look away.

And then I realize: Maybe I *do* have something in my metaphorical jacket pocket. Sitting here in this park, beside Reid, learning more about him, letting some of my own lowest feelings out into the open air—I don't even have to pretend to feel cheerful and light. I can actually . . . *be* cheerful and light.

My mouth curves into a smile, and I nudge him gently, teasingly, with my foot. I try to ignore the way touching him, even in this completely platonic way, doesn't feel all that much like teasing to me.

"Would you say . . . would you say that money is the . . . *common denominator* for your colleagues?"

For a second, he says absolutely nothing, and I think, *Nice job, Meg. It wasn't the time to be light and cheerful. With a* math *joke.*

But then he looks over at me, blinks once, and he . . . he *laughs*. A real, full laugh. An in-person laugh.

And it is the most gorgeous combination of sounds, the same sounds I heard him make when we walked together on the phone the other night: that groan, but this time at how utterly terrible my joke was. That warm, tight chuckle, a bit louder this time, then quieting and giving way to a sigh, a small exhalation of air. A sigh of *relief.*

It's the best sound I've ever heard. Nothing I could ever put in letters. I frolic right past another warning clutch in my heart.

"Thank God you laughed! That's one of maybe ten math terms I know. Want to hear the others?"

He smiles, breathing out only the chuckle now.

Let's walk for blocks and blocks, I'm thinking. *Let me make bad math jokes to you all day. Wait until you hear the one about stochastic calculus, which is basically me trying to pronounce it.*

"You feel better?" he asks.

"I do." I look over at the signs that have kept us company through this, our new not-game. "Anyway, these don't have the colors we need."

I swing my legs off the bench, stand up, and smooth my shirt down before grabbing my purse, telling him with my body that I'm ready to keep going.

"Meg," he says from behind me, and I turn, look back down to where he still sits, his body curved forward. His face is turned up to me, his eyes serious but dancing with the fluttering shadows from the canopy of trees overhead.

"Yeah?"

"Your friend . . . I don't believe she doesn't want to be your friend anymore. I think she must—" He breaks off, lifts a hand and runs it through his hair, something I've never seen him do. "She must have something going on, with herself. I'm sure she'll come around."

Oh, no. It's a big pendulum swing back. We're probably in one-second-from-crying territory now. Reid's quiet vote of confidence on this—even in spite of the fact that he's never met Sibby, that he's giving me all the benefit of the doubt, that he's admitted, not ten minutes ago, that he doesn't have all that much experience with friendship himself—it gives me so much comfort. I don't even know if I believe it, really, but—God. God, it helps to hear it.

"I hope so."

He stands then, and the movement puts us close to each other, unexpectedly so. Both of us seem to take the same quick inhale, and his hands rise to cup my elbows, as though to steady

me, and I guess it's a good thing, because *whoa*. *Both* of my elbows at the same time. I feel that touch like starbursts beneath
my skin, between my legs.

My eyes rise to his. His head is tipped down, the hair he
smoothed back curling over his brow again. When he breathes
out, I feel the fine strands of hair around my face quiver.

I feel so many things, so much more than I did this morning.

"What I mean to say is . . ." He pauses, those blue eyes searching mine. "What I mean to say is, I think anyone would want to
be your friend."

Friend.

The way Reid says this word—I want to draw and redraw it,
capturing how it sounds from his lips. I want to ask him to say it
again, so I can watch. So I can know if I'm seeing too much in
those letters when he says them.

I *must* be, right?

Friend is not starbursts in your elbows. *Friend* is not face-
pressing. *Friend* is not thinking about how a so-often-stern,
sometimes-laughing set of lips would taste.

Something in my body must've changed, straightened, because Reid drops his hands from me, though I still feel those
starbursts. *Do it again*, I want to say, but instead I take a half
step back and fix him with what I hope is a normal, unaffected
smile.

"Even you, huh?" I manage. And even though I know Reid
would've said it more directly, I hope he knows what I'm really
asking. I hope he knows I'm asking whether he's forgiven me
for those seven hidden letters.

He puts his hands in his jacket pockets. He looks at me for a
long time.

"Even me," he says, finally. And then he adds, quietly, the
most perfect, special fragment, the one I know I'll be drawing
for days and days. "Especially me."

Chapter 10

"Wow," Lark says, staring down at the pile of sketches in front of her. "This is a lot."

She doesn't say "a lot" as though she's happy about it, and given what I know about her decision-making capabilities, I suppose that's fair enough. Maybe I should've done fewer treatments, or streamlined her options. But I can't say I regret it.

Because everything laid out in front of us here? The bold, brightly colored compositions, the different iterations of the lettering Lark picked? The mix-and-match styles, the shapes I've formed with different letter arrangements?

All of it means I'm finally, *finally* unblocked.

Almost every idea on these pages I owe to the game, to the time Reid and I spent together last Saturday after the park. With my cramps abated and a new lightness between us as we'd walked and snapped photos, my pendulum had swung strongly in the direction of "needing tacos," and since I'd pretty much abandoned any modesty when it came to my period feelings, I'd told Reid immediately.

"I think there's a place around here you'd like," he'd said. Sadly, he had not touched my elbow again as he led the way.

Happily, though, "like" had been an understatement. The restaurant had been inspiration city—signs painted on the walls everywhere I looked, bold and bright, advertising *Cervezas* and *Micheladas* over the bar, *Tortillas* and *Salsas* and *Tostadas* in the dining room. Even some of the mirrors on the walls had been painted, one with a gorgeous, vintage-looking script that I'd sketched right away, flipping over the half sheet of paper we'd been given to check off our taco order.

We'd sat at the sticky-surfaced table, the bar loud at our backs, and shared everything we ordered. We ate food that was as bright and delicious as the signs around us. Ripe, pale-green avocado. Perfectly roasted, gold-yellow corn. Bowls of deep-red salsa. Dark, spicy black beans. The translucent purple of chopped red onions.

In between bites of food, we'd talked. It's clear Reid's least favorite topic is his job, but he'd told me more about his family, and I'd even gotten him to tell me about the pool smell: he swims laps at the gym every single morning, five a.m. to six a.m. After he finishes, he eats the same breakfast each day: three eggs, one sliced tomato, one banana, one cup of—"Let me guess!" I'd interrupted—hot tea. And he'd listened with interest while I'd told him all about my first few months in New York—well, leaving out the crying parts—exploring the city with Sibby.

It was easy and honest and fun, and I'd felt Reid's *Especially me* sparking like electricity in my fingers the whole time.

I'd drawn all through the train ride home, and I've kept drawing. At cafés, in between meetings with my regulars. At the shop, sometimes sitting and chatting with Lachelle or Cecelia, neither of them asking why I've been around more lately. At the apartment, in my room, sometimes with the occasional interruption from a text exchange with Reid—more pictures, more small games we've played. I've worked enough to have one complete treatment for the Make It Happyn job, something I'm pretty happy with, and I'd still managed to get time in for Lark's commission.

Now I lean away from it all, giving Lark a better view and an apologetic smile.

"It's possible I overdid it."

She smiles back—a knowing, indulgent smile, one that makes me think Lark and I could probably be friends.

"But remember, what we're looking for here is related to composition—a set of shapes that stick out to you. Try to ignore colors, for now."

With this direction, Lark eliminates a few entries. Even though I told her to ignore colors, I pay attention to where she lingers, for future reference. At one point, she sets the tip of her index finger to a pale-pink and pale-green juxtaposition, inspired by the drinks I'd insisted on ordering at the taco place: one lime soda, one watermelon soda. I'd tasted both first and passed the lime one to Reid.

"This one's not so sweet," I'd said. "But mine tastes like cavities." I'd taken a big drink just to see him shake his head in charming disapproval.

I look down at where Lark keeps her finger. Outside of the memory of the drinks Reid and I shared, this isn't really to my taste—it sort of looks as if I drew this for the Lilly Pulitzer catalog. But maybe Lark—in spite of the skinny black jeans she's wearing, the faded Ramones T-shirt that's too big for her—has a secret hankering for flower-patterned sundresses and sweaters tied around her shoulders.

"If you're into pastels," I venture, "that's a good option for the chalk wall."

She pushes the sheet away reluctantly.

"No, I'm into—you know. Black." She gestures down at her outfit. It looks as though she Googled "How to Dress Like a New Yorker."

"Sure, we can stay neutral. But even an accent—"

I'm interrupted by the sound of the front door opening and closing, the loud, warning beeps of the alarm system. At first I think it must be Jade, who'd taken off to run errands for Lark when I'd arrived, but then I hear a deep voice call out, "Goddammit! How do I shut this fucking thing off?"

Lark stiffens atop her stool, obviously surprised. When we'd set this meeting, she'd said Friday afternoon worked for her, that Cameron would be out late scouting locations for a new shoot he's working on. "Cameron," she'd said, going for the natural beginning to almost sixty percent of her sentences, "prefers if I handle everything related to the house." As though having to be involved in small decisions about what will greet his eyes every morning on the wall of his own bedroom is too much of a hardship for his artistic sensibilities.

There's another muffled curse from the entryway.

Lark gives me an embarrassed wince. "Sorry," she says, and then she calls, "Babe, remember? Put in the passcode!"

Silence. Lark seems to count to herself.

"Our first date?" she calls out.

More silent counting; then she slides off her stool. "I'll be right back."

The beeps are getting louder, closer together. I'd be nervous, I guess, to meet the half of this job who seems to be gumming up the decision-making works, but I'm too busy wondering if he'll be wearing that beanie and the leather bracelets.

When Lark and Cameron come into the kitchen, they've got those pinched-but-polite looks on their faces couples sometimes get, when you can tell they've shown up to a party after having a massive fight in the car about who always empties the dishwasher. My parents used to be super good at that look, always more polite than pinched. Lark and Cameron clearly need practice, but still—I feel an answering quiver of recognition, a discomforting familiarity deep inside of me.

"Hi!" I chirp, which is also how I used to deal with my parents. It's as though my brain has sent my mouth a message: *default to protocol.* I stand from my stool, stretching a hand out to Cameron. "I'm Meg Mac—"

"Look at you!" Cameron says, pumping my hand. I don't like it, that *Look at you!* As if I'm a toddler taking my first steps. "The Planner of Park Slope, right? We're pretty lucky getting you to this side of Brooklyn."

"Yeah, a whole two miles!" That works because I've said it so cheerfully, and Cameron smiles his bright white smile. He's not wearing the beanie, but he is wearing the bracelets, which look more ridiculous in person. I have the feeling he gave Lark the idea for her outfit, because he's got on a version of the same thing—black boots, dark jeans, vintage-looking black T-shirt. He's handsome—not Reid Sutherland handsome, though I guess that's an unfair standard for anyone to meet, given my personal preference for his face—but there's something off-putting about his good looks, how he matches them with an aren't-you-flattered-to-have-my-attention attitude.

"I mean, don't get me wrong," he says. "The Slope is great for families."

The Slope? I know from Cameron's IMDB page that he's from Malibu, so I'm pretty annoyed already. If Lachelle was here she'd be giving him a *look*, the kind of look where the two *o*'s are drawn as to-the-side eyeballs, but I nod my head in agreement. There's a strong smell of secondhand embarrassment coming off Lark, which at least is mitigating the smell of Cameron's too-strong cologne.

"I love the *feel* of it here, you know? It's so . . ." I already know what he's going to say next, and I brace myself for the impact of the irritation I'm about to feel. "Gritty," he finishes.

"Uh-huh." I drop his hand. I mean, okay. There's an IKEA not far from here; I think he can stop being so smug about Red Hook. "Well, it's really nice to meet you. You have a beautiful home." *That was built last year.*

"Still coming together, obviously." He puts an arm around Lark. "But I've got my princess here on the job."

One hundred percent of the sentences in my head now start with his name. Cameron is the worst. Cameron would never bring Lark a sandwich. Cameron probably doesn't know what a poem is. Cameron: ugh.

I nod and smile.

Lark ducks from under his arm, goes back to her stool. "Meg and I were looking over some things," she says, her voice cool. I get the sense she's trying to tell him to find something else to do, maybe to go put saddle soap on his bracelets or something, but instead he goes to the other side of the island and leans over my sketches. I go back to my seat next to Lark, giving her an encouraging smile.

"This for a kid's room, or something?" Cameron says, looking at the pink and green treatment. Another piece of jewelry has come loose from underneath the neck of his T-shirt. It's a shark tooth. On a thin rope of leather. Reid would *die*.

"Cam," Lark whispers sharply.

I give an airy, unbothered laugh, even though I'm thinking about weaponizing that thin rope of leather. "It's no big deal! I was explaining to Lark that these are helpful for seeing how we might set up the quote you choose for—"

"Yeah, the quote. I've got so many ideas about that."

"Great!"

Not great. I have the feeling that Lark's assertion that Cameron prefers her to deal with the house is not strictly true. He probably has tons of (terrible) opinions but wants her to execute them all. *On the job*, he'd said, as though she were his employee.

Beside me, Lark is shooting laser beams out of her eyes at Cameron.

"We're working on composition today, not the quote," Lark says. "I think I—"

But Cameron speaks over her.

"Do you know Nietzsche?"

"Not personally!" He absolutely doesn't get that I'm insulting him. That's how good I am at customer service, at putting on this act. I've picked up my pencil again, my grip on it overfirm, my palms clammy.

"He's a philosopher."

"Cam," Lark says. "I'm sure she knows that."

"So you've heard that quote, 'God is dead'?"

Lark runs two fingers along her hairline.

"You want 'God is dead' on your bedroom wall?" I ask.

"I want something *true*, you know?"

How about YOU'RE AN ASSHOLE. Not enough letters in *GOD*

IS DEAD to hide that, but I could think of something to get the job done.

Lark says, "We're not doing that."

Cameron looks at me as if we're in on something together, rolls his eyes, and says, "She's kind of a lightweight, this one."

And oh, man. It is so awkward. It's the kind of flippant, cruel remark that has ten layers of complication hiding inside of it. It's every time my mom said to me, during family dinners, "You know your father, he just *loves* his work," or every time my dad jokingly said to his employees at some boring holiday party, "My wife's favorite pastime is taking the fun out of things."

For a second, the room goes as silent as a grave. Lark's body is basically a headstone beside mine. She has not moved. It is unbelievable that I have not snapped my Staedtler in half with the force of my silent, suppressed anger.

Then Cameron laughs, clueless, turning to the refrigerator. I blink at his back, longing for laser beams, but I can't stand the silence. Can't stand that Lark's sitting there, probably humiliated.

"You know what?" I say to her, and to her only. I've kept my voice in the same register it'd been in before Cameron's little performance, as though nothing at all has happened to disturb our fun. "This is my favorite, too." I set my finger to the sheet of paper she'd been reaching for when Cameron interrupted her with his "God is dead" garbage.

Lark's face is flushed, but she smiles at me gratefully. "We made some progress today, right?"

I can tell she wants to wrap up, to get me out of here before Cameron does or says something else that's rude and patronizing.

And because I know that feeling, know how it is to pretend not to hear all the subtext that lies beneath a *he just* loves *his work* or to laugh uncomfortably at a hurtful joke about *taking the fun out of things*, I oblige. I tell her I'll work on this composition more, try it in different colors. I encourage her—pointedly, only her—to send me some ideas for quotes over e-mail. I shake Cameron's hand again and tell a bald-faced lie, because it was not at all nice to meet him, and I gather my stuff in my bag, tossing out a couple of self-deprecating jokes about its sloppy contents to break some of the tension that's hovering in the air.

But when Lark walks me to the foyer, the scene of Cameron's bonanza of cursing at a tiny type-pad that probably has more skills of human intuition than he does, I'm oddly unable to keep the ruse going. *Why are you with this guy?* I want to say. But I don't want to make her uncomfortable, don't want to shine an even brighter light on something she so clearly didn't want me to see.

"He's been under some stress lately," she says, before I can speak.

Default protocol is telling me to nod and smile again. But I must be all kinds of unblocked now, because I bypass it entirely and blurt, "That really sucked, what he said."

I only think fleetingly about whether or not he can hear me. I'm not sure I care if he does.

But I do care that Lark stiffens, her chin raising. She purses her lips and turns to the type-pad, punches in a code, and waits for a click before setting her hand on the doorknob. My face feels like I've stuck it against a hot oven door.

"I'll send you some of those quotes," she says sharply, and *oof*. Probably "God is dead" will end up in there, after this. The bright side, I guess, is that she's not firing me, but I feel such a potent, shaky-stomached feeling of dread. *Why did you say anything? Why couldn't you have left it alone?*

"Sure," I say. "Listen, I'm sorry if—"

"He's a good guy," she says, pointedly. "I know him."

I realize that Lark can absolutely be decisive when she wants to be. For example, when she wants me out of her house. When she's reminding me that I'm her employee, not her friend.

Nod and smile? Activated. I feel *ridiculous*.

"Oh, yeah," I say, stepping toward the open door. "I was being—" *Honest*, my brain supplies, but I don't say it. Instead I wave a hand dismissively. *I was being silly*, this gesture says.

"I'll give you a call next week," she says as I step onto the stoop, into the late-afternoon light. She doesn't sound much like she plans to call me next week.

"Absolutely," I say, nodding and smiling before I walk away.

♥ ♥ ♥

When I first moved to New York, one of the hardest things for me to get used to was not having a car.

It isn't that I thought I needed one—there're cabs and buses and the subway and your feet, obviously, and there's never anywhere to put one unless you're a billionaire or a person who doesn't mind having a lot of unpaid parking tickets. And it isn't that I've got some kind of American love affair with lengthy road trips, either, because I have a small bladder and a short attention span and also probably cannot be trusted to change a tire myself.

But getting my license at sixteen had been my most profound escape hatch, the thing that changed my life in relation to my parents' home the most. When tension would flare between them—more and more often as I got older, though back then I didn't really know why—I'd cheerfully call to them that I had an errand to run, or an extracurricular event at school, or some plan with Sibby. Then I'd grab the keys to my tiny, used Toyota and hit the road.

Sometimes I'd pick up Sibby; sometimes I'd go it alone. Either way, inside my car, I'd crack the windows no matter the temperature outside, a pressure release valve for all that tension, all the frustration I'd feel—at them for being so loud and messy with each other, at myself for being so quiet and accommodating. I'd queue up some pop-hits playlist, something where the beats were fast and the lyrics were easy to remember. I'd sing along, crowding out whatever words I'd heard between my parents, whatever words kicked around in my own head, desperate to be said out loud. I'd drive the suburban outerloop for as long as it'd take me to feel better.

City walking eventually became a substitute, though there were times, especially initially, when there were still so many strained conversations to be had with my parents (for example:

what to do with that old Toyota, once I told them I wouldn't be coming back), where all I'd want is an hour—thirty minutes, even—to be behind the wheel of a car. Going fast, wind in my hair, noise drowned all the way out.

After I leave Lark's, I really, really wish I had a car.

I'm rattled, that's the thing. For the rest of the afternoon, I run over those last few minutes in my mind, chastising myself for saying too much. I try to work, but that's a comically terrible idea. Letters—speaking and unpredictable—are the last thing I want to look at.

I want fresh air and a break from the words I shouldn't have said, and I want the kind of relief that only one person has made me feel in recent weeks.

So I call Reid.

"I guess I didn't think about the—lack of signs," I say to him now, as we stroll along my favorite part of Prospect Park, a curving path around Long Meadow. From here, you can look out over the vast expanse of green, the thick boundary of trees, and forget you're in a city at all, and even as much as I was longing for fresh air myself, I picked this specific place for Reid. Because I thought he'd enjoy it.

"It's fine." While it's not exactly curt, it's not exactly warm, either. It's not exactly, *I'm really enjoying this nature walk and this hot tea you brought me.* Beside me, he's *Masterpiece Theatre* stiff, the jacket of his suit—dark, dark blue again—draped neatly over his arm, his slim-cut white dress shirt doing everything to recommend swimming laps. But he's kept the sleeves down, buttoned at the wrists, still no concession to the warm air.

Maybe I've made a mistake, calling him—no matter that he'd texted me right back to tell me he'd come. No matter that he made me laugh with his reply, passing on my offer of a smoothie by telling me he preferred his fruit in "regular format." No matter that he walked up the subway stairs and *swoonshed*, as though he'd been waiting to see my face all week. Whatever made him agree to come, it hasn't been enough to chase away what I'm sensing is an awfully bad mood.

"No game, though," I say, and even to my own ears my voice

sounds false, almost manic in its effort to stay light, to pressure valve my way out of this frustrating, tension-filled day. "Maybe we can play—"

"Meg," he interrupts. "Are you okay?"

I shove my smoothie straw in my mouth, suck up more of its mango-banana sweetness to stall. Once I swallow I smile and— *oh no*. Nod. "Sure," I add.

"You seem—" He breaks off, clears his throat. "Different. Sort of . . . wired."

My cheeks heat in spite of the cold drink. I'm running through the stream of chatter I've kept up for the last half hour—the nice night, the guy who's passed us on a unicycle a bunch of times, my curiosity in general about people who play Frisbee. I should know by now I can't hide anything from Reid, not really. What he sees, what he hears—he asks about.

I shrug. "A lousy day at work, that's all."

"Your sketches didn't go well?" That he asks—that he knew— is a reminder of how much closer we've been over the past week, how much we've stayed in touch.

"They were fine. It's . . . a difficult client. Not a big deal."

"Difficult how?"

I feel cornered. I don't want to say anything about Lark, anything that would violate the privacy that's so important to her. So I settle for putting the blame where it really belongs.

"He's rude," I say, keeping my eyes up and ahead, on all the signless placidity surrounding us.

Reid pauses on the path, his body going still.

"Rude how?"

Standing there, Reid doesn't look all that different from the man who came into the shop all those weeks ago. Cold, determined, impatient. Looking for answers. And what am I going to say, that I went to a client's house and judged her marriage? That I think she's living a worse mistake than the one I so recklessly, secretly warned him about? That'll be a great reminder for him, I'm sure.

This is worse than being cornered. It's like being in a minefield, danger in every step I take.

"Well, first of all," I say, trying for a joke, "he wears these bracelets."

Reid blinks. "Pardon?"

I sigh. "Never mind. It's hard to explain."

"Meg." He manages to make that single syllable sound shorter than usual. "Just be—" He breaks off and shakes his head in exasperation, and I can tell it's not with himself. "Was he rude to you?"

Oh.

He's being—protective? I definitely don't want Reid to go all the way to Red Hook to punch Cameron in the face, but I am also not entirely opposed to adding this to my growing library of Reid-specific fantasies. *Alas*, cravats, pistols at dawn.

"He was rude to his wife. In front of me. It's not my favorite thing, being around that kind of tension."

I should ask Lachelle to make me a calligraphy certificate for Understatement of the Year. It'll be worth it, if Reid drops this.

At first I think he will, giving one of those tips of his head that I take as a cue to keep walking. But then he says, "So what did you do?"

"Nothing," I lie. "I made nice and got out of there. He's awful, and I'm pretty sure she knows it, but it's not really my business."

"Well," Reid says, and even from that one syllable I can hear an edge, an unkindness in his voice. "I suppose you could always hide it in some of your letters."

Everything—Reid, the park, my heart—everything goes still. Maybe the smoothie in my belly doesn't, but I sure wish it would. This is it—this is the confrontation I've been dreading with him. This is the one I'd stupidly let myself think we wouldn't need to have, ever since his perfect, quiet *Especially me.*

Today of all goddamn days.

Reid lifts his hand, scrapes it through his hair. "Forget I said that."

For a few seconds all I can do is stare at him. I'm stunned and shocked and hurt.

And then—then I'm suddenly so *angry. I'm* the mine, long-buried but still explosive, and I have definitely, definitely been stepped on. *Why couldn't you have left it alone?* I'm thinking, for the second time today, but this time all my frustration is leveled at the person standing in front of me. The person who *never* lets me keep it light. The person who's unblocked me into all this trouble.

"Forget you *said* it?"

"Yes," he answers. As though this is a perfectly reasonable request.

"This is what we're doing here? This is you being my . . . my *friend*? Waiting for your perfect opportunity to bring it up again?"

"No, I'm not. I'm not holding it against you. I've—listen, I've not had a good day."

"What does that have to do with me?"

"It doesn't." He takes a breath. "It's just that . . . some days, here, it feels to me like no one says what they mean. No one means what they say."

"Here?"

"Here," he repeats, gesturing to the air around us with his to-go cup. "This city."

I blink with a fresh wave of hurt. My hidden letters, his hatred of this city. *This,* this whole entire thing is what I should have left alone all those weeks ago. I shouldn't have taken that card as a sign. All these walks we've been on, and nothing, *nothing* has changed between us.

"It's not the city," I say, my voice hard, harsh—unrecognizable even to me.

He opens his mouth to speak, but I cut him off.

"You think you know it here? Your extensive network of people on *Wall Street*?" All my disdain, I put it into those italics. "At your big job that you never talk about, anyway?"

He stares at me, his jaw clenched.

"It's not the city," I say again. "It's the way people *are.* Not everyone says exactly what they're thinking all the time, in the most blunt way possible. People have to be nice to some jerk at their job so they don't get fired. Or they have to grin and bear it while a family member is being obnoxious so they don't make it worse. Or they have to put up with some annoying personality trait a friend has, because it's not the worst thing, in the grand scheme of things. People are only trying to . . . they're trying to *protect* themselves."

My mouth snaps shut, my face flushes. *Too much, again.* I've unblocked myself into another dimension, and that shaky-stomached feeling is back.

"Meg," Reid says softly, and this sympathy—it humiliates me further. All I can think of is distracting him from it.

"You think it's not easy to understand *here*," I say, loud enough that I think a few heads turn. "But that's not everyone else's fault. It's *yours*."

As soon as it comes out of my mouth, I know. I know it's a direct hit, the worst thing I could have said to him. I think of Cameron, saying to Lark the exact thing that seemed to hurt her the most. I think of my parents. I think of *myself.*

Neither of us says anything for a few seconds. We both seem to have to stay still to absorb the shock.

"Maybe we ought to forgo the rest of this walk," he says, finally.

"Reid, let me—I didn't say that right."

"You said it right." These four words—they are so sans serif they slice me in half.

He raises his head, quickly scans our surroundings. The park is busy, the sun not set yet.

"Will you be all right getting home?"

I nod, still shocked. I couldn't add a smile if I tried.

But when he starts to turn, I make my second—or third, or fourth, who even knows by this point—impulsive move of the day. I reach out to stop him, and I don't know what happens—don't know if I jerk back in surprise at myself, or if he's startled, or if some electric current lives between us—but suddenly Reid's cup of tea is upturned, spilling across his arm, all the way up to the crook of his elbow. All over the white expanse of his perfect shirt.

The cup hasn't even finished rolling on the ground before Reid has yanked open the buttons at his wrist, his face set in pained tolerance. I'm close enough to feel the heat from the liquid that's soaking into his skin.

"Oh, no! I'm so sorry!"

I set my smoothie on the ground, take his suit jacket from his arm before it slips. He pulls his sleeve to his elbow, getting the hot fabric off his skin.

"Reid," I breathe, failing to keep the alarm out of my voice. "What happened?"

Because this, what I'm looking at—this cannot be a burn from that tea. Along the edge of that forearm I've longed to see, there's a bright red patch of skin that tracks from the middle of his wrist to the bend at his elbow. It's wet from the tea, but I can tell it must've been dry before—it must've been itchy and uncomfortable and so, so painful.

I look up. Reid's face is blank, severe. He holds out his hand for his jacket.

"Nothing."

"That's not nothing. Have you seen a—"

"It's nothing. A psoriasis flare. I'm used to it." He's pulling on his jacket, his movements stiff. It can't be comfortable, putting that wet sleeve inside the tailored lines of the jacket.

I'm watching closely enough that I see him cringe, minutely, as it settles over his skin.

"Reid."

"Don't," he replies. I see the word in my head, shaped as a set of double doors closing—**D-O** on one side, **N-T** on the other. A tiny sliver of space between, narrowing and narrowing as they shut in my face.

He bends, picks up his now-empty cup, and gives me one brief nod of farewell.

And before I can think of any words to stop him, he's gone.

Chapter 11

"It's the guy, isn't it?"

Lachelle has basically shouted this at me across the small table we're crammed around at Cecelia's favorite neighborhood restaurant, a vegan place that serves all-organic cocktails and menu items featuring an abundance of kale. It's Friday night, and the place is packed with regulars, but also with the many guests who've come out for a happy hour in honor of Cecelia and her husband Shuhei's anniversary. When I'd walked into the somewhat shabby, too-small space, determined to stay at most for an hour so I could get back to my very important schedule of staring at blank pages and moping, I'd been met with a crush of people, the room noisy with conversation and the sizzle of the grill at the back, wafting delicious, spicy food smells into the dining room.

I'd pasted a smile on my face and felt a clenching pang of longing for Reid.

Reid who has been ignoring me for a whole week.

"What guy?" I say, and Lachelle throws a kale chip at me.

About a half hour ago, after I'd given my gift to Cecelia and Shuhei, smiled and small-talked my way through the rounds, I'd started inching toward the exit, toward the silent safety of my apartment. Sibby's at Elijah's tonight, probably opening up an advent calendar of "days until I move away from Meg," and I'd been thinking of how much I needed to tidy my bedroom, evidence of my newly returned block everywhere. Crumpled paper on the floor, half-done sketches scattered across the desk, pens left outside their color-coded cups.

But then Lachelle had spotted me—why did I wear this dress with gold Hello Kitty faces on it?—and had pointed at her table's empty chair. "You're staying, Meg," she'd said. "I'm not going home until after the kids' bedtime, and you're the only person here other than Cecy I know well enough to talk to for another hour."

That'd been fair enough, so in spite of the self-imposed exile I've been in for days, I'd taken a seat. And once I'd settled in, I'd been grateful for the way Lachelle had taken over with a very long story about her very passive-aggressive sister. By the time I'd ordered my second cocktail, I'd thought, *Well, this is better than moping, at least.*

But now? Now there's a kale chip stuck to one of my Hello Kitty faces, and Lachelle is looking at me like she knows exactly what guy, and my moping plan is mocking me for abandoning it.

"The guy you went on a date with last month."

I pick off the kale chip. "It wasn't a date."

"Okay. But it was the guy, then?" She smiles, self-satisfied. "I knew something was wrong with you this week when you came in for supplies."

I sigh, resigned. I open my mouth, thinking I'll say, *We're just friends,* but then I close it again. The expression doesn't seem right for what Reid and I are.

Or were.

"I don't think it's going to work out." That feels—accurate. It's not going to work out with me and Reid, whatever "it" is. These last seven days of silence have proven that.

"He lives in the city," I add, which I figure will be effective as an explanation, since Lachelle thinks people from Manhattan should have to get a passport before they come to Brooklyn.

It doesn't work. "Yeah, that's a real barrier, given all the mass transit options. What's the problem, really? No job? Lives with his parents? Oh, is he in a band?"

That last one makes me smile, imagining Reid in a band. "No, none of those. He works on Wall Street."

Lachelle's eyes widen comically. "I hope you only met him in public," she says, clearly remembering the day I'd been headed to the Promenade. "That'd be terrible, having you get murdered by an investment banker on my conscience. A friend of mine went out with one who wanted her to dress up like that blue woman from the comic book movies. He was going to pay for her to get painted all over, scales and shit."

"He's not an investment banker. He's a quant."

"I don't know what that is, but he's probably still got something wrong with him." She takes a drink of her martini. She's wearing a gauzy black cape and a pair of beaded hoop earrings. I suddenly feel as if I'm on a field trip and she's the chaperone.

"He doesn't. He's a nice guy. A really nice guy."

A nice guy with a great face and terrific shoulders and a completely frank way of dealing with menstrual cramps. A nice guy whose feelings I hurt.

A nice guy who hurt mine.

"Oh?" I can see that question mark expand—a big, metallic party balloon, hanging right over our heads.

I take another sip of my cocktail. I'm buzzy in my joints, something that only ever happens when I have liquor. I set it down and push it away. I know when I've had enough, and the last thing I need is to go home to drunk moping. Still, I can feel the way it's loosened my tongue, my inhibitions.

"We had a fight."

Lachelle stares at me. "What do you mean, you had a fight?"

"Oh, thank goodness," Cecelia says, swooping in and taking one of the fake-bacon-wrapped water chestnuts from the plate in front of Lachelle.

She groans in satisfaction. "I keep forgetting to eat," she says. "Meg was telling me about this fight she had with a guy she's dating."

Cecelia's stare somehow makes me feel more embarrassed, enough that I don't even bother correcting Lachelle again. I mean, okay, I haven't dated much since I started the planner business, but Cecelia's looking at me as though I've torn off my nun's habit.

But then she says, in almost exactly the same tone as Lachelle, "You had a fight?"

I nod miserably, silently running through its worst moments all over again. That awful thing I'd said to Reid, that look in his eyes. That terrible splash of liquid on his skin. The only letters that have come easy to me this week are *s, o, r, y*. I sincerely hope my clients aren't on the lookout for hidden apologies that have nothing to do with them.

"Wow," says Lachelle. "I've never even seen you get irritated, and that includes the time your movie star client made you sit in the back room for ten thousand hours over one set of treatments."

"It wasn't ten thousand," I mutter, but my face heats at this mention of Lark, who hasn't totally ghosted me, but she has sent me two e-mails saying she hasn't had time to call to set up our next meeting. I wonder if she's asking Cameron for quotes to use in my termination letter.

"I get irritated," I add, thinking of Cameron and his terrible quotes.

Lachelle laughs. "I'm sure you do. But you don't show it."

"It's a wonderful quality," Cecelia says. "You're still the best person I ever had work the desk."

"Hey," says Lachelle.

"But I agree," Cecelia adds. "It is . . . unexpected."

Under their gazes, I'm the malfunctioning machine I've felt like all week long. A normally cheerful Meg-Bot that's finally short-circuited itself into a show of temper. They've removed the tiny screws for the cover of my control panel. They are staring right in there, surveying the damage.

"What did you fight about?" says Lachelle. "Was it the marginal tax rate? Those guys hate that."

"No, he . . ." Called me out. Said what he meant. Pushed and pushed, until we couldn't keep it light anymore. "Irritates me," I finish, half-heartedly.

"Dump him," says Lachelle. "There's already a bunch of men out there to be irritated with, and that's just on the Internet."

"Shuhei irritates me all the time. On our first date he told me I was using the wrong fork to eat my salad."

Lachelle looks at Cecelia as if she's revealed that Shuhei has a tail. "Which hospital did you take him to after?"

Cecelia smiles. "We irritate each other in the right ways. I probably wouldn't have managed more than three words if he hadn't said that stupid thing about the fork; I was so shy when I first moved here." She sends a dreamy look across the room toward where Shuhei stands. He seems to sense it, looking up at her and smiling.

"That's a good point," Lachelle says. "I irritated Sean into going to yoga with me, and now he has fifty percent less back pain."

"So does he irritate you in the right way?" says Cecelia, raising her eyebrows. Someone from over by the bar calls her name, and she groans. "I have to mingle. Come by the shop next week, okay? I want to know how this works out."

I nod and accept her hug, wondering if now it'll be time to tighten my screws and get out of here. But when she weaves her way back through the crowd, Lachelle takes over the eyebrow-raising.

"Does he, then?"

I think about his curious questions, his teacup-turning, his very disappointing opinions about dessert. I think of all that, and I want to say, *He does.*

Instead I shake my head.

"It can't be good that he gets me worked up that way. I mean, I *yelled.* In Prospect Park."

Lachelle snorts. "Believe me. You're not the first person to yell there."

She's not even finished speaking before I start again, propelled by my buzz or by my block or by my utter exhaustion at having thought about this all week.

"I said things to him I regret. I hurt him." I swallow, curl my hands back around my glass again, if only to have something to hold on to.

"Meg, take it easy on yourself. Everyone loses their temper sometimes." I look up at her, her soft, nonjudgmental smile paired with a gently furrowed brow of concern.

"You know what you said before about never seeing me get irritated?"

"Sure, but—"

"No, you're right. It's on purpose that I'm this way." I clear my throat. "When I was growing up, my parents—they fought a lot. Loud fights, quiet fights, whatever. Nothing physical, and they were good to me, but they were awful to each other a lot of the time. They couldn't wait to leave each other. My whole life, I tried to stay above the fray."

"That sounds terrible."

I shrug. "Lots of people have parents who don't get along. But when I got older—" I break off, reaching a limit, something I don't want to say. It's astounding how much I've told her already. Maybe my cocktail has truth serum in it.

"When I had my own fight with them," I say, adjusting for my limit, "I guess . . . I felt so out of control. We all said things we can't take back, and nothing's ever been the same. So I really try to—I keep the peace with people. I don't like the way it makes me feel, to fight."

Lachelle leans back, looking at me with some blend of sympathy and surprise, the latter probably because I've spent most of the years I've known her talking to her about pens and window displays, new shops in the neighborhood, sales at stores we both frequent. And that old chestnut, the weather.

"Of course you don't. No one's ever taught you how to do it."

I make what I hope is a sarcasm snort, though I suspect it sounds pretty unpracticed. "I told you. I learned from the masters."

"No, you didn't. I haven't been married for as long as the happy couple over there, but I've been with Sean for fifteen years, and I had to learn to fight with him the same way I had to learn how to fight with my sister, and with my roommate in college. Even a few times with Cecy."

Surprise must show on my face at that last one, and she shrugs.

"She could've won that window competition, you know. The point is . . . sometimes fighting isn't about leaving, it's about staying. It takes practice to get it right, and it's painful, but if you want to stay with people, you do it."

Something sparks in my circuit board then, some wire livening with its new connection. I haven't fought with anyone in years and years, have shoved down even the smallest inclination. Boyfriends I drifted away from for one thing or another— one who lied to me about smoking cigarettes at night, one who never let me finish a sentence before trying to complete it for me, one who I always suspected was seeing someone else, too. No great losses, but it wasn't as though I tried to press the point. Worse is the thought of friends I have scattered throughout Manhattan and here—including Lachelle, including Cecelia— who I've kept at a distance. I had Sibby, after all. Sibby who already knew all the hard things about me, and I'd never have to fight with her.

Except I do, I think, straightening up in my chair, suddenly feeling starkly, shockingly sober. I have to start a fight with Sibby, if I want us to stay friends after she leaves. I have to continue a fight with Lark, if I want us to become friends.

And I have to finish a fight with Reid—I have to do it *right* this time—if I want us to . . .

If I want us to be more than friends.

It's a revelation, but it's not an easy one. Even at the thought of it—more confrontation, more moments of getting it wrong— my palms feel clammy, my fingers weak. I think fleetingly about my desk at home, the wasteland of attempts and failures from the last week. Holding a pencil has felt like holding a thousand pounds of weight.

"Practice," I repeat, and I can hear the way it sounds disbelieving, suspicious.

"Listen, Meg," she says, reading my tone. "You didn't come to this city and teach yourself your craft and start your own business because you're weak. And you don't make nice with your clients and get them to trust you the way they do because you're weak, either. You practiced getting along with people. You can certainly practice not getting along with them, too."

It's part compliment, part assignment, and Lachelle delivers it with the unbothered confidence of a person who has had a ton of practice being right about everything from your back pain to your window display to your deep-seated emotional damage. She looks quickly down at her watch and her eyes widen. "Shit," she says. "I better go."

I'm grateful for the small distractions of wrapping up the evening—both of us settling our bills, waving quick goodbyes to Cecelia and Shuhei. It gives me a few minutes to process what Lachelle has said, to consider what I have to do, to let myself feel a fragile hope.

When we get outside, Lachelle taps out a quick text message to Sean to let him know she's on her way. Then she looks up at me again and says, "I think you should call him."

That fragile hope dissipates. I may not have spent the last seven days planning to practice my confrontation skills with Reid, but I *have* made an effort to apologize.

"I tried," I admit. "He sent it to voice mail. Three times."

Lachelle winces, as though she's picturing the same thing I have—Reid looking down at his phone, seeing my name pass across the screen. Pressing the button that reads DECLINE. Helvetica Neue. Cold as ice.

"What'd you say in your messages?"

I blink at her. "Nothing, since I'm under fifty and this is the twenty-first century. Who leaves messages?"

She laughs. "Fair. But I think you should try again." She lifts a hand in acknowledgment of the Uber she called pulling up at the curb. "Maybe what's wrong with him is that he likes voice mails."

When she's gone, I stand under the restaurant awning for a few seconds, my phone in my hand, wondering if nine thirty on a Friday night is too late to start practicing. I've got no doubt I'll get sent to voice mail again, but this time, I have to listen all the way through his crisp, short message. I have to wait for the beep, I have to—

The phone I'm holding rings.

For a second I stare down at it as though it has some kind of magical power. Since I don't recognize the number it's probably a telemarketer, but I guess all my cruel imaginings related to hitting the decline button have warned me against doing the same.

"Hello?"

There is an unholy amount of noise on the other end. I have to move it away from my ear.

"Meg?" A woman's voice shouts through the clamor. "Meg Mackworth?"

"Hi, yes, this is Meg." I try to make my voice loud enough to compensate for wherever she must be. A shouting convention, by the sound of it.

"Hey, I'm Gretchen. I tend bar over at Swine? You know it?"

"Uh . . ." I don't have much of a nightlife these days. And if I did, I'm guessing a place called Swine would not be part of it.

"Brooklyn!" she yells. She tacks on an intersection to narrow it down for me.

"Okay?"

"Do you know a guy called Reid?"

"I do!" I press a finger to my ear, now desperate to hear better, a bolt of anxiety landing straight in my stomach. "Is he all right?"

She laughs. "He's fine and dandy. Probably he wouldn't want me calling you, but I think he might've lost his phone or something."

"Oh," I say, confused. Who would ever describe Reid as "dandy"? Why is he at a bar called Swine? And, for the purposes of my absolute selfishness in regard to this particular matter, did he lose his phone before or after my attempts to reach him?

"I don't—I'm not sure why you're calling me?"

"Well, honey," Gretchen says, laughing over a loud clatter of ice being put into a glass. "He just tried to pay his bar tab with your business card."

♥ ♥ ♥

It isn't where I'd want to have my first fight practice.

Swine is the kind of bar that might make a tourist happy, that might make it into a guidebook for its gimmicky theme, its eagerness to attract a crowd. Oddly enough, the exterior is something Reid and I might've snapped a photo of on a walk— a white brick wall with bold, black block lettering, a big drop shadow with diagonal grading, a crude but clever outline of a pig, its various good-for-food parts blocked out and labeled in a thin slab serif. Over an arched opening in the wall there's a curving script indicating a "Biergarten," a patio from which plumes of woody smoke rise into the night sky.

But outside of its clever lettering, everything else about this place tells me Reid—and I—would've wanted to keep on walking. So far as I can tell, there's about ten million people in that Biergarten, and every man I can see is wearing some version of the same outfit: boat shoes, no socks, cropped-style khakis or slim-cut shorts, pastel-colored shirts. I almost check my phone to see if I've teleported out of Brooklyn into some college town's rush week.

It's so incongruous to imagine Reid here that I don't let myself wonder at my surroundings for long. I push through the heavy front doors into the non-Biergarten part of this sideshow and am met with a wall of noise. The crowd in here is different, more skinny jeans and beards, even a few leather bracelets.

So it's pretty easy to find the man I came for.

He's at the end of the long, dark-stained wood bar, wearing his weekend jacket over his weekend T-shirt and jeans. To any-one else, I'm sure his posture looks out of place: upright, overly formal. But I realize I know Reid's body so well that I can see how his broad shoulders hunch, ever so slightly, over the short glass of amber-colored liquid in front of him, the fingers of one hand curled around it.

That doesn't look right, I think, ridiculously. *It should be a cup of tea.*

It's this final incongruity that propels me forward, no thought to whether this'll end in a confrontation. I only want him *out* of here, out of this place where he doesn't belong. I take the empty stool next to him and right away he turns his head to me, his eyes widening briefly, those barely hunched shoulders straightening immediately.

"Meg. Hello."

He seems all the drunker for pretending not to be. His voice is extra deep, extra stern, and I should not be attracted to that, given that he's probably compensating for an inclination to slur. But there's no helping it: He sounds *great.*

"Hey there, Reid." I catch the bartender's eye, give her a wave of acknowledgment that I made it. She smiles and makes a discreet gesture to the register and I nod, indicating that I'll take the check.

"You've got cats all over you," Reid says.

I look down, remembering the gold Hello Kitty faces. I truly wish I was wearing something less absurd, but when I look back up at Reid he doesn't have the perplexed furrow in his brow I expect. Instead he's got a sloppy version of that *swoonsh,* as though he is entirely charmed.

As though we haven't fought at all.

And I admit—I'm tempted to give in to it. *Yes,* part of me is thinking, *look at my silly dress and forget about Prospect Park. Finish your drink and we'll walk it off, look at some signs together. We'll forget this ever happened. We'll never talk about it again.*

Instead I ask him the most direct question I can think of at the moment. "Did you lose your phone?"

He meets my eyes, his crooked smile fading. "No, I left it at home. I needed a break from it."

I swallow, feeling stung. Three calls isn't *that* many. Still, I stay in my seat.

I *stay.*

"From work," he clarifies, seeming to read my mind. He

turns his glass a quarter-turn, but makes no move to pick it up. "I called in sick today."

I search his face and realize there's something more drawn about it tonight, the already-carved planes along his cheeks sharper than when I last saw him. As with his posture, his face probably looks perfect to the untrained eye—but I can tell the difference. I wonder if he's been across the river all week, as blocked with his numbers as I've been with my letters, adding up sums that don't make sense. Like me, he ended up at a bar with a drink in his hand, but unlike how it turned out for me, no one here—with the exception of Gretchen—looks even half as cool as Lachelle.

"Are you okay?" I ask.

He seems to ignore the question. "I've never done that before, called in sick. I'm sure it'll cause—" He breaks off, shakes his head, and starts over. "What you saw, in the park. I get the flares when I'm stressed."

"Reid," I say quickly, almost sharply. I'm curious—I'm so, so curious—but I suddenly feel as clear about how this night needs to go as I've ever felt about anything. Reid this way, not quite himself—this is no time to practice, because this isn't a fair fight. I'll settle the bill; I'll get him a cab. I'll insist he calls me tomorrow. "We can talk about this later."

Reid starts to speak again, but I get an assist from Gretchen, who shows up with the bill. I'm reaching into my bag for my wallet but am surprised when I look up to find Reid holding out a credit card to her.

"I thought I paid," he says, but it's not accusatory. It's . . . confused.

She slides my business card back across the bar to him, and for a good five seconds the three of us are frozen in an awkward tableau—me with my oversized wallet, some random receipt stuck in the zipper, Gretchen with her hands on her hips, her heavily lined eyes moving back and forth between these two proffered payments, Reid's head tipped down, his gaze frozen on the business card.

Like it's a sign.

"Oh," he says finally, and it's almost as if I can *sense* him sobering up. Realizing how his sort-of friend Meg showed up to the same bar as him on a random Friday night.

"Sorry, man," Gretchen says, shrugging. She smiles as she plucks his card from his fingers. "Thought you needed an assist."

Reid watches her go, and I watch the wash of pink spread across his cheeks.

"It's fine!" I say, tucking my wallet back into my bag. "I was out, anyway."

"Meg," he says quietly, too quietly for the rising tide of noise all around us. "I'm sorry."

I wave a hand. It's ridiculous that I'm so embarrassed, but I am. I rushed over here as though he needed rescuing, so eager to see him again. "It's like I said, I was—"

"No," he says, and he has to lean in so that I can hear him. He went swimming today; I can tell. I let my eyes close for a beat longer than a blink, relishing that now-familiar smell, but open them when he speaks again. "I'm sorry I didn't call. That I didn't answer your calls."

I send up a silent plea of exasperation—to Lachelle, to Gretchen, to the fates—for giving me the *most* complex practice problem for my first try at fighting with Reid. Should I let him keep going? Should I interrupt to tell him how sorry *I* am, how it was my fault, how I never meant to hurt him? Should I tell him again that this isn't the time, that he's been drinking, that it's too loud and annoying in here? Or will that make it worse; will that make me seem rude, dismissive, distant?

"I thought of calling," he says, taking advantage of my quiet, anxious indecision. He reaches up and rubs a hand through his hair, messily enough that it sticks up on the right side. "Every day, I thought of it. But then I'd think about what you said. About people trying to protect themselves."

"I was wrong," I blurt, even though it's going to be no use right now explaining to him what I learned tonight—about myself, about other people.

But it doesn't matter, because he keeps going. Gretchen brings back Reid's card and receipt, but he doesn't even seem to notice; he keeps his blue eyes so focused on me. When there's a new round of shouts from somewhere in the rear of this swine-filled bar, he leans even closer.

"I don't do that. Protect myself. I'm"—he swallows—"honest to a fault, that's what Avery used to say. To my own detriment. To the detriment of people around me."

I tense at this mention of Avery, of the past between me and Reid she brings up, of a shared criticism we've both, apparently, leveled at him. I feel a new spike of guilt, a desperate urge to run from this pain I caused him.

But I stay.

"Then I went out walking today," Reid says. "I walked across the Bridge. I walked all around Brooklyn. And I realized something."

No, wait, I want to say. *Wait, I realized something, too.* But *God,* it is so loud in here, and Reid is so close, and his voice sounds so good. . . .

"I realized I'm not always honest with you."

I lean back, enough so I can look in his eyes. It doesn't sound like a good thing to say, this *I'm not always honest with you.* But somehow, the way Reid says it—the letters take on a new meaning. As though if you drew them all out, you'd find something. Something you'd actually want to see.

"But you . . ." I say, my voice too quiet for this clamor, and Reid ducks his head, brings his ear closer to my lips so he can hear me. "You always say what you mean."

He leans back again, his eyes tracing over my face—my eyes, my nose, my mouth. *Please forget I'm wearing Hello Kitty faces,* I think.

"I don't. Because if I did—"

Somewhere down the bar a glass breaks and someone shouts an unintelligible expletive, but neither of us moves. I'm watching Reid's mouth in case I have to lip-read what he says next.

"If I did, I would say that last week I watched every video you've got on your website so I could hear the sound of your voice again. I would say that a woman stood next to me on the subway and I think she used the same shampoo as you, and I could hardly breathe for how much I missed you. I would say that I walked around all day with a Meg-shaped shadow beside me, and I only came in here because of the signs outside, and so I wouldn't call you up at nine o'clock on a Friday night and beg you to talk to me again—about Frisbee, the weather, the name for that piece of a letter you told me about—"

"A spur," I whisper, because *holy shit*. This is the best fight of my whole *life*.

He nods, his face so serious. "A spur," he repeats.

Then he drops his eyes to the bar, to my card, and adds one more thing.

"I would say I like you so much, Meg."

And then—right then, the real fight breaks out.

Chapter 12

"A couple of stitches ought to do it."

The doctor leaning in to take one final look at Reid's eyebrow has the efficient, slightly impatient demeanor of a woman who has seen a whole lot worse, and who probably has a whole lot worse waiting for her out in the lobby of this urgent care. She reaches up a latex-gloved hand and touches her index finger to the lump forming around the cut on Reid's brow, and I see his jaw clench tightly against the pressure she's put there.

"Sorry, big guy," she says, lowering her hand and leaning back, pulling off her gloves. "The good news is, I don't think you're concussed."

"I told you I wasn't," Reid says, sullenly.

"Yes, that was helpful. To have your expert medical opinion." She looks over at me and rolls her eyes.

I really love this doctor.

She moves over to the tablet on the pale-green laminate counter, tapping in a few notes from her exam, and I realize that it's the first time in at least a couple of hours that I've taken a deep, relieved breath. All through the cab ride here, my big bag basically a clown car for the steady stream of tissues (clean! I'm not an animal, or your grandma) I'd handed over to Reid to press against his gushing cut, my body and brain had felt electrified, all my thoughts and actions a new, supercharged kind of Meg-Bot mechanical:

Noise, crowd, push, punch.

Blood, door, outside, cab, doctor.

Reid. Fight. *Bar* fight.

Swine, as it turned out, had lived entirely up to its name when it came to the majority of its patrons, who rudely interrupted the most romantic confrontation of my life by starting a brawl over a game of air hockey. It'd started somewhere in the back, some mysterious place where the pastel-shirt guys and the beard guys apparently met, deadlocked in their angry, competitive feelings toward each other over various table games and probably also their relative success levels at late capitalism. Maybe if my eyeballs hadn't been turning into giant red hearts I would've noticed how that rising tide of noise was being matched with a new press of people making their way to the front.

Instead, I'd only noticed when one of the pastel-shirt guys, courtesy of one of the bearded guys, had landed like a projectile into the back of Reid's stool.

And that's when I learned that Reid Sutherland—despite his stoicism, despite his civility, despite his slight inebriation—absolutely knows how to fight.

His reflexes had been superhero-fast, one hundred percent not-intoxicated fast. He'd stood from his stool, all his height blocking me from the encroaching crowd, and for one brief, mindless second, I'd done the thing I've been wanting to do for weeks: I'd pressed my body close to his.

In the seconds after—it must've only been seconds, though it'd felt much longer—the chaos had been overwhelming, somehow managing to be both an in- and out-of-body experience. I'd felt it when a cold splash of beer had landed on the back of my dress, and I'd heard my own brief yelp of surprise as I'd jumped away from Reid's body in shock. I'd felt it when his body had then briefly knocked into mine, the force of the stray elbow to his brow that's brought us here, and I'd heard his grunting exhalation of pain.

And then I'd seen something change in the line of his back—a broadening, a stiffening.

A preparation.

But had I really felt it when he'd turned and grabbed me by the wrist? When he'd tucked my body close to his, when he'd put an arm around my shoulders and started to shove his way through the crowd of angry, sloppy patrons? Had I really seen it right, when one of those patrons threw a lazy, misdirected punch in our direction? Had I truly heard Reid—*quite late* Reid!—mutter a quiet, frustrated "*Fuck*" through clenched teeth before he'd moved me out of the way? Had that been real, him ducking that punch, him pulling back his arm and making a fist as the guy started coming again?

Could I actually have felt the force of that ham-fisted, sloppy-drunk guy thudding to the ground at my feet?

"What about his hand?" I say now, in the firm, no-nonsense voice I seem to have had since we walked in here, and the truth is, I'm still surprised to hear it. A *literal* fight, and I feel stronger than I have in ages. In the lobby my hand had been rock-steady as I'd filled out Reid's paperwork, quietly but quickly asking him questions that he would answer stiffly, his voice muffled from the fresh, icy-cold compress the check-in nurse gave him.

"I'm okay, Meg," Reid says, his voice low and soothing. For a split second some of my newfound strength falters. *I like you so much, Meg*, he'd said, but he's been quiet ever since, and if I look at him now—if I see that bruised, bloody brow, the one he got for me—I may not be able to stay focused on the most important thing, which is making sure he's okay.

I keep my eyes on the doctor, waiting for her answer.

"In this case, the patient and I agree. His hand looks fine." She directs her next comment to him. "Someone must've taught you to make the right kind of fist."

Reid gives a bored shrug worthy of pastel-shirt guy. This

slight air of sullenness is the only lingering symptom of his former inebriation. He has looked stone-cold sober from the moment that man hit his stool, though the energy bar I forced him to eat (another gem from my bag) and the ten tiny cups of water I made him drink out in the lobby probably helped.

"I'm going to grab an NP who's got a steadier hand than me to stitch you up, okay?" Then she turns to me again, speaking as though Reid isn't in the room. "Keep an eye on him tonight. If he seems disoriented, or has light sensitivity, or complains of nausea, give us a call."

"She's not—" Reid begins, but I cut him off. Reid may have punched a guy in the face (better than pistols at dawn, I am now assured) before I could get clocked by an errant fist, but I'm ending this night as rescuer-in-chief. I got him to this urgent care, and I'm going to be the one who wakes him up every hour to shine a light in his eyeballs, though that is probably not what this doctor means about checking for light sensitivity.

"I will," I say. "He's staying at my place."

In my periphery, I see Reid turn his head sharply toward me.

"Great," says the doctor, snapping the cover closed on her tablet. "You all have a good night, and try to stay out of trouble." The door shuts behind her with a decisive click.

And then Reid and I are alone—truly alone—for the first time in a week.

"Meg, you don't have to—"

This time, it's me who turns sharply, and I finally let myself take in the full force of his bruised face. My heart clutches, but I don't wince. Somehow I know—as though I've been practicing for a lot longer with Reid than I realized—that if I show pity toward him right now, he'll fight me so much harder.

"You're staying with me. You don't even have your phone."

"I have my MetroCard. And my feet."

"You're about to get *stitches*." I cross my arms over my chest, and I register how strange it feels to do it. I don't think I've ever stood this way in my whole life. It's weirdly satisfying. "Where *did* you learn to punch like that, anyway?"

I don't ask so much because I care, but because I'm trying to distract him from arguing with me about staying over tonight.

He blinks down at his hand. "My older brothers. To help me at school." He pauses, then looks up at me with an expression of such naked embarrassment that I immediately uncross my arms.

"Please don't think I do that often," he says.

"I don't," I say quickly, feeling some of the fight drain out of me. "Of course I don't."

"Or . . . drink that way. It's rare. And I hadn't eaten all day. I only had—"

"Reid, it's fine."

Oh, man, the sad eyes. Forget it, I'll never win this argument. Maybe I can pay one of these nurses to go home with him, if the thought of staying with me is so awful.

"You—" He shifts on the bench, the paper covering the vinyl crinkling beneath him. "You've barely looked at me since we got out of there. If I scared you, or if the things I said—"

That fast, my own reflexes take over, some protective instinct I have for him, and I cross the tiny space, putting myself right in front of him. I wait until he raises his eyes to mine again, then reach out my hand—oh, it's shaky now—and set it on top of his.

I see his chest expand with the breath he takes.

"You didn't scare me. None of it scared me."

It's not all the way true, of course. It *was* scary, but not in the way he means. It was scary to see him again, to confront him again. It was scary to remember parts of our fight, to feel the hurt feelings that still exist between us. But I stayed, and if I can make him stay tonight—

"None of it?" he asks, looking down at our hands.

I know what he's asking. *I like you so much, Meg.*

"None of it."

He moves, turning his wrist so our palms press together, so his fingers link with mine. I swallow reflexively. *Holding hands with Reid,* I think, routes through the city unrolling in my head like a map on a table. *What if I never want to walk any other way?*

"But I think we should come back to this tomorrow," I say. "When you're feeling better."

For once, it doesn't feel like I'm avoiding anything. It feels like Reid is coming home with me tonight to sleep on my couch and to get annoyed with my nocturnal nursing efforts, and it feels like we'll wake up tomorrow and practice at this in the clear, completely sober light of day.

"Did she move out yet?" he asks quietly.

I feel my brows lower in confusion. "Sibby?"

He tips his downturned head in a small nod.

"No, but usually on Fridays she stays with—"

I don't finish before his shoulders slump in relief, his head dropping forward even more. With him sitting on the table, and me standing here, the top of his bent head is right at the level of my chin.

I realize what he must be worried about.

"She wouldn't care, anyway. We've lived together a long time. Both of us have had . . . uh, overnight guests before."

Reid's hand squeezes mine gently. He's holding my hand as though I belong to him. As though we belong to each other.

"A few more weeks," I say, and for the first time since I got the call about Reid I think about Sibby moving out, about the other fight I have waiting for me, and I take a breath through my nose. "I think the official date is on a—"

"I was worried," he says, interrupting me. He lifts our joined hands, holding them in the space between our bodies, and *oh.* His breath tickles the back of my hand. My sensitive, sensitive hand. Where all my talent and all my most secret thoughts come from. It's like having clinging, confining bandages removed.

"Worried?"

"I kept thinking," he says, his voice lower now—either my closeness or maybe the fatigue finally setting in. I take a step forward and shift our hands, making a small, inadequate pillow out of the back of mine for his brow. He takes the hint, letting the uninjured side of his forehead rest, warm and heavy, against my knuckles.

How must this look, this picture of us? A knight bowing in

service to his lady. I see my name in an illuminated, medieval-manuscript style.

MARGARET THE BRAVE

"I kept thinking," he says again, "it'd be hard for you, her leaving. And what if I missed it?"

"You didn't." My voice has lost all its steadiness, but it doesn't much bother me now. The hand that's not clutched to his—it lifts, seemingly of its own accord. I reach out and stroke my fingers through his thick mass of red-blond hair, and I think his whole body shivers. I think mine does, too.

"I'm so sorry I didn't call."

Reid the Repentant.

"It's all right," I say, stroking again. "Tomorrow, okay?"

"Tomorrow," he agrees, and then—as if to seal it—Reid lifts his head the smallest amount. Enough to press his lips against the back of my hand.

And that's how Reid and I rest after the fight, waiting to get stitched all the way back together.

♥ ♥ ♥

It's a bold move, going back to the park.

We don't so much plan it as we do walk our way to it, one of the many mutual, unspoken agreements we've come to over the course of last night and this morning. The promise we made to each other in that tiny treatment room—*Tomorrow*—has lived between us through every interaction we've had, something we both seem to be keeping sacred for full daylight, for full sobriety, for full assurance of no head injury. Inside the low-light, hushed quiet of my apartment, Reid had been polite, careful, helpful, a houseguest unsure of his welcome: *Your place is nice. I don't want to get blood on your couch. I can put the sheets down.*

In response, I'd tried to be easy and unbothered, nearly professional in my hangover-preventing, concussion-checking, of-course-you're-welcome-here care. Advil and a full glass of water to keep future headaches at a minimum. Quiet, hourly, tiptoed walks out into the living room to see his big, still-clothed body sprawled on my couch, half-covered by the blanket that I usually keep at the foot of my bed, his breathing soft and even. An extra towel and toothbrush in the bathroom, a fresh bar of soap in our tiny shower stall, a large T-shirt I got last year for free at the Northside Festival folded neatly on the counter.

All of it had gone a long way to establishing some way through for those awkward, sometimes charged moments in the early morning as we both woke and took turns showering and dressing in the incomplete privacy of the small space. When I'd emerged from my room, my hair still damp, the ends darkening the shoulders of my simple, gray cotton dress, Reid had looked up from where he waited for me on the couch, the stitched cut bisecting his brow, his jawline tight and shaded with scruff, his shoulders a few inches too broad for that borrowed T-shirt.

I thought if I let him look at me that way for too long, our *Tomorrow* promise to each other wouldn't involve all that much talking. It would involve that couch and Reid's scruff and the smell of my shampoo and our mouths and our hands and also, under the Saturday morning circumstances, Sibby probably walking in at a very inconvenient time.

I'd reached for my jacket and Reid had stood and reached for his own, and we'd made our way outside into the crisp, clear morning, the back of my hand still tingling from the feel of his lips on my skin.

"It's nice out today," Reid says, shifting his weight on the bench we sat on to finish our breakfasts—bagels from my favorite shop, coffee for me, tea for him, both of our to-go cups set carefully by our feet, as though they're weapons we've laid down. It's early enough still that the park is pretty quiet, no one else on the benches around us, most passersby either biking or jogging or on the kind of determined, headphone-accompanied walk that takes no interest in its surroundings.

"That's my line," I say, and he smiles softly.

"Meg, listen, I—"

"No, wait," I interrupt, because in between those tiptoed walks to check on him last night, I'd thought a lot about this morning, about how to finish this fight. I'd thought about everything Lachelle had said to me, and I'd thought about the things I have to say to make it so that Reid and I both try to stay. I *practiced.*

"I want to go first."

He nods, but I see the way he sets his jaw, a bulwark against what I think is some lingering embarrassment. I take a deep breath.

"The most important thing is that I'm sorry about last week. About the fight we had, and about how mad I got. What I said to you—it was really unfair."

"It wasn't unfair. It's like I said last night"—he clears his throat, lowering his eyes—"I'm well aware of my faults, especially the one you mentioned."

"It's not a fault," I say quickly, and he gives me a look I've never seen on his face, a cock of his head that looks a lot like sarcasm—a look that somehow telegraphs all the small moments where Reid's bluntness got the best of him: calling me a shopgirl. Scolding me for not having an umbrella. Asking me about my health insurance.

You know it is, that look says.

"Or at least it's no worse a fault than my own, which is . . . well, I guess it's one you already know about."

Reid waits, and for a couple of seconds, I do, too. I think about my parents and about Sibby, about how my fight with Reid pressed up against everything about my life that hurt before I came to New York, and about everything that hurts about it now.

"I hide things. My feelings about things in my life, or in the lives of people I care about. I hide them in my letters, and I hide them when I'm talking about the weather or Frisbee or whatever other thing I fill up the space with—"

"I like everything you talk about."

You know you don't, my look back to him says, and then I take a breath before I speak again.

"Last week," I begin, "I was really . . . I was trying so hard to hide, I guess. I was upset about this thing at work, and some things from my past it reminded me of, but instead of telling you that, I tried to distract you." I swallow. "That's something I'm realizing I do too much, to keep me—"

"I never meant you to feel unprotected," Reid says, his eyes full of regret. "I wouldn't ever want to make you feel that way."

"You punched a guy in the face for me last night," I say, my mouth curving into a teasing smile. "I feel pretty protected."

Reid ducks his head, his hair falling forward, skimming his stitched-up brow. "I only wanted you to—"

"Be honest," I finish for him. "Say what I mean."

His lips press together, which I take to mean agreement.

"I want to try that," I say. "Being honest. Talking about the things that are difficult. When I hide them—they seem to come out in other ways, anyway."

He moves, his body turning on the bench so we're facing each other more. He looks between us, where my hands have been idly toying with the strap of my bag.

And then he reaches out and takes one, pressing our palms together and linking our fingers, the same as he did last night. I close my eyes at the feel of it.

He'll protect you.

"Okay," he says.

"I have three points." I wince at how it sounds, this first attempt at saying what I mean. A little loud and slightly stiff, as though I'm about to start up a slideshow titled "Difficult Relationship Factors We Need to Address." Practicing for this in the mirror wouldn't have been the worst thing, if only six-foot-something of the man I'm trying to talk to hadn't been sleeping on my couch all night.

Reid smiles crookedly. "Three, huh?"

I smile back. "Three. This is a numbers game, Sutherland."

"Oh," he says softly, still smiling that *swoonsh*. "My specialty."

My specialty today. I've thought and thought about them, as if they were letters on a page: the order in which I'd say them. How I could make them strong enough, special enough, straightforward enough for Reid.

"One," I say, knowing his smile is about to disappear. "What you said last night, about your skin—"

He tries to preempt me. "I'm not embarrassed by it. I've had it for a long time. Obviously I'd prefer if I didn't, and I'd certainly prefer if you didn't find it un—"

"I don't find it anything except part of you. It's only number one because you said it gets worse when you're stressed, and your job—it always seems stressful to you. I see how you get, whenever it comes up. And if that's part of why things were so off with us last week, then I want to know about it."

Reid looks up from where our hands are joined, his eyes out on the wide expanse of park green as he answers me.

"My work is . . . stressful. Especially lately. When I came to see you last week, I'd had a particularly terrible day. When I looked back at it, afterward . . . I realized I should've passed on your invitation, gone home alone." He looks back at me, rubs his thumb over the back of my hand in a way that makes me shift on the bench, an inconvenient pulse of feeling between my legs.

"But I wanted to be around you. You're the only person here who doesn't treat me like I'm a calculator. When I'm around you, I don't think about numbers. It's a relief."

"And here I am with my numbers game," I tease, but I also use my own thumb to stroke his hand back, sorry for the stress he feels about his job. Honored that I'm as much a relief to him as he's been for me.

He smiles down at our hands. "I don't mind this one. What's two?"

Two is a hard one. I swallow.

"Two is—Avery. You, and Avery, and the wedding program." I watch his face, search for some grimace or sadness, something that'll give me an indication of how this one will go. "If you still hold it against me, Reid, it doesn't matter how much you may like me now. It doesn't matter how much we like each other. If you don't forgive me for those letters, and if you still have feelings for her—"

"I don't. I mean that I don't hold it against you. And I don't still have feelings for her. Please, let me make this clear to you."

"Okay," I say, because that is not going to be enough. I remember the way he's looked, sometimes, when she comes up. I remember the way he'd said she was beautiful, and powerful. "Make it clear."

He clears his throat. "Avery's father arranged for us to meet after she had been through a difficult time. A breakup with someone she'd been with since college, who had some problems with . . . ah, substances."

"Oh."

"I think he thought I'd be a good choice. Stable. Boring, probably." Reid gives a lift of one shoulder. "I thought being with her would help me find my way here, in some way. And I think she thought being with me would be easier. Undemanding, and . . . calm. But we were a terrible match, and we both knew it. For much longer than either of us was willing to admit."

"But you bought her that ring," I say, which is *ridiculous*. But it's the first time since he came back to the shop that Reid and I have had any meaningful conversation about him and Avery, about what happened between them. My memories of her, of them together, are shaped by that ring, by what it represented.

"That was not the ring I bought her, actually."

"What?"

"A week after we got engaged she came to a dinner we had planned with the new one. A gift for the two of us, from her father. An upgrade."

"Ouch," I say, grimacing, and he chuckles softly.

"She's a good person. I care about her, as a friend. But she's from another world, I guess. I thought, for a while, that I might try to fit into it, but we weren't for each other. You knew it as well as we both did." He pauses, strokes my hand, takes a breath. "As for your letters . . . well. Maybe I am glad to hear you're reconsidering the things you sometimes hide, but my frustration last week, it was not about you. It was about—"

"New York," I finish for him. "That's three."

He looks down at our joined hands. "New York," he repeats. For the first time in this numbers game, Reid looks well and truly unsure. *I'm leaving New York*, he'd said to me once, and I don't think all the games in the world could make him stay.

"This is home for me. This is where I built a life. And you're leaving."

There's a long pause, and I'd be lying if I said I wasn't holding my breath. I'd be lying if I said my heart didn't dip in disappointment at what he says when he speaks again.

"I'm here now."

It's an incomplete answer, a thing that won't be fully resolved between us—not today, and probably not ever. He may be here now, but what he means is that he's leaving later.

"I don't want to stop seeing you," he adds. "I'd see you any way you wanted. Only the walks, if that's all I can have."

It's not all you can have. The thought is immediate, but I say nothing, not yet. This will hurt, after all; I can tell already. I can have gone through all this work to make it so both of us stay—last night, this morning, anything that happens from this moment on—but in the end, he'll still leave.

"It'll probably never work," I say quietly, but I also desperately, desperately want him to convince me. "We're total opposites."

The hand that's not holding mine reaches out, and Reid sets a gentle finger to one of the buttons on my jacket.

"Letters, numbers," he says, a familiar beat to the words, as though he's saying *po-tay-to, po-tah-to.* "They're not so different."

I raise my eyes to his, and I'm not sure when we managed to get so close. Close enough that I can see the red-blond stubble along his jaw, close enough that I can smell my soap on his skin.

"Both codes," he adds. Then he moves his finger, tucking it under the edge of the button, tugging gently. The movement exerts no pressure, but I still lean closer to him.

"That's true," I whisper, and when I raise my eyes to his I can see the heat there. I want that heat. I want it, and right now, it doesn't matter to me if it'll hurt someday soon. It doesn't matter if this ends up being the fight of my life.

"We could do it on the count of three," I say, and he smiles, close-up and perfect and so, so sexy.

"This is your game." He leans in, but he doesn't kiss me. He puts his mouth right against my temple. "Picture it," he says, and somehow, I know exactly what he means. A code between us, the way we first talked to each other, even before we knew each other. My letters, and his ability to read them.

"One," he says.

And I see it, *o-n-e*, the *o* shaped in that space of skin between my hairline and the outer edge of my eyebrow, a looping, upward curve connection to the script *n* I'm imagining over the arch of that brow, which is where the feather-light touch of Reid's lips has moved. The *e* at the bridge of my nose, a slim, delicate, terminal curve that fades away rather than ending.

My breath shudders between my parted lips.

"Two."

He shifts, lets his lips rest softly against my cheekbone, and instead of pressing them there, he rubs them back and forth once, as light as a strand of my own hair in the wind, and I see that word, too, drawn in the same pink that's the color of my natural blush, the pink I turn when I'm warm or embarrassed or aroused. The *t*, the *w*, the *o*, all of them a heavily sloped italic. All of them on the way to somewhere.

"Reid," I whisper, and he moves his head back, traces his eyes over the spots where he kissed before looking into mine.

"May I?" he whispers back, and I let my eyes slide closed at this—the mannered, magnetic, *Masterpiece Theatre* perfection of it.

I nod.

"Three," he says, but I don't see any of those letters. I only feel the press of Reid's perfect lips against mine, and as soon as it happens, I know. I know that I could have my eyes closed this way and I'd still know Reid's kiss anywhere, because Reid's kiss is everything I like about Reid—firm and direct, with a sweetness you have to know to truly recognize. He sets one of his big, warm hands to the side of my neck, his palm pressing against the network of veins where the blood rushes to the surface for him, but with his thumb he lightly strokes the line of my jaw. His lips on mine tell me he wants more than a chaste, closemouthed kiss, but he waits until my tongue slips over his bottom lip to give me his own, and once he does, he makes that soft groan I've heard him make before, but this, *this* is the perfect version of it, the one I'll hear in my dreams for days and days.

I scoot toward him, moving to wrap my arms around his neck, and I'm barely thinking—barely thinking that we're in the park, that we're in *public*, that at any second some disgruntled jogger might shout a well-deserved *Get a room!* I kiss him and kiss him, my body growing desperate to get closer to him.

"This is the best game," I breathe between kisses, my chest rising and falling quickly. I'm practically panting out here, but I don't care. I want to keep his lips on mine; I want our tongues tangling; I want to press my whole self against him, and—unlike last night—I want to really feel it this time.

"Meg," he says, his forehead resting against mine, his own breaths coming faster now. "I have a number four."

I stiffen, worried we'll have to stop now, worried there's something I've forgotten.

But Reid keeps me close, kisses me once before he speaks again.

"Come home with me."

Chapter 13

No self-respecting New Yorker PDAs on the subway, and Reid and I manage—barely, it feels to me—to stay self-respecting.

But as soon as we're up the steps from the Herald Square station, Reid touches me again, taking my hand and keeping me close to his side as we navigate the not-yet-crowded sidewalks all the way to his apartment building, a nondescript brick mid-rise in Murray Hill, somewhat tired on the outside but updated with bland, modern renovations in the lobby. On any other morning, on any other day, I'd ask more than twenty questions about it all: *How'd you pick this? Do you know your neighbors? How long does it take you to get to work? Where's your dry cleaner?* This morning, though, my head is full of that kiss, my hand is full of Reid's, and all I want is to finish what we started.

As soon as the door to his apartment is closing behind us, I let him know it, turning to face him, tipping my head up for another kiss, and the best thing is that he doesn't leave any doubt that he's been wanting it, too, that he stood beside me on that train and felt every single passing touch of my body against his. He bends, his hands in my hair, releasing all the still-fresh shampoo scent he missed so much, and the noise that comes from his chest as he kisses me is guttural, impatient.

Hot.

"You don't want the tour?" he says when he pulls his lips from mine to take a breath, his chin ducking immediately to put his lips somewhere new, on the soft skin of my neck.

"Later I want the tour." I gasp at the way he's tasting me, his tongue tracing up that long column. "I'll ask you so many questions," I warn him.

"It's quite boring," he warns, kissing the corner of my mouth first, before he gives me his lips, his tongue.

"God, say that again," I say, almost a moan, and then realize I don't want to explain the *quite* thing, not when I could keep my mouth busy in other ways. "Never mind," I murmur hastily. "Nothing about you is boring."

He presses me against the wall by his front door, his hands at my waist and his mouth hungry on mine. We stay that way for so long, long enough that I push his jacket off his shoulders, long enough that he does the same to me, long enough that we both toe off our shoes, kicking them sloppily out of the way.

"Meg." His voice is gruff, and all of a sudden I realize I've gripped the firm, ropy length of his forearms; I'm squeezing there to hold myself steady while we devour each other, and for the first time I feel a rough texture beneath one of my palms.

"Oh," I say, pulling my hand away. "I'm sorry."

"No." He takes my hands in his and squeezes gently. "Touch me. Anywhere you want."

"Does it hurt?"

He shakes his head. "Not right now." He leans in, breathes against the skin of my neck. "Nothing hurts right now. I was going to ask if you wanted to go—

"Yes, to bed. That's where I want to go."

He leans back to look at me, and this time when he *swoonshes* I lift my hand to his face and set my thumb to that curving line on his cheek, the one I *know*, I *know* I'll be able to draw later.

"I'm trying it your way," I breathe, moving my thumb so I can lean in and press my mouth to that curve, so I can mimic it with my body, shaping myself to him. "Direct."

"I like it." He moves to pull me away from the wall; then he wraps his arms around my waist, lifts me off my feet, and carries me into his bedroom, never taking his mouth from mine.

And at first—*oh*, at first, I like it, too. I like it so much that I'm half-frantic with it. I don't take in any details of the space he's brought me to, because my eyes are busy on the parts of his body I reveal as I strip off his clothes—his stomach flat and ridged with muscle, a ladder of gorgeous, organized strength leading up to the heaven of his broad, smooth chest, broader even still by the way the muscles of his swimmer's back fan out. I spread my hands over his shoulders, feel the textures of his skin with a sort of buzzing electricity in my fingertips; I hear the way Reid's breath catches and quickens when I lean in to taste the clean-smelling skin of his neck. I'm so direct I can hardly wait, pulling him toward me as I back my way to the bed, barely pausing to let him get his hands on the hem of my dress, annoyed when getting it over my head means we have to stop kissing, the only solace the way Reid's hands feel on new parts of my bare skin—my waist, my rib cage, my shoulder blades. I reach behind me and unclasp my bra, delighting in the noise of pleasure Reid makes, the reverent, desperate way he whispers, *"Jesus,"* when I lie back on his bed.

But then—with our clothes mostly off and him on top of me, with my hips moving up in small, rhythmic pulses against the hard length between his legs—I suddenly feel a rolling, unwelcome crest of nervousness, a hiccup in my newfound directness that makes the rhythm break awkwardly, a stutter-stop I hope he doesn't notice. It's so good with him already, nothing I've ever felt with anyone else, his heat and the way he kisses me soft but holds me strong.

But it's started good before, and then I—

"Meg," Reid whispers softly, right against the shell of my ear. "Do you want to stop?"

"No!" It's too loud in the quiet room, my hands gripping at

his hips involuntarily, my eyes squeezing closed at the threat of impending confrontation over this.

"I want to keep going," I say, more softly now, nuzzling at his jaw, and he makes a low, humming noise against my skin, the sound a metronome for that beat I skipped, and I pulse my hips again.

But he presses up on his arms, moving his hard length away and looking down at me. "We can slow down."

I want to whimper without his heat, but before I can get the sound out he picks up one hand from where he's had it pressed against the mattress beside my head. He strokes his fingers slowly, carefully, right down the center line between my breasts, where my heart flutters beneath the skin.

"You seem nervous."

I blink up at him, then close my eyes again and shake my head, feel those fingers stroke, patient and soothing, against me. Of course he'd know. Of course he can read every code, every sign my body leaves for him.

"I'm not."

"Don't hide from me," he says, and I open my eyes, look up at his triple-take face, set in patient determination.

He'll protect you, I remind myself. *This is practice. This is staying.*

"I'm not easy," I tell him, wrapping my arms around his waist, my fingers trailing up those fanned-out muscles, a big, blank canvas for the nervous, directionless loops I draw there. "I mean that it's . . . not always easy for me to finish. To come."

I've worked up the courage to tell exactly two men this before. The first was after the third time I had sex with my high school boyfriend, an excruciating conversation that mostly included him asking me impatient questions I didn't know the answers to, all of them some version of "What should I do different?" as though I could produce an annotated diagram about my anatomy when I'd barely had enough sexual experiences to know the basics. Eventually, frustrated with my own limited vocabulary and his sullen, perfunctory responses, I'd simply stopped expecting to finish—with him or with the handful of guys I dated after him.

The second was a guy I'd gone out with two years ago, so sweet and kind and attentive on all of our dates until that one, when I'd told him and he'd said, with an undeserved, confident smirk on his face, "It's only because you haven't been with me yet, baby."

I'd texted Sibby with our this-is-a-bad-date signal and three minutes later, she'd called to pretend she had an emergency that I absolutely *had* to leave to help her with.

I never saw him again.

But Reid, he doesn't say anything at all at first. He only plants his hand back on the mattress and bends his head to kiss me again, his hair falling over his brow to tickle pleasantly across my forehead—another soothing, delicate touch.

"Okay," he says simply, between the kisses he presses against my mouth. For a while we get lost all over again, and I come back to my body. I don't think of anything except how good his warm skin feels on mine, how his shoulders make me feel as if I'm under the sturdiest shelter.

"Do you like what we're doing now?" he murmurs eventually, moving to kiss at the corner of my mouth, the line of my jaw, the skin beneath my ear.

I make a noise, something I hope comes out close to *Mmmm-hmmm*.

"Tell me what you like about it." *Direct, direct, direct.*

"I like you above me. And I like the way you kiss me. The way you work up to it, same as you did in the park." He does it again, now, that *one, two, three* pattern over my face, and I shudder out a breath, whispering to him again when he pulls his mouth away.

"I like the way you make me wait. That's how I am—everywhere on my body, I guess. I like the anticipation."

"Good," he says against my skin.

And *oh*, the way he says that *Good*. The sound says it's pleasure for himself and praise for me, all at once.

"More," he demands, pulling his mouth away, looking down at me with heat in his eyes, and I somehow know what he's asking me to do with that look, and I can hardly believe I want to. It's so intimate, so close, so honest.

It's what you'd do with someone you really, really trust.

And I realize, with certainty, that I trust Reid.

I take my hands from his body, and I put them on my own.

♥ ♥ ♥

It takes me a minute, long seconds where my palms rest somewhere safe, on the soft skin of my stomach, feeling myself inhale and exhale, gathering my courage, thinking of all the hidden parts of me I want to show Reid. It's broad daylight in here, Reid's window covered with a sleek, pale-gray shade that offers privacy but not darkness, and he'll be able to see everything.

But maybe that's right. Maybe that's exactly right, for me and Reid.

"I'm sensitive here," I whisper finally, letting one hand trace up, my fingertips lingering on the full underside of my breast, a curve of skin that always makes my nipples harden in response when I'm touched there. My face is hot, the skin on my chest dewing with sweat. I feel shy, exposed, but still unbelievably aroused. All I want is for him to tell me *Good* again; I want him to give me that *Good* with his hands and lips and teeth and tongue, so I'll show him everything.

I draw a single finger across my nipple, flicking it the way I'd want him to. He watches, his tongue darting out to lick at the corner of his mouth, his eyes hot and focused, and I know he's seeing me, reading me, cracking this code I'm leaving, letters on this page for him alone, and suddenly I have a new, powerful rush of feeling, a different sort of passion: I hate every man who ever made me feel I shouldn't say what felt right. I hate the way they didn't try to understand. I hate the way they made me feel demanding and difficult for asking them to do something they hadn't figured out on their own; I hate the way they got frustrated and impatient and wounded.

My hands grow rougher, more grasping, and Reid says "Good" again, and I forget about every other guy, ever.

"Where else," he says, the muscles in his arms straining tighter now, and I don't think it's fatigue.

I want to reward him for the way he's enjoying this, and for the way he holds himself back from it. For the way he doesn't say, *I'll take it from here.*

I raise my hips from the bed. "Take these off for me?"

He doesn't hesitate. He leans away from me and pulls my underwear down, and as soon as he's exposed the triangle of hair between my legs his jaw clenches, his body a study in restraint. Smooth, hard lines, fully upright. W-A-I-T, those lines spell.

"Show me," he says, and if it's impatience, it's exactly the right kind. It doesn't promise me anything but his desire, his enjoyment of this, wherever it goes from here.

My hand smooths down my stomach, lingers in the soft, curved space between my belly button and my pubic bone. I stroke my fingers there lightly, a tiny, gentle cursive, the same way I would at home, in my own bed, late at night.

"I like this to start." I already know I don't like it as much as I would if it were Reid's hand, Reid's fingertips.

He makes a noise, puts one knee back on the bed, but keeps his distance. My fingers skate down, and I know I'm more sensitive than I would be usually—one glancing touch from the soft pad of my index finger and my lower back arches from the bed. Reid sets a big, warm hand on the top of my raised knee, watching me with a hot concentration. God, that stitched-up brow, that bruise. I feel warm and liquid and desperate.

"Do you like being kissed there, too?" he says, after a few seconds.

"Sometimes." When it's hungry and unreserved, when it feels less about a technique for me than it is about some urgent, desperate need for him. "When I think . . . when I think the guy is into it."

"I'm into it," he says quickly, and I can't help but smile. I hope it's a smile of the sultry variety, but it's probably more the irrepressible joy variety. I close my eyes, picture Reid's head between my legs, those broad shoulders spreading me apart as he licks and sucks, and my fingers circle that firm nub with a faster, more insistent rhythm. Reid squeezes my knee, and I open my eyes again, stilling my fingers.

"I'm sorry," I say. "I'm so worked up."

"Don't be sorry. Don't—if this is all you want, you showing me what feels good—"

His saying it makes me realize how completely this is *not* all I want. Doing this—telling him, showing him—all of it has released me from the preoccupation with finishing. I want Reid to touch me; I want Reid *inside* of me, and I'm past caring if it gets me there. If it doesn't I'll happily take this same look in his eyes again as he watches me do it myself; I'll happily let him practice again and again and again.

"This isn't all I want." I remove my hands from my body, prop myself on my elbows to get closer to him. Beneath his gray boxer briefs I can see him, long and hard, stretching the material tight, and I get an entirely new face-pressing instinct when it comes to Reid, but that's going to have to wait until later, because I feel aching and empty between my legs, wet and worked up and *ready*.

"I want you. You and me, together."

He leans down to kiss me, his tongue sliding against mine, his arm coming to band around my lower back as he shifts me, moves me farther up the bed. When he's on top of me again, my hips rise to meet his immediately, and without the material of my underwear covering me, without that trace of anxiety, the contact between us makes me gasp in pleasure. He bends his head, his tongue tracing that curve I showed him on my breast with his tongue, the exact right pressure before he licks up to my nipple, his teeth grazing me, and when, a few delicious minutes later, he moves his hand between us, I can tell from his first touch he paid such good attention, such *close, close* attention, and I practically jolt off the bed in pleasure.

"Can you—" I gasp. "Can we practice that later? It feels so good, but I need . . ." I trail off, pressing against him.

"Say it, Meg."

My God, the way he does this, when we're this way together.

The way he's the right kind of direct. The way he makes it safe for me to be the same.

"I want you inside me."

He rewards me again, because we both know now the wait, the anticipation is over. He reaches his arm out, yanks the drawer of his small nightstand open for a condom, and within seconds he's shucked his underwear and sheathed himself, movements I watch with the same hungry intensity that he gave to me.

And when he settles between my legs and pushes forward— so slow, so perfect, so focused—it feels so good, right from the very first second, and I see what's happening inside of me. In my mind there's a gorgeous, dangerous £ taking shape, swooping across my thudding, happy heart, looping behind and around it, catching it unaware, holding it fast and tight.

In a sort of desperate, surprised panic, I clutch at Reid's sides, pulling him closer to me, relieved when the bolt of pleasure I get from feeling the full length of him inside of me scatters the rest of those too-soon letters from my mind as if they're pencil shavings I've blown from the page. Then all I can think about is the next thrust of his hips, the next roll of mine, the way we find such an easy, perfect rhythm together, like walking in sync, like reading the signs we share with each other—a touch here, a suck there, a gasp, a groan, a sigh.

I make a liar of myself, my release building fast and insistent.

"Reid," I breathe. "I'm close."

He ducks his head, presses his forehead into the now-tangled mass of my hair, gusting out a breath even as he—gorgeous, smart, always-paying-attention man—keeps the *exact* same pace, the one that's rocking me to a pleasure so intense I've never felt anything like it before.

"Good," he says again, and I'm so turned on by the way his breath comes short, the way it sounds as if he's speaking tight, almost through his teeth, holding fast to his control.

"Come with me," I beg. "Please, please, please."

And I don't know how he does it, Reid with his mysterious, magical numbers, but he does, every one of those pleas a count for him and his perfect, hard thrusts—

one
two
three
—and then I shatter, crying out my relief and release, feeling him tense and then shudder with his own, and when we both come down from it, our breathing heavy and our bodies sweaty and our limbs tangled together, I'm so sated and proud and exhausted; I'm so relieved to be back with him that I don't think either of us notices the way I'm tracing my fingers on his back, writing and rewriting that heart-holding £, the beginning of something special and rare and beautiful.

Something it's too soon to know if we can finish.

♥   ♥   ♥

It's still daylight when I wake up.

Alone.

In the cool quiet of Reid's bedroom, I'm tangled in his crisp, soap-and-swimming-pool-smelling white sheets, his dark navy coverlet a light, pleasing weight over my still-naked body. It'd be better, I think, to have him beside me—to have that weight be his arm around my waist, to stretch my sore muscles against the lean strength of his long body.

But it's okay to have this drowsy, waking-up moment alone, too. All alone, I don't worry about the blush rising to my cheeks, remembering everything that passed between me and Reid, hot and hard and honest. All alone I can press my hands over my face, feel the giddy smile spread across my cheeks. All alone I can do a goofy, whole-body wiggle, a celebration of what we did that first time, and the two times after (Reid is *definitely* "into it," one of those times proved), and an anticipation of all the things we still have yet to do.

I take a deep breath, quieting my body and taking in my surroundings for the first time. It's spare in here, almost ruthlessly so, a reminder of what Reid had told me about this place in those sated, soft-speaking moments before I must've drifted off. "I moved here after," he'd said, leaving Avery's name out of it. "I've never much thought of it as a home." Other than a narrow dresser in the corner, the bed and its lone nightstand take up most of the space. And besides my clothes—now folded neatly on top of that dresser—there's not much out and around. On the nightstand—clean-lined and dark, almost black wood— there's a sleek, brushed-steel light and a single hardback book, its cover shiny with a clear plastic sleeve, a label on the binding from the library. I lean up to see the title—*The Island at the Center of the World*—and peek inside the flap, and this, along with the slim gray bookmark (of course he uses a bookmark) sticking out from the top, tells me that Reid is halfway through a history of Dutch Manhattan during the seventeenth century. I close the cover and push my face into the pillow, wondering if I might have another orgasm from knowing this, from picturing Reid in this big bed at night, propped on this exact pillow, reading a library book, trying to understand something on his own about a city where nothing—nothing but me, maybe—makes sense to him.

But after a few seconds, the quiet in here—combined with the brutal plainness of it—starts to make me feel uneasy, as though I'm a temporary, unwelcome intrusion into the space. I look over at my clothes on the dresser, strain harder to listen for movement outside this room. Maybe he stepped out, maybe I should take this opportunity to leave before it gets post-sex awkward. I could write him a note, tell him to call if he wants. . . .

No, I tell myself, refilling my head with images and sensations from the last few hours. I sit up quickly and roll from the bed inelegantly, smoothing my mass of surely frizzy hair and reaching for the stack of clothes, bypassing everything in favor of the T-shirt I lent Reid. I pull it on and make my way out to the living space, the skin on my legs tingling with goose bumps as the bare soles of my feet meet the cool smoothness of the glossy parquet floors.

He's sitting on his couch, a low-to-the-ground, sharp-cornered, dark gray thing that looks absolutely terrible for naps or for sleeping off a night of drinking and fighting. His clothes look comfortable—a pair of light gray athletic pants, a white T-shirt, but he's sitting stiffly, his phone in his hand, the thumb that so gently soothed the back of mine only hours ago now flicking impatiently, irritatedly over its screen.

"Hi," I say.

Immediately his head raises, his thumb ceasing its movement. The soft relief in his eyes, the *swoonsh* he sends my way— it all goes a long way toward easing my mind about whether he wants me here still.

"You should've woken me up," I say, liking the way he watches me walk toward him, liking the way he reaches a hand out for mine and tugs me down next to him. The not-for-comfort couch is only improved by the way Reid pulls me so close to him, both of my legs hooking over one of his, absorbing his warmth, one of his arms lifting to come around me.

"I got more sleep than you last night," he says, leaning in to press a kiss against my temple, inhaling deeply, and there's that lovely, £-shaped tightening around my heart again at how good and natural and easy this feels.

But then the phone he's still holding pings in his hand, and his head falls back, his eyes closing in frustration.

"You missed a lot yesterday, huh?" I say, and he barely nods, the lines of his face so stark and grim that I can't help but reach out, trace the tip of my finger from his hairline down his forehead, over the strong slope of his nose and the soft rise of his lips. *This face,* I think, marveling at it all over again.

He nods again, his jaw clenching.

"It was a bad idea to be unreachable, I guess," he says.

I set the palm of my hand to his chest, stroking gently, feeling sorry. It's hard to see this tension up close. In his T-shirt, the patches on Reid's skin—the one I first saw last week, and another spot on his opposite elbow—are visible, and while it's a nice gesture to our new closeness, that he's not compelled to hide them from me, it's also a stark reminder of what he told me in that bar last night, that his skin flares this way when he's stressed, and that his job is the primary reason.

"Your job is—" I say, pausing to clear my throat, to blink down at where my hand rests over the steady beat of his heart. "Your job is why you're leaving New York?"

I see, in my periphery, the way his hand clenches around his phone.

"Yes," he says, plainly. Grimly. After a long pause, he adds, "I've agreed to see something through there. But then—"

"Then you'll leave."

It's not a question, and he doesn't answer. There's not really anything to say, not really anything to do but sit quietly for a moment, feeling the beat of his heart against my hand and forcing myself to imagine loosening those sneaky, surprising loops around my own.

"I can go," I say, after a few quiet seconds where Reid's phone pings twice more. "If you have to catch up on work."

I don't say it to be a martyr, or because I'm feeling sorry for myself. I say it because Reid really does seem to have work to do, and I don't blame him for that. And anyway, I have work of my own to do—sketches to return to, a new stirring in my mind and in my hands, and also work I'm determined to do with Sibby, and with Lark, too. I'd be wise to remember all of it—to remember that Reid is a temporary fixture, and always has been, no matter what's happened between us today.

But then Reid moves, flicking a button on the side of his phone before setting it on the squared-off arm of the couch. With his now free hand he reaches for my thigh and pulls gently, maneuvering me so I'm straddling his lap, the T-shirt bunched around my waist.

My hair falls forward, messy around my face, and Reid reaches up, pushing it back behind my shoulders, stroking it lightly in a way that makes my scalp tingle in pleasure.

"It can wait," he says, and I smile down at him, secretly pleased we don't yet have to call it a day.

"Yeah?"

"Yes," he repeats, but this time it doesn't sound plain or grim at all. He moves his hands from my hair so he can press them into my back, moving me closer to him. "Stay tonight?"

I lean in and kiss him, giving him my answer this way. When we finally break, long minutes later, he keeps only the barest space between our lips.

"You're the best part of this city," he whispers, and I close my eyes and kiss him again, lying to myself the whole time, telling myself I can keep this in *l-i-k-e* territory, telling myself that other, unruly, warning £ won't slice right through my heart when he leaves.

Chapter 14

"Oh, I like this, Meg."

In the back of the shop, Lachelle is peering down at my latest sketches for Make It Happyn, her expression serious, focused. This one, I'm excited about—Make It Happyn requires that one of my full-year treatments be a botanical, and it's long been one of my particular blocks. Earlier this spring, steeped in March and April misery, every floral attempt I'd made had felt pedestrian, familiar, too similar to the jobs I'd been doing for my clients.

But one Sunday morning not even a full two weeks ago now—specifically, the morning after the first perfect day and night I'd spent in Reid's bed—I'd woken up with a new idea. My botanical wouldn't be floral; it would be arboreal. Twelve months inspired by the trees in Prospect Park—almost two hundred species, per the park's website, and for days I've worked to study pictures, to reimagine their trunks and branches and leaves, to create whole new alphabets I could draw from for these monthly pages. It's not quite there yet, but I can feel that I'm on to something.

"No one else will think to have done trees," Lachelle says,

and this is the kind of response I've come to expect from her since I finally, last week, told her and Cecelia about Make It Happyn. Cecelia had responded with thrilled, congratulatory delight, and Lachelle had, too, for about fifteen seconds. Then her competitive streak had taken over, and since then she has been devoted to talking strategy, to looking at all my sketches and determining their fitness for winning this thing. Two days ago, she texted me with the name of another hand-letterer from San Francisco she thinks is up for the job. *He's all right I GUESS,* she'd texted, *but your stuff is better.*

"Yep," she says, nodding. "I like it a lot."

"But you don't *love* it," I say, and she slides her eyes my way, as though she's suspicious of my emphasis.

And the truth is, maybe she should be. **L-I-K-E,** after all, is a word I've been turning over and over a lot in my head over these last two weeks, trying to absorb it into my being, trying to keep it from becoming something else.

I only *like* being with Reid, I tell myself. I only *like* the time we spend together, walking and talking and eating and making lov—*like.* I only *like* the soft ways he touches me—holding my hand in his while we walk, or pressing his own on my lower back while we wait in line at some restaurant counter, or running his fingers through my hair at night before we fall asleep. I only *like* the rougher ways he touches me, too—gripping my hair or my hips when he's inside of me, tugging my body close to his when he wakes sleepily, finding we've strayed from each other in the night. I only *like* the secrets and sounds his body gives up to me when we're together—a hitch in his breath when I stroke him. A small, groaning shudder of pleasure when he first pushes inside of me. The rough, slightly scolding way he says *Meg* when I tighten my inner muscles around him, pushing him to an edge he doesn't want to go over yet.

And I only *like* the funny habits and sweet details I've learned about him: that he is an absolute monster about his wake-up time on weekdays, never hitting the snooze button even *once,* but always pulling the covers back over me neatly and pressing a kiss to my hair before he leaves. That he has a favorite tea brand. That he's never had a single library fine. That he will always call when he has to work too late for us to see each other, and that he will always sound frustrated and disappointed when that's the case.

Like, like, like, I tell myself, especially when any small reminder of his impermanence here asserts itself. A letter I spot on his refrigerator reminding him that he's not renewed the lease on the apartment that was only ever a placeholder for him, anyway. An awkward silence that falls on a walk when we pass an interesting sign for an off-Broadway show opening in September. The curt response I overheard him give on a work call—he gets so many work calls, and he never wants to talk about any of them—earlier this week: "It isn't going to be my problem, because I won't be there."

"What am I, getting married to it?" Lachelle says, interrupting my thoughts pointedly. She shrugs. "I think you need to do more with color. *Then* I'll probably love it."

"Done," I say, bending down to pencil in a reminder to myself in my notebook. When I straighten again, I give her a grateful smile before starting to gather up the pages. Cecelia and Lachelle are teaching a beginner's calligraphy class in the shop in about an hour, so I need to clear out.

When I'm tucking the final stack away, Lachelle gives me a gentle nudge and says, "You've made so much progress. And still almost a month to go."

"Yeah," I say cheerfully, catching a slight falseness in my tone that I hope Lachelle doesn't hear. The progress I've made on the job has, of course, been massive, especially compared to the weeks and weeks I spent completely blocked, and I'm definitely proud of it. I can sense that I'm not quite there—Lachelle is right; I *do* need to do more with color—but still, in my more confident moments, I wonder whether I might end up with more than three full treatments to choose from when it comes time for the pitch. For the first time since those early days after I'd gotten the call, I actually allow myself to imagine how it would be to get chosen for this, to have a line featuring these sketches in stores everywhere.

But with the exception of everything that happened with

Reid, there hasn't been much progress with the *other* work Lachelle encouraged me to do, because my opportunities to practice fighting—with Lark, with Sibby—have been nonexistent to minimal. Lark, for her part, is almost certainly trying to find a gentle way to fire me, because the e-mail I woke up to last Monday had asked if we could "press pause" on the project while she "made some other decisions about the house."

My reply—asking if we could get together for a meeting anyway—had gone unanswered.

With Sibby, I deserve more responsibility—once for staying with Reid on a night she was almost certain to be at the apartment, and once for chickening out at starting the conversation when she'd come home with Elijah in tow rather than by herself, as I'd expected. But by the end of last week—the same night, incidentally, that I'd seen that lease renewal letter on Reid's refrigerator—I'd felt a panicked sense of urgency about it all, chastising myself for dropping the ball. After all, Sibby was leaving soon, too. Sure, she'd be in the same city, but with the way things have been going lately, she might as well be whole states, whole countries away.

What was I doing, letting a summer romance with a leaving man I definitely only *like* get in the way of fixing this massive problem with my best friend?

I'd called her right away, that lease letter hovering somewhere over my shoulder. I'd even left a voice mail. "Sib," I'd said, my tone serious. "I need to talk to you. I'll be at home all day and night tomorrow. Call me and we'll find a time."

But she hadn't called me. She'd texted me back an hour later with the kind of polite, roommates-only text that's been a hallmark of her communication to me lately: *At Elijah's tonight and leaving super early tomorrow for the Hamptons with the Whalens. Should be back by next Saturday. Let me know if it's an emergency! If not, talk soon. Sorry about all the boxes at home!*

I'd felt my shoulders slump in disappointment as I'd read it.

I straighten them now, hefting my portfolio and my bag, watching as Lachelle starts setting out supplies for the class.

"I'm headed home to work," I say, determinedly, more to myself than to her. But I *am* determined, because if Sibby's coming back tomorrow, I'm going to be home to meet her. I've already told Reid I probably won't be free until Sunday, and my plan tonight is to tidy the apartment while I practice what I want to say to her. A night alone, I figure, will be good preparation, and when she gets back, we'll do this thing we've *both* been hiding from.

"Take it easy," Lachelle says. "Rest your hands."

"Yep," I say, waving at her as I go, wishing that the work I had ahead of me was as easy as the work I've been doing with my hands lately.

I make a quick stop off for groceries, indulging in an old best friend tradition of picking up a few of Sibby's favorite things, too, because I figure she'll appreciate that after being away. It's Friday afternoon crowded, but Trina behind the counter still makes time to tell me she got rid of the infection in her belly button ring and celebrated by getting a new piercing "somewhere private." Thankfully for me and everyone else in line behind me she does not offer to show it to me. When I get to my place, our post office guy has our bank of mailboxes open, so I sit on the steps and chat with him—he loves a good weather talk—while I wait for him to get to our apartment's delivery.

My phone pings when he's finishing up and I check it as I'm waving goodbye to him, smiling as I see I have a new message from Reid.

I'll miss you tonight, it says, because Reid texts direct, the same way he talks direct. *I hope it goes well. Call if you need me.*

You only like *him, Meg,* I tell myself as I stare down at it, that heart-tightening £ tugging again.

L-I-K-E, I spell in my head.

But right as I'm getting ready to respond, my screen flashes with a different four-letter *L* word, and not the one I've been trying not to feel.

L-A-R-K, it reads, and that's the first indication I get that my weekend is about to go a lot differently than I'd planned.

♥ ♥ ♥

Here's the thing: It is not easy preparing your home for an unplanned visit from a princess.

Lark's voice on the phone had been soft, friendly, maybe even embarrassed—so different from the sharp way she'd spoken to me the last time I'd seen her. She was in the neighborhood, she'd said, and was hoping she could stop by the shop.

"I'm at home now, but I could get back there quickly," I'd told her. "But it'll be a full house—there's a class happening there right now. How about we meet at a—" I'd begun, then remembered her reluctance about pretty much everywhere else.

"I could come to you," she'd said, filling up the awkward silence, and two minutes later I'd been texting her my address, frantically running through a mental list of all the stuff I needed to pick up.

I can't do much about the boxes that fill up the corners of the space, but I do my best with everything else. A quick cleanup of the kitchen, a grab-and-dump-elsewhere strategy of dealing with the mail I've let stack up on our breakfast table over the last few days, a flustered attempt at tidying the coffee table and couch, which shamefully—because Reid came over here last night—involves me shoving one of my bras between the cushions. My face heats at the reminder of that particular interlude, which ended with me on my knees and Reid with his hands in my hair.

When I buzz her up I use the last few seconds to look over the space (well, and to fan my hot face), acutely aware of how small and cluttered it'll still probably look, given that townhouse-tower she's used to.

But when I open the door to her, I'm reminded: Lark isn't really a princess, and her townhouse isn't really a tower. She's five foot two of regular person, with a self-conscious smile and—if I'm not mistaken—a sheepish look in her eyes, and seeing her stand there on the closest thing I've got to a front porch, I suspect she feels about as awkward as I did the last time we saw each other.

"Come in," I tell her, ushering her to my somewhat-sagging couch. I cheerfully list every type of beverage I have in my refrigerator, but really I know she'll pass. I'm already bad-habitting my way through this, stalling away from the confrontation I remind myself I'm determined to have—even if it wasn't the one I was planning on practicing for.

"Thanks for letting me come by," she says, when I've finally taken a seat on the other side of the couch. She has her hands clasped tightly on her lap, and her throat bobs with a swallow.

Not for the first time, I think Lark and I probably have more in common than I would've ever thought.

"Sorry I haven't called," she says breezily. "I got really busy working with this new decorator Jade hired, and we had a quick trip up to Toronto for a shoot Cam is doing, and there's been so much shopping to—"

"Lark," I interrupt. Seeing her struggle through this performance—it somehow stops me cold from even attempting my own. "It's okay. I get it."

She looks at me with a mute, embarrassed regret that makes me want to change the subject for her. Instead I say, "I know I spoke out of turn at our last meeting."

She blinks at me, then lowers her head for a minute, smoothing lint off her black jeans.

"No," she says finally, her chin raising. "*He* spoke out of turn. I was so embarrassed he acted that way in front of you. Not just . . . you know, what he said about me. But also his—" She breaks off, presses her lips together.

"His really bad quote idea?" I supply, sending a smile her way.

She raises a hand to her hairline, wincing and then breathing out an exasperated laugh. "I don't know *where* he gets this stuff. Every time I get close to finalizing an idea for the house, he comes up with something so . . . so *disruptive*."

My own smile fades. *He's doing it to control you*, I'm thinking. *He's doing it to make you feel unsure of yourself.*

"I hope you push back on that," I say, and this time, I don't put any cheer at all in my voice. "I hope you don't think of yourself as a . . . a lightweight."

"I don't," she says, and the quickness and confidence of her answer reassure me somewhat. Then she lowers her head again, looks down at her clasped hands. "But I'm pretty lost here. In New York, I mean. The truth is, I'd really only just gotten used to LA."

"It's pretty different, I imagine."

She looks up, gives me a sardonic, closemouthed smile. *You have no idea*, this smile says.

"I had more people there, you know? We moved here, and I—he's the *one* person."

I give a soft laugh. "Believe me. I relate."

"You moved here for a guy?"

"No, I moved here to . . . to start over. But when I came, I only knew one person." My eyes trace over to the boxes dotting the space of this much-loved, much-memoried apartment, and I try to press down another inconvenient feeling of urgency.

"At first," I say, "I really only saw the city through her. It took me a while to find my own way." I don't tell her that I'm one hundred percent sure Sibby has better eyes to see the city through than Cameron does.

"It does get easier, once you get out there," I add.

She nods, but her expression is distant. I think about everything I know about Lark: how she seems to think fitting in here means wearing head-to-toe black. How she thinks anyone in Brooklyn would really care if she went into a coffee shop. How she somehow thinks Cameron—a man who wears a shark-tooth necklace!—is more qualified to make it here than she is.

"You know," I say, keeping my voice light, the right kind of light for this, its own kind of confrontation. "I know this city pretty well. Anytime you want to get out, you should let me know."

"Really?"

"Of course."

"That's really nice, Meg. Especially after the way I acted. I'm so sorry for that."

"You don't have to apologize." Even as I say it, though, I know it's incomplete. I know it's not all I have to say. I'm making her feel better, but not myself.

I take a deep breath.

"But I do think—if you want us to keep working together on your house—I'd prefer if I'm taking direction from one person. It's difficult, in my position, when there's a lot of conflict over the commission. I totally understand if that doesn't work for you."

There's a long, awkward pause before she speaks again. It's possible I can hear the dust motes talking to one another; that's how quiet it seems in here as I wait for her to tell me whether the deal is off. It doesn't matter that I'm coming off a great couple of weeks of work for Make It Happyn: at this moment, Sibby's packed boxes feel encroaching, a reminder of why it's important for me to keep this job, too. My body seems to straighten, to take on a preparatory posture. I think of Reid, wondering if this is how his body feels to himself all the time. It must be exhausting.

"My other friends don't like him, either," Lark says, finally. "Back in LA."

My other *friends*. I hear this as the gesture I think it is, a reciprocation of my *Anytime you want to get out* offer. Lark considers me her *friend*, not just her employee.

I shrug. "Well, hey. It was only one meeting."

I don't say it because I think Cameron improves over time; I am almost certain he doesn't. I say it because—as her new friend, I guess—I don't think it would help, right in this moment, to pile on.

I think it would help her to hear something else.

"Think of yourself as having two people here, at least, okay?"

She looks over at me and gives me her closemouthed smile. "Thank you," she says softly. She swallows again, her face flashing with emotion briefly before she arranges it again into something neutral, unaffected. Then she looks over at me and breathes out a small, sarcastic laugh.

"Men," she says, rolling her eyes. "Am I right?"

I blink in surprise, seeing this side of Lark, this more Princess Freddie side of her. But I recover quickly. I know this is a fragile step in this new, fledgling friendship.

"Maybe that should be the quote for the wall," I say, doing my best deadpan Reid impression.

She tips back her head and laughs, no covering her mouth this time, and then I laugh, too, and it's the kind of laughing that takes you by surprise, the kind of laughing you do not because the thing that got you started is particularly funny, but because you're in the presence of someone else's laughter, because there's a point at which the laughter *itself* becomes funny.

Lark lifts a hand and sweeps it, palm out, in a big arc in front of her face, as if she's revealing a marquee. She says "MEN" again, like she's announcing a big show, and it's somehow the funniest thing. I see it

M-E-N

made of lightbulbs, and I laugh harder; I think of the whole thing flaming to life in a blaze of glory. I hold up a fist, making the popping noise I imagine as my fingers burst open, each bulb—well, except maybe one, one very special bulb—burning out in a loud, disappointing flare, and what's funnier is that I think Lark gets it, and she leans forward with her laughter, clutching at her sides, and we laugh and laugh, and I guess that's why I don't hear it when the door opens.

I guess that's why I miss Sibby coming home.

Chapter 15

"Holy shit."

I'm almost positive it's not what Sibby would intend to say upon meeting one of the idols of our childhood, but one look at her standing in the doorway tells me that Sibby is probably not in the best space to be intentional. I've lived through enough returns-from-the-Hamptons to know Sibby is probably coming off a stressful few days with the Whalens, since Tilda only likes the pool, the kids only like the beach, and Mr. Whalen only likes himself and his laptop. Even in her shock I can see that Sibby's come home having had it; she's got at least two stains on her T-shirt, her sunglasses are the only thing keeping her curls in any semblance of order, and that usually sharp black wing on her left eyelid has seen better days.

"Sib," I say, standing from my spot on the couch. "Hey, welcome back."

Instead of acknowledging my greeting, Sibby stares at Lark, her mouth ajar. For a second her gaze bounces purposefully around the room, as if maybe she's wondering if there's a pop-up tent somewhere in here. It's awkward, but I sympathize. At least I had advance warning about meeting her.

"This is Lark Tannen-Fisher," I add, ridiculously. "She's—"

"Princess Freddie," Sibby says, which is . . . you know, definitely not what *I* was planning to say.

Lark winces.

"I mean," Sibby says, "that was our favorite movie."

I look back at Sibby, surprised. Nothing has been "our" favorite anything in a long time. But I'm pretty sure she's still in an everything-I-say-is-unintentional space.

"Well," Lark says, standing and smoothing her (black) shirt. She's arranged her face in such a way that you'd think someone has pointed a camera at her. "I really appreciate that."

"Lark, this is Sibby, my—"

"It's Sibyl," Sibby corrects me, abandoning her small roller suitcase and stepping forward to reach out a hand. They shake, Sibby smiling broadly, but Lark keeps her camera-face on. She looks as though she's about to say what designer she's wearing, or that she's "just happy to be nominated."

I'm uncomfortable on Lark's behalf, but I'm also immediately protective of Sibby, because I know once the surprise wears off she'll be completely pissed at herself for calling Lark Princess Freddie. She will also probably not be happy once she notices that eyeliner. She definitely will wish she was wearing a clean shirt.

"I've been doing some work for Lark," I say, to fill in what might be a millennium of hand-shaking silence. "She's new to the area."

"Oh. Well, that's wonderful. She's the best, our Meg."

Our Meg? That's two "ours" in probably two minutes, and this one doesn't even make sense, unless Sibyl is the royal-we queen of a land called Sarcastia, because based on the tone of her voice, she does not seem to have meant the compliment.

"Yes," Lark says, and I think she also senses the tone, because she slides her eyes my way briefly before looking back to Sibby. "It was nice to meet you."

"Sure," Sibby says, having shifted her posture to seem completely unaffected, almost—cool. "Welcome to the neighborhood."

"Thank you," says Lark, equally cool, before turning to me. "Meg, I'll call you?"

"Yes!" I say, scrambling forward, ushering her around Sibby's abandoned luggage to the door, and while we say our goodbyes I can feel Sibby in the room behind me, a living shadow now, and even though this has been Apartment Number Awkward for months, this time, I can tell, I'm not going to turn around to polite, distant, everything-is-fine Sibby.

When I look back at her she's standing with her arms crossed over her chest, her head cocked to the side. The color is high in her cheeks.

"Princess Freddie, huh?" she says in that same tone.

It's so irritating that I think of correcting her, of saying, *Her name is Lark*. Instead I shrug. "Yeah, it's a job that came up a while back."

"I kind of can't believe you wouldn't say anything to me about it."

Immediately I open my mouth to apologize, to give her some excuse that puts all the blame on me, or that at least absolves her entirely. *I've been so busy*, I could say. *She's a pretty private person*, I could say.

But instead I press my lips back together and remember that this is the opportunity I wanted to have this weekend. Sure, it's not what I practiced for, but it still has to happen, and maybe especially now. Even in spite of the way she's acting at the moment, I *know* her. She's embarrassed and hurt and she's still my very best friend.

I *have* to make it better.

"There haven't been many opportunities to tell you anything lately," I say.

She stares at me. "You could've texted me."

Sarcastia speech must be catching, because the first thing I think to say is, *Texting is your way of doing things, not mine*. Instead I take a breath and try to calm the predictable roiling in my stomach.

"Texting isn't how I want to tell you things," I say.

There's a long pause where Sibby simply looks at me, as though she's trying to decide whether it's worth it, to do this.

And it almost breaks my heart when she uncrosses her arms and shrugs, moving toward her luggage. "We've both been really busy, I guess."

I move to stand in front of her suitcase.

Because she's worth it, to me.

"Sib. Don't do that. Let's finally talk."

She stills, crosses her arms again. But I can tell she's surprised. "Listen, I know it makes it weird, that I'm moving out."

"That's not what makes it weird. It's been weird for *months*. I don't want to pretend it's not anymore."

Her face softens, and she drops her eyes to our weathered floors. "It's probably—you know how it is, when you get into a new relationship. Elijah and I—"

"It's not Elijah. This is before Elijah. You know it is."

That softness in her face vanishes. She raises her chin. "Meg, you're making this too big of a deal. I've changed, you've changed. That happens sometimes."

You know how it is? That happens sometimes? Like she's *educating* me, in some way, about friendship in general. About our friendship in particular. I once held this woman's hair after she threw up from one wine cooler at senior prom. I got on my hands and knees on the floor of the Union Square station to help her find one of her favorite earrings even though the pair had only cost fifteen dollars. I've held on to grudges against anyone who's ever done her the slightest wrong. I know what friendship is.

I know I haven't made it too big of a deal.

"It doesn't happen to us," I say, proud of the way I've kept my voice calm. "I want to know what changed between *us*. I want to know why you stopped wanting to hang out. I want to know why you stopped talking to me about your day. I want to know why you constantly brush me off."

"It'll be better when I'm in my new place, okay?"

I feel my brow lower in confusion. "How will it be better?

How do you really think we're going to spend more time together that way?"

She gusts out an exasperated sigh. "Can't you leave this alone?"

It's a version of something I've heard before. From my parents, especially that final year I was at home. From myself, anytime I've wanted to avoid something difficult. *Leave it alone, Meg,* and there's still a part of me that wants to listen.

But I'm different now. I don't only protect myself anymore. I press. I practice. I *stay.*

"No, I can't."

For long seconds, I don't think she'll answer. I think she'll simply turn on her heel and walk the short distance to her boxed-up bedroom. And if she does, I guess I'll have to accept it. I can't force her to talk to me, to fight with me. But at least I'll know I tried.

"I want to work this out, Sib. It can't be worse than how it's been—"

"I'm *jealous,* okay?" she says, cutting me off. But her voice, in contrast to her words, isn't a sad, sorry confessional. I see that *jealous* as a sword: the *j* a curved, elaborate hilt, the letters rising out of it slanting and sharp-edged, narrowing and narrowing to the most precise, painful point.

I blink at her, stunned. "Jealous?"

It doesn't compute, not with me and Sibby. We made fun of girls like that. We rejected that kind of thing with elaborate celebrations of each other's accomplishments, always. Always, until . . .

"Because of my business?" I say, tentatively. I think back, months ago. When the *Times* article came out, Sibby and I went for a fancy dinner, the kind you make a reservation for. We drank champagne. We toasted The Planner of Park Slope, and we went to a new show she'd been dying to see. She *had* celebrated it. But after . . .

After, she *did* start getting distant.

At first, I feel a sense of relief. Jealousy is awful between friends, but Sibby and I can get past it. If I tell her how it's been—the pressure I've been feeling, the isolation I'd felt for so long. The worry over the block, the Make It Happyn deadline. If she knew . . .

But then she makes a derisive, annoyed noise, and I don't feel any relief at all.

"Your business, sure," she says. "Your *life.*"

"What about my life?"

She closes her eyes briefly, shakes her head, and I think she might be retreating, readying herself to cut this conversation off.

But then she opens them again.

"New York was *my* dream, Meg," she says, her voice hard, but tinged with sadness. "My whole life, I planned to come here. I love you, and I'm glad you're successful. But . . ." She trails off, and for one miserable, horrible second, I see her chin quiver. I step forward, on instinct, but she holds a hand up.

"But after all this time, I'm still nannying. I spent years in dance classes, in vocal lessons. The most I use them now is to entertain two kids who'll probably have forgotten about me by next summer, because they'll have some new version of Miss Michelucci."

This part, it's not new. Sibby and I have spent hours talking through her dashed hopes, her disappointments, her frustrations. We've cried over shitty auditions and lost parts together, ranted about her nannying job and its various annoyances. But the way it's directed at me now, the way it's an *indictment* of me, somehow—that *is* new. New and awful.

"I worked so hard to get here, Meg. You didn't even like the city. You . . . *fell* into it."

Something must pass over my face, some trace of the devastation I feel at being told that this is what Sibby thinks of me, and of my work. She raises a hand to her forehead, rubs her hand across it in exhaustion.

"I know you work hard, okay? I know you do. But you came here, and within a *year* you had people lining up for you. We move to Brooklyn and it's hardly any time at all before you're practically famous here. You start a whole new business." She gives a breathy, exhausted laugh, looks toward the couch where Lark and I sat. "You're friends with a *movie* star."

"I'm sorry," I say, but even as I'm saying it, I know it's not right, or at least it's not all the way right. I'm sorry for the way Sibby feels, but I don't know if I should be sorry for why she feels that way, for how my work has made her feel. I'm speechless. I have no idea what to say, where to even *start*, to confront this.

"So," she says. "You're happy to know it? The entire, petty truth of it? It makes the friendship so much better to have that out in the open?"

"It's not petty," I stumble out. "And it is better. It's better if we don't . . . if we don't hide things from each other. I'm really trying not to do that."

"That's great for you, Meg. But you know, some things are better to hide. I didn't *want* to tell you this. I wanted to work on moving past it, on my own, because I *know* it's not fair to you, and I know it's small of me. It's *humiliating*," she says, her voice cracking, her chin crinkling again. But immediately she tightens it, takes a breath through her nose.

"I'm happy with Elijah, and I'm happy I'll have some new opportunities in the city. *That* is what is going to help. Not . . . not *this*."

"I'm sorry," I say again, flustered now. I'd thought I was being so brave, pushing this. Now I'm confused, unsure, worried I've hurt her worse. "I didn't know. I didn't know it was this."

Part of me is saying, *Stop, don't push her.* But another part of me is so worried about losing her. I'm so deep into this confrontation that I don't know *how* to stop it now.

"Sib, if we could only—"

But I break off when I see the look on her face. She is . . . *exasperated*. With me, with this apartment, with this entire conversation. "Of *course* it's this," she says, as if she can't believe I wouldn't have realized. As if I was selfish not to have.

I almost apologize again, because maybe I *was* selfish. Maybe this was my fault. The not knowing, but also the not . . . the not leaving it alone. When I open my mouth again, hoping to say this in some halfway coherent way, Sibby speaks before I can, her voice hard, harsh.

"Not everything is some big 'I'm not your real mom' scandal, okay?"

All of the air is sucked out of the apartment, out of both of us. Sibby looks absolutely shocked that she's said it, that she's brought up the worst possible thing.

The family secret that brought me here.

The secret, I guess, that led to me encroaching on her New York City dream.

I don't know if I look shocked. I don't even know if I feel shocked. After all, I've been here before, and recently, too. This is where pushing, where fighting can lead. I've known it all along.

It can hurt.

It can hurt so, so bad.

"That's beneath you," I say, my voice cracking.

The tears filling her eyes spill over, tracking in gray-black tears down her cheeks. "I know. I'm sorry."

I know she is, and it's more than the tears that tells me so. It's in the set of her shoulders; it's in the way she's rubbing her thumb up and down along her index finger, a nervous habit. It's in the way she looks at me, full of regret.

The part of me who sat across a table from Lachelle and took her very good advice, the part of me that made certain I confronted Reid before I slept with him, the part of me that, not even a half hour ago, told Lark about my boundaries related to my work—that part of me is saying, *Stay. Stay and work it out.*

But that part of me is pretty new. That part of me doesn't have enough practice for this.

So I do the thing that feels most necessary for escaping this awful, awful hurt.

I leave.

♥ ♥ ♥

It's too soon.

Too soon to show up unannounced.

Too soon to cry in front of him.

Too soon to tell him the reason why.

And yet.

I left my apartment with nothing but my big, sloppy bag and my big, sloppy feelings, and I took the same walk—well, in the other direction—Reid took two weeks ago, all the way across the soaring, spectacular Brooklyn Bridge. Somewhere along the way I'd noticed, with a distant sort of awareness, all the lettering scribbled along its various beams, graffitied proclamations of protest, of identity, of love. I'd thought, *That should interest you*, but still I'd turned my eyes down, watching my shoes pass determinedly, rhythmically, over the worn wooden planks.

Once I'd descended into the city, it'd been firmly in the middle of rush hour—Lower Manhattan in honking, people-swarming action, a busy anonymity that'd felt unusually welcome to me. It was hard not to walk straighter amid all that focus, all that determined hustle to get home after a pressured workweek, and so maybe that's why I'd descended the subway steps at City Hall without stopping to consider the *too soon-ness* of what I was about to do.

It isn't until I'm outside his building that the full force of what I've done, where I've come, hits me. I hold my phone as though it's hot to the touch, switching it back and forth between my hands, uncertain. Text him and say I'm here? Text him but don't say I'm here? Forget texting him altogether and walk away, walk off the rising threat of a sob that's been swelling behind my sternum since Sibby spoke to me?

Before I have time to decide, though, he's there, striding up the street in that perfect, upright way: dark suit, the jacket folded and draped neatly over his arm. Another white shirt, fitted slim, the top button undone, the sleeves buttoned at the wrists. Blue tie, loosened, pulling to the right from the strap of the bag crossing his body.

Face, face, face.

And as soon as I see him, my own crumples.

I don't know how he gets to me so fast, but he does, his arms coming around me, his body curving over mine, his voice low and soothing in my ear.

"Meg, honey," he says, and I think, *Too soon?* But I also don't think that. I think Reid calling me *honey* is actually exactly like honey. Slow and thick and golden.

A balm.

I *like* it so much.

"What happened?"

"Sibby," I manage, my face against his perfect shirt—*why* am I always messing up his nice shirts?—and for a few seconds he only holds me tighter, closer.

"Let me take you inside," he says, and I nod against his chest, probably making the makeup/tears/snot-smearing situation worse, but he doesn't seem to care. He keeps his arm around me as he lets us into the building, his posture straightening as we enter the lobby, as if he's daring anyone around to look at me, to judge me for loudly sniffling, for unceremoniously swiping my hands across my face.

Inside he takes my big, sloppy bag and settles me on his too-stiff couch; he shuffles around his kitchen and returns with a cup of tea, holding it in his two hands as though it is his very own heart, and that makes me cry even harder, and for long minutes afterward all he does is sit next to me, his arm around my shoulders strong and warm and soothing, the cup of tea unfurling its steaming comfort into the air from its spot on the coffee table.

And then I tell him about the fight.

He's quiet for almost all of it, and that's what I expect—Reid's always been a good listener, a determined listener, and even as I'm telling it I can feel the way he hears it, the way he hears all the pauses at the hardest parts, the way he feels my breath catch with tension.

But when I tell him about the worst thing—*some big "I'm not your real mom" scandal*—he stiffens and leans away from me, tipping my face up to his.

"What does that mean?" he says, his brows lowered in concern, or maybe something closer to anger. I feel an unexpected, new pang of sadness, but strangely, it's not about my parents, about the "scandal" Sibby referred to. It's about Sibby, Sibby and Reid, about how telling him this story means something forever about how he'll feel toward her. My very best friend and my . . .

Nope, I scold myself. *You only like* him, *remember?*

But I tell him anyway.

"It means that when I was nineteen I found out my father was a serial cheater. And that . . . well. That I was the result of one of his . . . affairs, I guess? Though that's probably too strong a word for it. I think it was one night."

The rest of it, surprisingly, comes easily. I tell Reid about my parents' constant fighting: how for long, lonely years of my childhood I didn't know any different, I thought it was how all parents were. I tell him about how it worsened as I grew older: more distant but also more snide, the passive-aggressive barbs they would trade with each other through a veneer of politeness. I tell him about how I'd tried to be their arbiter and their adhesive; how I'd always been good at stopping them from fighting; how even in spite of their unhappiness with each other, they had at least seemed to share a happiness with me.

And then I tell him about my birth certificate.

"I was supposed to have it for school," I say. "Really, I was supposed to have it even before classes started, but my parents kept putting me off about it. My mom called the school, somehow talked them into letting me start without it. And my dad—he said he'd lost it, had thought it was in a safe he kept at work. We'd have to order a new one, he'd said, but every time I'd ask about it, worrying about registering for the next semester, he'd put me off."

Just leave it alone, Meg.

Reid's jaw tightens, and he moves, tucking a strand of hair behind my ear.

"Anyway, I guess I should've known—or I don't know, suspected—earlier. There'd been some difficulty when I got my driver's license, too, but I guess I hadn't really paid much attention. I don't know if I got old enough, or curious enough, or what. So I requested a new one."

I still remember looking at it. Fourth line down, MOTHER'S NAME. *This is a mistake,* I'd thought, staring down at the letters there, precise and mechanically made. Who was Darcy Hollowell?

My mother's name is Margaret, I'd thought. *My mother's name is the same as mine.*

But even as I'd thought it, I'd known. I'd felt it click into place as if it were a puzzle piece, a thousand tiny inconsistencies from my childhood suddenly making a painful sort of sense.

Those letters were *true.*

This part of the story, of course, is the worst: the revelation and what it led to, my parents presenting a unified front in the face of my sobbing outrage, the way they'd gently condescended to me as they'd presented their explanation. My father and an "indiscretion." A woman who'd decided to carry her pregnancy to term, but would place the baby up for adoption. My mother, who had struggled with her own ability to get pregnant, who had wanted to have a child for years and years.

And me, an imperfect solution.

More and more imperfect as the years went on, apparently: my dad still full of indiscretion, and my mom increasingly full of resentment—at him and, I suspected, at me. I *was* their adhesive, but in the worst possible way.

They'd been stuck together for *years.*

"Meg," Reid whispers at a certain point, all sympathy, and that gives me the strength to finish it cleanly, no more tears.

"It was a relief for them, in the end. Sort of a . . . 'the truth will set you free' situation, I guess. They told me that night they'd be divorcing. I'd never seen them get along better, when they told me. Like peas and carrots."

It had been, ultimately, what had hurt the most. That I'd been some kind of excuse for them, for staying together in a household that was poisoned by their fighting. That they'd used me, in a way, to keep themselves from having to make a decision about their marriage.

I had *screamed* at them. The worst night of my life. I left for New York the next week. Six months later, overwhelmed with curiosity, I'd contacted Darcy Hollowell and had gotten a very short, very polite reply that ended with a wish for me to "reconcile" with my parents and to "have a happy, healthy life."

It hadn't been difficult to see the hidden message there, and we've never been in touch again.

When I finally sag back against him, my cheek resting on his broad chest, I notice that there's no more swirling, rising steam from the teacup. I feel guilty for not drinking it, Reid's heart-in-hand offering, but his body has been the best kind of comfort, even though it feels stiffer now. Even though he hasn't said anything in a long time.

Too soon to tell him, probably.

But finally, he speaks again, his voice soft. "Did you ever forgive them?"

I close my eyes, thinking. It's taken years between us, to get back to a decent place, a place where I call each of them regularly. Longer with my dad, and it's still only the weather and the Buckeyes when we talk, and of course the occasional slip when I'm sending him a hand-drawn message of congratulations. With my mom, it's the weather, too, but also garage sales and trips she goes on and a man named David she calls her "companion," which is somehow both slightly gross and not-so-slightly adorable. I go home for Christmas, and I bounce awkwardly between their new houses: my dad and Jennifer and Jennifer's three bichon terriers in a house so similar to the one I grew up in that I hate sleeping there. My mom and her tidy, tiny-gardened townhouse, a few things of David's tucked away discreetly in her closet, happier than she ever was when I was still at home.

"I understand them," I say, after a minute. "I think they love me. I think they were trying to protect me."

"And themselves," he adds.

I nod, and feel a fresh press of tears behind my eyes. It feels impossible that I have any at all left, but it's a reminder of what brought me here in the first place.

"That's what Sibby's been trying to do. Protect herself. And I couldn't let it go. I—"

"She shouldn't have said it," Reid says. "There's no excuse."

I close my eyes and nod, and I'm not sure if it's because I agree or because I've entirely exhausted myself. That fight with Sibby might as well have happened *days* ago, *years* ago, for all the strange, sad distance I feel from it. When I try to think of what I'll do next to try to repair the damage, nothing comes to mind. My brain is a slate that's been wiped entirely clean—dull black and not a piece of chalk in sight.

I think fleetingly about my sketches, my deadline, dreading the thought of trying to return to them when I feel this way. I'm so tired that I suspect I could fall asleep right here, with this too-soon man I like so much holding me.

Except.

"Your couch is awful," I say, sitting up and wriggling my butt against it. "It's like sitting on pizza boxes."

He laughs softly, clearly surprised at the change in topic. "It came with the place."

"Ew." I dramatically hold out my arms so my skin is no longer touching it and wonder idly if someone in this building has a blacklight we can borrow.

He reaches out, gently rubs his thumb across my cheek. "It was new. This is a furnished rental."

Oh.

It's another one of those reminders for me, the ones I've been trying so hard to take to heart about Reid's impermanence here. The *too soon-ness* of this whole evening reasserts itself. It'll *always* be too soon with me and Reid, because Reid is leaving.

I drop my arms, hoping the motion hides my sigh. Suddenly, coming to this apartment feels like as bad of an idea as staying in my own. I open my mouth to say something—maybe a casual *Let's go get a sandwich and walk and pretend this never happened*— but Reid interrupts me.

"Do you want to go for a drive tomorrow?"

I blink at him.

A drive.

How could he possibly know?

"We could get out of the city," he says, a note of caution in his voice. "For some fresh air. Distance, you know?"

"Yes, I know *exactly*." At the very thought of it—wind in my hair, buildings and trees streaking past the windows, a break from everything here—I feel lighter already. I almost bounce on this pizza box couch.

"Where would we go?

Reid clears his throat, shifts as if he also hates this couch. "I've been meaning to get down to Maryland before—well, I haven't been in a while. It's a short trip, under three hours if we leave early enough."

"Oh. To meet your family?"

"We could—that is, I could say you're a friend from the city."

When I don't answer right away, he stands, gathering the teacup from the table. "It's too soon, I'm sure."

"Reid." I still him with a hand on the outside of his thigh, the closest place to him I can reach from where I sit. He looks down at me, that faint flush on his cheekbones. *Too soon*, he'd said, his mind a mirror of my own.

The loop around my heart squeezes, a warning and a warming all at once. This is no way to protect myself, probably, crossing another threshold of closeness with Reid. Leaving the safe haven of the city, the only place we've ever known each other. Seeing him with the people who made him who he is.

But tonight, he held me while I cried. He listened to me talk about my falling-apart friendship and my fallen-apart family. He knew exactly what I needed. He protected me.

"I'd like to go," I say.

His eyes light—same as the blue sky outside your windshield on a clear day.

"You're sure?"

"Oh, yeah. A drive like that? Think of the games we could play."

His mouth pulls to the side, that funny concentration face he has. "License plates. Highway signs. Billboards."

I shrug casually, standing up and taking the teacup from his hands. I take a sip of its now-cool, bottom-of-a-flowerpot taste, and wince dramatically just to hear Reid laugh quietly again.

I press up on my tiptoes and kiss him, reaching up a hand to touch his sandpapery, long-day-on-the-job cheek, and he immediately pulls me closer. When I pull my mouth away from his, I move so I can whisper in his ear.

"Sounds to me like it's right on time."

Chapter 16

"Well, I think it's time for tea, don't you?"

Cynthia Sutherland asks this question of the table exactly one hundred and twenty minutes after our arrival at the Sutherland family home, a small, well-maintained ranch in a somewhat run-down northeast Maryland suburb. Normally, counting the minutes—okay, counting anything, really—isn't my style, but over the last two hours I've learned, bit by bit, how keeping track of numbers might be important in a household like this one.

Mostly it's a matter of the residents themselves. Cynthia, Reid's mom—a petite, smiling woman with a head full of dark curls who retired from her job as a high school teacher only last year—has the kind of time-aware, resources-aware efficiency of a woman who has raised seven children in a three-bedroom, two-and-a-half-bathroom house. In her kitchen, every move she makes seems calculated to get the most from the space; at her dining table, every turn in conversation she directs seems calculated for balance, for making sure no one dominates. Maybe it ought to seem disconcerting, too mechanical, but somehow it doesn't. It only seems as though you've been put in the hands of someone capable and kind, someone who wants to make the most of her time with you.

Thomas Sutherland—a man who looks so like an older version of Reid that I'd stammered in shock at his initial, sternly put "Good afternoon" to me—is more literally a numbers guy, an accountant who works out of a tidy home office at the front of the house. He's quiet, observant, blunt when he speaks, and within three minutes of learning about my work he asked me whether I was careful about the deductions I took for my supplies. My lips had quirked in a smile, my eyes catching Reid's across the table, and for a second I think we'd both forgotten about numbers, remembering instead letters he once wrote to me: *I was nervous.*

Finally, there's Reid's sister, Cady. Twenty years old with long hair in mermaid shades of pink, blue, and purple, a dye job that would cost hundreds of dollars at even the cheapest salons in New York, and only six months to go in the cosmetology program she's in. Cady—bright and talkative and obviously something of a mystery to her more reserved parents and brother—counts herself in years of distance from her older siblings, none of whom are here for our spontaneous visit. Eight years younger than the youngest, Seth; ten years from Ryan; eleven years from Reid; thirteen from Owen; sixteen from the twins, Connor and Garrett. These numbers, it's clear, matter to her, some way that she defines herself in relation to siblings who are so much older than her, and even though I don't have any experience with that kind of count, I get the sense that in her adolescent years, Cady probably felt very much like an only child.

To that, I can definitely relate.

"My mom always has tea after a meal," Cady says to me now, by way of explanation. If Cady is a mystery to her parents, it's clear she knows they might be a mystery to a guest, and since I've arrived, she's made herself something of a guide to me, dropping in context at any possible moment of confusion. When Reid softly asks Cady about some paperwork related to her school, she proudly (and loudly) announces to me that Reid pays her tuition. When Thomas silently hands Reid a quarter-folded section of the newspaper, Cady rolls her eyes and explains that Thomas does a Challenger game in there every day, something Reid got him into a couple of years ago after a back injury.

"Now I see where he gets it," I say, smiling at Reid again as we all stand. I watch every Sutherland around this table stack and gather their two lunch plates and their three pieces of silverware in the exact same way, and I quietly mimic it, inwardly charmed by all the tiny signs being revealed to me, all the codes that seem to lead me right to the heart of Reid, the everyday habits that help make up who he is.

It's surprising, I guess, that I haven't felt more nervous, more of an interloper here. But after last night—all my tearful revelations to Reid, all the trust I'd put in him—I get a strange sense about this visit. Maybe we both know it's all too soon, but Reid has brought me here to give me something back, some comparable level of exposure to what I gave to him. The drive would have been enough to make me feel better, more stable about what had happened with Sibby—the snacks he stopped to get me after we picked up the rental car, the way he chuckled at my pop-song singing, the lines of his face when he wears a pair of sunglasses, the hand he kept on my thigh as we sped along the highway, finding signs. But the addition of this visit has been the most tender, vulnerable offering. Reid giving me something I didn't even know I needed.

We settle in the small living room, meticulous and symmetrical, for tea. On the wall across from where I sit is a gallery of Sutherland family photos—several that show the family's growth over time, expanding by an order of small, chubby baby every other photo or so. The most recent ones are almost class-photo-like in their population—all of Reid's siblings, but also various partners and children. None of them, I notice—with a not-small amount of relief—feature Avery.

"Thomas and I both came from large families," Cynthia says to me, when she catches me looking. "I know it seemed silly, to a lot of people, that we had so many children." She hands me a cup of tea, her cheeks flushing in the exact same spot Reid's do.

"I don't think it's silly," I say, even though I definitely want to get ten extra birth-control shots at the very thought of it. "I think it looks like it would've been fun."

"Fun," Thomas says, deadpan.

Reid *swoonshes*, hides it by taking a sip of his tea.

"We always planned it," Cynthia says, sending a warning—but somehow still loving and indulgent—glance Thomas's way.

"I mean," Cady says, laughing, "*I* definitely wasn't planned."

I smile over at her. "Me neither."

"You know, what you really want to see is *this*," Cady says, leaning forward to pull a photo album from the lower shelf of the coffee table.

"Cady," Reid says.

"This is payback. Recall your visit home on the weekend of my senior prom."

Reid's face goes stern. "He needed a reminder," is all he says, stern and protective, and I feel an inconvenient pulse of desire.

Involuntarily, my eyes drift to his brow, unstitched now but still bisected by the tiny line of his mostly healed cut. He seems to notice, raising that eyebrow at me in gentle teasing, as though he can read my mind.

I turn my focus to the photo album, my face heating.

"*Anyway*," Cady says, directing her mom to sit on the other side of me. Within seconds I've set my tea down—the truth is, it still has the taste of gardening to me—and I have the photo album in my lap, Cady and Cynthia providing commentary on the assembled pictures. I try to keep my mind only on the details they're happily sharing with me, but really I'm distracted by the flush of warmth I feel at being included in this specific way, the way that says, *Welcome to our family history.*

L-I-K-E, I spell to myself, just in case.

But when Cady turns the page from the set of pictures featuring Reid as a baby, I feel my heart squeeze from the loops of that other, more-than-L-I-K-E £ I try so hard to ignore.

"Oh," I say softly, staring down at the photo in front of me.

It's Reid as a small, small boy, maybe at five or six. His cheeks are pink, his hair closer to red than the reddish-blond it is now. I can't see the blue of his eyes because he has them squeezed tightly shut, and that's because his smile is so, so big, his top and bottom baby teeth showing, bright white and even, slim spaces between them. He looks small and joyful, full of a feeling too big for his body, and in his hands he clutches a miniature chalkboard bearing his name.

Written in *bubble letters*.

"I did this for all the kids on their first day of school," Cynthia says, pointing to it. "Not very expert, compared to what you do!"

"No," I say, transfixed by the image. "It's wonderful." I can't help but laugh. "Bubble letters! It suits him."

I never would have thought it, only a couple of months ago— serious, sans serif Reid. But it *does* suit him. Here, he looks fair to bursting with happiness, the colorful straps of his little-boy backpack like banners of celebration.

"He was so excited for school," Cynthia says. "He couldn't *wait* to start."

Across the room, Reid clears his throat, and I look up to see him turning his teacup one-quarter. I remember that day in the city, another time when Reid offered something else of himself to comfort me. *I was difficult in school,* he'd said. I lower my eyes back to the picture, feeling a pang for the way this little boy's excitement was quashed by everyone who didn't try to understand him.

"He wanted to be a teacher," Cady says. "Did he tell you that?"

She doesn't say it as if it's a test, as if it's somehow the way she's going to see whether I ought to be taken seriously here as a possible girlfriend to Reid. Still, it feels important, a piece of Reid's history I've been missing.

So I look up at him, instead of answering her.

"You wanted to be a teacher?"

He shifts in his chair, that slight flush on his cheeks. "Yes." He pauses, swallows. "Later, a . . . a professor."

I notice Thomas, sitting in a chair matching Reid's, take a sip of his tea before turning his sharp-edged profile to the window. For a fleeting moment I feel a stretch of time collapse, and I'm back in that Nolita restaurant, seeing the look on Reid's face when he'd first told me about John Horton Conway and his math-making games.

"What changed?" I say.

Thomas looks back at me, the corner of his mouth twitching. For the most part, he's been polite but cautious with me today, a fact that felt, if not wholly comfortable, at least familiar. It figures that the first noticeably positive response I'd get out of him would be for asking such a direct question.

No one even tries to answer for Reid. Thomas turns his tea-cup one-quarter, a tiny clink breaking the silence.

"My math skills are better than my people skills," Reid finally says. "I wasn't very successful as a TA."

"Weren't you"—I pause, because my counting skills aren't any quicker from being in this house for a single afternoon—"nineteen when you started graduate school?"

"Eighteen," Thomas says, his voice clipped.

"I finished college in three years," Reid clarifies for me.

"So . . . probably about the same age as the students you were teaching?"

Reid shrugs. "I moved into research positions later. It was a better fit."

My eyes drift back down to the photo album in my lap, to little boy Reid and his too-big backpack and too-big smile. That bubble-lettered chalkboard clutched in his tiny hands.

"I thought he should have kept trying," says Thomas, and I look up again, noticing the stiff tension between the two of them.

"I thought I should make money," Reid replies.

"You've been there for six years," Thomas says. I think I catch something, some brief movement of his eyes down to Reid's arms, to the skin there. "You've made enough money."

I look back and forth between them, some distant awareness that I'm too invested in this to be uncomfortable about it, to feel my usual apprehension over this kind of simmering conflict. Instead I'm thinking about how odd it is—to see Reid be so stalwart about his work, about making money. In the city, with me, his disdain for both has been so pointed, so consistent. And how odd it is that Thomas seems to know nothing about what Reid has been telling me since the very first day we got reacquainted: that his time in New York—*because* of his disdain for both of these things—is nearly up.

Reid clears his throat again, and for a split second our gazes tangle, and I get that sense again. *This is for you*, his eyes tell me. *This is because I trust you, the way you trusted me.*

Maybe it's not a smiling moment, with all this tense energy in the air, but I send him a soft smile anyway. I don't bother trying to ignore the £, or what it stands for.

"Not this again," says Cady, exasperated.

"Gosh, *really*," adds Cynthia, her voice all at once annoyed and amused.

Thomas says nothing, but he does send an apologetic look Reid's way, and with that, it's over, this obviously recurring flare in their family. Nobody seems particularly bothered; nobody tries to leave the room or pick another fight. Nothing essential between them—their trust in each other, their love for each other—seems shaken, and I clutch this observation to myself, something else Reid and his family have given me today. Some knowledge, some hope that eventually, Sibby and I will be able to talk about this difficult thing between us again, and that it won't spell the end of us, the end of our friendship, the end of our chosen family.

I blink down at the photo album, collecting myself. Maybe my companions notice, but no one seems to mind. Cady simply turns the page, and Cynthia starts telling me about the next picture, and just like that, I somehow get the sense I'm now one of their number.

♥   ♥   ♥

"So, this is your bedroom."

"This is my *old* bedroom," Reid says.

We're in the finished basement of the Sutherland house, a

massive but low-ceilinged space that's partitioned off into a laundry room, a storage closet, a half bathroom, and this larger space. It's clear that it's been transformed since Reid's childhood years, now the kind of neutral guest room that seems cobbled together from old furniture and decor.

"It used to be two sets of bunk beds," he says. "A desk over there." He points to the far wall, where there's a simple dresser set beneath the one source of natural light in here, a narrow rectangle of glass block that's now, this late at night, mostly a black ripple, twinkles of light from the dim bedside lamp like stars dotting its uneven surface.

"Cozy," I say, crossing to sit on the bed, propping myself on my palms as I gently push my way to the middle of it. I lean back on my hands, my feet crossed at the ankles, and study Reid, who's still leaning in the doorway.

"You're okay," he says, "that we're staying?"

It was only meant to be a day trip, this visit. But the afternoon had stretched on, in the most natural of ways, all of us forgetting to count the minutes during tea and conversation. When talk had turned to my work, Cady had begged for me to consider designing a business card for her, a request I'd told her I didn't even need to consider, and two hours later, I'd sketched her three different treatments. I'd accepted her thrilled hug of thanks, but the real prize had been the way Reid—coming to look at the final product—had bent to press a kiss to my temple before whispering his gratitude in my ear. By then, it'd only seemed natural for Cynthia to ask us to stay for dinner, which had turned into after-dinner cleanup, which had turned into a game of gin rummy, apparently a long-held tradition in the Sutherland household.

And then it'd been so late, and Cynthia had insisted.

"Very," I say, smiling. "I've had fun."

"Good."

That single word—every time I hear it in his low voice, I'm back in his bed, beneath him, and despite the fact that his parents and his sister are in bedrooms that are only a flight of stairs and a hallway away from us, I can't help but shift restlessly now, suddenly feeling all the affectionate but chaste ways he's touched me since we walked into this house.

Something changes in Reid's eyes—some flare of heat I recognize—as he looks at me.

"You're not coming in?" I say, innocently. But I am not being innocent.

"Depends."

"On?"

"On whether you make the very poor decision to change into a pair of my sister's pajamas," he says dryly, nodding toward the neatly folded shorts-and-top set Cady had given me, along with a small tote of extra toiletries.

"Oh?" I reach out, lift up the shirt from the top of the stack. "But this tie-dye would match my eyes. Anybody's eyes, really."

He crosses the threshold, pulling the door closed behind him before he comes to me and takes the shirt gently from my hand. Then he pauses and looks at the whole stack, and in a swift movement he pushes it off the side of the bed onto the floor, dropping the shirt on top of the now-messy pile. I look down at it, then up at him, my mouth agape.

"I've never seen this side of you," I tease. "Rebellious. *Messy*, even. I think you're trying to seduce me."

He leans over me, his hands planted on either side of my hips, and gives me my favorite *one two three* kiss. When he pulls back and looks at me, his eyes dropping to my quickened pulse point, his smile is crooked, mischievous. It's his game face.

I shift again, pressing my legs together.

"It must be because I'm breaking an old rule. No girls in our bedrooms."

"Your adolescence must've been a trial," I say, leaning up to kiss his neck, sucking gently.

He nudges along my jaw so I'll tilt my head back, leaving my neck exposed to his warm kisses. "I did a lot of math in my head."

I laugh softly, my hands lifting to his sides, and for long, delicious minutes we kiss, Reid's mouth on mine hungry, his hands growing restless, impatient. But when he lowers himself onto me farther, when our hips roll to meet each other's in the rhythm we've perfected together, the bed protests, a squeak so loud it could absolutely wake the dead.

I stiffen immediately. As though I am impersonating the dead.

Game over.

Reid groans again, this time right against the skin of my neck, his body tight with frustration, and I breathe out a quiet laugh, rubbing my hands over his back, trying desperately to ignore—to not rub against—the rock-hard, denim-covered length between his legs that is still resting against a *very* sensitive place between my own. I'm concentrating on slowing my panting breaths and my quick, aroused heartbeat when he speaks again, his voice low and gruff and desperate.

"Christ, I wish we were home."

Before I can stop myself, I stiffen again, my hands on Reid's back stutter-stopping in surprise before I move them again, trying to smooth over the thrill that had gone through me at his words.

I wish we were home.

In the city.

Something in Reid's body has changed, too, and I know he's registered the shock of what he's said. The mistake he's made, calling New York *home.* After a second he moves away from me, rolling onto his back so we're side by side on the bed. The small stretch of space between us feels like miles, like the distance we traveled only this morning, or like the distance Reid will travel—wherever he goes—when this summer is over.

But then he reaches for my hand, linking our fingers together.

We stay that way for a long time.

"What my dad said before," he says finally, and I turn my face to him, gaze at his profile. "That I should have kept trying."

"Reid," I say, keeping my voice quiet to match his. "You were so young."

"I'm not anymore. I think about it, sometimes. Whether I

should try again. When all this—when I finish with everything, at my job. I have money saved. I could afford it, to . . . try."

"Being a teacher?" I say.

He nods.

"I think you'd be a great teacher. You have the best ideas. You—"

"In New York," he interrupts, and I think my hand might jerk in his, an involuntary squeeze. Never, *never* has Reid said anything even close to this. Never has New York been an option for him beyond this summer. Somehow, the fact that he's mentioning it now, here—in a home I know he misses—makes it seem so much more significant.

I swallow.

"You hate New York," I say.

"It's growing on me."

It isn't the most ringing of all endorsements, and he keeps his eyes up on the ceiling, his face set in concentration, as though he's trying to work out the most difficult problem. As though it's full of numbers up there, and he's searching for an impossible solution.

I turn my face up to that blank space, too. I think about walking with Reid in the city. He's eased up, sure. He still loves the food and I think he's come to appreciate the signs, too. But I haven't forgotten the way his jaw clenches in the crowds, his irritation in the city's loudest, brightest spaces.

"You have to love it," I say cautiously, not wanting to hope. Not wanting to push, not this time. Not about this. "I think you have to love it to stay."

I see my words float up to the place where we're both staring. It wouldn't be difficult at all, to hide something in them. It's all there, after all, everything I'm not really saying, everything I've been trying not to let myself think.

The *I*, the *love*, the *you*. The *stay*.

I feel him turn his head toward me. "I love things about it," he says.

I take a deep breath and tear my eyes away from the ceiling, from my imaginary letters. I look at him, and I remember what he told me that night in the bar, that he doesn't always say what he means.

But neither of us says it. Neither of us says what I hope we're both thinking, what I hope is written on both of our hearts.

"It's soon," I say instead.

He nods again. "And I don't know if I can stay."

We leave it at that for a while, the suburban quiet all around us, our hands still intertwined. I think I can feel Reid's mind turning and turning. I think I can feel him tensing up, trying to solve this.

Getting blocked.

"Reid," I whisper, tugging on his hand. "You want to play a game?"

He looks over at me. He's got a trace of the sad eyes, but he *swoonshes* anyway.

"I already beat you twice at gin rummy," he says.

I scoot down the bed, standing at the foot of it. I pull on his hand and he doesn't resist. He sits up, and now I'm facing him, looking down at him. I take a step back, pulling my shirt over my head, tossing it on the heap of discarded pajamas. Next, my bra.

Reid's breath catches as he watches me.

"What are the rules?" he says, his voice rough.

I undo the button on my jeans. "Sit," I say, nodding toward the carpeted floor.

He stands first, pulling off his shirt. I see the bulge in his jeans, and I wonder if he's not going to play by the rules. I wonder if he's going to walk forward, if he's going to press me against the door at my back. Honestly, that would be fine, too—I've already learned, in the shower last week, that Reid does good work standing up—but I want to be in charge of this game.

After a beat, he follows my directions.

I slide my jeans and underwear down my legs.

"The game is we stay quiet," I whisper, stepping in the space between his stretched-out legs. "We don't make a sound. We don't say anything."

Anything like *I love you.*

Anything like *Stay.*

I lower myself onto him, straddling his lap, reaching between us to unbutton his jeans, to slide down his zipper. I watch him the whole time, and he's clenched his mouth shut, the muscles on either side of his jaw ticking in concentration. He's already playing.

He won't say a word.

He lifts his hips and I lean forward, my hands going to the edge of the bed to steady myself while he shoves down his jeans, pulls a condom from his wallet. I take it from him, tearing it open and fitting it over his length, and he tips his head back, closing his eyes and clenching his fists when I stroke him once. When I release him, he moves his hands, one settling at my waist to keep me raised above him, one moving between my thighs to touch me in the way that gets me wet, that gets me close.

But I stop him, pulling his hand away, keeping it locked with mine. I look down at him and shake my head. Then I move my other hand and stroke him again, once, before lowering myself onto him, a slow stretch that would've gone easier had I let him keep touching me. But I want it, this stretch, this patient accommodation my body has to make to his. I like how much work it takes to stay quiet; I like the silent signs we have to send each other—a hand I rest on his shoulder to tell him I need to go slow, a hand he moves to my lower back, urging me to tip forward for a better angle.

When he's fully inside of me, we breathe in sync, a warm relief between us, but at the first move of our bodies the bed protests again, this time a quiet *thunk* against the wall it's pushed up against, and both of us still, our eyes locked. This time, we're not stopping; I can tell by the way Reid looks at me, hot and focused and determined. His arm tightens low around my back, and he shifts us forward so his back isn't against the bed.

And with that move, everything is different, the first time we've ever had sex this way—no leverage at his back or mine, nothing to hold on to but each other. It's an effort, more so because we're playing by the rules, staying silent. We go slow—so, so slow—small pulses of his hips up to thrust into me, measured rocking of my hips in his lap to get the friction I need. I don't know how long it takes, because neither of us is marking the time, keeping track. It feels like floating, like being untethered.

Like writing without letters.

Like counting without numbers.

It feels like love.

And even when it reaches its peak—when I breathe through my slow, shuddering climax against his neck, when he grips me tighter and stiffens through his, when we clutch at each other in the aftermath with some new, shocked awareness between us . . .

Even then, neither of us breaks the rules.

Chapter 17

Lark is speechless.

In the back of the shop, Lark sits with the planner I've finished for her open on the table, her eyes tracking over the pages she turns slowly, carefully. I've looked at what's in those pages dozens of times myself over the last few days, so mostly I watch her face as she experiences it—the pastels I've chosen, mostly pinks and greens, the occasional rose gold accents. The small, wide-set, lowercase scripts that unfurl across the headers, and the narrow, close-set, all-caps sans serif that marks out the days. The delicate illustrations that dot the corners of some of the pages—a tiny splash of starbursts here, a single flower in a simple bud vase there. All of it is quiet, understated. Sweet and soft but also sturdy and sophisticated.

"This is very . . ." she begins finally, touching her finger to the corner of one page. "This is so . . . me," she finishes, a note of wonder in her voice.

I smile, relieved. "I'm so glad. That's what I was going for."

A few weeks ago, I might not have been able to design a

planner that was this right for Lark. But since that day at my apartment, a lot has changed between us. Sure, she's not yet up for coffee shop visits, but she will go on the occasional walk—half-planned tours through parts of Brooklyn that even I don't get to all that often. Sometimes I tell her things about the neighborhoods, about clients I have in various spots around town; sometimes she tells me things about LA or about the actors she's known and worked with. We talk occasionally about the job—the walls that she's *still* not ready for me to start on—but mostly we simply get to know each other in the kind of tentative, non-heavy-topics way of a new friendship. For the most part, she avoids bringing up the living land mine that is Cameron, who's been in and out of town on location shoots, but I notice the way her mood fluctuates according to his movements—she's lighter, more talkative, more adventurous when he's gone.

It's been good to have the company, because the relationship between me and Lark isn't the only thing that's changed since I got back from Maryland with Reid. First of all, Sibby's gone, moved in to her new apartment with Elijah, her last day at home over a week ago now. When I'd come back that Sunday, flushed with all the feelings for Reid I was no longer ignoring, Sibby was home, waiting for me. And I could tell that she'd practiced, the same way I had. "Meggie," she'd said, using her long-dormant nickname for me, "I didn't mean what I said, bringing up your family that way."

"I know you didn't," I'd answered, and I'd meant it. I'd forgiven Sibby even before I'd gotten all the way across the Bridge that night we'd fought, but forgiveness didn't really fix what was wrong between us. She may not have meant it, about my family, but she *had* meant everything else. And that meant the only kind of fighting I could do, the only kind of practice that would help her, was the kind where I gave her the time and space away from me that she'd wanted, until she was ready—*really* ready—to talk again. She'd seemed relieved, for those last few days of being my roommate, that we could play polite for the time being, that I was willing not to press it. On move-out day,

I'd helped her carry the last few boxes down to the rental truck Elijah had waiting at the curb, and we'd hugged each other tight, both of us holding back tears.

"It'll be better, Meggie," she'd said, and I'd nodded my chin against her shoulder, hoping she was right.

I'd gone back upstairs to my echoing apartment, but only briefly. Maybe it would've been the braver thing, to stay there alone that first night, but instead I'd packed a bag and gone to Reid's, using the key he'd given me. I'd stayed up late, working on my final Make It Happyn sketches while sitting on his terrible couch, hoping he might get home before eleven.

Because that—Reid working with this fixed, flared intensity— that is the other thing that's changed since Maryland. In some ways, it's as if he and I are still playing by the rules I set that night in the basement. We don't say anything about New York, about him staying. We don't wonder aloud about whether it's too soon, whether it's even possible. But clearly, something has shifted for Reid, and it doesn't matter that I see him less lately while he keeps these long hours.

Because I know that this shift is, at least in part, about me. About us.

"I have to see this through," he tells me, late at night, holding me close. "And then . . ."

But he always trails off, the game still in play. It's just that now, the game seems more serious between us than ever.

"Hey, ladies," Lachelle says, coming into the back room and setting her bag on the chair next to me. That must mean it's close to Lachelle's four o'clock client meeting, and also close to when I need to get on the subway.

"Look what Meg finished," Lark says, turning the planner toward Lachelle. They're kind of an odd pair, Lark and Lachelle, but each time Lark comes to the shop, Lachelle always gives her a warm, teasing welcome—calling her princess and asking her about her throwing arm.

"Ooooh," Lachelle says, leaning down. "This is so you!"

"That's what I said, too!" Lark says, delighted. "Meg, I want you to do one of these for my sister. She—"

"Nuh-uh," says Lachelle. She hooks a thumb at me as though she's my first base coach. "This woman has a *very important* deadline in two days. Nothing until that's over."

"Oh, that's right," Lark says, because now she knows about my deadline, too. "Well, after—"

"Actually," I say proudly, "I'm finished. I scanned all the sketches this morning. They're ready to go."

It's so hard to believe my pitch is almost here. When I think about where I was this spring, how utterly blocked I was, how different things were—it's a miracle I've actually got something to present. Something I'm so proud of. Like Reid, I've been working hard, too, more determined than ever to succeed at this pitch, as though getting it is somehow just as important for him, for us, to stay.

"Cough 'em up," says Lachelle, holding out a palm. "I want to see what you decided about the colors for the tree stuff."

I wave a hand. "They're back at home. I want you to see it all together. We're still on for the run-through tomorrow?"

"For sure," Lachelle says. "You should come, princess. Cecy and I are going to set it up back here like a conference room. Meg's going to do the whole thing."

"Really?" Lark looks back and forth between us. "That would be okay?"

"Absolutely," I say, still struck by Lark's insecurity, the way she's always worried about her welcome somewhere. "The more the merrier."

"Bring your boyfriend," Lachelle says, nudging my shoulder with her hip. "I'm dying to meet him. I'm definitely going to ask him about the marginal tax rate."

I laugh, but feel a thread of discomfort. I need to tell Cecelia and Lachelle about Reid, about how I met him. But I've been putting it off, and whether that's because I'm still ashamed about what I'd done that had brought him back in here, or because I'm worried that Reid and I won't make it past this summer—that's a mystery that's hidden even from me.

"He'll probably have to work." And anyway, he's seen them all already. When we're together, I show him the latest. When we're not, I snap photos and send them to his phone. No matter how busy he gets, he's always interested.

"Capitalism," Lachelle says, shaking her head. Then she peeks out to the front of the store, spotting her clients talking with Cecelia. "All right, get out, you two. I have money to make."

Lark and I both laugh, scrambling dramatically to pick up our things. On our way out, I wave at Cecelia, who's still chatting with Lachelle's clients, but she pauses long enough to mouth, *Tomorrow?* at me, and she gives me a thumbs-up when I nod.

"They're so nice," Lark says, when we're out on the sidewalk. I open my mouth to agree, but she speaks again. "I've been wondering if I should think about going back to work, you know?"

"Yeah?" I know my eyebrows are probably halfway up my head. Lark *never* talks about working as though it's something she's planning to do again. It's always about past projects, past goals she's set aside. Scripts Cameron doesn't like for her.

"I used to love being on set. I loved being around people."

"I think you should go back, too, if you want to. You're so talented."

She gives me her closemouthed smile. "You think?"

"Please. It wasn't our favorite movie for nothing," I say, ignoring the twinge I feel at having repeated Sibby's words. "Why not call your agent?"

"Maybe," she says, but she looks unsure.

On impulse, I reach a hand out, palm up, same as Lachelle. I look meaningfully at the planner Lark's still holding against her chest. When she hands it over, I shove a hand in my bag, come up with one of the Microns littering the bottom. I flip open the cover, page to tomorrow's spread. *Call agent*, I write, then hand it back to her.

"Great," she says, in that sarcastic way she sometimes has. "My handwriting is going to look like garbage in here now."

I snort a laugh, tucking my pen away.

"You're a good friend, Meg," she says. And then she reaches out her arm and pulls me into a hug.

For a second, my twinge becomes a full-fledged ache of sadness, thinking of Sibby—how we haven't been such good friends to each other lately, and how much I still miss her.

But Lark's hug is a comfort, a hope, like a lot of things I have in my life these days. I squeeze her back.

"Okay," she says, when we pull away. "You're going to meet your beau, yes?"

"Yes," I say, my face heating. "He works late, so we're going to have a quick dinner break."

"Ugh," Lark says genially. "You two."

I smile, my face flushing, liking the sound of that particular number.

Hoping I can keep counting on it.

♥ ♥ ♥

I meet Reid at South Street Seaport, the same place he once ducked away to find a set of letters to photograph for me to tell me about his day. This time of year, when the whole city is thick with tourists, it's probably more crowded than it was on that long-ago evening. It's been a gorgeous day, too—not too warm, a breeze off the water, and the sun is still out—so there's probably a higher-than-average turnout of city dwellers here, too.

That long-ago evening and what Reid spelled out to me that night—*TENSE*—makes me expect to find him in the same state, especially given the crowds, but I'm pleasantly surprised to find that he's not. When he finds me at our agreed-upon spot along one of the piers, he's got his white shirtsleeves rolled up, his tie shoved messily in his pocket, and he leans down to give me a soft kiss on the mouth before pulling back and looking over my maxi dress.

"Cute," he says, setting his forefinger to one of the tiny peaches patterned across it, but really he's looking at the expanse of skin—my shoulders, my chest—revealed by its thin straps.

"Good day?" I say, as we head toward a taqueria nearby. Reid doesn't seem to notice the clumps of people who occasionally get in our way; he moves us deftly through them, our hands linked together. I try to suppress the kind of stirring optimism I seem to call up whenever I see Reid act this comfortable, unbothered way somewhere in the city. I look for signs in everything—signs he's starting to do more than tolerate it, signs that he thinks of it as a possible home.

"Busy," he says mildly. "Still a lot to do."

"That sucks," I say, but he only shrugs.

"It may not be much longer until I can—well, until I finish up."

"Yeah?"

"Yes," he says, looking down at me as we get into a long line. He clears his throat. "I think—well, they're bringing in some new people. That ought to take some of the load off."

"Money people or math people?"

He *swooshes*. "Too soon to tell, I guess." He opens his mouth to say something else, then closes it. "How'd it go with Lark?" he finally asks, when he speaks again.

He's done this a lot lately, these not-subtle shifts away from saying too much about this project he's on, the one he's trying so hard to finish up. It'd bother me, maybe, under any other circumstance, but I think Reid is trying, as best he can, to protect me. To not get my hopes up about this, about his future plans. About whether he'll be able to stay.

So I indulge him, hoping for the best. I tell him about the planner and about the new plan for her to come see my rehearsal pitch tomorrow. He looks full of regret when I tell him Lachelle invited him along, but I promise I'll do the whole thing for him another time. We order food and find a spot outside to enjoy it, Reid still managing to eat with a napkin draped tidily over his lap, as though the breeze that keeps blowing mine away doesn't even bother trying it with him. He shows me a picture on his phone that came through earlier, his brother Owen and his young daughter Rae at a Brownie event, and I make him, not for the first time, remind me about the names of all his nieces and nephews.

When we're finished, he pitches our trash and comes back to sit beside me, draping an arm along the back of the bench, his hand tucking under the messy length of my haphazard ponytail to rest on the nape of my neck. He makes a low hum of disapproval when he squeezes there, and maybe it's wrong, out here in the open air, but I hear it as if it's a bedroom sound.

"Meg," he says, his voice stern. Bedroom stern. "You need to stretch more."

A common refrain these last few weeks, when he finds me hunched over my sketches. I purse my lips and reach a hand out, stroking my thumb under the soft, darkened skin beneath one of his eyes.

"You need to sleep more," I say. I like this, how this is—it's a real *you two* moment, two people taking care of each other, counting on each other.

He lowers his hand a couple of inches, presses his fingers into some of the tightest muscles. I wish I could say I made a bedroom sound in response, but my grunt of pleasure-pain probably sounds more like I'm changing a tire.

He chuckles.

"Finish early tonight," I say. "I'll let you give me a massage. I'll give you one back."

He looks over at me, his mouth crooking. "It's tempting," he says. But then he looks away from me, out into the crowd of people milling around. "I do have to go back, though."

I sigh, disappointed but understanding. I'll go back to Brooklyn tonight; I'll keep practicing my pitch. I'll see Reid tomorrow, maybe, or this weekend, after the pitch is done. No matter how it goes, I want to celebrate it with him. After all, it's his games that helped me get started on it in the first place.

He leans in, presses a kiss to my mouth. "Soon," he says, even though these days it all feels not soon enough.

"Okay," I say, standing and shaking out my dress. I set my hands on my hips and look back at him. "Well, at least let me get an ice-cream cone first."

The whole trip out here feels more than worth it to see Reid's expression when I order something called a Salty Pimp, a caramel-vanilla soft serve dunked in chocolate. It's a mess to eat, absolutely a disaster in the warmer weather, and every three licks or so, as we walk in the direction of his office, I hold it out to him and offer him a bite, even though I know he's never going to take one.

"Man, you're missing out," I say teasingly, delighting in his smiling refusal before taking another sloppy lick. We're close to our destination now, and I'm pretty sure I have some chocolate at the corner of my mouth, but there doesn't seem to be a whole lot of point in getting it now. Best wait until the cone is finished, and anyway, however much Reid doesn't eat sweets himself, he seems to love watching me have them, and I want to lighten his mood as much as possible before he has to go back to work. "After those spicy tacos? I can't believe you—"

I stop myself, feeling Reid's posture change beside me, a straightening that puts a slice of space between us. I look up at him, notice that his face has lost all the softness of before as he looks straight ahead. He is *Masterpiece Theatre* Reid. Many-months-ago Reid.

I follow his eyes.

For a good five seconds—five this-feels-like-being-buried-alive seconds—not a single one of us in this terrible eye-contact triangle moves.

Avery Coster looks exactly the way I remember her—beautiful and composed, but not cold or distant. Everything she's wearing looks plain but also deeply expensive: a lightweight cream sweater, a pair of cropped, dove-gray pants, pale-pink slides that don't—in spite of where she's standing right this second—look like they've ever seen the surface of a New York City street. Either she just had a blowout or she has made a deal with a being from the underworld in exchange for her mortal soul.

Reid clears his throat, and all of us take a step forward, as though we've all simply accepted that this isn't allowed to be only an eye-contact meeting.

"Meg," Reid says. "You remember Avery."

I say *nothing*. I don't even nod and smile. I am absolutely shocked; I feel as though I've walked into another dimension. In this particular dimension the hemline of your dress is wasted with city street dirt and you can't remember when you washed your hair last and there's a high-calorie dessert called a

Salty Pimp running down your left hand when you run into—
in a city of almost *two million people!*—the ex-fiancée of the man
you're currently sleeping with.

This dimension is called *Absolute Bullshit.*

"Hi!" I blurt, happy to at least have recovered my powers of
speech. "Yes, of course I remember. Hi."

Not great powers, alas.

"Meg," Avery says politely, her eyes *not once* looking at my ice-
cream cone. "It's very nice to see you again."

It doesn't sound chilly, or false. It sounds . . . *nice.* As though
she doesn't mind running into Reid at all. As though she doesn't
mind running into him with me, a woman who designed the invitation for her wedding—*their* wedding—that never happened.
If she was uncomfortable or surprised at first, that seems to
have entirely faded away.

"Oh! Oh, same. It's great to see you, too."

"Business is good?"

"Yeah, it's great. Thank you."

She gives me a genuine nod, a genuine smile. "That's wonderful. So many of my friends were so disappointed that you
got out of the wedding business before they had their big days.
Please reach out if you're ever back in it."

I blink in surprise, feel another trickle of cold soft serve slide
between my fingers. Now that the initial shock has worn off, I'm
relieved. Relieved and . . . reminded, I guess. This is awkward,
but it's not awful. I *like* Avery. I liked her when she was my client.
I don't have any reason not to like her now, and I don't have any
reason to have the kind of frantic, fight-or-flight response I'm
trying to get better at ignoring whenever things get tense.

"I will, absolutely." But deep down, I know I won't. I'm out of
the wedding business. I know how good those sketches I'm going to present are. I know, somewhere in my bones, that I'm on
the cusp of something brand new.

Avery turns her head toward Reid now. "I wondered why you
weren't at the office," she says, her voice friendly. "I stopped in
to see my father."

There's a too-long pause, and for the first time I shift my

eyes to look up at him, too. I don't know what I expect to see—maybe a version of the set, vacant mask he had before, the one he gets when he's uncomfortable. Maybe something closer to her expression—something warm and unbothered, the face you'd expect to see on half of a couple who split amicably, mutually, in all the ways that Reid said.

I don't expect him to look so . . .

So *wrecked.*

My stomach swoops and turns. My eyes dart around the sidewalk, desperate for a trash can, where I can get rid of this Salty Pimp. It's possible I'll never eat an ice-cream cone again.

Reid is still looking at Avery as though he's seen a ghost.

The most beautiful, powerful ghost.

He blinks, clears his throat again. "I stepped out for a dinner break," he says, as though he owes her an explanation.

She smiles. "Good for you. You always had terrible work-life balance."

He still does! I want to say, but that, of course, is ridiculous. This isn't a women-who've-dated-Reid street fair. I stay quiet, clutching my cone. I have never felt more out of place in my whole life, and given my personal history, that is really saying something.

"I still do," he says, his voice grim.

Avery rolls her eyes. "That's Daddy's influence on you."

Reid's Adam's apple bobs with a heavy swallow.

"Yes," is all he says.

Avery looks back and forth between us, entirely unbothered. "Well, good to see you both," she says, stepping toward the curb, where a dark sedan I didn't even see waits for her. She's already half-hidden behind the door being held open for her when Reid manages to speak again.

"Yes," he repeats. "You as well."

I step away from him when the car pulls away, spotting a trash can where I can finally pitch the cursed ice-cream cone. My hand is still sticky and damp, and with my clean one I reach into my bag, digging for hand sanitizer. *Give him a second,* I think to myself. *Of course he would feel uncomfortable. They were going to be* married, *after all.* I think of Sibby's cutting words, reminding me that not everything is some big scandal.

Maybe I don't press on this one. Maybe I give it time.

"Meg," he says, coming to stand beside me while I needlessly shake my tiny bottle of all-this-is-going-to-do-is-move-the-soft-serve-*around*-your-hands hand sanitizer.

I give him a toothy, false smile. I'm so out of practice that it feels unfamiliar on my face, more of a grimace. He's not even pretending. He looks as shocked, as upset as he looked only a few minutes ago.

"Are you all right?" I ask him.

"I'm fine." But as with my grimace-smile, it's not all that convincing. "I hadn't expected to see her."

"Well," I say brightly. "Her dad *does* work here."

I see him swallow again. "Yes."

Both of us step out of the way of a group of pedestrians. We are in the worst possible spot, doing the worst possible thing, blocking foot traffic. We've gotten so good at not doing that together, whenever we're on our walks. Nothing feels *fine.* Least of all, Reid.

"Hey. You want to walk some more? You seem—"

"I'm fine," Reid repeats. Then he looks down at me, his gaze softening. "It was a shock, that's all. Perhaps she . . ." He trails off, reaches to tug at cuffs that aren't rolled down. He looks even more bereft not to have found them at his wrists, where he expected them. "Perhaps she changed her hair."

I furrow my brow. Avery's hair looked the same as always. Which is to say, it looked perfect.

I have never seen Reid this lost. This indirect. This . . . dishonest.

"Listen, Reid, I'm sure that was—"

"I should get back in there." He starts unrolling his cuffs, folding them back down over his taut forearms. "I probably—I should get back in."

"Sure, okay. But we can talk about this later, if you want. I can go back to your place, wait for you there? I brought work with me, and—"

Reid clears his throat, buttons one of those cuffs. "I'll be late."

"Okay." I wait for a few seconds, watching him. Wondering if he'll add something. If he'll say, *But yes, wait for me there.*

He doesn't.

"I'll call you," he says instead. Then he meets my eyes with his own, and with one blink he eliminates the sadness I know I saw there. Now he looks blank, entirely unmoved. "Do you want me to get you a car?"

"No, I'll be . . . um, fine."

I almost walk away. But before I go, Reid catches my hand, pulls me toward him. When he's got me close he wraps his arm around my lower back, gathering me against him, something desperate in his hold, something reminiscent of that night in his old bedroom. He has to lean down to put his mouth close to my ear.

"I'm sorry," he says, so quiet that I have to strain to hear him. "Thank you for coming here. For having dinner with me."

I pull back, setting a hand against his cheek and looking into his eyes. They're all mixed up now. Part sad, part sorry. I try to put a question in mine.

"We'll talk about it," he says. "I promise. But I have to get back in there."

I nod and smile, press my mouth to his in a brief kiss. It should make me feel better, I guess, that he acknowledged it. I'm giving it time; he's giving it time. It's *not* a scandal. It's only something uncomfortable, something he maybe needs to work through on his own. And he did promise to talk about it.

But when I finally walk away, I have the most sinking, unpleasant feeling.

I have the feeling that I can't count on that promise at all.

Chapter 18

On Friday afternoon, I'm sitting on a cushy love seat outside of a rented conference room inside a huge, swanky Midtown hotel. Behind a set of double doors across from me, nine members of the Make It Happyn creative team are apparently settling back in after a long lunch they've taken, having heard two other pitches this morning. When I'd arrived fifteen minutes ago, checking in with the front desk per the e-mailed instructions I'd received last week, a hotel staffer had made a quick phone call, and within minutes I was being greeted by a young, energetic assistant named Daniel, who'd updated me on "the team's" morning while escorting me to my waiting spot. Daniel had offered me coffee or tea or Pellegrino, as well as a sleek promotional booklet about Make It Happyn's parent company, a Florida-based crafting retailer that mass-produces everything from yarn to scrapbooking tools to jewelry-making supplies. Daniel had called me "Miss Mackworth" three separate times and had also told me he was "rooting" for me, though something tells me he might've said the same thing to the other two artists who were apparently here before me.

I take a deep breath, trying to ignore the nagging feeling that I don't belong here, that something's off.

I should be feeling one hundred percent confident. In the portfolio resting beside me are my originals, ready to be displayed on the conference table, the same way I'd done yesterday during my practice run in the cozy familiarity of the shop. On top is my tablet and the adapter I purchased especially for this, ready for the projector I'd gotten an e-mail confirmation about two days ago from a Make It Happyn assistant (who was not Daniel). On my body is a trendy, dark denim A-line dress, accessorized with a sunny yellow belt and brushed-gold bangles on my wrist, hoops in my ears. And most importantly, in my head is the pitch itself, practiced and refined, praised by my small audience of friends in the shop.

But something *is* off.

Not for the first time today, I'm tempted to break a promise to myself, to pull out my phone and check my messages. But over the last two days, ever since South Street Seaport, all it's been is a distraction, a preoccupation, almost a compulsion. I've been checking it too regularly, staring at the messages from one particular person, looking for something hidden in the bland, polite words that have come through.

I'm sorry I didn't have time to call
I'm headed in early this morning
I have to be here late again

Each time I've gotten one, I've felt a creeping sense of dread, familiar to me from months of similar polite brush-offs from Sibby. I cling to the two phone calls Reid and I have had in between these messages—one yesterday afternoon right after my practice run, and one at 7:05 this morning, precisely five minutes after my alarm had gone off. During both, he'd told me how sorry he is for having to work. He'd told me he misses me. He'd asked if I was ready, if I was nervous, if I'd been stretching. He'd deflected when I'd asked him if he was all right. "Busy," he'd said. "Tired."

Last night, when I'd been doing a final run-through alone in my apartment, my intercom had buzzed, and my heart had skipped a beat in hopeful excitement. But it'd only been a delivery—a dozen yellow roses, a card with unrecognizable handwriting. *Meg*, it had read, in the messy script of some flower shop employee. *You're ready for this. We'll celebrate your pitch tomorrow, I promise. —Reid*

But I'm not reassured about that promise. We still haven't gotten to the other one, after all.

I'd tossed the card, kept the flowers.

Nothing's off, I reassure myself, plaiting my fingers in my lap. *You* are *ready for this. You want this. Don't get distracted. Don't let yourself get blocked.*

I concentrate on my breathing, counting out my exhales. Briefly, I close my eyes, taking Cecelia's suggestion from yesterday that I visualize myself in the room, presenting confidently.

"Meg?" a woman's voice says before I get all that far in my visualization.

The dark-haired woman who's come to get me introduces herself as Ivonne, my first contact with Make It Happyn, and she is as bold and vibrant in person as her voice was on the phone. Her summery dress is patterned all over with bright pink flowers; her high heels—which add four inches to her petite frame—match. She seems *thrilled* to finally meet me, and I get a jolt of you-don't-have-to-visualize-it confidence.

And the mood in the conference room is similarly welcoming. I miss the natural light of the shop, miss being surrounded by my friends and the beautiful, comforting tools of my trade, but the team is talkative as I set up, all of them complimenting me on my work, my social media. Within minutes my originals are spread out on the table, each one covered with a matte black sheet of paper, which I'll ask members of the team to reveal as I move through the presentation I'll be projecting on the screen. The scans are good, but it's not the same as seeing them on paper.

And then I begin.

I do it exactly as I rehearsed yesterday, introducing myself and my city walk-inspired pitch. I start with the vintage-inspired treatment, lettering for the headers like old signs, the colors muted and sometimes patchy, a faded effect that took forever to get exactly right. Then the trees—my lovely, gorgeous trees— branches and leaves growing across the pages, complemented by small, simple serifs that don't steal the focus. The final reveal is my favorite, my most recent addition, designed and refined over the last two weeks or so, when Reid's long hours had me longing for those not-too-warm spring days of walking. Each month a secret, subtle tribute to a different neighborhood we'd walked together, lettering inspired by its architecture or its attitude, lightly drawn lines linking one page to the next, as though they are train routes or street grids on a map. Maybe you'd see it if you knew New York, maybe you wouldn't. But every page is unique, and each time you turn one, you feel as if you've genuinely *moved*. You're in a whole new place, but some- how, you're still in the same general space.

When I did this pitch in front of Cecelia, Lachelle, and Lark, their faces had been a blend of pride and awe, big *ooh*s and *aah*s when I'd change the slide, when I'd cue them to reveal a sketch. Cecelia, in particular, had wiped her eyes when I finished, had told me how proud she was of how much I'd grown, how much my art had developed.

I get it, that the Make It Happyn folks have to be more cir- cumspect, but I'm not all that far in when I see the mood in the room shifting, when I notice a few cocked heads, a few fur- rowed brows. At first, I check my visuals—is the projector work- ing right, are the sketches turned the right way, did anything get damaged?

But everything looks exactly the way I intended it to.

So something is *definitely* off.

"What excites me about these sketches," I say, moving into the final part of my presentation, "is that they tell more than a color story, or a seasonal story, or the occasional holiday story. They're cohesive, gender neutral, and—"

"Miss Mackworth," a man in one of the corner seats inter- rupts, and I swallow, feeling a fresh wave of nerves. I clutch at my tiny projector remote like it's a lifeline.

"Yes?"

"These are beautiful pieces, and your talent is clear. But I think I speak for everyone when I say that what you've presented us with here is surprising, given the work we're used to seeing on your website and social media."

"Bill," says Ivonne, her tone warning. But when she looks back at me and smiles, there's a gentle encouragement there that seems condescending. "Go ahead and finish, Meg," she says, as though the rest is a formality, or a generosity. *She came all this way,* her tone seems to say.

I look back and forth between them, and for a second my old instinct comes roaring back—to smooth this over, to placate. To continue on as though I haven't noticed anything at all is uncomfortable here.

But I'm going to fight for this work.

I turn my head to the projector screen, feign a few seconds of contemplation, as if Bill has revealed a great mystery about my own work to me.

"Actually, that's a great point, Bill. This is very different from what I've been doing with my custom planners. I'm known for . . . something more traditionally whimsical, you might mean?"

He tips his head in acknowledgment, and a few of his colleagues nod in agreement, too.

"I absolutely could have produced those kinds of treatments for you, and it would have fit in really nicely with your existing lines. But I think if you're making an investment in creators, you want their lines to stand out from what you have. When Ivonne first called me for this opportunity, I studied what you have on the shelves, and it's beautiful, and functional. And these days, it's also the same kind of work you can see on hundreds of hand-lettering accounts all over social media, by amateurs and professionals alike. What was most exciting about this opportunity for me"—I break off, laughing a little at myself—"well, once I got over a *tiny* bit of creative block—was the thought that my version of a line could offer something new. Something that's accessible to everyone, but also something that's uniquely me. And since these lines are based on creator names, this seemed like the right direction to take."

I take a breath when I finish, noticing that Bill doesn't look all that impressed with my answer. Ivonne is making some notes, though whether that's a good sign or not, I can't quite tell. Some of the others at the table are looking again at the sketches, and I can only hope they're seeing them with new eyes.

I get a few questions, most of which seem pretty generic, and a light round of applause. Ivonne stands to thank me, shaking my hand and telling me how glad she is I came in, how talented I am.

But she doesn't say that I'll be hearing from her.

It doesn't truly hit me until I walk out—that heart-sinking feeling that it didn't go well at all. They wanted flowers and fairies, more brush-lettering, more *Bloom Where You're Planteds*. The other night, talking to Avery during that awkward run-in, I'd felt so sure of myself, so sure I was on the brink of something, so proud of the way I'd pushed myself to create something new, so pleased with the sketches I'd produced.

But now I feel close to the way I did in those moments right after—when I'd finally looked up at Reid and seen the expression on his face. It's part disappointment, part foreboding. It's the sense that I've read everything wrong, that I've misunderstood.

Make It Happyn didn't want something new, something that required my creativity. All they wanted was more of the same, and I blew it.

I keep my head up as I walk to the hotel lobby, refusing to crumple, even though I've got *real* crumply thoughts, my impending covering-the-rent problem being the most immediate. I'll need to add planner clients, and soon. I'll need to think about hours at the shop, maybe. It would help if Lark would want to move on the wall commissions, though God knows I'm not going to press it. I duck into a bathroom to change into flats before braving the trip home, and notice my hands shaking with adrenaline. It seems fair enough to break my promise to myself now, since the pitch is over. I root inside my bag for my phone.

As soon as I tap the home button, all I see is stacked notifications. Three voice mails, over a dozen texts.

All from Reid.

Reid, who knows where I've been this afternoon. Reid, who would never want to interrupt.

Immediately, I feel sick with worry.

And as soon as I start reading, I see I have every reason to.

♥ ♥ ♥

This city loves a scandal.

And as scandals go, the Coster Capital investment securities fraud is a big one.

It all started to unravel this morning, apparently. 9:36 a.m., if you wanted to be precise about it, and the newspapers, at least about this, certainly seem to want to be. That's when the FBI, along with members of the New York City Business Integrity Commission, entered the building where Reid has been employed for the last six years. Within two hours, they had seized every single computer from the company's three-floor office space. They had also boxed up every single piece of paper in Alistair Coster's office, as well as every single piece of paper in the office of his long-serving assistant. They had taken photographs; they had posted notices to the office's sleek double-entry glass doors. For all of that time, Mr. Coster—one of the city's most successful businessmen and one of its most generous philanthropists—had been allowed to wait in a conference room with two FBI agents, so long as he did not attempt interactions with any of his employees.

And then he was marched, in handcuffs, out the front doors, only a few steps away from where I'd stood two nights prior.

Where I'd stood talking to his daughter.

It isn't the first time, of course, that some high-flier finance guy in Manhattan has gone down for fraud. In fact, I'm pretty sure it isn't even the first time this year. But the Coster story has a lot to recommend it, even for people who don't know anything about the numbers, even for people who find it difficult to understand the complicated financial scheme that's apparently been defrauding investors for over a decade, lining the Coster family pockets in the meantime.

No, you could get interested in the Coster scandal even if you don't know what "futures" are, even if you've never heard of "blue chip" stocks, even if your financial experience is limited to balancing your own checkbook.

You could get interested because of Reid Sutherland.

His name is everywhere, and not just on my phone.

Meg, his first voice mail had said. *Please, call me.*

Meg, said the second, his voice quieter, more strained. *Something unexpected has happened. If you could call me, before you look at the news today.*

The third hadn't bothered with my name. Reid spoke quickly, almost in desperation. *I may not have access to my phone for some time,* he'd said, as though he was seconds away from this particular fate, as though he was holding up a finger to someone trying to take it from him. *But I will explain this to you. I promise*—that's three promises, now—*I will explain it.*

His texts had been more of the same—desperate in tone, but pointedly vague, revealing nothing more than his hope to speak with me, his concern over my seeing the news, his warning that he might be unreachable.

And because he is, in fact, unreachable—my hands shake each time I try to get ahold of him—I have to rely on the other places where I can find his name.

In the initial stories—the ones I missed when the news was breaking—Reid Sutherland is little more than a principled drone, a Coster employee who noticed something suspicious and quietly reported it. In those stories, Reid's name is small, easy to scroll past if you were so inclined. It's embedded—in tiny, unremarkable, roman fonts—in long columns of impenetrable detail about Coster and his scheme. Unless you knew him—unless your heart was pounding in shock and confusion for yourself and worry and fear for him—you might forget Reid Sutherland's name altogether.

But as the story unfolds, you can see the letters stretch to fit him; you can see the moment the press learned that he was more to Coster than an employee. One sub-headline teases it in bold, brutal type:

Whistleblower Sutherland Almost Married into Coster Family

After that, Reid is everywhere, an unforgettable part of the scandal, packaged for easy consumption by a media machine looking for a more click-worthy angle than the incomprehensible numbers. A one-time child prodigy who kept himself separate from his coworkers, most of whom thought him stern, humorless, distant. A brilliant analyst who'd risen in the ranks quickly, eventually spending eleven surprising months (some coworkers had taken bets on how long it would last) engaged to Alistair Coster's socialite daughter, until a quiet, seemingly amicable breakup not long before the wedding. A nerves-of-steel hero who spent the last six months working with authorities, never betraying even a hint of disruption to his regular work.

I spend an exorbitant amount of money to click through these stories. One part of it is the price I pay to get through paywalls, to make sure I don't reach an article-per-month limit on any major news site I visit. But the other, more outrageous price is the fare for a sweltering, stale-cigarette-smelling cab ride all the way back to Brooklyn, because I am not losing cell service for any length of time during a subway ride. I sit in the back, sweating from the heat and the panic, barely noticing the traded honks of frustration as we crawl through Manhattan, hardly registering when we break free of the worst of the snarls, finally crossing the Bridge. I pause in my reading over and over, sending Reid messages I can sense already he won't be able to respond to.

Are you okay
Please, call me again
Reid, this is crazy

By the time the cab pulls up at the curb outside of my building, my battery is getting low and my once-polished presentation outfit is crumpled and damp. I barely think about my portfolio of sketches as I pull them from the back of the cab, barely remember the disappointment I felt at the Make It Happyn committee's response. I'm sure it'll come roaring back soon, but for now my head is spinning. I think, fleetingly, of all the things Reid has been hiding from me, all the conversations we'll have to re-do. But mostly I focus on all he must be facing, the desperation and pressure he must have been feeling.

Not just today.

But for the whole time I've known him.

When I stumble into my apartment, dropping everything I'm holding haphazardly, I realize I have never been more grateful to be living alone. I'm ruthlessly sloppy as I tear through it, grateful that I don't have to explain this to anyone, because right now, *I* can't explain it, not without more information from Reid. I change into jeans and a T-shirt, pull my humidity-ruined hair into what I am sure is an appallingly messy bun. I shove clothes into a backpack, because it's the only thing I can think to do—to use my key, to wait for Reid at his apartment. They've taken his phone, apparently, but certainly he'll be allowed to go back to his apartment? After all, it's not *him* who's done something wrong.

My phone rings inside my bag, and I curse its roomy depths as I try to unearth it. *It has to be him*, I'm telling myself, trying to force a sense of relief I don't feel.

But it's not him.

"Hey, Cecelia," I say when I pick up, my voice sounding reedy to my own ears. I need to get some water before I leave; I'm probably dehydrated.

"I promise I was going to call—" I begin, because I *did* promise. I said I'd call as soon as I left the hotel. She and Lachelle are both working today, and they've probably been waiting.

"Meg, you're all right?" Her voice sounds unusual—concerned, but also somewhat impatient.

My brows lower in confusion. I'm *not* all right, but why does she sound as if she already knows that? Does she know someone connected to Make It Happyn, somehow? Did someone give her a heads-up it didn't go well?

"I'm . . . look, it didn't go great, I don't think, and I will tell you all about it, but I have to—"

"No, I mean that . . . well, I've gotten a call about . . . about your name in the news?"

In a day full of ominous feelings, it's almost surprising to know I'm capable of being even more deeply weighted with dread.

"*My* name?" I repeat slowly. My mouth somehow feels both dry and full of saliva.

"I'm going to send something over to you, okay? And then I think we should talk. When you can."

I nod, even though she can't see me. It doesn't feel possible that I could know what's coming, but somewhere deep down, I do.

"Okay," I manage.

The link comes through only seconds after we disconnect. I sit on the couch, plugging my phone in to give it some much-needed juice. I recognize the site—a Manhattan-based gossip blog that occasionally gets national traction, but mostly covers stories focused on the rarified air of the city's elite. Even a cursory glance at the words in the link text make me swallow in fear.

I click, and read it in full.

Coster's Scorned Almost-Son-in-Law Couldn't Get Over His Ex

Everything about this article—if it can be called that—is like reading the earlier stories through a cracked, distorted mirror. Here, Reid is no genius, no nerves-of-steel hero. He's a guy with a grudge, smart but vindictive, always insecure. *"Everyone knew she was out of his league,"* one of the article's anonymous sources says. *"He knew it, too. He was wrecked when they split."*

I keep scrolling, shoving the thought of Reid's reaction to

Avery—*wrecked*—two nights ago out of my mind, getting to the place where my name becomes a part of this horrible scandal.

> Sources close to the Coster family say that Sutherland resisted Avery's decision to call off their planned wedding, even going so far as to accuse others of sabotaging their relationship. Several people who knew the couple recall his certainty that their already-completed wedding program—designed by Meg Mackworth, the lately-in-demand "Planner of Park Slope"—contained a hidden message that the marriage would be a "mistake." "Who thinks there's a hidden message in their *wedding program*?" one source we talked to said. "Clearly, the guy has a screw loose. I'm pretty sure it'll come out that he's the one behind this so-called fraud."

No, I want to shout at this stupid, wrong rectangle, immediately defensive of Reid. I can see it, how this angle will take off, how it will spread like wildfire. Of course the *numbers* won't be interesting. Of course the breakup with a beautiful, beleaguered socialite will be.

But this isn't how it went!

Or at least, it isn't . . . *quite* how it went, not so long as Reid has been telling the truth. About him, about Avery, about the feelings between them.

And he *has* been, right?

Except . . . Reid never told me he'd shown anyone else those hidden letters. Reid never told me anyone else knew about them at all.

Don't panic, I chide myself. *He promised he'd explain.*

I take a deep breath, deciding this could be so much worse. Sure, my name is tied up in this, but no one will *believe* this accusation about a hidden message. It's like this so-called friend says: Who *would* think that?

Then I read the next paragraph.

> Maybe Sutherland does have "a screw loose," but there's at least some evidence to suggest he wasn't paranoid about Mackworth's program. We got ahold of one of these never-used programs, and once you start looking for it, the "mistake" is pretty clear. Did The Planner of Park Slope know

something Ms. Coster didn't? We've reached out to Mackworth—who we hear is still in touch with Sutherland—via her website, and to the shop where she used to peddle her secret-code scribbles, but so far, haven't heard back.

Beneath it, there's a photo of the program, marred with red circles around every letter featuring one of my cleverly drawn, traditionally whimsical characters.

There it is, for the whole world to see. The word, the pattern, the code.

The mistake.

♥   ♥   ♥

I don't know how long I sit on my couch, frozen in shock, but I know that by the time I move again—minimally, only to grab the remote for the TV—the light outside is waning and dusky. Beside me, my phone continues to light at regular intervals—unknown number after unknown number, and every time, my stomach leaps and turns with stress. *It could be Reid,* I think, every single time, but that hope didn't serve me well the first four times I answered and found myself immediately confronted with a reporter.

Confrontation after confrontation, living in every corner of that phone.

But not the one I'm desperate to have.

Notification after notification.

But not the one I'm desperate to get.

He doesn't call. He doesn't text. He doesn't e-mail. It is profoundly clear that he is not at home.

All I can do is wait.

I need to deal with my clients. I need to call Cecelia, Lachelle. *Lark,* my God. What must Lark, who guards her privacy so completely, be thinking? And I didn't think I had much chance at all with Make It Happyn after today's presentation—my gorgeous, not-what-they-wanted sketches—but now? Now I'm sure the idea of hiring Meg Mackworth exists somewhere on a continuum of *never* and *not if she were the last hand-letterer in the whole, entire universe.*

I think of running. A rental car, my hastily packed bag. Some way to simply . . . *go*. To get away from this awful exposure, this hidden thing I don't want to face. Every time I try to move, though, something—*something*—makes me stay.

The television lights up the darkening room, and I flip through the channels until I find it, coverage of the Coster arrest. The story seems to repeat at regular intervals, on a rotation with the day's other biggest news stories. When I see it for the fifth time—the room around me totally dark now—I very nearly have the visuals memorized. First, Coster himself, being led out of the building, his eyes cast down, his gray hair mussed. Then, stills of him in happier, more successful times—shaking hands with the mayor, smiling on the red carpet on the night of a New York City ballet opening, posed with his wife on the steps of the Met. Next comes his mug shot, then a clip from outside his Upper East Side home, which was apparently also raided this afternoon.

And then comes Reid.

There's a single clip of him, and I can only guess it's played on every local station. For this one, the chyron is dark blue, and the lettering identifying Reid is slim, all caps, white. *COSTER WHISTLEBLOWER REID SUTHERLAND,* it reads, and I'm relieved, at least, that the television media isn't going with blaring, base "scorned fiancé" headlines.

But nothing else about this clip is relieving. There's so little to see of him in it: He's surrounded by people in dark suits, one on either side of him and two at his back, one who moves in front, arm outstretched to block the crush of people who are holding cameras and video equipment. On my third time seeing this clip, I notice that the two men on either side of Reid—their faces set in frustrated impatience at the click-clamor surrounding him—have a length of clear, curling wire descending behind their ears. Security. For *Reid*.

It doesn't take me three times to notice every single thing about him, though. Pale, stoic, stern, his blue eyes blank when they—for the briefest of seconds—flicker upward to the camera lenses. Dark blue suit, white shirt, his gray tie straight, tight against his collar. In the very last seconds of this clip, when two of the photographers stumble over each other, jostling their surrounding colleagues and putting the men around Reid on high, tense alert, Reid raises his hand to his hair, and the very worst thing is revealed for the most fleeting of seconds. A flaring patch of skin that peeks from beneath the cuff of his shirt.

My heart breaks every time, and I think if I was left in charge of myself, I might wait for this clip to replay all night, just to let it break over and over again. Just to feel close to him in this small, unsatisfying way.

But I'm not left in charge of myself. Because this time, as soon as the clip is over, I hear the lock on my door turn.

And when I look up, I'm staring into the sympathetic eyes of my very best friend.

Chapter 19

I wake up knowing Sibby is still in the apartment.

My bedroom door is mostly closed, a sliver-crack of light peeking along its length. But through it, I can hear her in the kitchen, dishes clinking lightly in that particular way that suggests someone is trying to be quiet. When I take a deep inhale, I can smell the heady aroma of her favorite strong coffee. It sounds and smells like so many other mornings I've had in this apartment—Sibby up early for work, me sleeping off a late night of sketching.

But of course it's not like other mornings.

At first, I give in to the disappointment—the realization that I haven't woken up to find that yesterday was all a terrible dream. I burrow deep into my covers, briefly indulging in my desire to hide away from all the ways last night had gotten unaccountably worse—still no word from Reid, but *lots* of words from other people. Reporters who'd flooded my voice mail and my inbox. Clients who'd done the same, apparently scanning their planners for hidden messages, finding things I'd certainly never hidden. One had been convinced that I'd written *He's cheating* among the letters in her June spread. The truth is, I didn't even know she was seeing anyone. Another thought I'd hidden *Botox*, and wanted to know whether I was making an accusation or a suggestion. "That's a good one," Sibby had said, as she'd scrolled through the phone she'd commandeered from me shortly after her arrival. But I'd never hidden that word, either.

Still, I have a lot to answer for. And also, I want a lot of answers.

Slowly, I uncurl my body from the ball I've tucked myself into, tossing off the covers. I know I can't hide from this forever, and anyway, Sibby being here last night let me do a lot of hiding already.

My body feels achy with fatigue as I pull on a light wrap over my pajamas, and my eyes are swollen and stuck-together-feeling. I don't know when I finally fell asleep last night, but I do know that I'd been crying—steady streams of tears as Sibby and I had lain next to each other in the dark, the saddest version of our old sleepovers. In a cracking, barely whispered voice, I'd told her everything. About Reid and Avery and the program, about Reid and me and the walks. Even about that £ around my heart, and what it truly stands for.

She'd held my hand and listened. When I'd finished, she'd said, her voice cracking, too, "I didn't even know you were seeing anyone." And then she squeezed my hand tight and whispered, "I'm so sorry."

"Hey, Sib," I croak to her when I come out from my quick stop in the bathroom. I shuffle over to the couch and slump onto it. As progress goes, it's minimal, but it's better than staying in bed, at least.

She's wearing her clothes from yesterday, her face scrubbed clean of makeup, and as soon as I'm settled she comes over, holding out a glass to me.

"Water before you're allowed to have coffee," she says, and I'm guessing this is the voice Sibby uses on her young charges. I can't say I mind it at the moment. I take the glass and drink deeply, mostly because I want that coffee so bad.

"Thanks. Did you check the news?" I move to stand.

She puts a hand up, stilling me, but her eyes are still full of sympathy. "There's nothing new. Stay where you are. I'll get your coffee."

She bustles away, and I lean my head back and close my eyes, listening to her move around the kitchen while I try—dimly, groggily—to come up with some kind of plan for today. The list of people I need to call—the list of people itching for a confrontation with me—seems endless, and even as I try to work through it, my mind keeps going to Reid. It's odd, how I can hold in my looped heart such conflicting emotions: my overwhelming concern for him, my worry that he's in trouble, hidden away somewhere and unable to be in touch. But also, my devastation over the things he's apparently hidden from me—not the work stuff, because it's clear he had to be secretive about that, but the personal stuff. What he must have told others about the program, about my letters. The way he left me so . . . so *exposed* to all these revelations.

So unprotected.

He should have warned me. Somehow, he should have warned me.

"Okay," Sibby says, breaking into my thoughts. "Coffee. Instant oats, extra maple syrup."

I lift my head and take it from her, notice that she's poured me a pretty small cup. I know her well enough to know she's still managing me here—worried about giving me too much caffeine when I'm already this anxious. In spite of all my sadness, I feel my lips twitch with a smile as I take my first sip.

"Here's what I'm thinking," says Sibby, sitting beside me, pulling up her feet and criss-crossing her legs. "We get you a second line for your phone today. We'll call the people you know to give them the new number, but this way, all the random stuff will go to the old one. You can record a new voice mail for it, basically a polite *fuck off.* I already disabled the comments on your social media, but I think if we . . ."

She rattles off the rest of her ideas, and every single one of them is good. It's the same way she'd handled things in the first hour or so after she'd come last night—a force of nature with my phone, answering calls and providing the briefest of responses, depending on who was on the line. For clients, a simple "I'm taking messages for her." For reporters or bloggers or other randoms, a curt "No comment," followed by her speedy blocking of the number. She'd even called both of my parents, though thankfully, it seems pretty clear my part in this scandal is going to stay local. She'd swept in like a superhero, my most devoted champion.

I'd been grateful and comforted. But now, uneasiness sweeps through me as I listen to her talk. Maybe it's taking me a while to work up to the worst of my to-do list, but right now, sitting here with Sibby, one of the items on it becomes crystal clear.

"Sib," I say.

"Yeah?" Her wingless eyes are guileless as she looks at me, maybe some slight surprise that I've interrupted her. This morning, and last night, too, she's the old Sibby. Not distant, not polite. Vibrant and bold and big-talking, ready for anything, as though the last few months never happened.

I clear my raspy throat.

"Do you think it's easier to . . . to be friends with me, when it's this way? When I need you more, I mean. Do you think . . ." I stir listlessly at my oatmeal, trying to think of the right way to put this. "Do you think we maybe learned to be friends this way, and then when it wasn't so . . ."

I trail off again, but I'm not trying to be indirect. I just know that Sibby's thinking of all the same things I am, all the ways our friendship was formed and forged according to who we were when we were so, so young. Me on that bus with my Pepto-Bismol, nervous to be away from home, and her at a new school, ready to assert herself as strong and in control. Me on the threshold of an apartment in Hell's Kitchen, needing a new home, and her settling into one, eager to be the city expert to one person, at least.

Me now, and her now.

There's a long pause.

"I don't know, Meg. Maybe."

I nod. It isn't a definitive answer, but it's an honest one. For both of us, probably.

"But if it is true," she says, "then we ought to change it. We ought to learn to be friends a different way. Because I love you, and I miss you so much."

My eyes well with tears. "Me too, Sib."

Sibby scoots closer to me and for a while we sit quietly, her side pressed up against mine while I force myself to eat. The to-do list looms, and my heart is still broken. But maybe a tiny bit less so now. Maybe Sibby and I are strong enough to form and forge something new. To change.

"Okay, though," she says. "The second phone line *was* a good idea."

I snort. "It was. I'll call after I'm finished eating."

And I think we both feel pretty glad that we don't have to do *all* the changing today.

♥　♥　♥

A few hours later, I'm hugging Cecelia goodbye in the small entryway of her townhouse, still sniffling in spite of my best efforts. By this point, my eyelids probably resemble throw pillows, but at least some of the tears I've shed over the last hour have been tears of relief, because Cecelia—generous, wonderful person that she is—has forgiven me.

After I'd finished my breakfast, I'd gotten serious about dealing with the things *I'm* actually in control of in this awful situation, and this confrontation with Cecelia had been right at the top. Thankfully, she wasn't working today, and had eagerly agreed to my request to meet, offering up her own place—as though she could sense that I was cautious about being out.

It hadn't been easy, apologizing to Cecelia—no excuses, and only explanations insofar as they helped her to understand how all this had happened. I'd told her that I would do whatever I could to help her repair any fallout for the shop; I'd reassured her that I would answer for any work I had done while I'd been working for her. I would accept if she never wanted me in the shop again.

And I'd thanked her for all that she'd done for me, for trusting and believing in me. I'd told her I was sorry to have let her down so completely.

"Oh, Meg," she'd said, her eyes soft and mischievous. "I don't mean to be ironic, but . . . listen, you made a *mistake.*"

Still, Cecelia has a business to run, and together we make some decisions about how best to minimize the damage. As awful as it is to consider, I'll avoid the shop for a while, at the very least until the dust settles, and maybe for longer. If Cecelia gets calls from past clients, she will gently remind them that I was employed as an independent contractor and have sole responsibility for the work I produced. She will send them to the contact form on my website, and when she can, she'll give me a heads-up about anyone who she thinks might be particularly irate, though thankfully, there's been nothing that extreme as of yet.

"This doesn't mean we won't see each other," Cecelia says, squeezing me one more time before pulling back. "Come over next week, and we'll all have dinner."

"Oh, you don't have to—"

"Meg," she says firmly. "You're more to me than the letters, okay?"

I swallow back fresh tears at this kindness, barely managing a genuine nod and smile.

When I step out onto the street, I pull out my phone, sending a quick text to Sibby to let her know I'm on my way. She's still back at the apartment, and has insisted on staying for a couple of days to help out, asking Elijah to drop off a weekend bag for her. While I've been at Cecelia's, she's been doing some preliminary handling of my e-mail backlog, deleting anything from reporters and flagging messages from clients that I'll need to reply to soon. After I get home, my plan is to reach out to Lark, bumped up in the confrontation-priority queue after I spoke to Lachelle on the way over to Cecelia's. "What do I have to be mad about?" she'd said. She'd encouraged me to remind Cecelia that all publicity is good publicity before telling me I owed her my whole sob story over vegan cocktails.

Even though I should probably stash my phone and leave it alone until I get back home, I can't help checking out the cache of newly missed calls, and as I walk I listen to—and mostly delete—voice mails. The problem with the second phone line idea, I'd realized, almost as soon as I'd gone to set it up, was that it wouldn't relieve me of the compulsion to check constantly for something from Reid, who might be trying to reach me from a different number.

Except he hasn't.

Maybe I could try to call . . . the FBI? I'm thinking, ridiculously, as I press delete on yet another garbage press inquiry. *How does one call the FB—*

I stop in my tracks when I hear the beginning of the next message, which is so entirely unexpected—not even on the confrontation list—that I don't even pause to listen to the whole thing before dialing the number back.

"Meg!" Ivonne's voice is high and excited when she picks up after only a half ring. "I'm so glad we were able to connect. I tried calling you yesterday from the hotel, but your phone must have been blowing up!"

She makes it sound as if this is the greatest thing, one's phone "blowing up." One's *life* blowing up.

"Uh, yes." I swallow, then try again, attempting to be more cheerful. I thought I was finished at Make It Happyn, and now I might need this job more than ever. If they want whimsy, I guess I'll find a way to give them whimsy.

I offer an empty, false laugh. "Yeah, definitely! It's been wild."

Wildly terrible. Wildly devastating. Wildly heartbreaking.

"Listen, the team and I met last night, and you're our top, top pick for this. We're so excited to bring you on."

"Wh—really?" I should leave it at that, but I don't. Instead, I say what I'm thinking. "It seemed like the sketches I presented didn't work for you."

"This is a moment we need to move on," she says, as though I haven't spoken at all. "You're on the verge of a brand transformation."

"Yes, I agree, but I thought the ideas I proposed—"

"Hidden messages," she interrupts. "It's brilliant. We want to do a whole line. We're thinking messages of motivation, maybe one over the course of each month? I'm sure you could work it out—I saw that program! Anyway, we think it could be a hit, especially if we do it quickly. Sort of a game for our consumers, you know? It's terrific."

A game.

That quickly, my house-of-cards confrontation schedule collapses all around me, fresh pain about Reid punching through my chest. Every game I played with him had felt so sincere, so honest, so special. And every game had led to *work*—and to a relationship—that was sincere, honest, special. Now all of it feels trivialized, false. My name and Reid's tied together in some shallow, scandalous narrative, and I can't even speak to him to find out what's true and what's not. All my effort and creativity for Make It Happyn reduced to this, a half-baked offer to turn my mistakes into money.

This is such a *mess.*

"Meg?" Ivonne says. "Are you still there?"

Part of me wants to give her a hard no, to simply hang up at this ham-handed proposal, maybe even to block her number, too. But I've been self-employed in this city for too long to do anything that reckless, and anyway, I feel dangerously close to one of those blurting, I've-reached-my-limit outbursts that's gotten me into so much trouble before.

I compose myself enough to make an apology, and a request to call her back, given what I describe as "some distraction" in my current circumstances. She laughs congenially and agrees—*ha ha ha, isn't scandal* hilarious?—but asks that I call her first thing Monday.

"Sure," I promise before hanging up, though I don't see how I'll have any more clarity on this issue by Monday.

It's a slog to get home. It's muggy and gray, my personal worst weather combination, and anyone who's out in it seems like they don't want to be, including me. Sure, I'm glad I got to talk to

Cecelia, but maybe that's enough for the day. Maybe I could let myself hide for a bit longer, hand over my phone to Sibby until tomorrow, while I wait and hope for Reid to call.

That hiding—it's what I want most as I trudge up the stairs to my apartment, feeling the energy leak from my bones. When I open the door, I'm head down with headphones on, hiding, hiding, hiding, but my day of confrontation isn't quite over yet, because when I finally pull them from my ears and look up, I see that it's not only Sibby here in the apartment.

It's Lark, too.

And in her hands, she has her planner.

♥ ♥ ♥

"I did *not* hide anything in there," I blurt immediately, because I guess I've finally snapped. I wish this proclamation—which is true—seemed more convincing, but since I have actual beads of sweat on my forehead, I'm sure I look like Lying Witness Number Four, sent over here from central casting.

"Well, this is awkward," says Sibby, grimacing as she looks between me and Lark. "In this case, I can *literally* say I've been there." She gestures to where I'm standing.

Lark laughs.

Wait . . . she laughs?

"What's going on here?" I say, my gaze now the one ping-ponging between them. They look like they're about to put on face masks and watch *The Princess Tent*. Honestly that's a pretty good idea, but I still can't figure out what's happened here since I left.

"Lark came to check on you," says Sibby. "She was worried."

"I read the news and thought I'd come over," she says. She holds up her planner. "I was showing Sibby what you'd done for me while we waited for you to get back."

Sibby? It's Sibby now?

"Why have I never hired you to do a planner?" Sibby says, gesturing to Lark's. "This one is gorgeous."

"Because you use an app," I say.

"Point," says Sibby, holding up a finger. "How'd it go with Cecelia?"

I rub at my sweaty temples. "You guys, I need a minute. What is—are you two friends now?"

"We had a nice talk while we waited for you," Lark says. "You didn't tell me Sibby was auditioning again."

I gape. "I didn't know she was."

Sibby waves a hand. "I'll tell you about it. A small production. Who knows if I'll get it."

"Sib, that's so great. What's the—"

Sibby snaps her fingers, as though she's trying to wake me out of a hypnosis. "Focus, Meg."

I drop my bag, take a few steps, and sink onto the area rug, sitting across from their spots on the couch. "It went okay with Cecelia. But on the way home I got offered the Make It Happyn gig."

They both get excited at first, until I fill them in on the details, adding some extra padding to my throw pillow eyes with a few additional tears.

"Ugh," says Sibby. "You can't take it."

"I don't know if I can *not* take it. I'm going to lose so many clients because of this. People trust me with a lot of details about their lives. And they're right to be angry. To be suspicious of me."

"Lark was suspicious," Sibby says, and my stomach drops.

"Lark, I was serious. There's *nothing* in there. I haven't done this in months. I was going through—"

"Suspicious is the wrong word," Lark says reassuringly. "I was . . . hopeful?"

"*Hopeful?*"

Lark cracks the planner, presses her thumb against the pages so they shuffle past in the way of a flip-book. She shrugs. "I stared at every page, every letter. When I got to the end I realized I was looking for something pretty specific."

"God," says Sibby. "The suspense is *killing* me here."

Lark smirks, but then she looks at me. "I think it's not working out with Cam. Or it's not working out in New York. I'm not sure which."

"Oh, Lark," I say.

"Well, it's not New York's fault," Sibby says, defensively, and

I can't help but smile. But then I feel another pang of sadness about Reid, Reid and Sibby. It would have been fun, to watch them argue about New York, to teasingly pile on him about it. But maybe that will never happen now.

I refocus on Lark. "Did something happen?"

She shrugs. "No, but . . . I mean. You've met him."

"Yikes," says Sibby. What Reid and Sibby would one hundred percent have in common is absolute derision for a shark-tooth necklace.

"I don't know if it was ever right between me and him," Lark says. "I don't know if we can work it out, either. I don't even know if I *want* to." She looks down again at the planner, smooths her hand over the cover. "I think maybe I was hoping you had the answer."

"I definitely don't," I say, and I mean it. I am the last person to be advising people about their relationships. "But I will talk through it with you as much as you want. If you need that."

"She's good at that," says Sibby. "One time she lettered me a gorgeous pro/con list about getting a tattoo."

"I think that's why I've been stalling about the wall. I'm sorry for that, by the way. But I—"

"Lark, it's completely okay. If that house isn't your home, we shouldn't do it."

"But you could use the money."

I purse my lips, lower my brows in a look of censure. "We're not doing that, Lark. We're friends." I borrow a line from Cecelia. "You're more to me than the jobs, okay?"

She nods, lowering her eyes, and I send a glance toward Sibby, relieved when I see that she looks totally comfortable. If seeing Lark here had been painful for Sibby before, it certainly doesn't seem to be now.

"Okay," Sibby says. "She *does* need money, though, if she's not going to do this"—she pauses to prepare her big voice—"*extremely bad* job idea. Meg, what if I—"

I cut her off before she can suggest anything ridiculous, such as calling her dad. It strikes me suddenly how many things have changed—not only in the last terrible, stressful day and a half, but also in the last few months. One gray day in spring, a man I never thought I'd ever have occasion to see again came through the doors of the shop and confronted me about my letters, and I felt as isolated as I'd ever been in my life. Now, it's a gray summer day and it feels as if the whole city knows about my secret, but at least I'm not facing the fallout alone.

"I can handle this," I say, feeling a whole lot more capable than I did when I walked in here. "I need to . . . start over, I guess. I've done it before, right? I'm going to start contacting my clients, and I'll try to reassure them the best I can, though it'll probably be difficult to—"

"I could help," Lark says.

Sibby and I both watch as she holds up the planner again, waving it in the air. "I'll do some social media posts about this to start."

"Oooh," Sibby says, and there's not a trace of jealousy in her voice. I get the sense of something important here, some shift in our pattern—Sibby not looking to take over, to be the one in charge. "Yes, this is good."

"And you meet your clients out, right? At coffee shops?"

"Uh, yes?"

Lark nods. "Maybe I could show up for the difficult ones, you know? I'm not saying everyone would care, but I still have a good deal of Princess Freddie power to my name. I could be a character reference. I mean, not a movie character. I'm not going to come in costume. You know what I'm saying."

I blink at her. "But you . . . What about your privacy?"

She shrugs again. "That's why I'd be a good reference, right? I trust you with my stuff, so they can, too."

"Lark, this is too much."

"It's not. It's like you said. We're friends."

"Oh!" Sibby exclaims. "Are we going to have a sleepover now? Because we absolutely should."

"I can swing it," Lark says. "I'll call Jade and ask her to bring me some things."

"Who's Jade?"

"My assistant," Lark says, and Sibby's eyes go wide.

"Oh, my God," she says, smooshing all her syllables together in excitement. "We have *so* much to talk about."

From my spot on the floor, I watch them chat easily, and I feel warm all over at the sight. *This is love, too,* I tell myself, reminding that aching mark on my heart. These friends who are here for me, who are helping me pick up the pieces after this scandal.

But even so, all night I wait for a call, a text, an e-mail.

All night I feel like someone I love is missing.

Chapter 20

I guess I leave because I'm looking for a sign.

In the early light of Sunday morning, I rise from the massive pile of blankets and throw pillows (not my eyelids, which have been modestly improved by, of all things, two moist teabags laid gently over their swollen surface) haphazardly arranged on my living room floor. Pretty much all of my bones hurt from sleeping in this arrangement, even a few I wasn't aware I had, but I don't suppose I'd trade it. Sibby's still down there, the comforter from my bed pulled up over her head, only her pouf of black curls visible on the pillow. On the couch, Lark is sprawled—in true princess style—limbs askew, mouth open, a gentle snore punctuating her breaths. Neither one of them stirs when I move, and I'm guessing that's because they stayed up much later than me. I'm pretty sure I'd drifted off sometime during the fifth episode of *The Bachelorette* binge-watch, and as I tiptoe into the kitchen I fleetingly wonder if I ought to check the freezer for one or more of my bras.

Instead, I immediately check my phone, which is, at this point, almost certainly a fool's errand. There's still nothing from him, and nothing new from the news or gossip blogs—only the same basic information, repackaged to seem like there's something additional. Keeping the clicks coming.

I could start working, I suppose, could start setting up these coffee-shop meetings Lark plans to help me with. But this early on a Sunday—well, on a Sunday at all, probably—I'm probably not going to hear much back. And anyway, at this particular moment, when my heart—still looped with that inconvenient £—is tight and aching, work would only be another kind of hiding. If I'm missing Reid so much, I might as well do the one thing that'll make me feel closest to him.

Quietly, I wash my face and brush my teeth, avoid everything in my closet with any kind of frolicsome pattern, and shove my feet into a pair of sneakers that'll keep my feet comfortable. I snag a piece of scrap paper from my desk and in my own un-adorned, unremarkable handwriting, I write a simple message.

Going for a walk. Back soon. xo —Meg

I leave it on a throw pillow beside Sibby before I leave.

Outside the morning sky is clear. It's already warm, but nothing like yesterday's sweaty soup-fest, and I focus on the fresh air as I walk for blocks and blocks. All the signs are familiar to me, and I can't think of a single game to play. I think of Reid that night at Swine, telling me he walked with a Meg-shaped shadow beside him, and once it's in my head, it's all I can imagine—my relationship to this city and its signs changed forever now, a memory of Reid with me in so many places.

He did give you signs, I keep thinking, each time I wrestle with the shock of what's happened. His disdain for his work, his stress over it, his reluctance to talk about the details. His phone—the trouble it had caused to be away from it, even for his so-called sick day. His *money people, math people* frustration. His insistence that he would leave New York by the end of the summer, his seeming difficulty comprehending how he might stay.

But it's the other signs I struggle to read without him here beside me. That last time I saw him, and the look on his face when he saw Avery. His determination when he came to see me at the shop, coded program in hand. Was it less amicable with her than he'd told me? Had he told everyone about what he had seen in my letters, and had he sought me out, at least at first, because he couldn't get over her?

No, I think, almost desperately. *No, you have other signs.* Everything he and I shared. Every way he ever touched me. Every time he walked with me, made love to me. Those were signs, too. *Remember them*, I tell myself. *Remember them while you wait.*

But if I could only *hear* from him. Call, text, e-mail. *Anything*.

It's what I'm thinking as I wind my way back home, my skin dewy with sweat now, my feet growing tired. I forgot my sunglasses, so now I squint against the brightening morning sun, and when I'm only a few buildings away from my own, the light grows almost blinding as it glints off the hood of a car that's parked out front. I raise my hand to shade my eyes, annoyed. That's a no parking zone; there are signs everywhere.

But as I approach, I notice someone standing beside it, as though she's guarding it from any cop who might try it with a ticket. She frowns down at her watch, clearly impatient, and maybe that wouldn't be so unusual except that when she looks up, she catches sight of me and I get the eerie certainty that I'm the person she's been impatient for. She straightens, her eyes on me like I'm a flight risk.

And maybe I am. I'm not ashamed to say I really and truly think about turning and walking in the exact opposite direction. Is interest in my small part in this story high enough that a reporter could've actually tracked down where I live?

But once again, something makes me stay.

I walk toward her, steeling myself for confrontation.

"This is a no parking zone," I say bluntly. Reid would be proud of that, I think.

The woman raises a dark eyebrow. "You're Margaret Mackworth?"

I raise an eyebrow back. "You're . . . ?"

The right side of her mouth hitches. "Your roommate told me you'd be coming back. I'm Special Agent Shohreh Tirmizi. I work for the FBI."

She doesn't pause to allow me to process that information. She simply pulls a leather fold from her pocket and shows me an honest-to-God badge. A badge! Now that I've seen that, I decide she has many other law enforcement-type qualities, at least such qualities that exist in my imagination. She has a suit on like Olivia Benson from *SVU*! Also she is tall.

"Yes," I say. "I'm Meg. Is he—"

But she doesn't wait for me to ask my question. "My partner and I have been working with Reid Sutherland for the last eight and a half months."

I blink at her. "I thought it was six."

"Don't believe everything you read in the papers."

Somehow, from her tone, I get the sense she's not just talking about the timeline information.

"Is he okay?" I say before she can cut me off again.

"He's fine. He's had a lot of statements to give after the arrest. And given some of the accusations circulating about him in the press—" She breaks off and gives me a meaningful look, as if she knows all about the way I clicked through the gossipy stories containing those accusations: Reid and his revenge mission; Reid orchestrating some kind of numbers-game setup of Alistair Coster.

"Well," she finishes, "we're trying to limit anyone's access to him for a few days."

I furrow my brow. "But I'm not—" I don't know how to finish that sentence. I'm not anyone? I'm not trying to access him, to ask him whether some parts of those stories are true?

I clear my throat after I trail into silence, and she simply looks at me again, taking my measure. Or maybe she's using some sophisticated interrogation tactic on me. Honestly, if it's the latter, it's pretty effective, because for a second I consider telling her about the time I shoplifted a Werther's Original from the bulk candy section at the grocery store. When I was eight.

"I don't have any information for you," I say, finally, submitting to her considerable powers. "He never told me—"

"I know that," she says, and the way she says it tells me she knows Reid, trusts him. "I came because he asked me to."

For the first time since Friday, my heart leaps with hope.

From the inside of her Olivia Benson jacket, Agent Tirmizi draws out an envelope, stuffed thick with paper. Even from here I can see Reid's handwriting across the front: *Meg.*

A letter. Of course.

Even though I want to reach out and snatch it, to run up to my apartment and shut the door while I pore and pore over it, I wait until she holds it out to me, and I take it from her hands gently.

"Thank you," I tell her.

She has that assessing look again. "You should thank me for more than this letter."

I blink at her, confused. She really seems as though she's waiting for something specific.

"Um . . . oh!" I say, struck with an idea that doesn't seem all that good, but at least it *is* one. "Yes. Thank you for . . . your service?"

This feels awkward. I am obviously also against financial crimes, but you know. This seems kind of insistent, under the circumstances.

For the first time, she seems to take pity on me, or maybe that's the face she makes when she's trying not to laugh.

"Reid mentioned you to me earlier this spring," she says.

"He did?"

She nods. "After you'd e-mailed him to meet. It was—that came at a critical time. Reid had met with us several times that week."

"Oh." I try to imagine what those meetings would have been like. Would they have been in a windowless room, one table, two chairs, Reid and an FBI agent facing each other beneath an industrial light fixture? Or would Reid have been ushered into a bland but comfortable conference room? Would they have

poured him tea, spoken to him gently, encouragingly? I suppose I could ask Agent Tirmizi, but as with so many questions I
have—I only want to ask them of Reid.

"I suggested he might want to take you up on your offer. To
give himself some relief from all this."

I blink down, let my eyes slide closed for a few seconds so I
can think of Reid that first day at the Promenade. His weekend
clothes, his stern face, his sad eyes. *Someone did tell me recently I
ought to try keeping my mind occupied.*

I feel the weight of the letter in my hand, let the pad of my
thumb pass over the exact spot where Reid has written my
name. I wish he had pressed harder. I wish I could feel some
relic of his hand's movement over these letters. I notice that it's
not sealed, the envelope's flap only tucked inside, and I look up
at Agent Tirmizi.

"I read it," she says, shrugging. "Following protocol, for his
good and yours."

"Of course," I say, my face flushed, my fingers tight around
the envelope.

"I always wanted my wife to write me love letters."

My heart *thunks thunks thunks* in anticipation. Agent Tirmizi
seems nice and all, and I'm sure it's a disappointment about her
wife, but I'd really like her to leave now. I'd really like to read
this letter alone.

"She's more of a Post-it note stuck to the refrigerator kind of
woman."

"Yeah," I say, as though I know anything about her wife. I
only want to *go*, but I suppose running from a literal FBI agent
would be a poor decision. Anyway, I'm already tired from all
the walking I did.

"A few years ago, though, she got me a book of them. Famous
love letters."

Wow, okay. Does she also want to give me an inventory of the
contents of the refrigerator that her wife leaves the Post-its on?
Or can I finally, please, *please* go upstairs and read this—

"What I'm saying is, I've read a lot of them."

She has a small smile on her face that hints she's been stalling me on purpose, making me sweat this. I hope they do put her in those windowless rooms sometimes to make the bad guys squirm. They probably leave with their eyelids looking like throw pillows, too. But I keep my eyes fixed on hers, my feet steady where I stand, and her smile widens briefly.

Approvingly.

She nods toward the letter, then looks me straight in the eye. "That one's a good one."

And when she turns to open the door of her car, I know she's not just talking about the letter.

Chapter 21

Dear Meg,

Sending you this letter may be a mistake.

That's what Agent Tirmizi told me when I asked her whether I could write to you. She reminded me, in stark terms, that I have caused a great deal of difficulty in your life, difficulty you were not able to prepare for or decide for yourself. She has warned me that all this means you might have reason not to keep a letter from me private, that you might have reason to sell a letter I send to you. Knowing you as I do, I don't believe this is a great risk, but if it is— if it is a mistake, Meg, it is a mistake I won't regret making. It is a mistake for which I would deserve the consequences, and if this letter shows up on some website tomorrow, or the next day, or any day after that, I hope you know I would not blame you.

Whatever it is that I deserve, what is more important is that you deserve to know about the many mistakes I have made over these last several months. As I am sure Agent

Tirmizi will mention to you, I have been quite isolated since Friday, and while I have spent a great deal of my time answering and re-answering questions, I have also had a great deal of time to think about those mistakes. I enumerate them. I work them out like equations. I work backward through each step. I try to see all the places I went wrong.

I suppose the first and worst one is that I came to the shop this spring to see you, which has, to my profound regret, exposed you to this scandal in ways that, as I hope this letter will make clear, I was foolishly, selfishly unprepared for. That evening, I knew, from the second I walked through the door of the shop, that I would be withholding something from you, because I knew I could not tell you the full story of what I had seen in your letters. Everything I have told you about Avery and me was true: I did disappoint her. I was quiet and overly reserved, sometimes too blunt, and as a guest at the many social commitments that were important to her, I never could quite master the kind of social interaction that she needed in a partner. As I told you that day in the park, we each had our reasons for attempting the relationship, and we each had our reasons for knowing it wasn't working. The letters in your program confirmed what I always knew.

But they did something else, too. This is what I could not say, and still will not be able to say fully, not for some time. What I can tell you is that in the months prior to the wedding, something had been on my mind at work, something involving the group within the company that worked on investment securities. I could not understand the returns this group was producing so consistently. I could not understand how the math worked, though I did not expect to find anything untoward. Initially, I think I might have been looking for some kind of game to play, something that could connect me to the math I grew up loving so much. As you may have gathered, I have not felt connected to that in a long time. So here was a problem in front of me, and I could only find the solution by trying, again and

*again, to work backward—to reverse engineer the numbers.
At first it was challenging, the most challenging math I had
done in ages, and I enjoyed working on it.*

*Eventually, though, I realized that it was not, in fact,
challenging math. It was impossible math. I could not
understand the numbers because the numbers did not make
sense. I cannot say here to whom I brought this information
first. What I can say is that, initially, I was told that I had
only uncovered a simple mistake, one that I was assured
would be fixed.*

*Once, you told me that when you are feeling most
inspired, you see letters sketch themselves in your mind all
the time—at night when you're falling asleep, first thing
in the morning when you wake, when you're walking or
waiting for the train or cooking or eating. I suppose that's
the closest way of describing how I felt, for weeks afterward.
In the pool, I could see the numbers in my head. I could
picture them, swimming along as smoothly as I was, except
every once in a while, a splash, a missed stroke.*

*So that word, "mistake"—it stuck with me, even as I
wanted to trust what I had been told about it being fixed.
It stuck with me even after Avery and I split up, after I'd
tried to convince myself that the code in the program was
only about our relationship. It stuck with me enough that
I checked the math again. It stuck with me enough that I
agreed, at a certain point, to check these numbers as part of
a larger investigation, about which I can say no more here.*

*When I first came to you, Meg, I never thought that there
would be any reason for my curiosity about your letters
to cross paths with the numbers work I have been doing
regarding this case. I told myself you and I would speak
once, and I would get some answers, and we would go our
separate ways. But of course I should have known this was
a mistake, too. The first time I ever saw you—when I was
sitting next to a woman I was supposed to marry—I knew
I felt something for you, something for the way you smiled*

and talked and drew. I deluded myself thinking I wouldn't feel the same way when I saw you again this spring. When you found my card and e-mailed me, I should have said no. When you walked away from me in Midtown, I should have let you go. I should have known that every time I let myself get closer to you, you were getting closer and closer to the risk for this exposure, this scandal. But I suppose I got greedy, and given what I have accused some of my colleagues of, I certainly see the irony. I wanted—even for a little while—to be around your smile and your conversation and your talent, and eventually, your way of seeing this city. And then I wanted everything else. Your kiss, your body close to mine, your love. I wanted your forever.

Last week, when we saw Avery on the street—I know what you must've thought then, and I dread what you certainly must think now. I know that my reaction to seeing her, my shock at seeing her, must be confirmation for you of everything that's now in the papers about me—that I am a scorned party in a relationship that went wrong, that I could not let her go, that my feelings for her are what led to my involvement in this case. It is true, as I have always told you, that I cared about her, that I still care about her. When I saw her, I was reminded, in a concrete way, how she would be hurt by all this, how her life would change because of her father's crimes. I was reminded of how I would be, at least in part, responsible, and I hated and still hate to know this. I hate to think that she is suffering because of what I have helped reveal about her father.

But my care for Avery does not account for the full extent of my shock in that moment, because right then, I could see—though not fully—the potential for how this scandal might touch you. I could see that, when the story eventually broke, Avery might remember seeing us together. I could see that your name might eventually be drawn into this story, as a person who is now involved with me, and as a person who was once involved, however briefly, with my and

Avery's wedding plans. I knew already (I had been warned already) that there was potential for blowback on me, that the press might treat me as though my motivations were not pure. But I did not truly see, until that moment, that there would be blowback on you.

I thought I could protect you. And I was a fool.

That foolishness extends to another of my mistakes, the one that has surely caused you the most pain. It is my worst lie of omission, something I should have told you much sooner, and something that probably would have never mattered at all had I not come to see you that first day, had I not let myself get involved with you. I did tell Avery about what I had seen in the wedding program. At the time, this seemed to me to be the right thing, the honest thing to do. I showed her what I'd seen and told her I thought we should talk about the wedding and whether we should get married at all. She did not believe what I had seen in your letters was intentional. She believed that I was seeing what I wanted to see, that I was looking for some kind of sign. But still, she admitted she was relieved. It wasn't easy or comfortable, but we did part on good terms, and I did not think she had ever told anyone else about that program. I did not think anyone—other than me, and her—had a copy of it. But of course Avery and her family are in a desperate situation. And of course they have many friends in which to confide, friends who are eager to defend them. I am a convenient target. Anything I have been involved in now must seem like fair game to them. All of it, Meg—all of it should have occurred to me sooner.

I need you to know that I did try, desperately, to stop this. When I left you that night, even before I'd had any thought about that program, I called Agent Tirmizi and begged her to let me tell you. I begged her for some way to help me make sure my mistakes would not be irreparable. But as it turns out, Agent Tirmizi and her colleagues also had to keep many things hidden from me, including other sources

*they had, and a newly accelerated timeline for arresting Mr.
Coster. I believed I had time to explain things to you, Meg.
I made that promise to you fully intending to keep it. And
if what I write next gets me into trouble with the people who
read this letter before it gets to you, so be it: I would have
broken my promises to them to keep my promise to you. I
would have told you everything after your pitch. (How was
your pitch?) I would have risked everything to warn you.*

*This is probably all the explanation I'll be allowed to give
you, unless I want this letter marred with black stripes of
redaction or worse. But there is more I have to write, and I
hope you will keep reading.*

*Last night I stayed awake for hours, worrying for you,
wondering how it must be for you—reading all this in the
news and not being able to reach me, all my promises to you
unfulfilled. I kept thinking about what signs you'd send me
now, if you'd write to me and tell me you thought it was all
a mistake, too. I keep thinking, what if you writing that
word all those many months ago wasn't because you were
warning me, or Avery? What if you were somehow warning
yourself? What if you knew, somewhere deep down, that I
would be a mistake in your life?*

*I hate to think it. But it might be true, and I am so sorry.
I have brought to your life the kind of secrecy and upheaval
you never wanted to experience again. The consequences
you may suffer to your business and to your heart I will
regret for the rest of my life. I have spent all these months
involved in the investigation of a man who made selfish
choices, choices that have ruined the lives of the people
around him. When all this began, I never thought it would
end with me feeling that I had something in common with a
man as dishonest as Alistair Coster. But now I see so clearly
that I do.*

*I don't know how to explain that thinking of all this—
enumerating all these mistakes, writing them out in the
dusty chalkboard of my brain, even knowing I won't ever be*

able to solve any of them—is the only thing comforting me right now. I feel closer to you with this word in my mind, I guess, because in spite of everything, your letters saved me. And while I am sure it doesn't seem so now, the message you sent to me, or to Avery, or to yourself—in the end, it will have done a great deal of good for a lot of people who stood to lose so much.

It's funny, isn't it, what happens to a word when you write it over and over again? You see it differently. I've always thought of the word "mistake" as meaning an error, a miscalculation. But now that I'm finishing this letter to you it reminds me of something I should have told you before. For most of my life, whenever I wasn't with my family, I felt, somehow, mis-taken. Mistaken as cold or rude or boring or distant. All my best intentions, in school, at work—mistaken. But you were the first person in this city who made me feel I was more. To be able to see this city through your eyes, to be able to play games with you and laugh with you, to have you tease me about my tea and my posture and my terrible couch, to watch you create so many beautiful things—it has been the only thing that has made me feel like myself in these last months. It is more than I have deserved, but I am still so grateful.

When I sat down with this blank pad of paper, I wished I could send you a sign, something I could hide in this apology that would tell you how much you have meant, still mean, always will mean to me. But I don't suppose I have much of a stomach for hiding things anymore, and while there is not much I am looking forward to about the days to come, being able to be honest again—being able to say exactly what I mean—is one thing about this I do embrace.

So: I am sorry. I am sorry, and I love you, and the time I have spent with you has been the best time of my life. No matter where I go after this, I will never take a step without wishing you were walking beside me, and I will never see a sign without wishing you were there to see it with me.

Maybe there is one sign I could send you, even though it

won't be your favorite kind. But I've always been better with numbers, Meg, and the numbers I have written below—I think they should be easy to decode.

And they will be scored on my heart forever.

All my love,
Reid

Chapter 22

I'd stared at those numbers for a long time.

I hadn't even bothered to go inside with Reid's letter. I'd read it right there on the sidewalk, alone, through a blurry sea of tears, and when I finished I'd read it all again. Then I'd taken out my phone, bypassing every single worthless notification on it.

I may not know much about numbers, but I know, in spite of what he kept hidden from me, everything I need to know about Reid.

And so he'd been right. The numbers *were* easy for me to decode.

And they'd told me what to do next.

From the passenger seat of the last rental car on the lot, a creaky, amenities-limited two-door Ford, Sibby reads off directions to me, occasionally getting distracted by her repeated fiddling with the radio, an old habit that used to make me grind my teeth in frustration back when we were teenagers. Now I'm too nervous, too focused to care much. Crammed into the tiny backseat is Lark, my phone held up to her ear as she talks to

Lachelle. "She didn't let us see it," she's saying, and I think I can hear Lachelle's shout of protest from here. "I *know*," Lark says.

"Tell her we'll call back," I say. "I think we're getting close." I jut out an elbow to dislodge Sibby's arm from where she's toying with the tuner again, trying to find something worth singing to. "What next?" I ask her.

With the help of Sibby's Google Mapped directions, it's only a few more turns before I'm pulling into the lot of a nice but nondescript-looking hotel in New Jersey, one of those ones with "suites" for extended stays.

"This is it?" says Lark, poking her head between the seats and ducking to peer out of the windshield.

"It has to be it," I answer.

"Jersey," Sibby says. "Why would they bring him here?"

"Cam did this movie once about witness protection," Lark says. "Maybe it's that."

"He's not going into witness protection," I say, but I guess I don't really know. "Anyway, they'd take him farther away than Jersey for that." *Barely two hours,* I reassure myself, thinking back over the drive here. *I'm sure he's* quite *safe.*

I unbuckle my seat belt and open my door, but Sibby stops me with a hand on my forearm. "Want to check your hair first?"

I roll my eyes, but also I flip down my visor and check my reflection in the tiny, cloudy mirror there. Listen, it is definitely not great, but it's also not as though Reid cited normal-sized eyelids or brushed hair as a reason he loves me.

He loves me.

I quickly smooth my unruly hair, mostly to assuage Sibby's concerns, and start to get out again.

"Meggie," Sibby says, and I look over at her again. "You're good, right?"

It's not the first time she—or Lark—has asked since I'd flung myself through the apartment door, the pages of Reid's letter clutched tight in my hand, my mind already racing toward what I needed to do next. Both of them, in their own ways, had made sure I slowed down, had made sure I'd thought it through. Sibby, who'd seen me through the revelation of another big scandal once upon a time, had furrowed her brow in worry. "This is a lot to handle, Meg. This kind of secret from someone you—" She broke off, apparently cautious about repeating everything I'd told her on Friday night. "Someone you felt so strongly about."

Lark, too, had been tentative. Maybe she'd been optimistic yesterday—with our girl-power sleepover on the horizon—about how I could salvage my business, but in the light of day, she'd been more hard-nosed about it. "Being in the news, Meg," she'd said with the serious expression of someone who knows what it's like to be in the news. "It can be a lot to navigate. And if it's between your work and him . . ."

She'd trailed off then, pressing her lips together, and I think Sibby and I both had gotten the sense that Lark had her own choices in mind, too.

"I'm good," I tell them both now, keeping my voice firm, the same way it'd been when I'd answered them back in the apartment. When I'd told them how determined I was to do this.

How certain I was.

"Want us to go in with you?" Lark says hopefully. Now that we've taken this drive together, talking through it the whole way, they seem certain, too. As invested in this as I am.

I stand, turning back to them with one hand on the open car door, ducking so I can see them both.

"I love you guys for driving here with me, but I think I need to go in there alone."

They both look crestfallen, but Sibby says, "Understood. We'll wait right here. We'll come up with something to kill the time."

I smile. "Play a game," I say, tossing her the keys. "There are signs everywhere around here. I'll call you."

I hear them call *Good luck!* to me in unison as I head toward the entrance, my palms sweaty with nerves. No matter how certain I am about this, it's still going to be a fight. Maybe to get to him, and maybe once I *do* get to him, too. And after—after, there are still so many fights to have, against all of the enemies that Reid's amassed over the last forty-eight hours.

The lobby is as bland as the exterior—mostly neutral, with those awful punctuations of standard hotel lobby maroon. In a small, clean, open dining room off to my right, a few guests sip coffee and read newspapers, and I can only hope all of them are completely skipping the financial section. I head over to the front desk, steeling myself.

The man behind the counter is named Gregory—*not* Greg, a fact about which he will be clear if you slip up—and his attitude does not match his *May I Help You?* name tag. Still, I can't say I blame him, what with how insistent I'm being.

"Young lady," he says, after we've already gone back and forth a few times. "I've told you, there's no one here by that name."

"Old man," I say, even though Gregory is *maybe* only a decade or so older than me. But he can try it again with this *young lady* shit. "I *know* there is."

Isn't there? I keep my head held up, determined not to falter. I picture the numbers in my head. I *know* what they meant.

"Ma'am," a man's voice says from behind me, and it is not a nice-sounding *ma'am*. It's sort of a you're-about-to-be-arrested *ma'am,* and for a second all the numbers fly out of my brain. I see those two *a*'s like a pair of handcuffs, that apostrophe transformed into a chain.

Well, so be it. I'm in the news already.

I turn to face the voice.

"Yikes," I say without thinking, my head tipping back to look at the massive man standing in front of me. He's wearing a black suit, a dark tie, the same as the men on television who surrounded Reid. But unlike those men on television, he's significantly older, maybe in his late fifties. He is cue-ball bald, but he has the thickest gray mustache I've ever seen in my life. I am almost certain he carries handcuffs.

"Ma'am," he says again, as though to remind me. "I'm going to need you to step away from this counter."

"I'm looking for a guest here. His name is Re—"

"If you could come with me," he cuts me off, turning on his heel and walking toward the lobby's elevators. I follow him, but don't resist the impulse to give Gregory a pretty smug look.

When I catch up, he's already pressed the button for the elevator.

"Is this witness protection?" I say.

He looks at me out of the side of his eyes. "Yes," he says dully. "It's this one hotel. The Witness Protection Hotel. For all the witnesses. Ever."

"You're funny," I say. "But I'm not getting on this elevator unless I see some identification."

God! I am so good at this. I wish Agent Tirmizi were here.

The man sighs and takes out one of those leather folds and shows it to me.

"Vic, huh?" I say. "Sounds fake."

His mustache twitches. "You want to see Mr. Sutherland or not?"

"I do," I say. Then I keep my mouth firmly shut for the entire elevator ride, though it is definitely a challenge not to bring up the weather.

Down the long hallway I follow the massive width of Vic's back, reaching into my back pocket to take out Reid's letter. I'm holding it tightly in my hand when Vic stops in front of a door.

When he reaches his huge fist up to knock, he pauses and gives me one last look, and the best way I can describe this look is to say it's like having a raw piece of steak (with a mustache) judge you for being annoying while also asking whether you're really sure you want to go through with this. I guess over the last few months I've learned not to judge people solely by the expressions they wear on their faces, but Vic here could really benefit from some gentle giant training.

I swallow nervously.

But I'm still as certain as I was a few hours ago, as certain as I was when I left Sibby and Lark in the car. So I nod once, the way I've seen Reid do a hundred times. A firm tip of my head.

Vic thuds the side of his fist against the door.

But it's not Reid who answers. It's just another random man in a suit. He's rail-thin, a string bean to Vic's slab of beef. He looks back and forth between us as though we are the worst room service team to ever show up to this door.

"Sutherland has a visitor," Vic says in a low voice.

"*How?*" String Bean says.

Vic shrugs.

"I'll take care of this, Micah," says a woman's voice I recognize, and the guy called Micah steps to the side. In my periphery I see Agent Tirmizi approach, but I don't look to her.

Because now I can see Reid.

He's standing with his back to the window, his white shirt untucked but buttoned at the wrists, his suit pants wrinkled, but his dress shoes on. He looks at me with that fixed, focused intensity I've missed so much, but he holds his body still and upright, his jaw set tight. *Protecting himself.*

"Meg, nice to see you again," Agent Tirmizi says. "Oh, let her in, Micah. Vic, take off for the night. Thanks for the heads-up about her. Sorry you got waylaid on your way out."

I tear my eyes from Reid, look up and give Vic what I hope is a look of thanks for rescuing me from Gregory's extreme competence at keeping secrets. His mustache twitches, and I take that as a "you're welcome" before stepping into the room, barely restraining myself from running over to Reid. But since there's a lot of tension right now between Agent Tirmizi and this Micah person, I hold off.

"Did you tell her to come here?" says Micah.

Agent Tirmizi snorts. "Are you kidding?"

"She didn't," I say. I carefully unfold the letter, shuffling pages until I get to the last one. "It was in—"

Micah raises a hand to his brow. "You *insisted* on reading the letter," he says to Agent Tirmizi, "but you let an *address* slip your notice?"

"It wasn't an address," I say to them, but I make sure I'm looking at Reid. "It's coordinates."

Lines and lines of lovely, loving code. The shop, where he first found me. The Promenade, where we first made our plan. The Garment Worker, and the awning where we hid from the rain. A tiny, always crowded restaurant in Nolita, a bright mural on Bowery. Off Sixth Avenue, the quiet refuge of Winston Churchill Square. A taco joint in the East Village. The broad, beautiful green of Prospect Park. A bar, an urgent care, my apartment building and his.

More and more numbers, for every place in the city that means something to me and Reid.

And then one row of them, approximately two hours out of place.

The numbers that led me to this hotel.

My eyes brim with tears again, and Reid's jaw ticks with tension. His hands in his pockets look like they clench in frustration at the distance we're being forced to keep from each another.

"Guess I missed it," Agent Tirmizi says, but I don't think she did. I think she's a not-so-secret romantic. "Anyway, you're his attorney," she adds. "You should be protecting his interests. He's allowed to see people."

Micah looks back and forth between Reid and me, and then Reid and Agent Tirmizi. He sighs. Obviously I've never met him before, but I can see signs of fatigue all over his face. I imagine he's had a stressful few days, too.

"I wanted to get through the rest of this stuff today," he says apologetically, and for the first time I notice the setup of the room, the round, four-seat table that's littered with documents. I don't know what all of it is—statements or evidence or whatever Reid's been stuck taking care of, but I know he absolutely should get a break.

"Please," Reid says, the first word he's spoken since I came in this room. His voice is hoarse-sounding, and I think of the line from his letter, the one where he said he begged. *I begged her.* "Please, let me have a few minutes with her."

Agent Tirmizi moves over to the table, stacking papers. After a beat, Micah follows her, and for what feels like actual centuries Reid and I stand in our respective spots, our eyes on each other while we wait. The £ on my heart is fully unfurled into the word it's always wanted to be.

Love, Love, Love, it beats.

"You know where to find us," Agent Tirmizi says as she heads to the door.

Micah delays a beat, stops, and murmurs quietly to Reid, probably some reminder about what he can and can't say. He gives me another apologetic look before he finally passes through the door Agent Tirmizi is holding open.

And when it clicks shut behind them, Reid and I are finally alone.

♥ ♥ ♥

"Meg," he says immediately. "Please don't cry."

"Am I crying?" I say. "I hardly notice anymore."

He raises a hand through his hair. "I am so—"

"Reid," I interrupt him. I step farther into the room, pausing briefly to set the pages of his letter onto the bed. But then I move to him. I stand directly in front of him and look at his gorgeous, stern, triple-take face. His sad eyes. I reach out and circle my fingers around each of his wrists. I tug his hands loose from his pockets.

"It's okay," I say.

He lowers his head, his hair falling over his brow.

"I have done so much damage," he says, almost a whisper.

"It's okay," I repeat, and I step into him more. I pull his wrists toward me and wrap them around my lower back.

And then I put my arms around him.

The best way to describe what happens to Reid's body next is to say that he . . . *slouches*. As though he has been relieved of the most massive weight on those broad shoulders, he bends over me, his back curved, his head pressed into my hair, his arms holding me as though I'm the one thing in this whole entire world keeping him upright. Beneath my hands his back expands and contracts with great, heaving breaths, and I tighten my arms; I hold him together through whatever this is. I want to say, *Reid, don't cry*, but also I want to tell him he can cry all he wants.

I don't know how long we stand this way. Long enough that Reid's breathing regulates, long enough that I loosen my arms, switching from clutching him tight to rubbing my palms up and down the broad, tight muscles of his back, long enough that I'm sure we both grow stiff and achy, our height differential never more uncomfortable than when we stand like this. When he pulls back from me, he keeps his head tipped down, and I take his hands from my waist, pull him over to the bed. We sit beside each other, the pages of his letter between us.

He clears his throat. "Thank you. For coming all this way."

"You told me to."

He still won't raise his eyes to mine. "It was . . . an impulse," he says, running a hand through his hair again.

"It was a good one. I loved your letter."

His eyes flick upward, a question in them. Then he lowers them again. "Meg, I am sure I have made such a mess of your life. I'm afraid to ask what you've been through, these past couple of days."

"The worst of it was not knowing if you were okay. Everything else, I can handle."

Maybe I say this more confidently than I deserve to, given some of my lower moments over this past weekend.

But right this second, Reid doesn't need to know about those.

Reid shakes his head. He idly toys with the buttons at his wrists, as though he's considering undoing them. "There was this window," he says quietly. "After they took my phone, I mean. I had to turn it over for a couple of days. Anyway, there was this short window of time where I could call you. And then I . . ."

He trails off, stops with the buttons. His face flushes. "I couldn't remember your phone number. In my phone, you're the letters of your name. I'd never memorized the number."

He sounds so utterly stunned by this. I can imagine him somewhere, a phone clutched in his hand, his heart thudding in panic, numbers failing him.

"And then it was chaos. For hours and hours."

"It must've been awful," I say. I reach out, over the pages of the letter. I gently unbutton his cuffs for him, and he watches silently until I finish.

"Once your name hit the news, I—well, I'm reasonably sure I threatened Vic. To let me go to you. It's all something of a blur."

"Wow. I've seen you throw a punch, Hotshot, but I'm pretty sure you're not a match for Vic."

For the first time since I've gotten here, I see the barest flicker of the *swoonsh*, but then it fades. "I can't imagine what you thought."

I swallow. I could lie, but the pages between us are all about honesty. A contract, or rules for a game. And I'm not breaking them.

"I didn't know what to think, at first. I admit that I . . . I guess I felt some doubt. About what you'd told me, about you and Avery. About who you'd told about the program."

He looks up at me. "You have a lot of reason to doubt people," he says. "You can't know how sorry I am that I'm now another one of those people."

"Reid, I don't doubt you. Not now."

But I can tell he doesn't quite believe me. He looks down again, to his now-unbuttoned cuffs. I reach out, tug gently on one of them.

"Reid," I say again. "I know you. I know your heart. You were under so much stress, and maybe you made some mistakes. But I know you didn't mean for this to happen." I rest my hand on top of his letter. "I believe you."

"How, Meg?" His voice is low, raspy from the tears he'd shed against my body. "I hid so many things from you."

I shrug. "I hid things, too."

He looks up at me, his gaze dismissive. "The program is nothing, Meg. That's over. You know I don't—"

"I didn't mean the program."

He shakes his head. He's still fighting me so hard. "You didn't hide anything like this." He gestures idly to the now-empty table.

I don't bother to look over at it. I keep my eyes fixed on him.

"I hid that I'm in love with you. That I've been in love with you. For a long time."

I pick up the pages of his letter, move them to the other side of me. Then I shift, turning to the side, moving closer to him. I put my hand on his cheek, turn his face toward mine. I look into his sad, disbelieving eyes. His shoulders are still tight with tension. Stoic, stern, *Masterpiece Theatre* Reid. He never has been quite what he seemed on the outside, but I always knew that. I always saw something else inside him. From that very first day.

"I love you," I repeat, and he closes his eyes. I lean in and press a kiss to his temple, trail my lips over his scarred brow. *One*, I don't say. I move to his cheek, brush my lips back and forth there. *Two*, I don't say. I pause with my lips in front of his. *Three*, I'm begging him silently, but I don't move.

Then he whispers, "I love you, too."

And he kisses me.

Every kiss I've ever had with Reid has meant something—lust, welcome, comfort, reassurance, even love. But this is the first kiss I've ever had with him that feels like a promise, a commitment. It's soft and unhurried at first, and at one point, Reid has to reach up to gently swipe yet another tear from my cheek. But when he licks at my lips, it grows more intense, more desperate, all our fear and confusion from these last few days living between us as we cling together.

We won't be apart again, this kiss says.

We stay.

But eventually, I pull back. I'm not even sure if this is Reid's hotel room, and something tells me Agent Tirmizi would not approve of us having sex on her bed, not to mention Reid's lawyer. Also, I haven't forgotten that two of my friends are tooling around New Jersey in a rental car, waiting for news from me.

And anyway, I don't think we can leave these promises at a kiss.

Reid clutches both my hands in his. "I don't know how, Meg," he says, "but I promise you, I will fix it, whatever's been done to your business because of this."

Wrong promise.

"No, you won't." I make my voice as stern as his usually is.

He looks at me, startled.

"I'll fix it myself," I say. "I'm not taking the Make It Happyn job, but I—"

"You got it?" he says, his eyes lighting with pride, with relief.

"Sort of." I briefly—as gently as possible, under Reid's current guilt-ridden circumstances—explain their offer, the "hidden messages" concept.

"You could do it, Meg," he says quickly, before I've finished. "Please don't—"

"I'm not turning it down because of you. It's not what *I* want. It's not what I worked for, these past few months. It's not what all those walks with you helped me see. About myself, and about what I'm capable of."

My heart swells when I see that curve in his cheek, another almost-there *swoonsh*.

"I promise," I tell him, "I've got a plan for my work, my business. Or at least the beginnings of one. You have to focus on what's coming up for you, and—"

The curve disappears, and his brow furrows again.

"It's going to be hard for a while, Meg. For me, it'll be hard. I don't know how I'll keep you out of it, now that your name is in this."

"Reid, I'm trying to tell you. You don't *have* to keep me out of it. If you're in it, I'm in it. We're in it together."

It's going to be such a fight, I already know it. The trial, the press. The gossip. It's going to be so uncomfortable. It'd be so much easier to leave.

"But," I add, and his hands tighten immediately, briefly on mine. I rub my thumbs over his skin, soothing him. "You need to know, I'm not leaving New York. I ran away from one home because of a scandal. I'm not doing it again."

There's a long pause.

"Good," he says finally, a firm tip of his head. "I'm not leaving New York, either."

"No?"

He shakes his head.

"But you ha—"

"I love it here," he interrupts. "You're here."

I furrow my brow, remembering our night in Maryland, remembering all of Reid's frustrations with the city—the noise, the crowds, the gray, the dirt. There's all that, and now this—this spotlight on him. This reputation that will follow him.

"I don't know if that's enough," I say. "For you to stay."

"It's enough," he says, immediately. "It's everything." He leans in, kisses me again. "But there's also all those numbers in my letter to you. Every place we ever went to together. I love those places. It's like I said, Meg. I would've kept those places close to me forever. Even if you'd never wanted to see me again."

He pauses, wipes another tear—this one, happy—from my cheek. "And also, still the food."

I smile, looking into his not-sad eyes. "You made a joke," I say.

He gives me a real, fully formed, honest-to-God *swoonsh*.

I press my thumb to it, and for these few borrowed minutes, a break in the storm we both know we're going to have to weather, Reid and I feel perfectly like each other's shelter. The only two people in the world who understand each other this well. Letters, numbers.

The perfect code.

"Reid," I whisper to him. "It wasn't a mistake."

"No," he says, resting his forehead against mine. "It was a sign."

Epilogue

It wasn't part of the plan, to return to the wedding business.

In the back room of the shop, I sit in the same seat I've sat in so many times before, a gallery of pages set out in front of me. It's all there, mockups for each part of the job: save the dates, invitations, place cards, and even—oh, yes—a *program*. Across from me sits a couple who for weeks has been poring over ideas and suggestions, a couple who came in today hoping to see all of those ideas transformed into something special. Something unique, cohesive, *them.*

It's so familiar.

And yet.

"Oh, Meg. This is *perfect*. It's all so . . . it's so . . ."

"Whimsical?" I say, grinning across the table.

Sibby looks up from the sketches, her eyes bright and her grin matching mine. "Yes," she says. "That's exactly it. Whimsical! Isn't this whimsical, Eli?"

"Yes?" Elijah says from beside her, looking back and forth between us. I'm reasonably sure he doesn't really know why anything he's looking at qualifies as "whimsical," but he looks happy nonetheless, as he has through every one of the preparations having to do with his wedding to Sibby.

Over the last year and a half or so, as Sibby and I have worked on the new version of our friendship we found ourselves in after that day she came back to the apartment, part of the work we've had to do—in addition to the long, sometimes painful conversations, in addition to establishing new routines and new traditions—is to learn about the parts of each other's lives we missed during the time we weren't close. For me, that's included getting to know Elijah better, and the best part about that is how much I like him, and in a way that's more than "at least he picks up after himself" or "at least he doesn't eat any of your food out of the fridge without asking." He's soft-spoken, content to let Sibby shine, but he's got a sly sense of humor and good taste in music, and whenever I go over to their place to watch *The Bachelorette*, he makes the popcorn.

"Now on the program," I say, moving that to the center, "I think with the metallic accents you've chosen for the illustrations, you should keep the information to a minimum. Your names, your parents' names, the—"

"Your name here, right?" Sibby says, cutting me off. She taps her finger beneath the lettering that spells out *Wedding Party*.

"Right," I say, looking up at her and smiling. She moves her hand from the program to squeeze mine briefly, her eyes welling with tears. I've seen it before, of course, emotional brides—those flare-ups of sentiment or stress or simple, pure happiness. But with Sibby I know the emotion of this moment is different. It's taken us a while, after all, to get here. A new version of being best friends, one that's not so rooted in our past—and past patterns—together.

I squeeze her hand back and go over a few more elements of the job, offer some suggestions for some additional changes. Then I stand, the same as I would have were this any old wedding job. It was always a good idea to step away for a few minutes, to give the clients some time to really see the work, without my presence looming.

I let them know I'll return shortly, taking one final look at the treatments from this more distant angle. I'm proud of how they turned out—the sleek, upturned serifs reminding me of Sibby's favorite winged-eyeliner look, the extra-tall ascenders on the complementary cursive reminding me of Elijah's height. Anyone who looks closely would see the hidden message here, the only one that matters:

Someone who knows Sibby and Elijah—someone who loves them—created these letters.

"They liked it?" Lachelle says when I come up to the front desk, taking in what I'm sure is my relieved smile. She's got three supplier catalogs open in front of her and a red Sharpie in her hand, her tidy *X*'s of interest marked next to the items she's considering for the shop.

Six months ago, Cecelia announced that she wanted less day-to-day involvement in the shop, since her kids would be headed off to college soon and she and Shuhei wanted to spend as much time with them as possible. After that, they planned to travel more, and so the timing seemed perfect. She wouldn't sell, but she would reorganize, shutting down the retail part of the store so that she could run it as a custom invitation business only, everything by appointment with either her or one of her contractors.

To Lachelle—and honestly, to me, though it wasn't quite my business—that idea had been outrageous, and she'd put up a big fight. A couple of times, in the weeks following Cecelia's initial announcement, I'd come into the shop, hunting down supplies, only to find the two of them orbiting around each other in strained politeness; *excuse me* this and *can you pass me the ink* that. Once upon a time, it might've made me nervous and uncomfortable enough to avoid the place altogether, but by that point, deep into the aftermath of Reid's revelations, I'd felt almost fireproof against life's petty confrontations.

And anyway, soon enough, they'd come to a solution—Lachelle would buy in, taking over retail and operations, and Cecelia would manage the contractors and the custom service.

Mostly, the shop runs the same way it always did—a steady stream of visitors and regulars, the usual upticks in custom services during wedding and holiday seasons. But Lachelle is changing things, too. A switched-up floor plan means more space for the new retail, more evening classes taught by some of the contractors, and—of course—a brand-new window display every month, all of them the likes of which this stretch of street has never seen.

"They love it," I tell her, and we both glance up at where Elijah and Sibby sit, their heads bent together, still smiling dreamily at my work.

"Young love," Lachelle says, shaking her head. "He probably still puts the toilet seat down."

I nudge her. "He's nice. Anyway, what are you ordering? Those samples I tried from—"

"I'll tell you what I'm *not* ordering," she says, capping the Sharpie and crossing her arms before facing me.

"I *knoooooow*," I groan, pulling my phone from my pocket. "I'll check again."

I refresh my e-mail, watching new messages stack and stack, until I've got to scroll through to search for the name I'm looking for.

"Oh, wait!" I exclaim, straightening as I quickly scan the message from the print supplier I've been working with for the last few months. A smile spreads across my face as I see the good news. "Two weeks, they say. A full restock."

"Whew," Lachelle says. "Things are getting *desperate* over there."

She gestures toward the somewhat empty-looking table at the front of the store, the special placement Cecelia and Lachelle have reserved for me since the new line launched three months ago. I may not be part owner of this shop with my two friends, but the sign that proclaims this store the "birthplace" of the new Meg Mackworth line makes me feel warm with contentment, included in the most perfect possible way.

Despite this evening's sojourn in the back of the shop, I'm not really back in the wedding business. Instead, I'm back in my own business, a new version of it that I've had to rebuild, somewhat, in the aftermath of the Coster Capital fallout. With a lot of determined, difficult work—and the occasional character reference from everyone's favorite princess—I'd managed to keep most of my clients. But there'd been costs to having my name in the news—time spent fending off the press, reconsideration of my website and social media, the realization that I couldn't keep up with enough new clients to make up for the losses.

So in the end, I didn't really have a choice. I'd needed to pivot.

I'd needed to find a way to do my work the way I'd wanted to do it. The way that I'd broken through my block for.

Lachelle and I both drift over to the table, and I start straightening the products that are left, a burst of pride going through me each time I see the logo I designed.

Harbinger, I'd called it, my new product line. Journals and planners, stickers and stationery, no hidden messages necessary. These pieces, they're the right kind of signs—letters that remind you of a place, a season, a feeling, an ambition. Letters that say more than the words on the page.

Lachelle can't keep them in stock.

"These are still my favorite," she says now, fanning out a diminished stack of soft-cover notebooks, part of my New York Parks series. Botanicals—they're always going to be popular, but I'm pretty proud that there's not a single *Bloom Where You're Planted* in sight. "But right now it's that pink houndstooth I can't keep in stock! I wonder why?" She grins over at me.

"She's the best," I say, smiling as I think of Lark, who's made sure to be photographed with her new Harbinger planner twice since she's gone back to LA—*without* Cameron—where she's started filming a rom-com series for a massive streaming platform. But even beyond those supposedly candid paparazzi shots, whenever she posts something on her social media from the set, she makes sure that planner is somewhere in sight—on the small banquette table inside her trailer, resting on top of the crinkled, marked-up pages of her script, on her lap while someone touches up her makeup, her hair up in huge, bright purple velcro rollers, or tucked under her arm while she and one of her costars pose for a goofy selfie.

Incoming <3, she always texts me, right before one of these posts goes up.

We stay in touch, texts and phone calls and twice, her visits back here. Secretly, I think me and Sibby and Lachelle all hold out hope she might come back to the East Coast for good. But each time I see her big, toothy smile in the California sunshine, I get the sense that maybe Lark is in her true home.

"What I'm thinking," Lachelle says, "is that it's time for coloring books. Exclusives, for this shop. I know you turned it down before, when all the trial stuff was happening, but now you could—"

We're interrupted by the door to the shop opening, and I sense him even before I look up to see him.

Still, I like to look up and see him there. Tall, lean, triple-take-face Reid, his eyes lighting on me immediately, not a trace of sadness in them.

"Good evening," he says seriously, always more formal when there are other people around.

"Oh, here he is," says Lachelle. "Listen, I need your help with this payroll software. Now there's this whole section about allowances for—"

"Lachelle," I say teasingly. "He's not a small business consultant."

"What's it matter?" she says. "He knows the numbers. So anyway, I need . . ."

Reid hasn't said anything beyond his initial greeting, but still he steps farther in, listening to Lachelle with a serious expression on his face, offering her the occasional brief nod of understanding as she recounts a long list of grievances about the tax code. This is, in fact, the primary way Reid and Lachelle had bonded, back when she'd first met him. She calls him Robin Hood most of the time, a tribute to his heroic whistleblower status, even though most of the time he also sees fit to clarify for her that he didn't steal from anyone.

"I only tried to point out the stealing someone else was doing," he says, usually with that slight flush on his cheeks.

I'm finishing my tidying of the display when I hear Reid offering his suggestions to Lachelle—the same steady, assured tone I'm sure makes him excellent at his new job. Within seconds she's thanking him, letting us know she's going to go "handle this" right now, before she forgets every single thing Reid said to her.

"Looking sparse," Reid says, nodding at the table.

I smile at him. "Quite," I say pointedly, and he *swoonshes*.

The startup at Harbinger had been something of a fight between me and Reid. I didn't have the funds on my own to get it going—the contract with the supplier, the more sophisticated software and scanning equipment I'd needed. But Reid—practical, numbers-minded Reid—definitely did, and all he'd wanted was to give me some of it.

"Think of what you've done for me," he'd said, practically begging me. But I hadn't really seen any of what he'd been referring to as something I'd done for him. It'd been for *us*. A way for us to start our lives even as we were weathering the storm. After a couple of months, it hadn't made sense for Reid to stay in his apartment. It'd made better sense to move into mine— farther away from the chaos of the Coster fallout, farther away from the job he'd used to have. Closer to the job he'd hoped to have.

Anyway, it wasn't as though he didn't pay rent.

Still, Reid said it was more—more I'd done, more I'd had to face for him. All the times I'd come with him to meetings, depositions, days in court, my head held high when reporters would shout questions at the both of us. All the *Let's walk around Brooklyn* games I'd distracted him with as he'd struggled with worry over Avery, who had—not long after her father's arrest— reconciled herself to the depth of his crimes. All the evenings I sat quietly with him after some other random "source" con-

nected to Coster claimed anew that Reid was nothing more
than a hack, a guy with an ax to grind. All the days I never gave
up, even when it seemed as if the attention was never going to
go away.

"We're not keeping a balance sheet here," I'd said to him
once, trying to keep my temper in check, trying to reason with
him in a way he'd understand.

It hadn't always worked, of course. There'd been a few
slammed doors, a few brooding, silent meals. A few days when
both of our nerves were strung tight, worn-out, where we
couldn't communicate with each other at all.

But we'd practiced. We'd stayed.

In the end, it'd been a compromise. Not a gift, but a loan,
one I've almost already paid back. Reid's feathers had been
ruffled, and my pride had been stung, but we'd made it work.

And sometimes—like right now, when he comes over to lean
down and give me a soft kiss of greeting—I think it's my best
work.

"How was today?" I ask him, smoothing his hair back from
his brow. He's never so polished coming from work anymore—
Wall Street Reid is long since gone. In the morning, he still
leaves the house early, ready for his daily swim, his work clothes
ironed and placed carefully in a hanging bag. But by the time
he's finished for the day, they're always more than a little rum-
pled.

"Difficult," he says with a smile. "They test me."

"They" are Reid's students, and we both know that the truth
is, he enjoys being tested.

In the months immediately after Coster's arrest, it wasn't
really possible for Reid to work. He was too tied up all the time,
too hounded by press inquiries, interview requests—none of
which he ever granted. But it was possible to quietly reach out
to many of his graduate professors, to make connections with
area colleges and universities who might be looking for lectur-
ers. To Reid's surprise—but to no one else's, really—many of
those colleges and universities were extremely interested in

having a crack at a famous analyst who could boost the profile of their departments with special lectures about Wall Street
whistleblowing.

But as with the dreaded press inquiries, Reid had passed,
opting instead for a couple of sections of Advanced Calculus
at a community college. The pay is garbage and the grading
so far seems endless, but Reid only ever says it's a "valuable"
learning experience. As near as I can tell, Reid is only being
"tested" insofar as the following he's developed—students who
want to stay after class, playing more of the games Reid has
designed for them, students who ask the kinds of questions
that can only mean they're interested, students who press him
about whether he'll be teaching any other classes in future
semesters.

Still, at night, Reid comes home and prepares for another
path, studying for his New York State teaching certification—
hoping, eventually, to land in one of the STEM schools here in
Brooklyn.

"I think maybe," he'd said to me once, "I could be good with
kids who love math. Or . . . or with kids who could learn to
love it."

I'd thought of that picture of Reid on his first day of school.
That bubble-lettered chalkboard and that irrepressible smile.
I'd told him I thought he could be good, too.

Now, I brush a patch of chalk dust from his sleeve, while he
looks toward the back of the shop.

"Ah," he says, smiling when he spots Sibby and Elijah, both
of whom have grown to be close, trusted friends of Reid's, especially after they'd shown him a lot of support in those initial,
tumultuous months. "Did she like it?"

"She loved it."

"Good."

Since it's been a couple of days since Reid and I have been
able to connect at home—both of us busy with work—I hear
that "Good" in all the wrong ways for a public venue, and I take
a step back from him.

"I'll go check on them one more time," I say. "And then we can go."

He catches my hand and pulls me back toward him.

"Now wait a minute," he says, and I feel my skin flush. *That* was unmistakably bedroom voice.

"Reid," I whisper sternly, but not all that seriously.

"I want to talk to you about what you left in my bag today," he says. He lifts it from over his shoulder, sets it gingerly on one of the bare spaces of the display table.

My heart taps in anticipation, the same way it always does for these moments. These games we still play together.

From the front pouch he takes out a folded sheet of paper, uncreases it, and sets it on the table.

"This letter," he says, pointing down to the words I wrote there this morning—all-lowercase cursive, long and looping swashes at the start of each word. "It's a very nice invitation to dinner this evening."

"Yes," I say formally. "There's a new noodles shop that's just opened three blocks from here." I gesture toward the words. "See? The lettering is all . . . noodle-y."

"I do see," he says, trying to hide his *swoonsh.* "But I see something else here, too."

"Oh?"

"It took me some time to decode it," he says. But I can tell he's lying. Sweet, stoic, playful Reid. Always up for a game.

He moves his body so he stands behind me, reaches his arm around me, and points.

"But I figured it out." Slowly, he moves his fingertips along the page, pausing briefly at each of the letters I've ever so slightly made stand out. It's only ever Reid I hide messages for now. My face heats as he moves through them, adding them up until they spell out a request. *Whew.* These words seemed a lot less dirty when I wrote them this morning.

"Did I get it right?" he says quietly, his breath tickling my neck. I shudder with frustrated pleasure.

"You always were good at reading codes," I say.

For the briefest seconds, his lips dip to press against that *one* spot—right there at my temple—and in his soft kiss I feel all the history we've made and are making together, all the letters and numbers we're writing out and counting up.

"And you, my love," he says, "were always good at sending them."

Acknowledgments

First, to readers: Thank you so much for inviting Meg and Reid into your imaginations and, I hope, into your hearts. It means so much to me to share this story with you, and I hope you'll share in my thanks to some very special people who helped me bring it into the world.

Two exceptional women deserve so much of the credit for *Love Lettering*. My agent, Taylor Haggerty, is the first person to have ever heard my idea about Meg and Reid and the secret code they shared, and throughout the process of my writing this book—everything from the very first synopsis to the very final sentence—she encouraged me by reading pages when I stumbled and rooting for me when I got back up again. Taylor, I adore you, and I am so grateful for everything you have done and continue to do for me.

I have been fortunate to work with the incomparable Esi Sogah on five books now, and for each one, she has applied her keen eye for character, for story, for sound, and for sense to every one of my sentences. But for *Love Lettering*, a book that challenged me in unexpected ways, Esi did so much more—

coaching me through the tough parts, accommodating me when I needed more time, and helping me see my way to the end more clearly than I would have been able to without her vision. And beyond all this: She is simply the most fun person to work with, the most fun person to know and be around. Esi, for all this and more, I owe you a front-row seat to some musical where you will take great joy in my hives of embarrassment.

The team at Kensington Books more generally has my sincere gratitude for believing in this book and for helping it make its way into the world so beautifully. For their work and support, I thank Michelle Addo, Lynn Cully, Jackie Dinas, Vida Engstrand, Susanna Gruninger, Sheila Higgins, Norma Perez-Hernandez, Lauren Jernigan, Samantha McVeigh, Alexandra Nicolajsen, Kristine Noble, Carly Sommerstein, and Steve Zacharius.

In the summer of 2018 I sat in a small, slightly overloud, somewhat poorly lit vegan restaurant in Brooklyn and met the brilliant Sarah MacLean for the first time, and to Sarah I owe a great debt—for loving this idea and for reading pages of it when I was stuck, and for becoming a devoted friend who has supported me a great deal. More generally, what I would say is that I am grateful, over these past few years, to have learned something that Meg learns in the pages of this book—being creative doesn't mean being solitary, and so many friends in the romance community deserve my thanks. I can name only a small fraction of them here, for this book especially: Olivia Dade (who deserves particular credit for teaching me this lesson most patiently, and for helping me shape the first half of this manuscript), Therese Beharrie, Alyssa Cole, Jen DeLuca, Elizabeth Kingston, Ruby Lang, and Jennifer Prokop. Thank you for being writers I admire, and more importantly, thank you for being friends who listen and encourage and celebrate. I can only hope that for you I have done a small share of what you have done for me.

To my family (immediate, extended, and in-lawed!)—thank you for believing in me, even when I am doing my level best not to believe in myself, and thank you for your patience and kindness each time I undertake a new project. To my lovely, supportive friends, who had to keep me from drowning in a difficult time—Amy (who read every page of this book, sometimes *as* it was being written), Elizabeth, Jackie, Joan, Niamh, Sarah, (other!) Amy—you are more precious to me than I could ever say. Your voices exist in this book, hidden messages of love I sent you along the way.

Finally, to my husband—I hope you'll take this as *quite* the compliment—you are and have been my inspiration, always. Thanks for spending hours chasing down signs with me in your not-favorite city, and thank you for never doubting I could turn those signs into something special.

Connect with 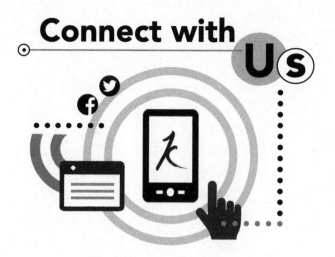 Us

Visit us online at
KensingtonBooks.com
to read more from your favorite authors, see books
by series, view reading group guides, and more.

Join us on social media

for sneak peeks, chances to win books and prize packs,
and to share your thoughts with other readers.

facebook.com/kensingtonpublishing
twitter.com/kensingtonbooks

Tell us what you think!

To share your thoughts, submit a review,
or sign up for our eNewsletters, please visit:
KensingtonBooks.com/TellUs.